The Wizard of Oz

In his fourteen books about Oz, three of which are collected here, Baum developed his vision of a socialist paradise. *The Wizard of Oz* (1900) introduces Dorothy, who arrives from Kansas and meets the Scarecrow, the Tin Woodman, the Cowardly Lion, and a host of other characters. *The Emerald City of Oz* (1910) finds Dorothy, Aunt Em, and Uncle Henry coming to Oz just as the wicked Nome King is plotting to conquer its people. In Baum's final novel, *Glinda of Oz* (1920), Dorothy and Princes Ozma try to prevent a battle between the Skeezers and the Flatheads. Tapping into a deeply rooted desire in himself and his loyal readers to live in a peaceful country which values the sharing of talents and gifts, Baum's imaginative creation, like all great utopian literature, holds out the possibility for change.

> "I am a writer today because I learned to love reading as a child—and mostly on account of the Oz books."
> —ELIZABETH GILBERT

PENGUIN THREADS

With paper and pen or needle and thread, storytelling has many traditions. Penguin's award-winning art director Paul Buckley presents Penguin Threads, a series of Penguin Classics Deluxe Editions inspired by the aesthetic of handmade crafts with specially commissioned cover art. Jillian Tamaki's embroidered artwork appears on *The Secret Garden* by Frances Hodgson Burnett, *Emma* by Jane Austen, and *Black Beauty* by Anna Sewell. Rachell Sumpter's hand stitched cover art appears on *The Wizard of Oz* by L. Frank Baum, *The Wind in the Willows* by Kenneth Grahame, and *Little Women* by Louisa May Alcott. Sketched in a traditional illustrative manner, then hand stitched, the final covers are sculpt embossed. Through story, style and texture, the Penguin Threads is an exciting chapter in Penguin's long history of excellence in book design, for true lovers of the book, design, and handcrafted beauty.

T0038672

PENGUIN CLASSICS ⓟ DELUXE EDITION

THE WIZARD OF OZ

LYMAN FRANK BAUM was born in Chittenango, New York, in 1856. In addition to publishing numerous children's books, he worked as a journalist, traveling salesman, horticulturalist, chicken breeder, theater manager, producer, actor, playwright, owner of a general store, and show window designer. His first book for children was *Mother Goose in Prose* (1897). In 1900 he published *The Wonderful Wizard of Oz*, which was a great success and inspired a musical theatrical version in 1902. Baum went on to write thirteen more Oz books, the last being *Glinda of Oz*, published posthumously in 1920. Although he is best remembered for the hugely popular Oz series, Baum wrote many other books as well, including *Father Goose* (1899), *The Life and Adventures of Santa Claus* (1902), and *Queen Zixi of Ix* (1905), as well as books published under various pseudonyms. In 1910, pursuing the burgeoning film industry as an outlet for more Oz stories, he moved with his family to Hollywood, where they lived until his death in 1919.

JACK ZIPES is professor emeritus at the University of Minnesota. A specialist in folklore, fairy tales, and children's literature, he has translated such works as the fairy tales of the Brothers Grimm and Herman Hesse, written more than twenty books of criticism, and edited numerous anthologies, including *Spells of Enchantment: The Wondrous Fairy Tales of Western Culture*. For Penguin Classics he has edited *The Wonderful World of Oz*, *Pinocchio*, and *Peter Pan*, and translated *Little Red Riding Hood*. He has been honored with the Distinguished Scholar Award by the International Association for the Fantastic in the Arts as well as fellowships by the Guggenheim Foundation and the National Endowment for the Humanities.

RACHELL SUMPTER lives and works on a tiny island in the Puget Sound, Washington, with her husband and fellow artist Jacob Magraw-Mickelson and their two children. Her work has been exhibited worldwide, including at the Jack Hanley, Allston Skirt, and Richard Heller galleries, and featured in *The Boston Globe*, *San Francisco Chronicle*, and *McSweeney's*.

L. FRANK BAUM

The Wizard of Oz

AND OTHER WONDERFUL BOOKS OF OZ:

The Emerald City of Oz

AND

Glinda of Oz

Edited with an introduction and notes by
JACK ZIPES

PENGUIN BOOKS

PENGUIN BOOKS
Published by the Penguin Group
Penguin Group (USA) Inc., 375 Hudson Street, New York, New York 10014, U.S.A.
Penguin Group (Canada), 90 Eglinton Avenue East, Suite 700, Toronto, Ontario, Canada
M4P 2Y3 (a division of Pearson Penguin Canada Inc.)
Penguin Books Ltd, 80 Strand, London WC2R 0RL, England
Penguin Ireland, 25 St Stephen's Green, Dublin 2, Ireland (a division of Penguin Books Ltd)
Penguin Group (Australia), 250 Camberwell Road, Camberwell, Victoria 3124, Australia
(a division of Pearson Australia Group Pty Ltd)
Penguin Books India Pvt Ltd, 11 Community Centre, Panchsheel Park,
New Delhi – 110 017, India
Penguin Group (NZ), 67 Apollo Drive, Rosedale,
Auckland 0632, New Zealand (a division of Pearson New Zealand Ltd)
Penguin Books (South Africa) (Pty) Ltd, 24 Sturdee Avenue,
Rosebank, Johannesburg 2196, South Africa

Penguin Books Ltd, Registered Offices:
80 Strand, London WC2R 0RL, England

The Wizard of Oz first published as *The Wonderful Wizard of Oz*
in the United States of America by George M. Hill 1900
The Emerald City of Oz first published by Reilly & Britton 1910
Glinda of Oz first published by Reilly & Lee 1920
This volume published as *The Wonderful World of Oz* with an introduction
and notes by Jack Zipes in Penguin Books 1998
This edition published in Penguin Books 2012

14

Introduction and notes copyright © Jack Zipes, 1998
All rights reserved

ISBN 978-0-14-310663-0
CIP data available

Printed in China

ALWAYS LEARNING   PEARSON

For Ken Silverman,
wizard extraordinaire

CONTENTS

INTRODUCTION

Home Sweet Home. When Dorothy Gale returns to Kansas at the end of her adventures in the Land of Oz, she declares that there is no place like home, and she appears content to be back on the farm with her Aunt Em and Uncle Henry. The MGM film based on *The Wonderful Wizard of Oz*, with which most people are nowadays more familiar than the novel, reiterates this message about home sweet home. But it is all a lie. Dorothy does not yet know what home is, and only those readers familiar with L. Frank Baum's fourteen fairy-tale novels about Oz know that home cannot be found in America. Home is Oz, a transcendent utopian paradise, that must be protected from America.

Of course, Baum himself was not certain what he wanted to do with Dorothy and Oz when he began writing *The Wonderful Wizard of Oz* in 1899. He wrote intuitively, and when his readers demanded more sequels, and he needed money and respite from financial pressures, he turned to Oz, constantly elaborating what he thought might be the ideal socialist society. Not that Baum was a conscious political thinker, but he was highly aware of what was missing in his life and in American society, and Oz gradually came to embody Baum's vision of a utopian world. But in order to understand this vision and why Baum was compelled to return time and again to Oz, it is important to trace the contours of his life, which lead from the East Coast to the West, from Broadway to Hollywood, with important stopovers in Aberdeen, South Dakota, and Chicago.

Born in Chittenango, New York, on May 15, 1856, with a heart defect, Baum was very much like the cowardly lion—all heart. He was the seventh of nine children, and his parents, Benjamin Ward Baum and Cynthia Ann Stanton, were from respectable, well-to-do families. His mother, a devout Methodist, ran the household as a stern disciplinarian. His father owned a barrel factory, which he sold in 1860 to begin a prosperous oil business in western Pennsylvania and upstate New York. This was the same year that the Baum family moved to Syracuse, and in 1861 Baum's father bought a fifteen-acre country home called Rose Lawn, outside Syracuse, and it was here that Baum spent idyllic days exploring the country and developing great interest in horticulture and chicken breeding. Because of his heart disease,

Baum was at first educated at home and was fond of reading fairy tales and Victorian literature. However, in 1868, his parents decided that he needed more structure and discipline. So, they sent him to Peekskill Military Academy, which he detested. In fact, due to the cruelty and corporal punishment that he experienced there, Baum lasted only two years, and in 1870, he returned to Syracuse, where he continued his education with private tutors, never obtaining a high school diploma.

When he turned fifteen, Baum received a printing press as a present, and he decided to produce a monthly magazine with his younger brother Harry. They called it *The Rose Lawn Journal*, and for the next three years they published stories, poems, riddles, articles, and advertisements. Already the young Baum, greatly influenced by Charles Dickens, showed a propensity for all kinds of writing and experiments. Never an idle dreamer, he always grabbed the initiative and sought to put his dreams into action. His dreams came to form his reality.

By 1873, Baum became editor of *The Empire*, a local paper, and also worked as a cub reporter for the *New York World*. After *The Empire* was forced to close due to loss of funds, he established his own print shop in Bradford, Pennsylvania, and wrote for the newspaper *The New Era* for several years. This work, however, was not entirely fulfilling for the imaginative and energetic Baum, who also worked as a salesman, bred chickens, and, as secretary of the Empire State Poultry Association, published a magazine called *The Poultry Journal*. In 1880, he began to manage the opera houses and theaters in New York and Pennsylvania owned by his father, and became involved as writer and actor, despite having no theatrical training. It took him little time to produce his first success, a sentimental musical play called *The Maid of Arran*, written in 1881 and based on William Black's novel *A Princess of Thule* (1874). Baum even starred in the production, which was mounted in Pennsylvania, Syracuse, and New York City in 1882, and he now became confident that he could have a career in the theater, which would be his life-long love.

In the meantime, Baum had fallen in love with Maud Gage, a student at Cornell, during a Christmas party at the home of his sister in 1881. Maud was the daughter of Matilda Joslyn Gage, who collaborated with Susan B. Anthony and Elizabeth Cady Stanton to write the four-volume *History of Woman Suffrage* (1881–86) and who was famous for her own work, *Woman, Church, and State* (1893). Highly educated and independent, Maud came from a different social environment than Baum, and yet they appeared to complement each other, she with her sober political ideas and practicality, and he with his boundless idealism and imagination. They were going to need both sobriety and idealism after their marriage, on November 8, 1882, due to a series of mishaps that would send them on a course of downward social mobility and financial need.

In 1883, after settling in Syracuse, Baum continued writing plays, but with little success. At the same time he worked as a traveling salesman for Baum's Castorine Company, the family oil business. Maud gave birth to Frank Joslyn Baum, the first of four sons, on December 4, and it appeared at that point that the family had a secure future. However, in 1884, Baum lost his shares in an opera-house chain through bad management and fire. He then opened up a small company to sell crude oil products in conjunction with his father's business. But his father's firm was failing because an accountant was cheating the company by falsifying the financial statements, thereby causing great losses. In 1885, Baum's father had a serious accident that left him semi-paralyzed. By the time Benjamin Baum died, in 1887, the business had collapsed, and the oil fortune had all but vanished. With a second son to feed—Robert Stanton Baum was born on February 1, 1886—and his prospects for a theater career rather dim, Baum decided to join the many Americans moving west at this time to take advantage of the land boom. Maud had two sisters and a brother living in Aberdeen, and Baum went to visit them in June of 1888 to determine what he might be able to do in South Dakota territory. By September he moved with his family and opened a general store called Baum's Bazaar. For the next three years he tried to establish himself in Aberdeen, but could not have picked a worse time, for the crops were failing and the farmers were about to plunge into several years of economic depression.

Though enterprising, Baum was a poor businessman and did not know how to manage the stocks in his store properly to make ends meet. In addition, he was generous to a fault and could not bear to force poverty-stricken customers or those who had come upon hard times to pay their debts. He also preferred spending his time telling stories to children outside the shop or supporting the local baseball team to running an efficient business. By January 1, 1890, he was obliged to close the store and look for a job more suitable to his talents and proclivities. He soon took over a weekly, *The Aberdeen Saturday Pioneer*, as publisher and editor. For the next year and a half, Baum wrote articles on social events, politics, sports, gossip, weather, and economics. Some of his editorials dealt with women's suffrage, theosophy, electoral campaigns, the church, horticulture, and husbandry. Baum had always supported the suffragette movement and came out strongly for women's equal rights. He was against organized religion and supported the Farmers' Alliance, criticizing the government and banking system for not lending greater support to the farmers. His most popular column was called "Our Landlady," which reported on conditions and people in a fictitious boardinghouse run by Sairy Ann Bilkins. Here Baum invented delightful stories that poked fun at well-known citizens in Aberdeen and included fantastic things such as electric blankets and flying machines. Yet, despite Baum's remarkable journalistic talents, the circulation of the weekly dwindled because people could not afford the luxury of a newspaper. Baum had to set his own type, lay out advertising, and do printing for other concerns. In March of 1891 he returned the paper to its original owner and resigned as editor.

When son number three, Kenneth Gage Baum, was born on March 24, Baum was desperate for a job. Fortunately he found one in Chicago as a reporter for the *Chicago Evening Post*. Within months, however, he left this job because his salary had been reduced and began working as a traveling salesman for the chinaware firm of Pitkin and Brooks. At this time the Baums (which included his mother-in-law, Matilda Gage) lived in a Chicago home that had no running water or bathroom, and Maud gave embroidery lessons at ten cents an hour to help support the family. Gradually Baum became the best salesman at Pitkin and Brooks and also helped customers design show windows. At the same time he continued writing stories and poems, which were published in local newspapers, joined the Theosophical Society, avidly attended baseball games, and supported populist causes, even taking part in a demonstration. In 1897, fatigue and nasal hemorrhages, signs of a stressed heart, caused him to retire as a salesman, and he assumed the editorship of *The Show Window*, the first magazine in America to be published for window decorators. As in everything else he did, Baum threw himself into this job with enthusiasm and became the secretary of the National Association of Window Trimmers. Imaginative and inventive, he wrote about and designed fascinating displays that would entice customers into stores. His experience in the theater played a major role here, for he envisioned the windows as scenes from fantastic plays and offered spectators a chance to change their lives through consuming the goods in the windows. But Baum was not interested so much in consumption as he was in writing and theater. Encouraged by his mother-in-law, who thought highly of his bedtime stories for his sons, he began producing children's books: *Mother Goose in Prose* (1897), illustrated by the famous Maxfield Parrish, *My Candelabra's Glare* (1898), and *Father Goose* (1899), his initial collaboration with W. W. Denslow, who had already established a reputation as a gifted illustrator in Chicago. All these books were relatively successful, but it was the publication of *The Wonderful Wizard of Oz*, with the marvelous illustrations by Denslow, in 1900 that enabled Baum to resign his position as editor of *The Show Window* and dedicate himself totally to writing and the theater. Actually Baum never intended to write a series of Oz books. He followed *The Wonderful Wizard of Oz* with *Dot and Tot of Merryland* and *American Fairy Tales* in 1901, *The Life and Adventures of Santa Claus* in 1902, and *The Enchanted Island of Yew* in 1903. It was not until 1904 that he published a sequel, *The Marvelous Land of Oz*. The reasons he continued the Oz story reveal a great deal about American culture and Baum's personal relationship to a utopian fantasy that literally took over his life. First, there had been a great demand for a sequel to *The Wonderful Wizard of Oz* by readers of all ages, and the huge success of the musical adaptation in 1902 stimulated even more interest in Oz. The play, which was a sentimental farce for adults and employed new characters and creatures such as Imogene the Cow instead of Toto the dog, had a long run on Broadway and inspired Baum to try his hand at other Oz plays. Second, Baum kept writing short stories and tales with characters similar to those in Oz, but his readers kept urging him to place them in Oz. Finally, when Baum ran into financial difficulty because his theatrical ventures floundered and because he liked to live extremely well when he had the money, he knew that sequels with dramatic possibilities would provide him with the funds he needed. Thus, he developed a curious relationship to Oz: it was his pot of luck to which he could turn when he needed money, and it was the means through which he had formed a bond with hundreds if not thousands of readers who wrote and gave him suggestions for characters, incidents, and plots. To his credit, Baum, who called himself the Royal Historian of Oz, gradually realized that after its creation, Oz did not belong to him. True, he had conceived this marvelous land and its inhabitants, but Baum had tapped a deeply rooted desire in himself and his readers to live in a peaceful country, one that maintained tolerance for the weirdest creatures and strange behavior in communities such as Crystal City, China Country, Time Town, Regalia, Blankenburg, and many others that were generally autonomous. That country was not America, and the more Baum cultivated the socialist utopian relations and principles of Oz, the more he and his readers shared this knowledge.

The 1902 play *The Wizard of Oz*, which was greatly rewritten by Julian Mitchell, the director, led to a dispute with W. W. Denslow about the "property rights" to Oz. For some time, Baum and Denslow had engaged in a kind of rivalry as to who should receive more credit for the creation of their books, especially *The Wonderful Wizard of Oz*. Since Denslow felt that he had been given a minor role in the production of the play and wanted a large share of the royalties, he split with Baum and went on to write and illustrate his own Oz books, which were not very successful. Since Baum had never truly appreciated Denslow's illustrations, he was satisfied with this separation, and he now focused on the play and his theater career. Just as the profits from the earlier *Father Goose* had helped the Baum family buy a summer cottage in Macatawa, Michigan, the success of the musical helped the Baums move into a more comfortable house in Chicago. In the meantime, Baum threw himself into theater projects. He finished *Search for Montague*, based on *Madre d'Oro an Aztec Play* (1889) by Emerson Hough, in 1903, but it was never produced. He wrote the playscript and lyrics for *Father Goose* and the prospectus for a new play, *The Maid of Athens*, which was printed but not performed. Finally, in 1904 he published *The Marvelous Land of Oz*, illustrated by John R. Neill, who would do the drawings for all the subsequent Oz books until his death in 1943 and who also wrote four Oz novels himself in the 1940s. In this first sequel to *The Wonderful Wizard of Oz*, Baum introduced such memorable characters as Ozma, the rightful ruler of Oz, Jack Pumpkinhead, the Saw-Horse, and Professor H. M. Woggle-Bug. This book is notable because it obliged Baum to provide more historical information about Oz, its laws, and characters and to sharpen his vision of a socialist utopian society. In addition, Baum began publishing a series of twenty-seven stories under the title "Queer Visitors from the Marvelous Land of Oz," which appeared with illustrations by Walt McDougall in the comic pages of the *Philadelphia North American*, the *Chicago Record Herald*, and other newspapers until February 1905. Soon there were all kinds of Oz novelties (sheet music, postcards, pins, and recordings) that furthered the distribution and sales of Baum's Oz books. In fact, the Woggle-Bug became something of a national fad and icon, leading Baum to publish *The Woggle-Bug Book*, illustrated by Ike Morgan, and to produce a play, *The Woggle-Bug*, in 1905 (which was not very successful).

During the next two years Baum continued to publish works that were not related to Oz. For instance, in 1905 he completed a musical, *The King of Gee Whiz*, with Emerson Hough; a traditional fairy-tale novel, *Queen Zixi of Ix*, which Baum thought was one of his best works; and a novel for adults, *The Fate of a Crown*, under the pseudonym Schuyler Staunton. The following year, after a trip with his wife to see Egypt and parts of Europe, he started a series for older girls with *Aunt Jane's Nieces* and *Aunt Jane's Nieces Abroad* under the pseudonym Edith Van Dyne and a series for older boys, *Sam Steele's Adventures on Land and Seas*, under the pseudonym Captain Hugh Fitzgerald. Yet, he could not abandon Oz, and over the next few years wrote *Ozma of Oz* (1907), *Dorothy and the Wizard in Oz* (1908), and *The Road to Oz* (1909). Nor could he abandon the theater, conceiving a traveling stage production called *Fairylogue and Radio Plays* in which he used slides, film, live actors, and music to tell Oz stories and other tales that he had written. He took this show on tour, opening on September 24, 1908, in Grand Rapids, Michigan, and closing on December 16 in New York City. Though the performances were well attended, Baum had underestimated the costs of staging such a large traveling show and consequently had financial troubles. Despite these problems, he invested in a film company and put all his energy into writing scripts for plays and in making films, the reasons why he decided to end the Oz series with *The Emerald City of Oz* in 1910. Of course, Baum did not want to abandon Oz entirely, nor could he. Rather he wanted to use the medium of film to realize his Oz fantasies, and it was important then to move to Hollywood, where the film industry was making great strides.

In December 1910, the Baums migrated to Hollywood and bought a home that they dubbed "Ozcot" with money that Maud had inherited from her mother. This was the house that Baum would occupy until his death in 1919, and it was here that he devoted himself to raising flowers and winning awards as an amateur horticulturist. Moreover, he returned to breeding chickens and kept Rhode Island Reds in his yard. But Baum was far from retiring as a country gentleman when he arrived in Hollywood and continued writing plays, filmscripts, and poems. Despite his productivity, he had to declare bankruptcy in June of 1911 because of the debts that he had accumulated from *Fairylogue and Radio Plays*. When his plight was made public, Baum received well over a thousand letters, mainly from young readers, who offered to send him money or help him in any way they could. But Baum would not accept charity, and the only way that he knew to recover from financial debt was to continue writing at a furious pace.

Not only did he publish two new fantasies for children, *The Sea Fairies* (1911) and *Sky Island* (1912), but he also produced numerous books for his boy and girl series and was involved in the stage play *The Tik-Tok Man of Oz*, which opened at the Majestic Theater in Los Angeles on March 31, 1912. The favorable reviews of this play and the demands of his readers influenced Baum to resume the Oz series, and on July 1, 1913, *The Patchwork Girl of Oz* was published, followed by *Tik-Tok of Oz* (1914), *The Scarecrow of Oz* (1915), *The Lost Princess of Oz* (1917), *The Tin Woodman of Oz* (1918), *The Magic of Oz* (1919), and *Glinda of Oz* (1920), the last two appearing posthumously. These works were all conceived by Baum while he was engaged in writing other Oz works either for the cinema or for the theater. Never one to give up, Baum had formed the Oz Film Manufacturing Company and used characters and motifs from *The Patchwork Girl of Oz*, which had also been made into a musical in 1913, for a film. Three other films based on Oz themes were produced in the coming years, and Baum also wrote various short stories based on Oz themes and characters. Even after he had a gall bladder operation in February 1918 and his heart condition worsened, causing painful tics to his face, Baum kept working on his Oz books. Finally, he suffered a stroke and died at his home in Hollywood on May 6, 1919.

It is tempting to read the trajectory of Baum's life as that of a late-nineteenth-century pioneer who heads west into open territory when his opportunities run dry on the East Coast. In fact, Baum's social and economic decline led to his decision to seek new and brighter opportunities in the Dakota Territory. When he suffered another setback during the depression years of the 1890s, he moved temporarily to Chicago, where he made and lost a fortune. Then, following his proclivity for experimenting with the latest technological inventions related to his art, he headed for California, as always with rose-tinted glasses, optimistic till the end of his days. He was an incredibly talented man with an indomitable spirit and drive, despite his heart condition. Journalist, printer, chicken breeder, actor, theater manager, playwright, oil salesman, owner of a general store, editor of a newspaper, window dresser, editor of a professional journal for window display, carpenter, inventor, cinematist, theosophist, supporter of the suffragette movement, baseball fan, owner of a film company, horticulturist, father of four sons, and devoted husband—throughout the journey of his life, Baum developed new qualities by trying to fill all these roles, and many of these experiences and qualities were incorporated into the Oz books. Like Dorothy, he traveled to discover his talents, and like Dorothy, he gathered friends around him, accepting their help, and helping them in return.

It is difficult not to idealize Baum, and when the first critical biography of his life is written, we may learn that he had an ugly and mean side. For instance, we already know that he wrote unkind remarks about Indians while living in Aberdeen. Certainly, he was not without his contradictions. But no matter what is discovered about Baum, it is important to note and perhaps to emphasize that his conception of Oz stemmed from a tragicomic vision of America and that Oz never stopped existing for him after the publication of *The Wonderful Wizard of Oz* in 1900. If we want to know his full vision and to know the profundity of Oz, it is necessary to read the fourteen Oz novels so that we can begin to grasp the cultural process that produced this peculiar *American* utopian fantasy.

Until recently, most critics read the Oz books as some kind of homage to populism and to socialist utopianism. However, during the last ten years several academicians have taken Baum to task for his contribution to the cult of consumerism in America, his anti-feminism, and his retrogressive political ideas. Since these writers raise some important and serious issues about Baum as an artist and the "ultimate" meaning of Oz, if there can be an ultimate meaning, they serve as a good starting point for reconsidering the Oz series as the year 2000 marks the 100th anniversary of the publication of *The Wonderful Wizard of Oz*.

In 1988, Stuart Culver began a shift in Oz scholarship with his essay "What Manikins Want: *The Wonderful Wizard of Oz* and *The Art of Decorating Dry Goods Windows*." He declared that "Dorothy's search for the home imagined by Populist theory takes place in a gaudy, artificial fantasy world that is given over entirely to the values of consumerism. Oz's green capital city, lying midway between the yellow wastes ruled by the Wicked Witch of the West and the blue land of the Munchkins, is a place of mixing and exchange" (101). Through a tour-de-force reading of Baum's *The Art of Decorating Dry Goods Windows* and his involvement in the window display industry, Culver sought to prove that all relations in *The Wonderful Wizard of Oz* are commodity relations and reflect capitalist exchange values that cater to the needs of commerce. In his interpretation, the characters are similar to manikins and are used to stimulate consumer desire. However, since this desire can never be entirely fulfilled, Baum's fantasy projects an ambivalent image in which the characters as customers (readers) are encouraged to buy commodities as false images and yet can never achieve the "genuine" identities they desire through consumption. Though Dorothy ultimately refuses to become trapped by commodity fetishism, she does want to "appease a decadent taste for spectacle in the purest sense of the word" (113). In *Land of Desire: Merchants, Power and the Rise of a New American Culture* (1993), William Leach was much more severe in his critique of Baum and accused him of endorsing some of the worst aspects of consumer culture at the turn of the century. "Baum introduced into his fairy tale a mind-cure vision of America quite at home with commercial development of the country. Baum could have criticized American society. He could have used his fairy tale as a means of drawing attention to economic suffering and racial injustice, to the alienating new forms of industrial labor, to the extravagance and greed of many Americans, and to the pooling of wealth and power that was becoming a distinguishing, abiding feature of American capitalist society (250). . . . More to the point, there is no trace of a critique of capitalism in *The Wizard of Oz*. The book is a totally upbeat American fairy tale that, far from challenging the new industrial society, endorsed its values and direction" (250–51). Both Leach and Culver maintain that America had undergone a major socioeconomic transformation at the end of the nineteenth century making the home into a site of consumption rather than production. As a result, advertising through show windows and the mass media were to turn women into "artistic" homemakers who could aesthetically arrange articles of accumulation acquired through the power of the male breadwinner. In this regard, all of Dorothy's contacts with the figures and places in the Oz books could be compared to the relations that "every girl" should cultivate as the perfect consumer. Culver focused his 1992 article, "Growing Up in Oz," on *The Land of Oz*, interpreted as an anti-feminist tract. Here Culver maintained that the plot serves to condition readers to establish their identities through shopping. This intriguing and complex novel reveals how the boy Tip is actually the Princess Ozma, and both Ozma and Dorothy join together to put down a revolt led by a female general. According to Culver, Ozma is developed into a type of figurine or image in the course of the novel that encourages readers to buy into commodity fetishism and accept the domestication of women. More recently, M. David Westbrook endeavored to rectify the political-economist approach to the Oz books in his 1996 essay "Readers of Oz: Young and Old, Old and New Historicist." While agreeing with Leach and Culver that commodity fetishism and exchange value determine the relations between the various characters within Oz, he finds that their critique is inadequate because "Ozian commerce, like textual commerce in general, operates according to its own laws, laws distinct from those that govern the circulation of merely physical commodities" (114). Westbrook focuses more on the relations between readers and the Oz texts and demonstrates that the meaning of Oz is conditioned by the consumption of the texts. "While Culver sees the act of reading fantasy as an act of consumption that alienates the child reader from authentic experience and from production," he concludes, "Baum asks whether readers are consumers or whether the reproduction of Oz in the reader's imagination should be considered a productive process in its own right. In the case of Oz, the answers to the questions raised both by Culver and by Baum's own texts can be found more easily in the local particulars of Oz's circulation as a textual commodity than in a generalized discourse of political economy" (118).

Although Westbrook does not sufficiently deal with the misreadings of the Oz books by Leach and Culver, his approach to the Oz books, with its reliance on reception aesthetics and readers' response theory, is an excellent starting point for understanding the significance of Oz as cultural icon. Therefore, reflecting upon his notions about "readerly cultural production" and "conceptions of cultural property" and how they have contributed to the formation of the meaning of Oz requires returning to the texts themselves to reconsider the social and economic relations that Baum established in the fictitious land of Oz to show that its compelling feature rests in the cultivation of gift exchange and a principle of hope.

Westbrook maintains that, without grasping how readers received and appropriated the Oz books, we cannot establish the value of Oz as cultural artifact and as commodity. His point is well taken. When Baum first produced *The Wonderful Wizard of Oz* with Denslow's drawings in 1900, he had no idea how successful this fantasy would be and how it would capture the imagination of young and old readers alike. Indeed, it was an immediate best-seller, and he and Denslow sought to capitalize on its success. Not only did they enhance Oz's exchange value as commodity with the production of the musical *The Wizard of Oz* in 1902, but they expanded the audience, for the play was directed mainly at adults. From this point on, the market for Oz consisted of children and adults, and Baum and Denslow created all sorts of novelties (posters, postcards, pins, music sheets, boxes, etc.) that would continue to pique the interest and curiosity of loyal followers and potential customers. But what were Baum, Denslow, and the publishers of the Oz materials piquing? Clearly, the fascination with Oz on the part of the children and adults cannot be solely explained by consumer desire. In fact, as Westbrook shows, the reader input that compelled Baum (and Denslow, and later Neill, who seem to be forgotten by Leach, Culver, and Westbrook in their critiques) to continue producing Oz books is highly significant in determining what Oz meant and means. Oz was and still is more than just a commodity. In particular, Baum gave Oz as a kind of gift to the public and cultivated Oz in a singular rapport with his readers, who saw in Oz an embodiment of social relations that were not possible in America. Many readers maintained a personal relationship with the author through letters that influenced Baum in his attitude toward Oz, which, as we know, he protected from encroachment by hostile forces.

Oz did not die after Baum's death. Ruth Plumly Thompson was appointed Baum's successor by Maud Baum and the publishers, and Neill continued illustrating the "official" Oz books until his death in 1943. In the meantime, numerous other writers and artists wrote Oz parodies, sequels, stories, and novels, and Oz films were produced, the most significant being the MGM production in 1939 with Judy Garland as Dorothy, Bert Lahr as the Cowardly Lion, Ray Bolger as the Scarecrow, and Jack Haley as the Tin Woodman. This film was not initially a great success, and the reception of the Oz books had undergone somewhat of a change in the 1940s with many librarians censoring the series either because of the positive images of witches or because of its alleged communist politics. But, in 1956, Oz returned to American consciousness with a vengeance when the MGM film was telecast to millions of viewers. Since then, it has been retelecast annually; new film adaptations have been made; and a video of the original MGM film has been reproduced. In addition, the International Wizard of Oz Club, formed by Justin Schiller in 1957, has flourished and sponsors Oz conventions and meetings, aside from publishing the important journal *The Baum Bugle* and other Oz-related works. Finally, talented writers such as Philip José Farmer (*A Barnstormer in Oz*, 1982), Geoff Ryman (*Was*, 1992), and Gregory Maguire (*Wicked: The Life and Times of the Wicked Witch of the West*, 1995) have commemorated Oz in novels that reflect different readerly and artistic appropriations of Baum's original utopian fantasy.

Although Oz as book and icon has been commodified throughout the twentieth century, it has also been exchanged as a gift to readers by its author/begetter and by readers to friends and other readers that transcends and subverts the commodity system. This creative act of gift exchange has endowed Oz with manifold meanings, but most of all, Oz has come to represent through readerly exchange and gift-giving a world other than what America is, no matter how different readers' responses have been. This otherness also depicts another form of relationship: the Oz novels display how people can relate to things and nature in a manner that was not and is not typical of how relationships have been formed and forged in America.

If we now focus on the texts, we can see how the Oz books themselves (as intended by Baum) have fostered a certain understanding of utopian otherness that may have a bearing on the way Oz has been received as a gift and interpreted by readers. Since Oz is generally associated with the first novel, *The Wonderful Wizard of Oz*, or with the MGM film, it is important to remember that all Baum's Oz books are connected and somewhat dependent on one another: they represent a creative process in which the characters share gifts and talents with one another and with readers to express the hope that base materialist and gendered interests need not determine the way people relate to each other. Oz as a utopian home is constructed from these relationships, and its gradual development in the early twentieth century serves as a counter model to the rise of capitalist commodity exchange.

The mistake that critics like Culver, Leach, and Westbrook make in their analysis of the Oz books is that they identify Oz with America and imagine that there is some sort of commodity exchange that determines how the characters and creatures in Oz will behave. Yet, Oz is clearly another world with its own peculiar social economy. It may be a lost continent or territory; it may even be an island surrounded by deserts. Whatever or wherever it is, it is not part of the United States. Nor does it have a unified monetary system and commodity exchange. In the first novel, Baum makes clear that Oz is *not* controlled by the Wizard, who only exerts power in the Emerald City. Nor does the Emerald City determine how people relate to each other outside its limits. If anything, the Wizard as *American* con man has colonized the city, duped its gentle and naive inhabitants, and introduced American standards and norms based on salesmanship and deception that ultimately will not work in the land of Oz as a whole. The qualities that distinguish most of the "native" inhabitants of Oz from the beginning are their gentleness, generosity, and tolerance. The Munchkins and Witch of the North are grateful to Dorothy for accidentally killing the Wicked Witch of the East, and their first act is to give Dorothy the silver slippers as a gift. They expect nothing in return, and they all want to help her find her way back to Kansas. The second thing that Dorothy receives is a kiss from the Witch of the North that will protect her. Soon she will discover that the Munchkins, who are all good farmers and raise large crops (in contrast to the situation in Kansas), do not use money. They share their food and provide lodging for Dorothy without thinking of charging her anything. Everything is free in Oz, and the value of life (the government, morality, ethics) depends on the economy of gift-giving that brings with it the obligation to give, accept, and reciprocate. Gifts are not only material objects but also spiritual qualities and talents. As Lewis Hyde has made clear in his superb book *The Gift: Imagination and the Erotic Life of Property*, "when gifts circulate within a group, their commerce leaves a series of interconnected relationships in its wake, and a kind of decentralized cohesiveness emerges (xiv). . . . a circulation of gifts nourishes those parts of our spirit that are not entirely personal, parts that derive from nature, the group, the race, or the gods. Furthermore, although these wider gifts are a part of us, they are not 'ours'; they are endowments bestowed upon us. To feed them by giving away the increase they have brought with us is to accept that our participation in them brings with it an obligation to preserve their vitality" (38). In contrast to the gift economy, Hyde argues, the capitalist commodity system is based on the exploitation of a gift and work for profit. It involves a negative reciprocity that brings about fragmentation, individualism, and clannishness.

Baum's first novel, *The Wonderful Wizard of Oz*, associates good with the vital progression of gift-giving and evil with hoarding and oppression. What is spectacular in this novel is not the spectacle of the show window but the extraordinarily gracious acts of the people and creatures who uncover false spectacle on their way to defining what Oz is as potential home. The three characters Dorothy meets and seeks to help on her way to the Emerald City—the Scarecrow, the Tin Woodman, and the Cowardly Lion—already possess the talents they think they lack. During their journey Baum shows that, by sharing their talents with one another, they can easily overcome adversity, and the irony of the first part of their trip is that they already are in full possession of their gifts when they meet the American con man who wants to manipulate and exploit them for his own selfish interests.

Culver and Leach exaggerate the significance of the commercialism of the Emerald City and argue that the commodity system is in full operation in Oz. Certainly, Baum describes Dorothy's first encounter with the city like this: "Many shops stood in the street, and Dorothy saw that everything in them was green. Green candy and green popcorn were offered for sale, as well as green shoes, green hats and green clothes of all sorts. At one place a man was selling green lemonade, and when the children bought it Dorothy could see that they paid for it with green pennies." This particular scene led Culver and Leach to generalize about Oz and some of the sequels as exemplifying consumer capitalism where the spectacle and illusion function to bind people to capitalist fetishism. However, the Emerald City is unlike most of Oz. It has been taken over by the American Wizard, who is responsible for deluding the people and instituting a market system. When he vanishes by the end of the novel, his system disappears with him: it is almost as though he is tied to the wicked witches, who use magic for their own benefit. All the Oz books pose one major question as their theme: how can the gift of magic be used to benefit the majority of people so they can live in harmony and foster respect for differences?

For Baum, magic was a powerful art form, and his own writing brought about miraculous transformations of his story line into even more extraordinary plots and characters as he sought to imagine a world that did not have to rely on deceit and transformation. In this respect, each one of the Oz novels deals with the issue of how to honor the gift of magic so that it is used properly, and with each Oz book, Baum gains a greater sense of how he wants to use his own "magic" to provide historical background for his utopian world and to illustrate how the gift of magic can foster communal cohesiveness and provide a true home for people. In his second work, *The Land of Oz* (1904), Baum establishes two key principles that will be significant for his future elaboration of what Oz is: magic can only be used by Glinda and Ozma for the good of the people; the art of magic as a nurturing force will be in the hands of women. Interestingly, Dorothy does not appear in this novel because Baum is more concerned with recording how Oz came to be and how it will be shaped in the future. The work joins together two plots that concern the machinations of the evil witch Mombi, who has transformed Ozma, the rightful ruler of Oz, into the boy Tip, and the rebellious forces of the female general Jinjur, who dethrones the Scarecrow. In the end, it is Glinda the Good who compels Mombi to restore Ozma to her real self, and who helps bring about the defeat of Jinjur. As Glinda tells Tip/Ozma, she refuses to deal in transformations, "for they are not honest, and no respectable sorceress likes to make things appear to be what they are not. Only unscrupulous witches use the art, and therefore I must ask Mombi to effect your release from her charm, and restore you to your proper form. It will be the last opportunity she will have to practice magic."

From this point on in the Oz sequels, the government of Oz will be determined by the soft and gentle magic of Ozma, assisted by Glinda and at times by the reformed Wizard, who returns in a later adventure. Though Baum clearly wrote *The Land of Oz* as a spoof of some of the worst aspects of the suffragette movement, he did not belittle women, nor did he reify them as manikins as Culver suggests. His own writing style and the governing style of Ozma/Glinda are strikingly similar: they are soothing and attentive to the peculiar desires and needs of characters. In all his works, the writing and magic appear to formulate psychological principles of object relations that are to guide parents in the nurturing of their children. Baum sets up a space, a unique environment, in which his young characters can play creatively and explore their potential for development in relation to a mother figure. As D. W. Winnicott has pointed out, "the potential space between baby and mother, between child and family, between individual and society or the world, depends on experience that leads to trust. It can be looked upon as sacred to the individual in that it is here that the individual experiences creative living" (11). Each novel creates its own space called Oz which is filled with the most eccentric and peculiar creatures and things, and Baum weaves their relations in such a way that their needs are respected and fulfilled without infringing upon the instinctual drives and needs of the others. If there is conflict—and there are always conflicts and adventures—the nurturing voices and wise responses of Ozma and Glinda the Good move the involved characters toward peaceful reconciliation. Creative exploration and artistic transformation of space into a home in which all the characters feel comfortable with themselves—this is the teleological force that guides all the Oz books and perhaps imbues the responses to Oz of readers and viewers during this past century.

In the next sequel, *Ozma of Oz* (1907), we have a perfect example of how Baum structured most of the novels in the series to emphasize magic as art and art as a manner of gift-giving that can induce positive reciprocity in the object relations of the characters. Here Dorothy is on her way to Australia with her sick uncle Henry when a storm strikes and causes a shipwreck. Saved by a chicken coop on the ocean, she encounters the talking hen Billina. They reach land—the Kingdom of Ev—and meet Tik-Tok the Machine Man, who tells them about the evil King of Ev, who has sold his wife and children to the Nome King. When Dorothy, Tik-Tok, and Billina enter the Kingdom of Ev, they are incarcerated by the vain and treacherous Princess Langwidere, the temporary ruler, who has more than thirty heads she can change to improve her looks—and she wants Dorothy's head. At this point, Ozma arrives to liberate Dorothy, Billina, and Tik-Tok. Eventually, they proceed to the Nome King's domain, where, with the help of the Tin Woodman and the Scarecrow, they capture the magic belt that gives the Nome King power. Once they free the Queen of Ev and her family through the use of Billina's eggs, which act like poison on the Nomes, they return to Oz. Dorothy gives the magic belt to Ozma, and Ozma wishes Dorothy back to Kansas, where her sick Uncle Henry still needs her.

Throughout the novel Dorothy, Billina, Tik-Tok, and Ozma give of themselves. They lend their talents to oppressed characters who are being exploited out of vanity, greed, and lust for power. Once again, magic is being abused to transform people into ornaments and artificial things. It is through the use of their gifts—Billina's eggs, the Scarecrow's intelligence, Dorothy's bravery—that the relations are changed, and that the individuals inside and outside Oz can pursue their goals without harm or hindrance.

As Baum responded to the events he depicted in the first three novels and the network of relations he created in Oz, he was compelled to explain more to himself and to his readers how and why Oz came into being, and how relations were determined. By the time he came to write *The Emerald City of Oz* (1910), he was ready to finalize all its features and to define this utopian world as a socialist projection because he had decided this would be his last Oz novel. Therefore, this book is perhaps the most significant of the series and the most innovative. It lays out the principles of Oz as a type of socialist paradise, an alternative to the United States, which by the end of the book must be made invisible because of encroaching technology and capitalist expansion. Kansas is depicted now as a *place of exploitation*, where Uncle Henry and Aunt Em are at the mercy of bankers. The narrative structure assumes a dialectical and thus a dramatic quality with a twofold plot: 1) Dorothy seeks to find a refuge for Aunt Em and Uncle Henry, and with the help of Ozma, she brings them to Oz for good and takes them on a tour of Oz to show them this splendid place and to explain the "object relations" of the different characters. This trip allows Baum to reintroduce most of the key charmingly eccentric creatures—the Wizard of Oz, the Shaggy Man, the Cowardly Lion, the Tin Woodman, the Scarecrow, the Hungry Lion, Jack Pumpkinhead, Billina, Tiktok, and Professor Wogglebug—as though in a grand finale in a musical show; 2) the Nome King amasses a large army with the Whimsies, Growleywogs, and the Phanfasms and attempts to avenge his previous defeat in *Ozma of Oz* by destroying Oz. His evil attitude can be likened to that of the bankers in America. He acts out of pure greed, and he wants to destroy a land that is not based on commodity exchange. Baum describes Oz very thoroughly in this volume to make sure that his readers understand what is at stake in the conflict:

> No disease of any sort was ever known among the Ozites, and so no one ever died unless he met with an accident that prevented him from living. This happened very seldom, indeed. There were no poor people in the Land of Oz, because there was no such thing as money, and all property of every sort belonged to the Ruler. The people were her children, and she cared for them. Each person was given freely by his neighbors whatever he required for his use, which is as much as any one may reasonably desire. Some tilled the lands and raised great crops of grain, which was divided equally among the entire population, so that all had enough. There were many tailors and dressmakers and shoemakers and the like, who made things that any who desired them might wear. Likewise there were jewelers who made ornaments for the person, which pleased and beautified the people, and these ornaments also were free to those who asked for them. Each man and woman, no matter what he or she produced for the good of the community, was supplied by the neighbors with food and clothing and a house and furniture and ornaments and games. If by chance the supply ever ran short, more was taken from the great storehouses of the Ruler, which were afterward filled up again when there was more of any article than the people needed.
>
> Every one worked half the time and played half the time, and the people enjoyed the work as much as they did the play, because it is good to be occupied and to have something to do. There were no cruel overseers set to watch them, and no one to rebuke them or to find fault with them. So each one was proud to do all he could for his friends and neighbors, and was glad when they would accept the things he produced.

Though there are evident contradictions in some of the Baum Oz novels that preceded *The Emerald City of Oz*—money is occasionally used, and there appear to be hunger and want, especially among the animals—all the sequels that followed this book tended to maintain the socialist principles outlined here, the assumption being that the Land of Oz must be protected at all costs. Oz is a wonder to behold, and the nurturing female rulers demonstrate that the art of magic or the magic of art can effectively be used to rearrange social relations for harmonious living.

What is perhaps most significant about the Oz books written in California from 1912 until Baum's death in 1919 is that Baum was literally compelled to write these novels because of the readers' demands for more Oz stories, Baum's own fascination with Oz, and his financial need. They were also written against a background of increasing industrial growth and expansion in the United States, floods of immigration to America, intense struggles over workers' rights, and World War I. While Baum made no direct allusions to these developments—after all he was writing mainly for children—it is clear that Oz as socialist paradise represents certain "good" values that are opposed by the "evil" machinations of characters that represent "American norms" such as genetic experimentation in *The Patchwork Girl of Oz* (1913), cruel oppression by the Nome King in *Tik-Tok of Oz* (1914), and the abuse of magic in *The Scarecrow of Oz* (1915), *The Rinkitink in Oz* (1916), *The Lost Princess of Oz* (1917), *The Tin Woodman of Oz* (1918), and *The Magic of Oz* (1919). Toward the end of his life, Baum appeared to be somewhat obsessed by the expropriation of magic and its misuse. Perhaps he was worried about losing his own "magic" as his health declined during these years and he was unable to bring some of his projects to fruition. Within his texts, however, the meaning is more social and political.

If magic is a "powerful gift" of transformation, it could be very dangerous if it were to fall into the wrong hands. In Oz, this power resides with Ozma, a mother figure, who, as though taking care of a large family, nurtures the talents of her subjects and animates them through her art to share their talents for the welfare of all. Thus, the final highly significant novel, *Glinda of Oz*, provides different societal models and different ways in which magic is used to resolve conflict. Here Baum did in fact allude directly to World War I in the first chapter, "The Call to Duty," when Ozma discovers that there is a war in her realm about which she had known nothing: "Being the Princess of this fairyland it is my duty to make all my people—wherever they may be—happy and content and to settle their disputes and keep them from quarreling. So, while the Skeezers and Flatheads may not know me or that I am their lawful Ruler, I now know that they inhabit my kingdom and are my subjects, so I would not be doing my duty if I kept away from them and allowed them to fight."

Whether the Flatheads are the Allies and the Skeezers the Germans and Austrians or vice versa does not matter, for Baum was more concerned in mocking war in general and ridiculing the perpetrators of the absurd war started by Queen Coo-ee-oh and Su-Dic (the Supreme Dictator), who are disempowered thanks to the collective action of Ozma and her friends. It is important that Ozma by herself cannot bring about a resolution to the conflict. She needs the aid of Glinda, Dorothy, the Patchwork Girl, and Reera the Red. In other words, these characters all lend their talents so that peace can return to Oz. As Ozma tells Dorothy at the beginning of their adventure, "no one is powerful to do everything."

With a fairy-tale structure similar to that of *The Wonderful Wizard of Oz*, this narrative depends on the reciprocal action of gift-giving. Ozma helps everyone by giving of herself and is in turn helped by her friends and strangers who partake of the generous and gracious spirit in which she operates. This is also the spirit that inspires so much fascination in the readers of the Oz books.

Though *Glinda of Oz* was Baum's last Oz novel, it was not really the last word on Oz. There is no closure to the Oz stories. Baum had tried to close down Oz with *The Emerald City of Oz*, but he failed wonderfully. To this day no one can prevent Oz from continuing because it stems from deep social and personal desires that many Americans feel are not being met in this rich and powerful country that is also known for its pauperization of children. In this respect, the fairy tale of Oz is truly a very *American* fairy tale in its projection of an oppositional space that holds out the possibility for the enrichment of children, and its reception over the past hundred years is also an American cultural phenomenon. Dorothy's pursuit of home is a successful one because she does not stay in Kansas. She did not allow herself or her aunt Em and uncle Henry to be ground to death by humiliating and inequitable conditions of labor on the great plains. She—and Baum—became magically touched by Oz in the first novel, and they experienced a resonating presentiment: home was not a nostalgic search for one's roots but a move forward into the unknown where one might design and designate home with others. Home could be defined in an active process of transforming social relations that would bring about personal fulfillment and a utopian societal model. As an icon of utopian home, Oz reveals how differences might shine and be truly appreciated and how a communal spirit might flourish. Together Baum's novels serve as utopian markers about our potential to realize home concretely in reality. In giving us Oz, Baum not only celebrated and enjoyed his own imaginative gifts, but he also invited us to join his quest and to reciprocate by keeping alive our hope for a land in which poverty and greed are banished.

Baum, Frank Joslyn, and Russell P. MacFall. *To Please a Child.* Chicago: Reilly & Lee, 1961.

Bewley, Marius. "The Land of Oz: America's Good Place." In *Masks and Mirrors,* 255–67. New York: Atheneum, 1970.

Billman, Carol. "I've Seen the Movie: Oz Revisited." In *Children's Novels and the Movies,* edited by Douglas Street, 92–100. New York: Ungar, 1983.

Brotman, Jordan. "A Late Wanderer in Oz." In *Only Connect: Readings in Children's Literature,* edited by Sheila Egoff, G. T. Stubbs, and L. F. Ashley, 156–69. New York: Oxford, 1969.

Carpenter, Angelica Shirley, and Ann Shirley. *L. Frank Baum: Royal Historian of Oz.* Minneapolis: Lerner, 1991.

Chaston, Joel D. "If I Ever Go Looking for My Heart's Desire: 'Home' in Baum's 'Oz' Books." *The Lion and the Unicorn* 18 (1994): 209–19.

———. "The 'Ozification' of American Children's Fantasy Films: *The Blue Bird, Alice in Wonderland,* and *Jumanji.*" *Children's Literature Association Quarterly* 22 (Spring 1997): 13–20.

Culver, Stuart. "What Manikins Want: *The Wonderful Wizard of Oz* and *The Art of Decorating Dry Goods Windows.*" *Representations* 21 (Winter 1988): 97–116.

———. "Growing Up in Oz." *American Literary History* 4 (Winter 1992): 607–28.

Erisman, Fred. "L. Frank Baum and the Progressive Dilemma." *American Quarterly* 20 (Fall 1968): 616–23.

Gardner, Martin. "The Tin Woodman of Oz: An Appreciation." *The Baum Bugle* (Fall 1996): 14–21.

Gardner, Martin, and Russell B. Nye. *The Wizard of Oz and Who He Was.* East Lansing: Michigan State University Press, 1957.

Gilead, Sarah. "Magic Abjured: Closure in Children's Fantasy Fiction." *PMLA* 106 (March 1991): 277–93.

Gilman, Todd. "Aunt Em: Hate You! Hate Kansas! Taking the Dog. Dorothy': Conscious and Unconscious Desire in *The Wizard of Oz.*" *Children's Literature Association Quarterly* 20 (Winter 1995–96): 161–67.

Greene, David L., and Dick Martin. *The Oz Scrapbook*. New York: Random House, 1977.

Griswold, Jerry. "There's No Place but Home: *The Wizard of Oz*." *The Antioch Review* 45 (Fall 1987): 462–75.

Harmetz, Aljean. *The Making of the Wizard of Oz*. New York: Knopf, 1978.

Hearn, Michael Patrick, ed. *The Annotated Wizard of Oz*. New York: Clarkson N. Potter, 1973.

———. "L. Frank Baum and the 'Modernized Fairy Tale.'" *Children's Literature in Education* (Spring 1979): 57–66.

———. "Preface." In *The Wizard of Oz*, edited by Michael Hearn, ix–xiv. New York: Schocken, 1983.

Hyde, Lewis. *The Gift: Imagination and the Erotic Life of Property*. New York: Random House, 1983.

Leach, William. *Land of Desire, Merchants, Power and the Rise of a New American Culture*. New York: Pantheon, 1993.

Littlefield, Henry M. "*The Wizard of Oz*: Parable of Populism." *American Quarterly* 16 (Spring 1964): 47–58.

McCord, David. "L. Frank Baum." In *Twentieth Century Children's Writers*, edited by D. L. Kirkpatrick, 91–93. New York: St. Martin's Press, 1978.

Mauss, Marcel. *The Gift: The Form and Reason for Exchange in Archaic Societies*. Translated by W. D. Halls. New York: W. W. Norton, 1990.

Miner, Harold E. "America in Oz: Conclusion." *The Baum Bugle* 20 (1976): 7–12.

Moore, Raylyn. *Wonderful Wizard, Marvelous Land*. Bowling Green, Ohio: Bowling Green University Popular Press, 1974.

Nathanson, Paul. *Over the Rainbow: The Wizard of Oz as a Secular Myth*. Albany: State University of New York Press, 1991.

Rahn, Suzanne. *The Wizard of Oz: Shaping an Imaginary World*. New York: Twayne, 1998.

Reckford, Kenneth. "Allegiance to Utopia." *The Baum Bugle* 32 (Winter 1988): 11–13.

Rockoff, Hugh. "The 'Wizard of Oz' as a Monetary Allegory." *Journal of Political Economy* 98 (1990): 739–60.

Sackett, S. J. "The Utopia of Oz." *Georgia Review* (Fall 1960): 275–90.

St. John, Tom. "Lyman Frank Baum: Looking Back to the Promised Land." *Western Humanities Review* (Winter 1982): 349–60.

Schuman, Samuel. "Out of the Fryeing Pan into the Pyre: Comedy,

Myth and *The Wizard of Oz.*" *Journal of Popular Culture* (Fall 1973): 302–304.

Vidal, Gore. "The Wizard of the 'Wizard.' " *The New York Review of Books* 24 (September 29, 1977): 10–15; "On Rereading the Oz Books." *The New York Review of Books* 24 (October 13, 1977): 38–42.

Wagenknecht, Edward. *Utopia Americana.* Seattle: University of Washington Book Store, 1929.

West, Mark I. "The Dorothys of Oz: A Heroine's Unmaking." *Stories and Society: Children's Literature in Its Social Context,* edited by Dennis Butts, 125–31. New York: St. Martin's Press, 1922.

Westbrook, M. David. "Readers of Oz: Young and Old, Old and New Historicist." *Children's Literature Association Quarterly* 21 (Fall 1996): 111–19.

Winnicott, D. W. "The Location of Cultural Experience." *Transitional Objects and Potential Spaces: Literary Uses of D. W. Winnicott,* edited by Peter L. Rudnytsky, 3–12. New York: Columbia University Press, 1993.

Zipes, Jack. "Inverting and Subverting the World with Hope: The Fairy Tales of George MacDonald, Oscar Wilde and L. Frank Baum." In *Fairy Tales and The Art of Subversion,* 97–133. London: Heinemann, 1983.

———. "Oz as American Myth." In *Fairy Tale as Myth/Myth as Fairy Tale,* 119–38. Lexington: University Press of Kentucky, 1994.

BOOKS BY L. FRANK BAUM

OZ SERIES

The Wonderful Wizard of Oz. Illustrated by W. W. Denslow. Chicago: George M. Hill, 1900.

The Marvelous Land of Oz. Illustrated by John R. Neill. Chicago: Reilly & Britton, 1904.

Ozma of Oz. Illustrated by John R. Neill. Chicago: Reilly & Britton, 1907.

Dorothy and the Wizard in Oz. Illustrated by John R. Neill. Chicago: Reilly & Britton, 1909.

The Emerald City of Oz. Illustrated by John R. Neill. Chicago: Reilly & Britton, 1910.

The Patchwork Girl of Oz. Illustrated by John R. Neill. Chicago: Reilly & Britton, 1913.

Tik-Tok of Oz. Illustrated by John R. Neill. Chicago: Reilly & Britton, 1914.

The Scarecrow of Oz. Illustrated by John R. Neill. Chicago: Reilly & Britton, 1915.

Rinkitink in Oz. Illustrated by John R. Neill. Chicago: Reilly & Britton, 1916.

The Lost Princess of Oz. Illustrated by John R. Neill. Chicago: Reilly & Britton, 1917.

The Tin Woodman of Oz. Illustrated by John R. Neill. Chicago: Reilly & Britton, 1918.

The Magic of Oz. Illustrated by John R. Neill. Chicago: Reilly & Lee, 1919.

Glinda of Oz. Illustrated by John R. Neill. Chicago: Reilly & Lee, 1920.

GENERAL

The Book of the Hamburgs, a brief treatise upon the mating, rearing, and management of the different varieties of Hamburgs. Hartford, Conn.: H. H. Stoddard, 1886.

Mother Goose in Prose. Illustrated by Maxfield Parrish. Chicago: Way & Williams, 1897.

By the Candelabra's Glare: Some Verse. Illustrated by W. W. Denslow and others. Chicago: Privately printed, 1898.

Father Goose, His Book. Illustrated by W. W. Denslow. Chicago: George M. Hill, 1899.

The Army Alphabet. Illustrated by Harry Kennedy. Chicago: George M. Hill, 1900.

The Art of Decorating Dry Goods Windows and Interiors. Chicago: The Show Window Publishing Co., 1900.

The Navy Alphabet. Illustrated by Harry Kennedy. Chicago: George M. Hill, 1900.

A New Wonderland. Illustrated by Frank Ver Beck. New York: R. H. Russell, 1900.

The Songs of Father Goose. Illustrated by W. W. Denslow. Chicago: George M. Hill, 1900.

American Fairy Tales. Illustrated by Harry Kenny, Ike Morgan, and N. P. Hall. Chicago: George M. Hill, 1901.

Dot and Tot of Merry Land. Illustrated by W. W. Denslow. Chicago: George M. Hill, 1901.

The Master Key: An Electrical Fairy Tale. Illustrated by Fanny Y. Cory. Indianapolis: Bowen-Merrill, 1901.

The Life and Adventures of Santa Claus. Illustrated by Mary Cowles Clark. Indianapolis: Bowen-Merrill, 1902.

The Enchanted Island of Yew. Illustrated by Fanny Y. Cory. Indianapolis: Bobbs-Merrill, 1903.

The Maid of Athens. Chicago: Privately printed, 1903.

Prince Silverwings. Chicago: A. C. McClurg, 1903.

The Surprising Adventures of the Magical Monarch of Mo and His People. Illustrated by Frank Ver Beck. Indianapolis: Bobbs-Merrill, 1903.

Queen Zixi of Ix: or the Story of the Magic Cloak. Illustrated by Frederick Richardson. New York: Century, 1905.

The Woggle-Bug Book. Illustrated by Ike Morgan. Chicago: Reilly & Britton, 1905.

John Dough and the Cherub. Illustrated by John R. Neill. Chicago: Reilly & Britton, 1906.

Father Goose's Year Book; Quaint Quacks and Feathered Shafts for Mature Children. Illustrated by Walter J. Enright. Chicago: Reilly & Britton, 1907.

Baum's American Fairy Tales; Stories of Astonishing Adventures of American Boys and Girls with the Fairies of their Native Land. Illustrated by George Kerr. Indianapolis: Bobbs-Merrill, 1908.

L. Frank Baum's Juvenile Speaker; Readings and Recitations in Prose and Verse, Humorous and Otherwise. Illustrated by John R. Neill and Maginel Wright Enright. Chicago: Reilly & Britton, 1910.

Baum's Own Book for Children; Stories and Verses from the Famous Oz Books, Father Goose, His Book, Etc., Etc. Illustrated by John R. Neill and Maginel Wright Enright. Chicago: Reilly & Britton, 1911.

The Daring Twins; A Story for Young Folk. Illustrated by Pauline M. Batcheler. Chicago: Reilly & Britton, 1911.

The Sea Fairies. Illustrated by John R. Neill. Chicago: Reilly & Britton, 1911.

Phoebe Daring; A Story for Young Folk. Illustrated by Joseph Pierre Nuyttens. Chicago: Reilly & Britton, 1912.

Sky Island. Illustrated by John R. Neill. Chicago: Reilly & Britton, 1912.

The Little Wizard Series. Illustrated by John R. Neill. Chicago: Reilly & Lee, 1914.

The Snuggle Tales. Illustrated by John R. Neill and Maginel Wright Enright. Chicago: Reilly & Britton, 1916.

Babes in Birdland. Illustrated by Maginel Wright Enright. Chicago: Reilly & Britton, 1917.

BOOKS PUBLISHED UNDER PSEUDONYMS

Floyd Akers

The Boy Fortune Hunters in Alaska. Illustrated by Howard Heath. Chicago: Reilly & Britton, 1908.

The Boy Fortune Hunters in Egypt. Illustrated by Emile A. Nelson. Chicago: Reilly & Britton, 1909.

The Boy Fortune Hunters in the Panama. Illustrated by Howard Heath. Chicago: Reilly & Britton, 1909.

The Boy Fortune Hunters in China. Chicago: Reilly & Britton, 1909.

The Boy Fortune Hunters in Yucatan. Chicago: Reilly & Britton, 1910.

The Boy Fortune Hunters in the South Seas. Chicago: Reilly & Britton, 1911.

Laura Bancroft

The Twinkle Tales. Illustrated by Maginel Wright Enright. Chicago: Reilly & Britton, 1906.

Policeman Bluejay. Illustrated by Maginel Wright Enright. Chicago: Reilly & Britton, 1907.

Twinkle and Chubbins; Their Astonishing Adventures in Nature-Fairyland. Illustrated by Maginel Wright Enright. Chicago: Reilly & Britton, 1911.

John Estes Cook

Tamawaca Folks, A Summer Comedy. Tamawaca Press, 1907.

Captain Hugh Fitzgerald

Sam Steele's Adventures on Land and Sea. Illustrated by Howard Heath. Chicago: Reilly & Britton, 1906.

Sam Steele's Adventures in Panama. Illustrated by Howard Heath. Chicago Reilly & Britton, 1907.

Schuyler Staunton

The Fate of a Crown. Illustrated by Glen C. Scheffer. Chicago: Reilly & Britton, 1905.

Daughters of Destiny. Illustrated by Thomas Mitchell Peirce and Harold DeLay. Chicago: Reilly & Britton, 1906.

Edith Van Dyne

Aunt Jane's Nieces. Illustrated by Emile A. Nelson. Chicago: Reilly & Britton, 1906.

Aunt Jane's Nieces Abroad. Illustrated by Emile A. Nelson. Chicago: Reilly & Britton, 1906.

Aunt Jane's Nieces at Milville. Chicago: Reilly & Britton, 1908.

Aunt Jane's Nieces at Work. Chicago: Reilly & Britton, 1909.

Aunt Jane's Nieces in Society. Chicago: Reilly & Britton, 1910.

Aunt Jane's Nieces and Uncle John. Chicago: Reilly & Britton, 1911.

The Flying Girl. Illustrated by Joseph Pierre Nuyttens. Chicago: Reilly & Britton, 1911.

Aunt Jane's Nieces on Vacation. Chicago: Reilly & Britton, 1912.

The Flying Girl and Her Chum. Illustrated by Joseph Pierre Nuyttens. Chicago: Reilly & Britton, 1912.

Aunt Jane's Nieces on the Ranch. Chicago: Reilly & Britton, 1914.

Aunt Jane's Nieces Out West. Chicago: Reilly & Britton, 1915.

Aunt Jane's Nieces in the Red Cross. Chicago: Reilly & Britton, 1915.

Mary Louise. Chicago: Reilly & Britton, 1916.

Mary Louise in the Country. Chicago: Reilly & Britton, 1916.

Mary Louise Solves a Mystery. Chicago: Reilly & Britton, 1917.

Mary Louise and the Liberty Girls. Chicago: Reilly & Britton, 1918.

Mary Louise Adopts a Soldier. Chicago: Reilly & Lee, 1919.

For the two most thorough bibliographies of L. Frank Baum's books, stories, plays, and other writings, see:

Douglas G. Greene and Peter E. Hanff. *Bibliographia Oziana: A Concise Bibliographical Checklist of the Oz Books by L. Frank Baum and His Successors.* Escanaba, Mich.: The International Wizard of Oz Club, 1988.

Michael Patrick Hearn, ed. *The Annotated Wizard of Oz.* New York: Clarkson N. Potter, 1973.

A NOTE ON THE TEXTS
AND THE ILLUSTRATORS

The three novels in this volume are based on the following editions:

1. *The Wonderful Wizard of Oz*. Illustrated by W. W. Denslow. Chicago and New York: George M. Hill, 1900.

2. *The Emerald City of Oz*. Illustrated by John R. Neill. Chicago: Reilly & Britton, 1910.

3. *Glinda of Oz*. Illustrated by John R. Neill. Chicago: Reilly & Lee, 1920.

Once Baum's books were ready for publication, they did not undergo many changes in the later editions. The cover pages and illustrations were changed here and there, depending on the publisher. The title of *The Wonderful Wizard of Oz* was altered in the second edition to *The New Wizard of Oz*. The first edition of *The Wonderful Wizard of Oz* was a splendid book: it had twenty-four tipped-in four-color plates and two-color textual illustrations throughout the entire volume. In addition, the binding was of cloth and stamped in color, and the book was encased in a decorative dust jacket. Although the rest of the Oz books were not as embellished as the first, Baum always insisted that the novels be published with ample illustrations and in striking formats.

His first significant collaboration with an illustrator was with W(illiam) W(allace) Denslow, one of the foremost innovative American illustrators at the turn of the century. Born in Philadelphia on May 5, 1856, Denslow studied art in New York and then worked as an illustrator for newspapers, magazines, theaters, and advertising companies throughout the States. By the time he arrived in Chicago in the early 1890s, he was a recognized free-lance artist and commercial illustrator. He met Baum in 1896 when they began work on *Father Goose*, which was very successful, thanks in large part to Denslow's illustrations. Denslow also drew the pictures for Baum's *Dot and Tot of Merryland*, and he and Baum helped finance the costly publication of the first edition of *The Wonderful Wizard of Oz*. After its publication, a rivalry between the two intensified, both claiming that the success of their books was due to their individual input. By 1902, as

Baum prepared to produce the musical of *The Wizard of Oz*, they argued over royalties and agreed to go their separate ways. Since Denslow was so well established as a commercial artist, his career did not depend on future collaboration with Baum. He did, however, publish a booklet with twenty-two color plates from *The Wizard of Oz* with a text by Thomas H. Russell, and he wrote and illustrated his own Oz book, *Denslow's Scarecrow and the Tin-Man* in 1904, followed by the publication of a comic strip "Scarecrow and Tin-Man" in Midwest newspapers such as the *Detroit Free Press* and the *Minneapolis Journal.* By this time, Denslow had moved to Ponquogue, Long Island, where he opened a design studio. Extremely wealthy from his numerous commissions, Denslow bought an island near Bermuda where he built a house and called himself King Denslow I of Denslow Island. He continued illustrating books on this island as well as designing books and advertisements. But his heavy drinking and free spending caused the quality of his work to decline by 1910. He died nearly impoverished on March 29, 1915. Though he has been somewhat neglected in scholarly interpretations of Oz, his great art nouveau work for *The Wonderful Wizard of Oz* is still considered a remarkable achievement in the history of book illustration.

After Denslow's departure, Baum needed a new illustrator when he decided to continue the Oz books in 1903. This time, the publishers Reilly and Lee found the artist, and they commissioned John Rea Neill to illustrate all the future Oz novels. Like Denslow, he was born in Philadelphia, on November 12, 1977, but his background and lifestyle were much different from that of the "Bohemian" Denslow. After studying at the Pennsylvania Academy of Fine Arts in 1895–96, Neill worked for various Philadelphia newspapers and, when he was contacted by Reilly and Britton in 1903, he had already established a name for himself as an illustrator of books, magazines, and children's stories. In his work for *The Marvelous Land of Oz* (1904), he followed Denslow's character depiction in broad outline but turned more toward a realistic if not naturalistic portrayal of the characters with fine ink and pen detail reminiscent of *Jugendstil.* Baum was very content with Neill's work, and Neill went on to illustrate all of Baum's Oz books and some of his other works as well. In addition, he did illustrations for stories in magazines such as *Ladies' Home Journal, The Saturday Evening Post, Boys' Life, Pictorial Review,* and *Argosy.* When Baum died in 1919, Neill continued to be the illustrator for all the Oz sequels written by Ruth Plumly Thompson. By this time he had established a studio in New York City. In all he illustrated over forty Oz books, and he even wrote and illustrated his own Oz works: *The Wonder City of Oz* (1940), *The Scalawagons of Oz* (1941), and *Lucky Bucky in Oz* (1942). He was working on a fourth Oz novel, *A Runaway in Oz*, when he died in September of 1943.

THE WIZARD OF OZ

This book is dedicated
to my good friend and comrade
MY WIFE

L.F.B.

INTRODUCTION

Folklore, legends, myths and fairy tales have followed childhood through the ages, for every healthy youngster has a wholesome and instinctive love for stories fantastic, marvelous and manifestly unreal. The winged fairies of Grimm and Andersen have brought more happiness to childish hearts than all other human creations.

Yet the old-time fairy tale,[1] having served for generations, may now be classed as "historical" in the children's library; for the time has come for a series of newer "wonder tales" in which the stereotyped genie, dwarf and fairy are eliminated, together with all the horrible and blood-curdling incidents devised by their authors to point a fearsome moral to each tale. Modern education[2] includes morality; therefore the modern child seeks only entertainment in its wonder-tales and gladly dispenses with all disagreeable incidents.

Having this thought in mind, the story of "The Wonderful Wizard of Oz" was written solely to please children of today. It aspires to being a modernized fairy tale,[3] in which the wonderment and joy are retained and the heartaches and nightmares are left out.

L. FRANK BAUM
Chicago, April, 1900

LIST OF CHAPTERS

CHAPTER 1

The Cyclone

Dorothy[1] lived in the midst of the great Kansas prairies, with Uncle Henry, who was a farmer, and Aunt Em, who was the farmer's wife. Their house was small, for the lumber to build it had to be carried by wagon many miles. There were four walls, a floor and a roof, which made one room; and this room contained a rusty looking cooking stove, a cupboard for the dishes, a table, three or four chairs, and the beds. Uncle Henry and Aunt Em had a big bed in one corner, and Dorothy a little bed in another corner. There was no garret at all, and no cellar—except a small hole, dug in the ground, called a cyclone cellar,[2] where the family could go in case one of those great whirlwinds arose, mighty enough to crush any building in its path. It was reached by a trap door in the middle of the floor, from which a ladder led down into the small, dark hole.

When Dorothy stood in the doorway and looked around, she could see nothing but the great gray prairie on every side. Not a tree nor a house broke the broad sweep of flat country that reached the edge of the sky in all directions. The sun had baked the plowed land into a gray mass,[3] with little cracks running through it. Even the grass was not green, for the sun had burned the tops of the long blades until they were the same gray color to be seen elsewhere. Once the house had been painted, but the sun blistered the paint and the rains washed it away, and now the house was as dull and gray as everything else.

When Aunt Em came there to live she was a young, pretty wife. The sun and wind had changed her, too. They had taken the sparkle from her eyes and left them a sober gray; they had taken the red from her cheeks and lips, and they were gray also. She was thin and gaunt, and never smiled now. When Dorothy, who was an orphan, first came to her, Aunt Em had been so startled by the child's laughter that she would scream and press her hand upon her heart whenever Dorothy's merry voice reached her ears; and she still looked at the little girl with wonder that she could find anything to laugh at.

Uncle Henry never laughed. He worked hard from morning till night and did not know what joy was. He was gray also, from his long beard to his rough boots, and he looked stern and solemn, and rarely spoke.

It was Toto[4] that made Dorothy laugh, and saved her from growing as gray as her other surroundings. Toto was not gray; he was a little black dog, with long, silky hair and small black eyes that twinkled merrily on either side of his funny, wee nose. Toto played all day long, and Dorothy played with him, and loved him dearly.

Today, however, they were not playing. Uncle Henry sat upon the doorstep and looked anxiously at the sky, which was even grayer than usual. Dorothy stood in the doorway with Toto in her arms, and looked at the sky too. Aunt Em was washing the dishes.

From the far north they heard a low wail on the wind, and Uncle Henry and Dorothy could see where the long grass bowed in waves before the coming storm. There now came a sharp whistling in the air from the south, and as they turned their eyes that way they saw ripples in the grass coming from that direction also.

Suddenly Uncle Henry stood up.

"There's a cyclone coming, Em," he called to his wife; "I'll go look after the stock." Then he ran toward the sheds where the cows and horses were kept.

Aunt Em dropped her work and came to the door. One glance told her of the danger close at hand.

"Quick, Dorothy!" she screamed; "run for the cellar!"

Toto jumped out of Dorothy's arms and hid under the bed, and the girl started to get him. Aunt Em, badly frightened, threw open the trap door in the floor and climbed down the ladder into the small, dark hole. Dorothy caught Toto at last, and started to follow her aunt. When she was halfway across the room there came a great shriek from the wind, and the house shook so hard that she lost her footing and sat down suddenly upon the floor.

A strange thing then happened.

The house whirled[5] around two or three times and rose slowly through the air. Dorothy felt as if she were going up in a balloon.

The north and south winds met where the house stood, and made it the exact center of the cyclone. In the middle of a cyclone the air is generally still, but the great pressure of the wind on every side of the house raised it up higher and higher, until it was at the very top of the cyclone; and there it remained and was carried miles and miles away as easily as you could carry a feather.

It was very dark, and the wind howled horribly around her, but Dorothy found she was riding quite easily. After the first few whirls around, and one other time when the house tipped badly, she felt as if she were being rocked gently, like a baby in a cradle.

Toto did not like it. He ran about the room, now here, now there, barking loudly; but Dorothy sat quite still on the floor and waited to see what would happen.

Once Toto got too near the open trap door, and fell in; and at first the little girl thought she had lost him. But soon she saw one of his ears sticking up through the hole, for the strong pressure of the air was keeping him up so that he could not fall. She crept to the hole, caught Toto by the ear, and dragged him into the room again, afterward closing the trap door so that no more accidents could happen.

Hour after hour passed away, and slowly Dorothy got over her fright; but she felt quite lonely, and the wind shrieked so loudly all about her that she nearly became deaf. At first she had wondered if she would be dashed to pieces when the house fell again; but as the hours passed and nothing terrible happened, she stopped worrying and resolved to wait calmly and see what the future would bring. At last she crawled over the swaying floor to her bed, and lay down upon it; and Toto followed and lay down beside her.

In spite of the swaying of the house and the wailing of the wind, Dorothy soon closed her eyes and fell fast asleep.

CHAPTER 2

The Council with the Munchkins

She was awakened by a shock, so sudden and severe that if Dorothy had not been lying on the soft bed she might have been hurt. As it was, the jar made her catch her breath and wonder what had happened; and Toto put his cold little nose into her face and whined dismally. Dorothy sat up and noticed that the house was not moving; nor was it dark, for the bright sunshine came in at the window, flooding the little room. She sprang from her bed and with Toto at her heels ran and opened the door.

The little girl gave a cry of amazement and looked about her, her eyes growing bigger and bigger at the wonderful sights she saw.

The cyclone had set the house down, very gently—for a cyclone—in the midst of a country of marvelous beauty.[1] There were lovely patches of greensward all about, with stately trees bearing rich and luscious fruits. Banks of gorgeous flowers were on every hand, and birds with rare and brilliant plumage sang and fluttered in the trees and bushes. A little way off was a small brook, rushing and sparkling along between green banks, and murmuring in a voice very grateful to a little girl who had lived so long on the dry, gray prairies.

While she stood looking eagerly at the strange and beautiful sights, she noticed coming toward her a group of the queerest people she had ever seen. They were not as big as the grown folk she had always been used to; but neither were they very small. In fact, they seemed about as tall as Dorothy, who was a well-grown child for her age,[2] although they were, so far as looks go, many years older.

Three were men and one a woman, and all were oddly dressed. They wore round hats that rose to a point a foot above their heads, with little bells around the brims that tinkled sweetly as they moved. The hats of the men were blue;[3] the little woman's hat was white, and she wore a white gown that hung in plaits from her shoulders; over it were sprinkled little stars that glistened in the sun like diamonds. The men were dressed in blue, of the same shade as their hats, and wore well-polished boots with a deep roll of blue at the tops. The men, Dorothy thought, were about as old as Uncle Henry, for two of them had beards. But the little woman was doubtless much older: her face was covered with wrinkles, her hair was nearly white, and she walked rather stiffly.

When these people drew near the house where Dorothy was standing in the doorway, they paused and whispered among themselves, as if afraid to come farther. But the little old woman walked up to Dorothy, made a low bow and said, in a sweet voice,

"You are welcome, most noble Sorceress, to the land of the Munchkins.[4] We are so grateful to you for having killed the wicked Witch of the East,[5] and for setting our people free from bondage."

Dorothy listened to this speech with wonder. What could the little woman possibly mean by calling her a sorceress, and saying she had killed the wicked Witch of the East? Dorothy was an innocent, harmless little girl, who had been carried by a cyclone many miles from home; and she had never killed anything in all her life.

But the little woman evidently expected her to answer; so Dorothy said, with hesitation,

"You are very kind; but there must be some mistake. I have not killed anything."[6]

"Your house did, anyway," replied the little old woman, with a laugh; "and that is the same thing. See!" she continued, pointing to

the corner of the house; "there are her two toes, still sticking out from under a block of wood."

Dorothy looked, and gave a little cry of fright. There, indeed, just under the corner of the great beam the house rested on, two feet were sticking out, shod in silver shoes[7] with pointed toes.

"Oh, dear! oh, dear!" cried Dorothy, clasping her hands together in dismay; "the house must have fallen on her. What ever shall we do?"

"There is nothing to be done," said the little woman calmly.

"But who was she?" asked Dorothy.

"She was the wicked Witch of the East, as I said," answered the little woman. "She has held all the Munchkins in bondage for many years, making them slave for her night and day. Now they are all set free, and are grateful to you for the favor."

"Who are the Munchkins?" inquired Dorothy.

"They are the people who live in this land of the East, where the wicked Witch ruled."

"Are you a Munchkin?" asked Dorothy.

"No; but I am their friend, although I live in the land of the North. When they saw the Witch of the East was dead the Munchkins sent a swift messenger to me, and I came at once. I am the Witch of the North."

"Oh, gracious!" cried Dorothy; "are you a real witch?"

"Yes, indeed," answered the little woman. "But I am a good witch, and the people love me. I am not as powerful as the wicked Witch was who ruled here, or I should have set the people free myself."

"But I thought all witches were wicked,"[8] said the girl, who was half-frightened at facing a real witch.

"Oh, no; that is a great mistake. There were only four witches[9] in all the Land of Oz,[10] and two of them, those who live in the North and the South, are good witches. I know this is true, for I am one of them myself, and cannot be mistaken. Those who dwelt in the East and the West were, indeed, wicked witches; but now that you have killed one of them, there is but one wicked Witch in all the Land of Oz—the one who lives in the West."

"But," said Dorothy, after a moment's thought, "Aunt Em has told me that the witches were all dead—years and years ago."

"Who is Aunt Em?" inquired the little old woman.

"She is my aunt who lives in Kansas, where I came from."

The Witch of the North seemed to think for a time, with her head bowed and her eyes upon the ground. Then she looked up and said,

"I do not know where Kansas is, for I have never heard that country mentioned before. But tell me, is it a civilized country?"

"Oh, yes," replied Dorothy.

"Then that accounts for it. In the civilized countries I believe there are no witches left; nor wizards, nor sorceresses, nor magicians. But, you see, the Land of Oz has never been civilized,[11] for we are cut off from all the rest of the world. Therefore we still have witches and wizards amongst us."

"Who are the Wizards?" asked Dorothy.

"Oz himself is the Great Wizard,"[12] answered the Witch, sinking her voice to a whisper. "He is more powerful than all the rest of us together. He lives in the City of Emeralds."[13]

Dorothy was going to ask another question, but just then the Munchkins, who had been standing silently by, gave a loud shout and pointed to the corner of the house where the Wicked Witch had been lying.

"What is it?" asked the little old woman; and looked, and began to laugh. The feet of the dead Witch had disappeared entirely and nothing was left but the silver shoes.

"She was so old," explained the Witch of the North, "that she dried up quickly in the sun. That is the end of her. But the silver shoes are yours, and you shall have them to wear." She reached down and picked up the shoes, and after shaking the dust out of them handed them to Dorothy.

"The Witch of the East was proud of those silver shoes," said one of the Munchkins; "and there is some charm connected with them; but what it is we never knew."

Dorothy carried the shoes into the house and placed them on the table. Then she came out again to the Munchkins and said,

"I am anxious to get back to my Aunt and Uncle. Can you help me find my way?"

The Munchkins and the Witch first looked at one another, and then at Dorothy, and then shook their heads.

"At the East, not far from here," said one, "there is a great desert, and none could live to cross it."

"It is the same at the South," said another, "for I have been there. The South is the Quadlings country."[14]

"I am told," said the third man, "that it is the same at the West. And that country, where the Winkies[15] live, is ruled by the wicked Witch of the West, who would make you her slave if you passed her way."

"The North is my home," said the old lady, "and at its edge is the same great desert that surrounds this land of Oz. I'm afraid, my dear, you will have to live with us."

Dorothy began to sob, at this, for she felt lonely among all these strange people. Her tears seemed to grieve the kind-hearted Munchkins, for they immediately took out their handkerchiefs and began to weep also. As for the little old woman, she took off her cap and balanced the point on the end of her nose, while she counted "one, two, three" in a solemn voice. At once the cap changed to a slate, on which was written in big, white chalk marks:

"LET DOROTHY GO TO THE CITY OF EMERALDS."

The little old woman took the slate from her nose, and, having read the words on it, asked,

"Is your name Dorothy, my dear?"

"Yes," answered the child, drying her tears.

"Then you must go to the City of Emeralds. Perhaps Oz will help you."

"Where is this City?" asked Dorothy.

"It is exactly in the center of the country, and is ruled by Oz, the Great Wizard I told you of."

"Is he a good man?" inquired the girl anxiously.

"He is a good Wizard. Whether he is a man or not I cannot tell, for I have never seen him."

"How can I get there?" asked Dorothy.

"You must walk. It is a long journey, through a country that is sometimes pleasant and sometimes dark and terrible. However, I will use all the magic arts I know of to keep you from harm."

"Won't you go with me?" pleaded the girl, who had begun to look upon the little old woman as her only friend.

"No, I cannot do that," she replied; "but I will give you my kiss, and no one will dare injure a person who has been kissed by the Witch of the North."[16]

She came close to Dorothy and kissed her gently on the forehead. Where her lips touched the girl they left a round, shining mark, as Dorothy found out soon after.

"The road to the City of Emeralds is paved with yellow brick,"[17] said the Witch; "so you cannot miss it. When you get to Oz do not be afraid of him, but tell your story and ask him to help you. Good-bye, my dear."

The three Munchkins bowed low to her and wished her a pleasant journey, after which they walked away through the trees. The Witch gave Dorothy a friendly little nod, whirled around on her left heel three times, and straightway disappeared, much to the surprise of little Toto, who barked after her loudly enough when she had gone, because he had been afraid even to growl while she stood by.

But Dorothy, knowing her to be a witch, had expected her to disappear in just that way, and was not surprised in the least.

CHAPTER 3

How Dorothy Saved the Scarecrow

When Dorothy was left alone she began to feel hungry. So she went to the cupboard and cut herself some bread, which she spread with butter. She gave some to Toto, and taking a pail from the shelf she carried it down to the little brook and filled it with clear, sparkling water. Toto ran over to the trees and began to bark at the birds sitting there. Dorothy went to get him, and saw such delicious fruit hanging from the branches that she gathered some of it, finding it just what she wanted to help out her breakfast.

Then she went back to the house, and having helped herself and Toto to a good drink of the cool, clear water, she set about making ready for the journey to the City of Emeralds.

Dorothy had only one other dress, but that happened to be clean and was hanging on a peg beside her bed. It was gingham, with checks of white and blue; and although the blue was somewhat faded with many washings, it was still a pretty frock. The girl washed herself carefully, dressed herself in the clean gingham, and tied her pink sunbonnet on her head. She took a little basket and filled it with bread from the cupboard, laying a white cloth over the top. Then she looked down at her feet and noticed how old and worn her shoes were.

"They surely will never do for a long journey, Toto," she said. And Toto looked up into her face with his little black eyes and wagged his tail to show he knew what she meant.

At that moment Dorothy saw lying on the table the silver shoes that had belonged to the Witch of the East.

"I wonder if they will fit me," she said to Toto. "They would be just the thing to take a long walk in, for they could not wear out."

She took off her old leather shoes and tried on the silver ones, which fitted her as well as if they had been made for her.

Finally she picked up her basket.

"Come along, Toto," she said, "we will go to the Emerald City and ask the great Oz how to get back to Kansas again."

She closed the door, locked it, and put the key carefully in the pocket of her dress.[1] And so, with Toto trotting along soberly behind her, she started on her journey.

There were several roads near by, but it did not take her long to find the one paved with yellow brick. Within a short time she was walking briskly toward the Emerald City, her silver shoes tinkling merrily on the hard, yellow roadbed. The sun shone bright and the birds sang sweet and Dorothy did not feel nearly as bad as you might think a little girl would who had been suddenly whisked away from her own country and set down in the midst of a strange land.

She was surprised, as she walked along, to see how pretty the country was about her. There were neat fences at the sides of the road, painted a dainty blue color, and beyond them were fields of grain and vegetables in abundance. Evidently the Munchkins were good farmers and able to raise large crops. Once in a while she would pass a house, and the people came out to look at her and bow low as she went by; for everyone knew she had been the means of destroying the wicked witch and setting them free from bondage. The houses of the Munchkins were odd-looking dwellings, for each was round, with a big dome for a roof. All were painted blue, for in this country to the East blue was the favorite color.

Towards evening, when Dorothy was tired with her long walk and began to wonder where she should pass the night, she came to a house rather larger than the rest. On the green lawn before it many men and women were dancing. Five little fiddlers played as loudly as possible and the people were laughing and singing, while a big table nearby was loaded with delicious fruits and nuts, pies and cakes, and many other good things to eat.

The people greeted Dorothy kindly, and invited her to supper and to pass the night with them; for this was the home of one of the richest Munchkins in the land, and his friends were gathered with him to celebrate their freedom from the bondage of the wicked witch.

Dorothy ate a hearty supper and was waited upon by the rich Munchkin himself, whose name was Boq. Then she sat down upon a settle and watched the people dance.

When Boq saw her silver shoes, he said,

"You must be a great sorceress."

"Why?" asked the girl.

"Because you wear silver shoes and have killed the wicked witch. Besides, you have white in your frock, and only witches and sorceresses wear white."[2]

"My dress is blue—and white-checked," said Dorothy, smoothing out the wrinkles in it.

"It is kind of you to wear that," said Boq. "Blue is the color of the Munchkins, and white is the witch color; so we know you are a friendly witch."

Dorothy did not know what to say to this, for all the people seemed to think her a witch, and she knew very well she was only an ordinary little girl who had come by the chance of a cyclone into a strange land.

When she had tired watching the dancing, Boq led her into the house, where he gave her a room with a pretty bed in it. The sheets were made of blue cloth, and Dorothy slept soundly in them till morning, with Toto curled up on the dark blue rug beside her.

She ate a hearty breakfast, and watched a wee Munchkin baby, who played with Toto and pulled his tail and crowed and laughed in a way that greatly amused Dorothy. Toto was a fine curiosity to all the people, for they had never seen a dog before.

"How far is it to the Emerald City?" the girl asked.

"I do not know," answered Boq gravely, "for I have never been there. It is better for people to keep away from Oz, unless they have business with him. But it is a long way to the Emerald City, and it will take you many days. The country here is rich and pleasant, but you must pass through rough and dangerous places before you reach the end of your journey."

This worried Dorothy a little, but she knew that only the great Oz could help her get to Kansas again, so she bravely resolved not to turn back.

She bade her friends good-bye, and again started along the road of yellow brick. When she had gone several miles she thought she would stop to rest, and so climbed to the top of the fence beside the road and sat down. There was a great cornfield beyond the fence, and not far away she saw a Scarecrow,[3] placed high on a pole to keep the birds from the ripe corn.

Dorothy leaned her chin upon her hand and gazed thoughtfully at the Scarecrow. Its head was a small sack stuffed with straw, with eyes, nose and mouth painted on it to represent a face. An old, pointed blue hat, that had belonged to some Munchkin, was perched on this head, and the rest of the figure was a blue suit of clothes, worn and faded, which also had been stuffed with straw. On the feet were some old boots with blue tops, such as every man wore in this country, and the figure was raised above the stalks of corn by means of the pole stuck up its back.

While Dorothy was looking earnestly into the queer, painted face of the Scarecrow, she was surprised to see one of the eyes slowly wink at her. She thought she must have been mistaken, at first, for none of the scarecrows in Kansas ever wink; but presently the figure nodded its head to her in a friendly way. Then she climbed down from the fence and walked up to it, while Toto ran around the pole and barked.

"Good day," said the Scarecrow in a rather husky voice.

"Did you speak?" asked the girl in wonder.

"Certainly," answered the Scarecrow; "how do you do?"

"I'm pretty well, thank you," replied Dorothy politely; "how do you do?"

"I'm not feeling well," said the Scarecrow with a smile, "for it is very tedious being perched up here night and day to scare away crows."

"Can't you get down?" asked Dorothy.

"No, for this pole is stuck up my back. If you will please take away the pole I shall be greatly obliged to you."

Dorothy reached up both arms and lifted the figure off the pole; for, being stuffed with straw, it was quite light.

"Thank you very much," said the Scarecrow, when he had been set down on the ground. "I feel like a new man."

Dorothy was puzzled at this, for it sounded queer to hear a stuffed man speak, and to see him bow and walk along beside her.

"Who are you?" asked the Scarecrow, when he had stretched himself and yawned, "and where are you going?"

"My name is Dorothy," said the girl, "and I am going to the Emerald City, to ask the great Oz to send me back to Kansas."

"Where is the Emerald City?" he inquired; "and who is Oz?"

"Why, don't you know?" she returned in surprise.

"No, indeed; I don't know anything. You see, I am stuffed, so I have no brains at all," he answered sadly.

"Oh," said Dorothy; "I'm awfully sorry for you."

"Do you think," he asked, "if I go to the Emerald City with you, that the great Oz would give me some brains?"

"I cannot tell," she returned; "but you may come with me, if you like. If Oz will not give you any brains you will be no worse off than you are now."

"That is true," said the Scarecrow. "You see," he continued, confidentially, "I don't mind my legs and arms and body being stuffed, because I cannot get hurt. If anyone treads on my toes or sticks a pin into me, it doesn't matter, for I can't feel it. But I do not want people to call me a fool, and if my head stays stuffed with straw instead of with brains, as yours is, how am I ever to know anything?"

"I understand how you feel," said the little girl, who was truly sorry for him. "If you will come with me I'll ask Oz to do all he can for you."[4]

"Thank you," he answered gratefully.

They walked back to the road, Dorothy helped him over the fence, and they started along the path of yellow brick for the Emerald City.

Toto did not like this addition to the party, at first. He smelled around the stuffed man as if he suspected there might be a nest of rats in the straw, and he often growled in an unfriendly way at the Scarecrow.

"Don't mind Toto," said Dorothy to her new friend; "he never bites."

"Oh, I'm not afraid," replied the Scarecrow; "he can't hurt the straw. Do let me carry that basket for you. I shall not mind it, for I can't get tired. I'll tell you a secret," he continued, as he walked along; "there is only one thing in the world I am afraid of."

"What is that?" asked Dorothy; "the Munchkin farmer who made you?"

"No," answered the Scarecrow; "it's a lighted match."[5]

CHAPTER 4

The Road Through the Forest

After a few hours the road began to be rough, and the walking grew so difficult that the Scarecrow often stumbled over the yellow bricks, which here were very uneven. Sometimes, indeed, they were broken or missing altogether, leaving holes that Toto jumped across and

Dorothy walked around. As for the Scarecrow, having no brains he walked straight ahead, and so stepped into the holes and fell at full length on the hard bricks. It never hurt him, however, and Dorothy would pick him up and set him upon his feet again, while he joined her in laughing merrily at his own mishap.

The farms were not nearly so well cared for here as those farther back had been. There were fewer houses and fewer fruit trees, and the farther they went the more dismal and lonesome the country became.

At noon they sat down by the roadside, near a little brook, and Dorothy opened her basket and got out some bread. She offered a piece to the Scarecrow, but he refused.

"I am never hungry," he said; "and it is a lucky thing I am not. For my mouth is only painted, and if I should cut a hole in it so I could eat, the straw I am stuffed with would come out, and that would spoil the shape of my head."

Dorothy saw at once that this was true, so she only nodded and went on eating her bread.

"Tell me something about yourself, and the country you came from," said the Scarecrow, when she had finished her dinner. So she told him all about Kansas, and how gray everything was there, and how the cyclone had carried her to this queer land of Oz. The Scarecrow listened carefully, and said,

"I cannot understand why you should wish to leave this beautiful country and go back to the dry, gray place you call Kansas."

"That is because you have no brains,"[1] answered the girl. "No matter how dreary and gray our homes are, we people of flesh and blood would rather live there than in any other country, be it ever so beautiful. There is no place like home."[2]

The Scarecrow sighed.

"Of course I cannot understand it," he said. "If your heads were stuffed with straw, like mine, you would probably all live in the beautiful places, and then Kansas would have no people at all. It is fortunate for Kansas that you have brains."

"Won't you tell me a story,[3] while we are resting?" asked the child.

The Scarecrow looked at her reproachfully, and answered,

"My life has been so short that I really know nothing whatever. I was only made day before yesterday. What happened in the world before that time is all unknown to me. Luckily, when the farmer made my head, one of the first things he did was to paint my ears, so that I heard what was going on. There was another Munchkin with him, and the first thing I heard was the farmer saying,

" 'How do you like those ears?'

" 'They aren't straight,' answered the other.

" 'Never mind,' said the farmer; 'they are ears just the same,' which was true enough.

" 'Now I'll make the eyes,' said the farmer. So he painted my right eye, and as soon as it was finished I found myself looking at him and at everything around me with a great deal of curiosity, for this was my first glimpse of the world.

" 'That's a rather pretty eye,' remarked the Munchkin who was watching the farmer; 'blue paint is just the color for eyes.'

" 'I think I'll make the other a little bigger,' said the farmer; and when the second eye was done I could see much better than before. Then he made my nose and my mouth; but I did not speak, because at that time I didn't know what a mouth was for. I had the fun of watching them make my body and my arms and legs; and when they fastened on my head, at last, I felt very proud, for I thought I was just as good a man as anyone.

" 'This fellow will scare the crows fast enough,' said the farmer; 'he looks just like a man.'

" 'Why, he is a man,' said the other, and I quite agreed with him. The farmer carried me under his arm to the cornfield, and set me up on a tall stick, where you found me. He and his friend walked away and left me alone.

"I did not like to be deserted this way; so I tried to walk after them, but my feet would not touch the ground, and I was forced to stay on that pole. It was a lonely life to lead, for I had nothing to think of, having been made such a little while before. Many crows and other birds flew into the cornfield, but as soon as they saw me they flew away again, thinking I was a Munchkin; and this pleased me and made me feel that I was quite an important person. By and by an old crow flew near me, and after looking at me carefully he perched upon my shoulder and said,

" 'I wonder if that farmer thought to fool me in this clumsy manner. Any crow of sense could see that you are only stuffed with straw.' Then he hopped down at my feet and ate all the corn he wanted. The other birds, seeing he was not harmed by me, came to eat the corn too; so in a short time there was a great flock of them about me.

"I felt sad at this, for it showed I was not such a good Scarecrow after all; but the old crow comforted me, saying: 'If you only had brains in your head you would be as good a man as any of them, and a better man than some of them. Brains are the only things worth having in this world, no matter whether one is a crow or a man."[4]

"After the crows had gone I thought this over, and decided I would try hard to get some brains. By good luck, you came along and pulled me off the stake, and from what you say I am sure the great Oz will give me brains as soon as we get to the Emerald City."

"I hope so," said Dorothy earnestly, "since you seem anxious to have them."

"Oh yes, I am anxious," returned the Scarecrow. "It is such an uncomfortable feeling to know one is a fool."

"Well," said the girl, "let us go." And she handed the basket to the Scarecrow.

There were no fences at all by the road side now, and the land was rough and untilled. Towards evening they came to a great forest, where the trees grew so big and close together that their branches met over the road of yellow brick. It was almost dark under the trees, for the branches shut out the daylight; but the travelers did not stop, and went on into the forest.

"If this road goes in, it must come out," said the Scarecrow, "and as the Emerald City is at the other end of the road, we must go wherever it leads us."

"Anyone would know that," said Dorothy.

"Certainly, that is why I know it," returned the Scarecrow. "If it required brains to figure it out, I never should have said it."

After an hour or so the light faded away, and they found themselves stumbling along in the darkness. Dorothy could not see at all, but Toto could, for some dogs see very well in the dark; and the Scarecrow declared he could see as well as by day. So she took hold of his arm and managed to get along fairly well.

"If you see any house, or any place where we can pass the night," she said, "you must tell me, for it is very uncomfortable walking in the dark."

Soon after the Scarecrow stopped.

"I see a little cottage at the right of us," he said, "built of logs and branches. Shall we go there?"

"Yes, indeed," answered the child. "I am all tired out."

So the Scarecrow led her through the trees until they reached the cottage, and Dorothy entered and found a bed of dried leaves in one corner. She lay down at once, and, with Toto beside her, soon fell into a sound sleep. The Scarecrow, who was never tired, stood up in another corner and waited patiently until morning came.

CHAPTER 5

The Rescue of the Tin Woodman

When Dorothy awoke the sun was shining through the trees and Toto had long been out chasing birds and squirrels. She sat up and looked around her. There was the Scarecrow, still standing patiently in his corner, waiting for her.

"We must go and search for water," she said to him.

"Why do you want water?" he asked.

"To wash my face clean after the dust of the road, and to drink, so the dry bread will not stick in my throat."

"It must be inconvenient to be made of flesh," said the Scarecrow, thoughtfully, "for you must sleep, and eat and drink. However, you have brains, and it is worth a lot of bother to be able to think properly."

They left the cottage and walked through the trees until they found a little spring of clear water, where Dorothy drank and bathed and ate her breakfast. She saw there was not much bread left in the basket, and the girl was thankful the Scarecrow did not have to eat anything, for there was scarcely enough for herself and Toto for the day.

When she had finished her meal, and was about to go back to the road of yellow brick, she was startled to hear a deep groan near by.

"What was that?" she asked timidly.

"I cannot imagine," replied the Scarecrow; "but we can go and see."

Just then another groan reached their ears, and the sound seemed to come from behind them. They turned and walked through the forest a few steps, when Dorothy discovered something shining in a ray of sunshine that fell between the trees. She ran to the place, and then stopped short with a cry of surprise.

One of the big trees had been partly chopped through, and standing beside it, with an uplifted axe in his hands, was a man made entirely of tin.[1] His head and arms and legs were jointed upon his body, but he stood perfectly motionless, as if he could not stir at all.

Dorothy looked at him in amazement, and so did the Scarecrow, while Toto barked sharply and made a snap at the tin legs, which hurt his teeth.

"Did you groan?" asked Dorothy.

"Yes," answered the tin man, "I did. I've been groaning for

more than a year, and no one has ever heard me before or come to help me."

"What can I do for you?" she inquired softly, for she was moved by the sad voice in which the man spoke.

"Get an oil-can and oil my joints," he answered. "They are rusted so badly that I cannot move them at all; if I am well oiled I shall soon be all right again. You will find an oil-can on a shelf in my cottage."

Dorothy at once ran back to the cottage and found the oil-can, and then she returned and asked anxiously,

"Where are your joints?"

"Oil my neck first," replied the Tin Woodman. So she oiled it, and as it was quite badly rusted the Scarecrow took hold of the tin head and moved it gently from side to side until it worked freely, and then the man could turn it himself.

"Now oil the joints in my arms," he said. And Dorothy oiled them and the Scarecrow bent them carefully until they were quite free from rust and as good as new.

The Tin Woodman gave a sigh of satisfaction and lowered his axe, which he leaned against the tree.

"This is a great comfort," he said. "I have been holding that axe in the air ever since I rusted, and I'm glad to be able to put it down at last. Now, if you will oil the joints of my legs, I shall be all right once more."

So they oiled his legs until he could move them freely; and he thanked them again and again for his release, for he seemed a very polite creature, and very grateful.

"I might have stood there always if you had not come along," he said; "so you have certainly saved my life. How did you happen to be here?"

"We are on our way to the Emerald City, to see the great Oz," she answered, "and we stopped at your cottage to pass the night."

"Why do you wish to see Oz?" he asked.

"I want him to send me back to Kansas, and the Scarecrow wants him to put a few brains into his head," she replied.

The Tin Woodman appeared to think deeply for a moment. Then he said:

"Do you suppose Oz could give me a heart?"[2]

"Why, I guess so," Dorothy answered, "it would be as easy to give the Scarecrow brains."

"True," the Tin Woodman returned. "So, if you will allow me to join your party, I will also go to the Emerald City and ask Oz to help me."

"Come along," said the Scarecrow heartily; and Dorothy added that she would be pleased to have his company. So the Tin Woodman shouldered his axe and they all passed through the forest until they came to the road that was paved with yellow brick.

The Tin Woodman had asked Dorothy to put the oil-can in her basket. "For," he said, "if I should get caught in the rain, and rust again, I would need the oil-can badly."

It was a bit of good luck to have their new comrade join the party, for soon after they had begun their journey again they came to a place where the trees and branches grew so thick over the road that the travelers could not pass. But the Tin Woodman set to work with his axe and chopped so well that soon he cleared a passage for the entire party.

Dorothy was thinking so earnestly as they walked along that she did not notice when the Scarecrow stumbled into a hole and rolled over to the side of the road. Indeed, he was obliged to call to her to help him up again.

"Why didn't you walk around the hole?" asked the Tin Woodman.

"I don't know enough," replied the Scarecrow cheerfully. "My head is stuffed with straw, you know, and that is why I am going to Oz to ask him for some brains."

"Oh, I see," said the Tin Woodman. "But, after all, brains are not the best things in the world."

"Have you any?" inquired the Scarecrow.

"No, my head is quite empty," answered the Woodman; "but once I had brains, and a heart also; so, having tried them both, I should much rather have a heart."

"And why is that?" asked the Scarecrow.

"I will tell you my story, and then you will know."

So, while they were walking through the forest, the Tin Woodman told the following story:[3]

"I was born the son of a woodman who chopped down trees in the forest and sold the wood for a living. When I grew up I too became a woodchopper,[4] and after my father died[5] I took care of my old mother as long as she lived. Then I made up my mind that instead of living alone I would marry, so that I might not become lonely.

"There was one of the Munchkin girls who was so beautiful that I soon grew to love her with all my heart. She, on her part, promised to marry me as soon as I could earn enough money to build a better house for her; so I set to work harder than ever. But the girl[6] lived with an old woman who did not want her to marry anyone, for she was so lazy she wished the girl to remain with her and do the cooking and the housework. So the old woman went to the wicked Witch of the East, and promised her two sheep and a cow if she would prevent the marriage. Thereupon the wicked Witch enchanted my axe, and when I was chopping away at my best one day, for I was anxious to get the new house and my wife as soon as possible, the axe slipped all at once and cut off my left leg.

"This at first seemed a great misfortune, for I knew a one-legged man could not do very well as a woodchopper. So I went to a tin-smith[7] and had him make me a new leg out of tin. The leg worked very well, once I was used to it; but my action angered the wicked Witch of the East, for she had promised the old woman I should not marry the pretty Munchkin girl. When I began chopping again my axe slipped and cut off my right leg. Again I went to the tinner, and again he made me a leg out of tin. After this the enchanted axe cut off my arms, one after the other; but, nothing daunted, I had them replaced with tin ones. The wicked Witch then made the axe slip and cut off my head, and at first I thought that was the end of me. But the tinner happened to come along, and he made me a new head out of tin.

"I thought I had beaten the wicked Witch then, and I worked harder than ever; but I little knew how cruel my enemy could be. She thought of a new way to kill my love for the beautiful Munchkin maiden, and made my axe slip again, so that it cut right through my body, splitting me into two halves. Once more the tinner came to my help and made me a body of tin, fastening my tin arms and legs and head to it, by means of joints, so that I could move around as well as ever. But, alas! I had now no heart, so that I lost all my love for the Munchkin girl, and did not care whether I married her or not. I suppose she is still living with the old woman, waiting for me to come after her.

"My body shone so brightly in the sun that I felt very proud of it and it did not matter now if my axe slipped, for it could not cut me. There was only one danger—that my joints would rust. But I kept an oil-can in my cottage and took care to oil myself whenever I needed it. However, there came a day when I forgot to do this, and, being caught in a rainstorm, before I thought of the danger my joints had rusted, and I was left to stand in the woods until you came to help me.

It was a terrible thing to undergo, but during the year I stood there I had time to think that the greatest loss I had known was the loss of my heart. While I was in love I was the happiest man on earth; but no one can love who has not a heart, and so I am resolved to ask Oz to give me one. If he does, I will go back to the Munchkin maiden and marry her."

Both Dorothy and the Scarecrow had been greatly interested in the story of the Tin Woodman, and now they knew why he was so anxious to get a new heart.

"All the same," said the Scarecrow, "I shall ask for brains instead of a heart; for a fool would not know what to do with a heart if he had one."

"I shall take the heart," returned the Tin Woodman; "for brains do not make one happy, and happiness is the best thing in the world."

Dorothy did not say anything, for she was puzzled to know which of her two friends was right, and she decided if she could only get back to Kansas and Aunt Em it did not matter so much whether the Woodman had no brains and the Scarecrow no heart, or each got what he wanted.

What worried her most was that the bread was nearly gone, and another meal for herself and Toto would empty the basket. To be sure, neither the Woodman nor the Scarecrow ever ate anything, but she was not made of tin nor straw, and could not live unless she was fed.

CHAPTER 6

The Cowardly Lion

All this time Dorothy and her companions had been walking through the thick woods. The road was still paved with yellow brick, but these were much covered by dried branches and dead leaves from the trees, and the walking was not at all good.

There were few birds in this part of the forest, for birds love the open country where there is plenty of sunshine; but now and then there came a deep growl from some wild animal hidden among the trees. These sounds made the little girl's heart beat fast, for she did not know what made them; but Toto knew, and he walked close to Dorothy's side, and did not even bark in return.

"How long will it be," the child asked of the Tin Woodman, "before we are out of the forest?"

"I cannot tell," was the answer, "for I have never been to the Emerald City. But my father went there once, when I was a boy, and he said it was a long journey through a dangerous country, although nearer to the city where Oz dwells the country is beautiful. But I am not afraid so long as I have my oil-can, and nothing can hurt the Scarecrow, while you bear upon your forehead the mark of the good Witch's kiss, and that will protect you from harm."

"But Toto!" said the girl anxiously; "what will protect him?"

"We must protect him ourselves, if he is in danger," replied the Tin Woodman.

Just as he spoke there came from the forest a terrible roar, and the next moment a great Lion bounded into the road. With one blow of his paw he sent the Scarecrow spinning over and over to the edge of the road, and then he struck at the Tin Woodman with his sharp claws. But, to the Lion's surprise, he could make no impression on the tin, although the Woodman fell over in the road and lay still.

Little Toto, now that he had an enemy to face, ran barking toward the Lion, and the great beast had opened his mouth to bite the dog, when Dorothy, fearing Toto would be killed, and heedless of danger, rushed forward and slapped the Lion upon his nose as hard as she could, while she cried out:

"Don't you dare to bite Toto! You ought to be ashamed of yourself, a big beast like you, to bite a poor little dog!"

"I didn't bite him," said the Lion, as he rubbed his nose with his paw where Dorothy had hit it.

"No, but you tried to," she retorted. "You are nothing but a big coward."[1]

"I know it," said the Lion, hanging his head in shame; "I've always known it. But how can I help it?"

"I don't know, I'm sure. To think of your striking a stuffed man like the poor Scarecrow!"

"Is he stuffed?" asked the Lion, in surprise, as he watched her pick up the Scarecrow and set him upon his feet, while she patted him into shape again.

"Of course he's stuffed," replied Dorothy, who was still angry.

"That's why he went over so easily," remarked the Lion. "It astonished me to see him whirl around so. Is the other one stuffed also?"

"No," said Dorothy, "he's made of tin." And she helped the Woodman up again.

"That's why he nearly blunted my claws," said the Lion. "When they scratched against the tin it made a cold shiver run down my back. What is that little animal you are so tender of?"

"He is my dog, Toto," answered Dorothy.

"Is he made of tin, or stuffed?" asked the Lion.

"Neither. He's a—a—a meat dog," said the girl.

"Oh. He's a curious animal, and seems remarkably small, now that I look at him. No one would think of biting such a little thing except a coward like me," continued the Lion sadly.

"What makes you a coward?" asked Dorothy, looking at the great beast in wonder, for he was as big as a small horse.

"It's a mystery," replied the Lion. "I suppose I was born that way. All the other animals in the forest naturally expect me to be brave, for the Lion is everywhere thought to be the King of Beasts. I learned that if I roared very loudly every living thing was frightened and got out of my way. Whenever I've met a man I've been awfully scared; but I just roared at him, and he has always run away as fast as he could go. If the elephants and the tigers and the bears had ever tried to fight me, I should have run myself—I'm such a coward; but just as soon as they hear me roar they all try to get away from me, and of course I let them go."

"But that isn't right. The King of Beasts shouldn't be a coward," said the Scarecrow.

"I know it," returned the Lion, wiping a tear from his eye with the tip of his tail; "it is my great sorrow, and makes my life very unhappy. But whenever there is danger my heart begins to beat fast."

"Perhaps you have heart disease,"[2] said the Tin Woodman.

"It may be," said the Lion.

"If you have," continued the Tin Woodman, "you ought to be glad, for it proves you have a heart. For my part, I have no heart; so I cannot have heart disease."

"Perhaps," said the Lion thoughtfully, "if I had no heart I should not be a coward."

"Have you brains?" asked the Scarecrow.

"I suppose so. I've never looked to see," replied the Lion.

"I am going to the great Oz to ask him to give me some," remarked the Scarecrow, "for my head is stuffed with straw."

"And I am going to ask him to give me a heart," said the Woodman.

"And I am going to ask him to send Toto and me back to Kansas," added Dorothy.

"Do you think Oz could give me courage?" asked the cowardly Lion.

"Just as easily as he could give me brains," said the Scarecrow.

"Or give me a heart," said the Tin Woodman.

"Or send me back to Kansas," said Dorothy.

"Then, if you don't mind, I'll go with you," said the Lion, "for my life is simply unbearable without a bit of courage."

"You will be very welcome," answered Dorothy, "for you will help to keep away the other wild beasts. It seems to me they must be more cowardly than you are if they allow you to scare them so easily."

"They really are," said the Lion; "but that doesn't make me any braver, and as long as I know myself to be a coward I shall be unhappy."

So once more the little company set off upon the journey, the Lion walking with stately strides at Dorothy's side. Toto did not approve of this new comrade at first, for he could not forget how nearly he had been crushed between the Lion's great jaws; but after a time he became more at ease, and presently Toto and the Cowardly Lion had grown to be good friends.

During the rest of that day there was no other adventure to mar the peace of their journey. Once, indeed, the Tin Woodman stepped upon a beetle that was crawling along the road, and killed the poor little thing. This made the Tin Woodman very unhappy, for he was always careful not to hurt any living creature; and as he walked along he wept several tears of sorrow and regret. These tears ran slowly down his face and over the hinges of his jaw, and there they rusted. When Dorothy presently asked him a question the Tin Woodman could not open his mouth, for his jaws were tightly rusted together. He became greatly frightened at this and made many motions to Dorothy to relieve him, but she could not understand. The Lion was also puzzled to know what was wrong. But the Scarecrow seized the oil-can from Dorothy's basket and oiled the Woodman's jaws, so that after a few moments he could talk as well as before.

"This will serve me a lesson," said he, "to look where I step. For if I should kill another bug or beetle I should surely cry again, and crying rusts my jaw so that I cannot speak."

Thereafter he walked very carefully, with his eyes on the road, and when he saw a tiny ant toiling by he would step over it, so as not to harm it. The Tin Woodman knew very well he had no heart, and therefore he took great care never to be cruel or unkind to anything.

"You people with hearts," he said, "have something to guide you, and need never do wrong; but I have no heart, and so I must be very careful. When Oz gives me a heart, of course, I needn't mind so much."

CHAPTER 7

The Journey to the Great Oz

They were obliged to camp out that night under a large tree in the forest, for there were no houses near. The tree made a good, thick covering to protect them from the dew, and the Tin Woodman chopped a great pile of wood with his axe and Dorothy built a splendid fire that warmed her and made her feel less lonely. She and Toto ate the last of their bread, and now she did not know what they would do for breakfast.

"If you wish," said the Lion, "I will go into the forest and kill a deer for you. You can roast it by the fire, since your tastes are so peculiar that you prefer cooked food, and then you will have a very good breakfast."

"Don't! please don't," begged the Tin Woodman. "I should certainly weep[1] if you killed a poor deer, and then my jaws would rust again."

But the Lion went away into the forest and found his own supper, and no one ever knew what it was, for he didn't mention it. And the Scarecrow found a tree full of nuts and filled Dorothy's basket with them, so that she would not be hungry for a long time. She thought this was very kind and thoughtful of the Scarecrow, but she laughed heartily at the awkward way in which the poor creature picked up the nuts. His padded hands were so clumsy and the nuts were so small that he dropped almost as many as he put in the basket. But the Scarecrow did not mind how long it took him to fill the basket, for it enabled him to keep away from the fire, as he feared a spark might get into his straw and burn him up. So he kept a good distance away from the flames, and only came near to cover Dorothy with dry leaves when she lay down to sleep. These kept her very snug and warm and she slept soundly until morning.

When it was daylight the girl bathed her face in a little rippling brook and soon after they all started toward the Emerald City.

This was to be an eventful day for the travelers. They had hardly been walking an hour when they saw before them a great ditch that crossed the road and divided the forest as far they could see on either side. It was a very wide ditch, and when they crept up to the edge and looked into it they could see it was also very deep, and there were many big, jagged rocks at the bottom. The sides were so steep that none of them could climb down, and for a moment it seemed that their journey must end.

"What shall we do?" asked Dorothy despairingly.

"I haven't the faintest idea," said the Tin Woodman; and the Lion shook his shaggy mane and looked thoughtful. But the Scarecrow said:

"We cannot fly, that is certain; neither can we climb down into this great ditch. Therefore, if we cannot jump over it, we must stop where we are."

"I think I could jump over it," said the Cowardly Lion, after measuring the distance carefully in his mind.

"Then we are all right,"[2] answered the Scarecrow, "for you can carry us all over on your back, one at a time."

"Well, I'll try it," said the Lion. "Who will go first?"

"I will," declared the Scarecrow; "for, if you found that you could not jump over the gulf, Dorothy would be killed, or the Tin Woodman badly dented on the rocks below. But if I am on your back it will not matter so much, for the fall would not hurt me at all."

"I am terribly afraid of falling myself," said the Cowardly Lion, "but I suppose there is nothing to do but try it.[3] So get on my back and we will make the attempt."

The Scarecrow sat upon the Lion's back, and the big beast walked to the edge of the gulf and crouched down.

"Why don't you run and jump?" asked the Scarecrow.

"Because that isn't the way we Lions do these things," he replied. Then giving a great spring, he shot through the air and landed safely on the other side. They were all greatly pleased to see how easily he did it, and after the Scarecrow had got down from his back the Lion sprang across the ditch again.

Dorothy thought she would go next; so she took Toto in her arms and climbed on the Lion's back, holding tightly to his mane with one hand. The next moment it seemed as if she was flying through the air; and then, before she had time to think about it, she was safe on the other side. The Lion went back a third time and got the Tin Woodman, and then all sat down for a few moments to give the beast a chance to rest, for his great leaps had made his breath short, and he panted like a big dog that has been running too long.

They found the forest very thick on this side, and it looked dark and gloomy. After the Lion had rested they started along the road of yellow brick, silently wondering, each in his own mind, if ever they would come to the end of the woods and reach the bright sunshine again. To add to their discomfort, they soon heard strange noises in the depths of the forest, and the Lion whispered to them that it was in this part of the country that the Kalidahs[4] lived.

"What are the Kalidahs?" asked the girl.

"They are monstrous beasts with bodies like bears and heads like tigers," replied the Lion; "and with claws so long and sharp that they could tear me in two as easily as I could kill Toto. I'm terribly afraid of the Kalidahs."

"I'm not surprised that you are," returned Dorothy. "They must be dreadful beasts."

The Lion was about to reply when suddenly they came to another gulf across the road; but this one was so broad and deep that the Lion knew at once he could not leap across it.

So they sat down to consider what they should do, and after serious thought the Scarecrow said,

"Here is a great tree, standing close to the ditch. If the Tin Woodman can chop it down, so that it will fall to the other side, we can walk across it easily."

"That is a first-rate idea," said the Lion. "One would almost suspect you had brains in your head, instead of straw."

The Woodman set to work at once, and so sharp was his axe that the tree was soon chopped through. Then the Lion put his strong front legs against the tree and pushed with all his might, and slowly the big tree tipped and fell with a crash across the ditch, with its top branches on the other side.

They had just started to cross this queer bridge when a sharp growl made them all look up, and to their horror they saw running toward them two great beasts with bodies like bears and heads like tigers.

"They are the Kalidahs!" said the Cowardly Lion, beginning to tremble.

"Quick!" cried the Scarecrow, "let us cross over."

So Dorothy went first, holding Toto in her arms; the Tin Woodman followed, and the Scarecrow came next. The Lion, although he was certainly afraid, turned to face the Kalidahs, and then he gave so loud and terrible a roar that Dorothy screamed and the Scarecrow fell over backwards, while even the fierce beasts stopped short and looked at him in surprise.

But, seeing they were bigger than the Lion, and remembering that there were two of them and only one of him, the Kalidahs again rushed forward, and the Lion crossed over the tree and turned to see what they would do next. Without stopping an instant the fierce beasts also began to cross the tree, and the Lion said to Dorothy,

"We are lost, for they will surely tear us to pieces with their sharp claws. But stand close behind me, and I will fight them as long as I am alive."

"Wait a minute!" called the Scarecrow. He had been thinking what was best to be done, and now he asked the Woodman to chop away the end of the tree that rested on their side of the ditch. The Tin Woodman began to use his axe at once, and, just as the two Kalidahs were nearly across, the tree fell with a crash into the gulf, carrying the ugly, snarling brutes with it, and both were dashed to pieces on the sharp rocks at the bottom.

"Well," said the Cowardly Lion, drawing a long breath of relief, "I see we are going to live a little while longer, and I am glad of it, for it must be a very uncomfortable thing not to be alive. Those creatures frightened me so badly that my heart is beating yet."

"Ah," said the Tin Woodman sadly, "I wish I had a heart to beat."

This adventure made the travelers more anxious than ever to get out of the forest, and they walked so fast that Dorothy became tired, and had to ride on the Lion's back.

To their great joy the trees became thinner the farther they advanced, and in the afternoon they suddenly came upon a broad river, flowing swiftly just before them. On the other side of the water they could see the road of yellow brick running through a beautiful country, with green meadows dotted with bright flowers and all the road bordered with trees hanging full of delicious fruits. They were greatly pleased to see this delightful country before them.

"How shall we cross the river?" asked Dorothy.

"That is easily done," replied the Scarecrow. "The Tin Woodman must build us a raft, so we can float to the other side."

So the Woodman took his axe and began to chop down small trees to make a raft, and while he was busy at this the Scarecrow found on the river bank a tree full of fine fruit. This pleased Dorothy, who had eaten nothing but nuts all day, and she made a hearty meal of the ripe fruit.

But it takes time to make a raft, even when one is as industrious and untiring as the Tin Woodman, and when night came the work was not done. So they found a cozy place under the trees where they slept well until the morning; and Dorothy dreamed of the Emerald City, and of the good Wizard Oz, who would soon send her back to her own home again.

CHAPTER 8

The Deadly Poppy Field

Our little party of travelers awakened next morning refreshed and full of hope, and Dorothy breakfasted like a princess off peaches and plums from the trees beside the river.

Behind them was the dark forest they had passed safely through, although they had suffered many discouragements; but before them was a lovely, sunny country that seemed to beckon them on to the Emerald City.

To be sure, the broad river now cut them off from this beautiful land; but the raft was nearly done, and after the Tin Woodman had cut a few more logs and fastened them together with wooden pins, they were ready to start. Dorothy sat down in the middle of the raft and held Toto in her arms. When the Cowardly Lion stepped upon the raft it tipped badly, for he was big and heavy; but the Scarecrow and the Tin Woodman stood upon the other end to steady it, and they had long poles in their hands to push the raft through the water.

They got along quite well at first, but when they reached the middle of the river the swift current swept the raft downstream, farther and farther away from the road of yellow brick; and the water grew so deep that the long poles would not touch the bottom.

"This is bad," said the Tin Woodman, "for if we cannot get to the land we shall be carried into the country of the wicked Witch of the West, and she will enchant us and make us her slaves."

"And then I should get no brains," said the Scarecrow.

"And I should get no courage," said the Cowardly Lion.

"And I should get no heart," said the Tin Woodman.

"And I should never get back to Kansas," said Dorothy.

"We must certainly get to the Emerald City if we can," the Scarecrow continued, and he pushed so hard on his long pole that it stuck fast in the mud at the bottom of the river, and before he could pull it out again, or let go, the raft was swept away and the poor Scarecrow was left clinging to the pole in the middle of the river.

"Good-bye!" he called after them, and they were very sorry to leave him; indeed, the Tin Woodman began to cry, but fortunately remembered that he might rust, and so dried his tears on Dorothy's apron.

Of course this was a bad thing for the Scarecrow.

"I am now worse off than when I first met Dorothy," he thought. "Then, I was stuck on a pole in a cornfield, where I could make believe scare the crows, at any rate; but surely there is no use for a Scarecrow stuck on a pole in the middle of a river. I am afraid I shall never have any brains after all!"

Down the stream the raft floated, and the poor Scarecrow was left far behind. Then the Lion said:

"Something must be done to save us. I think I can swim to the shore and pull the raft after me, if you will only hold fast to the tip of my tail."

So he sprang into the water and the Tin Woodman caught fast hold of his tail, when the Lion began to swim with all his might toward the shore. It was hard work, although he was so big; but by and by they were drawn out of the current, and then Dorothy took the Tin Wood-man's long pole and helped push the raft to the land.

They were all tired out when they reached the shore at last and stepped off upon the pretty green grass, and they also knew that the stream had carried them a long way past the road of yellow brick that led to the Emerald City.

"What shall we do now?" asked the Tin Woodman, as the Lion lay down on the grass to let the sun dry him.

"We must get back to the road, in some way," said Dorothy.

"The best plan will be to walk along the river bank until we come to the road again," remarked the Lion.

So, when they were rested, Dorothy picked up her basket and they started along the grassy bank, back to the road from which the river had carried them. It was a lovely country, with plenty of flowers and fruit trees and sunshine to cheer them, and had they not felt so sorry for the poor Scarecrow they could have been very happy.

They walked along as fast as they could, Dorothy only stopping once to pick a beautiful flower; and after a time the Tin Woodman cried out,

"Look!"

Then they all looked at the river and saw the Scarecrow perched upon his pole in the middle of the water, looking very lonely and sad.

"What can we do to save him?" asked Dorothy.

The Lion and the Woodman both shook their heads, for they did not know. So they sat down upon the bank and gazed wistfully at the Scarecrow until a Stork[1] flew by, which, seeing them, stopped to rest at the water's edge.

"Who are you, and where are you going?" asked the Stork.

"I am Dorothy," answered the girl; "and these are my friends, the Tin Woodman and the Cowardly Lion; and we are going to the Emerald City."

"This isn't the road," said the Stork, as she twisted her long neck and looked sharply at the queer party.

"I know it," Dorothy said, "but we have lost the Scarecrow, and are wondering how we shall get him again."

"Where is he?" asked the Stork.

"Over there in the river," answered the girl.

"If he wasn't so big and heavy I would get him for you," remarked the Stork.

"He isn't heavy a bit," said Dorothy eagerly, "for he is stuffed with straw; and if you will bring him back to us we shall thank you ever and ever so much."

"Well, I'll try," said the Stork; "but if I find he is too heavy to carry I shall have to drop him in the river again."

So the big bird flew into the air and over the water till she came to where the Scarecrow was perched upon his pole. Then the Stork with her great claws grabbed the Scarecrow by the arm and carried him up into the air and back to the bank, where Dorothy and the Lion and the Tin Woodman and Toto were sitting.

When the Scarecrow found himself among his friends again he was so happy that he hugged them all, even the Lion and Toto; and as they walked along he sang "Tol-de-ri-de-oh!" at every step, he felt so gay.

"I was afraid I should have to stay in the river forever," he said, "but the kind Stork saved me, and if I ever get any brains I shall find the Stork again and do it some kindness in return."

"That's all right," said the Stork, who was flying along beside them. "I always like to help anyone in trouble. But I must go now, for my babies are waiting in the nest for me. I hope you will find the Emerald City and that Oz will help you."

"Thank you," replied Dorothy, and then the kind Stork flew into the air and was soon out of sight.

They walked along listening to the singing of the bright-colored birds and looking at the lovely flowers which now became so thick that the ground was carpeted with them. There were big yellow and white and blue and purple blossoms, besides great clusters of scarlet poppies,[2] which were so brilliant in color they almost dazzled Dorothy's eyes.

"Aren't they beautiful?" the girl asked, as she breathed in the spicy scent of the flowers.

"I suppose so," answered the Scarecrow. "When I have brains I shall probably like them better."

"If I only had a heart I should love them," added the Tin Woodman.

"I always did like flowers," said the Lion; "they seem so helpless and frail. But there are none in the forest so bright as these."

They now came upon more and more of the big scarlet poppies, and fewer and fewer of the other flowers; and soon they found themselves in the midst of a great meadow of poppies. Now it is well known that when there are many of these flowers together their odor is so powerful that anyone who breathes it falls asleep, and if the sleeper is not carried away from the scent of the flowers he sleeps on and on forever. But Dorothy did not know this, nor could she get away from the bright red flowers that were everywhere about; so presently her eyes grew heavy and she felt she must sit down to rest and to sleep.

But the Tin Woodman would not let her do this.

"We must hurry and get back to the road of yellow brick before dark," he said; and the Scarecrow agreed with him. So they kept walking until Dorothy could stand no longer. Her eyes closed in spite of herself and she forgot where she was and fell among the poppies, fast asleep.

"What shall we do?" asked the Tin Woodman.

"If we leave her here she will die," said the Lion. "The smell of the flowers is killing us all. I myself can scarcely keep my eyes open and the dog is asleep already."

It was true; Toto had fallen down beside his little mistress. But the Scarecrow and the Tin Woodman, not being made of flesh, were not troubled by the scent of the flowers.

"Run fast," said the Scarecrow to the Lion, "and get out of this deadly flowerbed as soon as you can. We will bring the little girl with us, but if you should fall asleep you are too big to be carried."

So the Lion aroused himself and bounded forward as fast as he could go. In a moment he was out of sight.

"Let us make a chair with our hands, and carry her," said the Scarecrow. So they picked up Toto and put the dog in Dorothy's lap, and then they made a chair with their hands for the seat and their arms for the arms and carried the sleeping girl between them through the flowers.

On and on they walked, and it seemed that the great carpet of deadly flowers that surrounded them would never end. They followed the bend of the river, and at last came upon their friend the Lion, lying fast asleep among the poppies. The flowers had been too strong for the huge beast and he had given up, at last, and fallen only a short distance from the end of the poppy-bed, where the sweet grass spread in beautiful green fields before them.

"We can do nothing for him," said the Tin Woodman sadly; "for he is much too heavy to lift. We must leave him here to sleep on forever, and perhaps he will dream that he has found courage at last."

"I'm sorry," said the Scarecrow; "the Lion was a very good comrade for one so cowardly. But let us go on."

They carried the sleeping girl to a pretty spot beside the river, far enough from the poppy field to prevent her breathing any more of the poison of the flowers, and here they laid her gently on the soft grass and waited for the fresh breeze to waken her.

CHAPTER 9

The Queen of the Field Mice

We cannot be far from the road of yellow brick now," remarked the Scarecrow, as he stood beside the girl, "for we have come nearly as far as the river carried us away."

The Tin Woodman was about to reply when he heard a low growl, and turning his head (which worked beautifully on hinges) he saw a strange beast come bounding over the grass towards them. It was, indeed, a great, yellow wildcat, and the Woodman thought it must be chasing something, for its ears were lying close to its head and its mouth was wide open, showing two rows of ugly teeth, while its red eyes glowed like balls of fire. As it came nearer the Tin Woodman saw that running before the beast was a little gray field mouse, and although he had no heart he knew it was wrong for the wildcat to try to kill such a pretty, harmless creature.

So the Woodman raised his axe, and as the wildcat ran by he gave it a quick blow that cut the beast's head clean off from its body, and it rolled over at his feet in two pieces.[1]

The field mouse, now that it was freed from its enemy, stopped short; and coming slowly up to the Woodman it said, in a squeaky little voice,

"Oh, thank you! Thank you ever so much for saving my life."

"Don't speak of it, I beg of you," replied the Woodman. "I have no heart, you know, so I am careful to help all those who may need a friend, even if it happens to be only a mouse."

"Only a mouse!"[2] cried the little animal indignantly; "why, I am a Queen—the Queen of all the field mice!"

"Oh, indeed," said the Woodman, making a bow.

"Therefore you have done a great deed, as well as a brave one, in saving my life," added the Queen.

At that moment several mice were seen running up as fast as their little legs could carry them, and when they saw their Queen they exclaimed,

"Oh, your Majesty, we thought you would be killed! How did you manage to escape the great Wildcat?" and they all bowed so low to the little Queen that they almost stood upon their heads.

"This funny tin man," she answered, "killed the Wildcat and saved my life. So hereafter you must all serve him, and obey his slightest wish."

"We will!" cried all the mice, in a shrill chorus. And then they scampered in all directions, for Toto had awakened from his sleep, and seeing all these mice around him he gave one bark of delight and jumped right into the middle of the group. Toto had always loved to chase mice when he lived in Kansas, and he saw no harm in it.

But the Tin Woodman caught the dog in his arms and held him tight, while he called to the mice: "Come back! come back! Toto shall not hurt you."

At this the Queen of the Mice stuck her head out from a clump of grass and asked in a timid voice,

"Are you sure he will not bite us?"

"I will not let him," said the Woodman; "so do not be afraid."

One by one the mice came creeping back, and Toto did not bark again, although he tried to get out of the Woodman's arms, and would have bitten him had he not known very well he was made of tin. Finally one of the biggest mice spoke.

"Is there anything we can do," it asked, "to repay you for saving the life of our Queen?"

"Nothing that I know of," answered the Woodman; but the Scarecrow, who had been trying to think, but could not because his head was stuffed with straw, said quickly,

"Oh, yes; you can save our friend, the Cowardly Lion, who is asleep in the poppy bed."

"A Lion!" cried the little Queen; "why, he would eat us all up."

"Oh, no," declared the Scarecrow; "this Lion is a coward."

"Really?" asked the Mouse.

"He says so himself," answered the Scarecrow, "and he would never hurt anyone who is our friend. If you will help us to save him I promise that he shall treat you all with kindness."

"Very well," said the Queen, "we will trust you. But what shall we do?"

"Are there many of these mice which call you Queen and are willing to obey you?"

"Oh, yes; there are thousands," she replied.

"Then send for them all to come here as soon as possible, and let each one bring a long piece of string."

The queen turned to the mice that attended her and told them to go at once and get all her people. As soon as they heard her orders they ran away in every direction as fast as possible.

"Now," said the Scarecrow to the Tin Woodman, "you must go to those trees by the riverside and make a truck that will carry the Lion."

So the Woodman went at once to the trees and began to work; and he soon made a truck out of the limbs of trees, from which he chopped away all the leaves and branches. He fastened it together with wooden pegs and made the four wheels out of short pieces of a big tree trunk. So fast and so well did he work that by the time the mice began to arrive the truck was all ready for them.

They came from all directions, and there were thousands of them: big mice and little mice and middle-sized mice; and each one brought a piece of string in his mouth. It was about this time that Dorothy woke from her long sleep and opened her eyes. She was greatly astonished to find herself lying upon the grass, with thousands of mice standing around and looking at her timidly. But the Scarecrow told her about everything, and turning to the dignified little Mouse, he said,

"Permit me to introduce to you her Majesty, the Queen."

Dorothy nodded gravely and the Queen made a curtsy, after which she became quite friendly with the little girl.

The Scarecrow and the Woodman now began to fasten the mice to the truck, using the strings they had brought. One end of a string was tied around the neck of each mouse and the other end to the truck. Of course the truck was a thousand times bigger than any of the mice who were to draw it; but when all the mice had been harnessed they were able to pull it quite easily. Even the Scarecrow and the Tin Woodman could sit on it, and were drawn swiftly by their queer little horses to the place where the Lion lay asleep.

After a great deal of hard work, for the Lion was heavy, they managed to get him up on the truck. Then the Queen hurriedly gave her people the order to start, for she feared if the mice stayed among the poppies too long they also would fall asleep.

At first the little creatures, many though they were, could hardly stir the heavily loaded truck; but the Woodman and the Scarecrow both pushed from behind, and they got along better. Soon they rolled the Lion out of the poppy bed to the green fields, where he could breathe the sweet, fresh air again, instead of the poisonous scent of the flowers.

Dorothy came to meet them and thanked the little mice warmly for saving her companion from death. She had grown so fond of the big Lion she was glad he had been rescued.

Then the mice were unharnessed from the truck and scampered away through the grass to their homes. The Queen of the Mice was the last to leave.

"If ever you need us again," she said, "come out into the field and call, and we shall hear you and come to your assistance. Good-bye!"

"Good-bye!" they all answered, and away the Queen ran, while Dorothy held Toto tightly lest he should run after her and frighten her.

After this they sat down beside the Lion until he should awaken; and the Scarecrow brought Dorothy some fruit from a tree near by, which she ate for her dinner.

CHAPTER 10

The Guardian of the Gates

It was some time before the Cowardly Lion awakened, for he had lain among the poppies a long while, breathing in their deadly fragrance; but when he did open his eyes and roll off the truck he was very glad to find himself still alive.

"I ran as fast as I could," he said, sitting down and yawning, "but the flowers were too strong for me. How did you get me out?"

Then they told him of the field mice, and how they had generously saved him from death; and the Cowardly Lion laughed, and said,

"I have always thought myself very big and terrible; yet such small things as flowers came near to killing me, and such small animals as mice have saved my life. How strange it all is! But, comrades, what shall we do now?"

"We must journey on until we find the road of yellow brick again," said Dorothy; "and then we can keep on to the Emerald City."

So, the Lion being fully refreshed, and feeling quite himself again, they all started upon the journey, greatly enjoying the walk through the soft, fresh grass; and it was not long before they reached the road of yellow brick and turned again toward the Emerald City where the great Oz dwelt.

The road was smooth and well paved now, and the country about was beautiful; so that the travelers rejoiced in leaving the forest far behind, and with it the many dangers they had met in its gloomy shades. Once more they could see fences built beside the road; but these were painted green, and when they came to a small house, in which a farmer evidently lived, that also was painted green. They passed by several of these houses during the afternoon, and sometimes people came to the doors and looked at them as if they would like to ask questions; but no one came near them nor spoke to them because of the great Lion, of which they were much afraid. The people were all dressed in clothing of a lovely emerald-green color and wore peaked hats like those of the Munchkins.

"This must be the Land of Oz," said Dorothy, "and we are surely getting near the Emerald City."

"Yes," answered the Scarecrow; "everything is green here, while in the country of the Munchkins blue was the favorite color. But the

people do not seem to be as friendly as the Munchkins and I'm afraid
we shall be unable to find a place to pass the night."

"I should like something to eat besides fruit," said the girl, "and
I'm sure Toto is nearly starved. Let us stop at the next house and talk
to the people."

So, when they came to a good-sized farmhouse, Dorothy walked
boldly up to the door and knocked. A woman opened it just far
enough to look out, and said,

"What do you want, child, and why is that great Lion with you?"

"We wish to pass the night with you, if you will allow us,"
answered Dorothy; "and the Lion is my friend and comrade, and
would not hurt you for the world."

"Is he tame?" asked the woman, opening the door a little wider.

"Oh, yes," said the girl; "and he is a great coward, too; so that he
will be more afraid of you than you are of him."

"Well," said the woman, after thinking it over and taking another
peep at the Lion, "if that is the case you may come in, and I will give
you some supper and a place to sleep."

So they all entered the house, where there were, besides the
woman, two children and a man. The man had hurt his leg, and was
lying on the couch in a corner. They seemed greatly surprised to see so
strange a company, and while the woman was busy laying the table
the man asked,

"Where are you all going?"

"To the Emerald City," said Dorothy, "to see the Great Oz."

"Oh, indeed!" exclaimed the man. "Are you sure that Oz will
see you?"

"Why not?" she replied.

"Why, it is said that he never lets any one come into his presence. I
have been to the Emerald City many times, and it is a beautiful and
wonderful place; but I have never been permitted to see the Great Oz,
nor do I know of any living person who has seen him."

"Does he never go out?" asked the Scarecrow.

"Never. He sits day after day in the great throne room of his
palace, and even those who wait upon him do not see him face to
face."

"What is he like?" asked the girl.

"That is hard to tell," said the man thoughtfully. "You see, Oz is a
great Wizard, and can take on any form he wishes.[1] So that some say
he looks like a bird; and some say he looks like an elephant; and some
say he looks like a cat. To others he appears as a beautiful fairy, or a

brownie, or in any other form that pleases him. But who the real Oz is, when he is in his own form, no living person can tell."

"That is very strange," said Dorothy; "but we must try, in some way, to see him, or we shall have made our journey for nothing."

"Why do you wish to see the terrible Oz?" asked the man.

"I want him to give me some brains," said the Scarecrow eagerly.

"Oh, Oz could do that easily enough," declared the man. "He has more brains than he needs."

"And I want him to give me a heart," said the Tin Woodman.

"That will not trouble him," continued the man, "for Oz has a large collection of hearts, of all sizes and shapes."

"And I want him to give me courage," said the Cowardly Lion.

"Oz keeps a great pot of courage in his throne room," said the man, "which he has covered with a golden plate, to keep it from running over. He will be glad to give you some."

"And I want him to send me back to Kansas," said Dorothy.

"Where is Kansas?" asked the man in surprise.

"I don't know," replied Dorothy sorrowfully; "but it is my home, and I'm sure it's somewhere."

"Very likely. Well, Oz can do anything; so I suppose he will find Kansas for you. But first you must get to see him, and that will be a hard task; for the great Wizard does not like to see anyone, and he usually has his own way. But what do YOU want?" he continued, speaking to Toto. Toto only wagged his tail; for, strange to say, he could not speak.[2]

The woman now called to them that supper was ready, so they gathered around the table and Dorothy ate some delicious porridge and a dish of scrambled eggs and a plate of nice white bread, and enjoyed her meal. The Lion ate some of the porridge, but did not care for it, saying it was made from oats and oats were food for horses, not for lions. The Scarecrow and the Tin Woodman ate nothing at all. Toto ate a little of everything, and was glad to get a good supper again.

The woman now gave Dorothy a bed to sleep in, and Toto lay down beside her, while the Lion guarded the door of her room so she might not be disturbed. The Scarecrow and the Tin Woodman stood up in a corner and kept quiet all night, although of course they could not sleep.

The next morning, as soon as the sun was up, they started on their way, and soon saw a beautiful green glow in the sky just before them.

"That must be the Emerald City," said Dorothy.

As they walked on, the green glow became brighter and brighter, and it seemed that at last they were nearing the end of their travels. Yet it was afternoon before they came to the great wall that surrounded the City. It was high, and thick, and of a bright green color.

In front of them, and at the end of the road of yellow brick, was a big gate, all studded with emeralds that glittered so in the sun that even the painted eyes of the Scarecrow were dazzled by their brilliancy.

There was a bell beside the gate, and Dorothy pushed the button and heard a silvery tinkle sound within. Then the big gate swung slowly open, and they all passed through and found themselves in a high arched room, the walls of which glistened with countless emeralds.

Before them stood a little man about the same size as the Munchkins. He was clothed all in green, from his head to his feet, and even his skin was of a greenish tint. At his side was a large green box.

When he saw Dorothy and her companions the man asked,

"What do you wish in the Emerald City?"

"We came here to see the Great Oz," said Dorothy.

The man was so surprised at this answer that he sat down to think it over.

"It has been many years since anyone asked me to see Oz," he said, shaking his head in perplexity. "He is powerful and terrible, and if you come on an idle or foolish errand to bother the wise reflections of the Great Wizard, he might be angry and destroy you all in an instant."

"But it is not a foolish errand, nor an idle one," replied the Scarecrow; "it is important. And we have been told that Oz is a good Wizard."

"So he is," said the green man; "and he rules the Emerald City wisely and well. But to those who are not honest, or who approach him from curiosity, he is most terrible, and few have ever dared ask to see his face. I am the Guardian of the Gates, and since you demand to see the Great Oz I must take you to his palace. But first you must put on the spectacles."[3]

"Why?" asked Dorothy.

"Because if you did not wear spectacles the brightness and glory of the Emerald City would blind you. Even those who live in the city must wear spectacles night and day. They are all locked on, for Oz so ordered it when the City was first built, and I have the only key that will unlock them."

He opened a big box, and Dorothy saw that it was filled with spectacles of every size and shape. All of them had green glasses in them. The Guardian of the Gates found a pair that would just fit Dorothy and put them over her eyes. There were two golden bands fastened to them that passed around the back of her head, where they were locked together by a little key that was at the end of a chain the Guardian of the Gates wore around his neck. When they were on, Dorothy could not take them off had she wished, but of course she did not want to be blinded by the glare of the Emerald City, so she said nothing.

Then the green man fitted spectacles for the Scarecrow and the Tin Woodman and the Lion, and even on little Toto; and all were locked fast with the key.

Then the Guardian of the Gates put on his own glasses and told them he was ready to show them to the palace. Taking a big golden key from a peg on the wall he opened another gate, and they all followed him through the portal into the streets of the Emerald City.

CHAPTER 11

The Wonderful Emerald City of Oz

Even with her eyes protected by the green spectacles, Dorothy and her friends were at first dazzled by the brilliancy of the wonderful City. The streets were lined with beautiful houses, all built of green marble and studded everywhere with sparkling emeralds. They walked over a pavement of the same green marble, and where the blocks were joined together were rows of emeralds, set closely, and glittering in the brightness of the sun. The windowpanes were of green glass; even the sky above the City had a green tint, and the rays of the sun were green.

There were many people,[1] men, women and children, walking about, and these were all dressed in green clothes and had greenish skins. They looked at Dorothy and her strangely assorted company with wondering eyes, and the children all ran away and hid behind their mothers when they saw the Lion; but no one spoke to them. Many shops stood in the street, and Dorothy saw that everything in them was green. Green candy and green popcorn were offered for sale, as well as green shoes, green hats and green clothes of all sorts.

At one place a man was selling green lemonade, and when the children bought it Dorothy could see that they paid for it with green pennies.

There seemed to be no horses nor animals of any kind; the men carried things around in little green carts, which they pushed before them. Everyone seemed happy and contented and prosperous.

The Guardian of the Gates led them through the streets until they came to a big building, exactly in the middle of the City, which was the Palace of Oz, the Great Wizard. There was a soldier before the door, dressed in a green uniform and wearing a long green beard.

"Here are strangers," said the Guardian of the Gates to him, "and they demand to see the Great Oz."

"Step inside," answered the soldier, "and I will carry your message to him."

So they passed through the palace gates and were led into a big room with a green carpet and lovely green furniture set with emeralds. The soldier made them all wipe their feet upon a green mat before entering this room, and when they were seated he said politely,

"Please make yourselves comfortable while I go to the door of the Throne Room and tell Oz you are here."

They had to wait a long time before the soldier returned. When, at last, he came back, Dorothy asked,

"Have you seen Oz?"

"Oh, no," returned the soldier; "I have never seen him. But I spoke to him as he sat behind his screen and gave him your message. He says he will grant you an audience, if you so desire; but each of you must enter his presence alone, and he will admit but one each day. Therefore, as you must remain in the Palace for several days, I will have you shown to rooms where you may rest in comfort after your journey."

"Thank you," replied the girl; "that is very kind of Oz."

The soldier now blew upon a green whistle, and at once a young girl, dressed in a pretty green silk gown, entered the room. She had lovely green hair and green eyes, and she bowed low before Dorothy as she said,

"Follow me and I will show you your room."

So Dorothy said good-bye to all her friends except Toto, and taking the dog in her arms followed the green girl through seven passages and up three flights of stairs until they came to a room at the front of the Palace. It was the sweetest little room in the world, with a soft, comfortable bed that had sheets of green silk and a green velvet counterpane. There was a tiny fountain in the middle of the room, that

shot a spray of green perfume into the air, to fall back into a beautifully carved green marble basin. Beautiful green flowers stood in the
windows, and there was a shelf with a row of little green books.
When Dorothy had time to open these books she found them full of
queer green pictures that made her laugh, they were so funny.

In a wardrobe were many green dresses, made of silk and satin and
velvet; and all of them fitted Dorothy exactly.

"Make yourself perfectly at home," said the green girl, "and if
you wish for anything ring the bell. Oz will send for you tomorrow
morning."

She left Dorothy alone and went back to the others. These she also
led to rooms, and each one of them found himself lodged in a very
pleasant part of the Palace. Of course this politeness was wasted on
the Scarecrow; for when he found himself alone in his room he stood
stupidly in one spot, just within the doorway, to wait till morning. It
would not rest him to lie down, and he could not close his eyes; so he
remained all night staring at a little spider which was weaving its web
in a corner of the room, just as if it were not one of the most wonderful rooms in the world. The Tin Woodman lay down on his bed from
force of habit, for he remembered when he was made of flesh; but not
being able to sleep he passed the night moving his joints up and down
to make sure they kept in good working order. The Lion would have
preferred a bed of dried leaves in the forest, and did not like being
shut up in a room; but he had too much sense to let this worry him, so
he sprang upon the bed and rolled himself up like a cat and purred
himself asleep in a minute.

The next morning, after breakfast, the green maiden came to fetch
Dorothy, and she dressed her in one of the prettiest gowns made of
green brocaded satin. Dorothy put on a green silk apron and tied a
green ribbon around Toto's neck, and they started for the Throne
Room of the Great Oz.

First they came to a great hall in which were many ladies and gentlemen of the court, all dressed in rich costumes. These people had
nothing to do but talk to each other, but they always came to wait
outside the Throne Room every morning, although they were never
permitted to see Oz. As Dorothy entered they looked at her curiously,
and one of them whispered,

"Are you really going to look upon the face of Oz the Terrible?"

"Of course," answered the girl, "if he will see me."

"Oh, he will see you," said the soldier who had taken her message
to the Wizard, "although he does not like to have people ask to see

him. Indeed, at first he was angry, and said I should send you back where you came from. Then he asked me what you looked like, and when I mentioned your silver shoes he was very much interested. At last I told him about the mark upon your forehead, and he decided he would admit you to his presence."

Just then a bell rang, and the green girl said to Dorothy,

"This is the signal. You must go into the Throne Room alone."

She opened a little door and Dorothy walked boldly through and found herself in a wonderful place. It was a big, round room with a high arched roof, and the walls and ceiling and floor were covered with large emeralds set closely together. In the center of the ceiling was a great light, as bright as the sun, which made the emeralds sparkle in a wonderful manner.

But what interested Dorothy most was the big throne of green marble that stood in the middle of the room. It was shaped like a chair and sparkled with gems, as did everything else. In the center of the chair was an enormous Head, without body to support it or any arms or legs whatever. There was no hair upon this head, but it had eyes and nose and mouth, and was bigger than the head of the biggest giant.

As Dorothy gazed upon this in wonder and fear the eyes turned slowly and looked at her sharply and steadily. Then the mouth moved, and Dorothy heard a voice say:

"I am Oz, the Great and Terrible. Who are you, and why do you seek me?"

It was not such an awful voice as she had expected to come from the big Head; so she took courage and answered,

"I am Dorothy, the Small and Meek. I have come to you for help."

The eyes looked at her thoughtfully for a full minute. Then said the voice:

"Where did you get the silver shoes?"

"I got them from the Wicked Witch of the East, when my house fell on her and killed her," she replied.

"Where did you get the mark upon your forehead?" continued the voice.

"That is where the good Witch of the North kissed me when she bade me good-bye and sent me to you," said the girl.

Again the eyes looked at her sharply, and they saw she was telling the truth. Then Oz asked,

"What do you wish me to do?"

"Send me back to Kansas, where my Aunt Em and Uncle Henry are," she answered earnestly. "I don't like your country, although it is so beautiful. And I am sure Aunt Em will be worried over my being away so long."

The eyes winked three times, and then they turned up to the ceiling and down to the floor and rolled around so queerly that they seemed to see every part of the room. And at last they looked at Dorothy again.

"Why should I do this for you?" asked Oz.

"Because you are strong and I am weak; because you are a Great Wizard and I am only a helpless little girl," she answered.

"But you were strong enough to kill the wicked Witch of the East," said Oz.

"That just happened," returned Dorothy simply; "I could not help it."

"Well," said the Head, "I will give you my answer. You have no right to expect me to send you back to Kansas unless you do something for me in return. In this country everyone must pay for everything he gets. If you wish me to use my magic power to send you home again you must do something for me first. Help me and I will help you."

"What must I do?" asked the girl.

"Kill the wicked Witch of the West," answered Oz.

"But I cannot!" exclaimed Dorothy, greatly surprised.

"You killed the Witch of the East and you wear the silver shoes, which bear a powerful charm. There is now but one Wicked Witch left in all this land, and when you can tell me she is dead I will send you back to Kansas—but not before."

The little girl began to weep, she was so disappointed; the eyes winked again and looked at her anxiously, as if the Great Oz felt that she could help him if she would.

"I never killed anything willingly," she sobbed; "and even if I wanted to, how could I kill the Wicked Witch? If you, who are Great and Terrible, cannot kill her yourself, how do you expect me to do it?"

"I do not know," said the Head; "but that is my answer, and until the Wicked Witch dies you will not see your Uncle and Aunt again. Remember that the Witch is Wicked—tremendously Wicked—and ought to be killed. Now go, and do not ask to see me again until you have done your task."

Sorrowfully Dorothy left the Throne Room and went back where the Lion and the Scarecrow and the Tin Woodman were waiting to hear what Oz had said to her.

"There is no hope for me," she said sadly, "for Oz will not send me home until I have killed the Wicked Witch of the West; and that I can never do."

Her friends were sorry, but could do nothing to help her; so she went to her own room and lay down on the bed and cried herself to sleep.

The next morning the soldier with the green whiskers came to the Scarecrow and said,

"Come with me, for Oz has sent for you."

So the Scarecrow followed him and was admitted into the great Throne Room, where he saw, sitting in the emerald throne, a most lovely lady. She was dressed in green silk gauze and wore upon her flowing green locks a crown of jewels. Growing from her shoulders were wings, gorgeous in color and so light that they fluttered if the slightest breath of air reached them.

When the Scarecrow had bowed, as prettily as his straw stuffing would let him, before this beautiful creature, she looked upon him sweetly, and said,

"I am Oz, the Great and Terrible. Who are you, and why do you seek me?"

Now the Scarecrow, who had expected to see the great Head Dorothy had told him of, was much astonished; but he answered her bravely.

"I am only a Scarecrow, stuffed with straw. Therefore I have no brains, and I come to you praying that you will put brains in my head instead of straw, so that I may become as much a man as any other in your dominions."

"Why should I do this for you?" asked the lady.

"Because you are wise and powerful, and no one else can help me," answered the Scarecrow.

"I never grant favors without some return," said Oz; "but this much I will promise. If you will kill for me the Wicked Witch of the West I will bestow upon you a great many brains, and such good brains that you will be the wisest man in all the Land of Oz."

"I thought you asked Dorothy to kill the Witch," said the Scarecrow, in surprise.

"So I did. I don't care who kills her. But until she is dead I will not grant your wish. Now go, and do not seek me again until you have earned the brains you so greatly desire."

The Scarecrow went sorrowfully back to his friends and told them what Oz had said; and Dorothy was surprised to find that the great Wizard was not a Head, as she had seen him, but a lovely lady.

"All the same," said the Scarecrow, "she needs a heart as much as the Tin Woodman."

On the next morning the soldier with the green whiskers came to the Tin Woodman and said,

"Oz has sent for you. Follow me."

So the Tin Woodman followed him and came to the great Throne Room. He did not know whether he would find Oz a lovely lady or a Head, but he hoped it would be the lovely lady. "For," he said to himself, "if it is the Head, I am sure I shall not be given a heart, since a head has no heart of its own and therefore cannot feel for me. But if it is the lovely lady I shall beg hard for a heart, for all ladies are themselves said to be kindly hearted."

But when the Woodman entered the great Throne Room he saw neither the Head nor the Lady, for Oz had taken the shape of a most terrible Beast.[2] It was nearly as big as an elephant, and the green throne seemed hardly strong enough to hold its weight. The Beast had a head like that of a rhinoceros, only there were five eyes in its face. There were five long arms growing out of its body and it also had five long, slim legs. Thick, woolly hair covered every part of it, and a more dreadful-looking monster could not be imagined. It was fortunate the Tin Woodman had no heart at that moment, for it would have beat loud and fast from terror. But being only tin, the Woodman was not at all afraid, although he was much disappointed.

"I am Oz, the Great and Terrible," spake the Beast, in a voice that was one great roar. "Who are you, and why do you seek me?"

"I am a Woodman, and made of tin. Therefore I have no heart, and cannot love. I pray you to give me a heart that I may be as other men are."

"Why should I do this?" demanded the Beast.

"Because I ask it, and you alone can grant my request," answered the Woodman.

Oz gave a low growl at this, but said gruffly,

"If you indeed desire a heart, you must earn it."

"How?" asked the Woodman.

"Help Dorothy to kill the Wicked Witch of the West," replied the Beast. "When the Witch is dead, come to me, and I will then give you the biggest and kindest and most loving heart in all the Land of Oz."

So the Tin Woodman was forced to return sorrowfully to his

friends and tell them of the terrible Beast he had seen. They all wondered greatly at the many forms the great Wizard could take upon himself, and the Lion said,

"If he is a beast when I go to see him, I shall roar my loudest, and so frighten him that he will grant all I ask. And if he is the lovely lady, I shall pretend to spring upon her, and so compel her to do my bidding. And if he is the great Head, he will be at my mercy; for I will roll this head all about the room until he promises to give us what we desire. So cheer up my friends, for all will yet be well."

The next morning the soldier with the green whiskers led the Lion to the great Throne Room and bade him enter the presence of Oz.

The Lion at once passed through the door, and glancing around saw, to his surprise, that before the throne was a Ball of Fire,[3] so fierce and glowing he could scarcely bear to gaze upon it. His first thought was that Oz had by accident caught on fire and was burning up; but, when he tried to go nearer, the heat was so intense that it singed his whiskers, and he crept back tremblingly to a spot nearer the door.

Then a low, quiet voice came from the Ball of Fire, and these were the words it spoke:

"I am Oz, the Great and Terrible. Who are you, and why do you seek me?" And the Lion answered,

"I am a Cowardly Lion, afraid of everything. I come to you to beg that you give me courage, so that in reality I may become the King of Beasts, as men call me."

"Why should I give you courage?" demanded Oz.

"Because of all Wizards you are the greatest, and alone have power to grant my request," answered the Lion.

The Ball of Fire burned fiercely for a time, and the voice said,

"Bring me proof that the Wicked Witch is dead, and that moment I will give you courage. But so long as the Witch lives you must remain a coward."

The Lion was angry at this speech, but could say nothing in reply, and while he stood silently gazing at the Ball of Fire it became so furiously hot that he turned tail and rushed from the room. He was glad to find his friends waiting for him, and told them of his terrible interview with the Wizard.

"What shall we do now?" asked Dorothy sadly.

"There is only one thing we can do," returned the Lion, "and that is to go to the land of the Winkies, seek out the Wicked Witch, and destroy her."

"But suppose we cannot?" said the girl.

"Then I shall never have courage," declared the Lion.

"And I shall never have brains," added the Scarecrow.

"And I shall never have a heart," spoke the Tin Woodman.

"And I shall never see Aunt Em and Uncle Henry," said Dorothy, beginning to cry.

"Be careful!" cried the green girl; "the tears will fall on your green silk gown, and spot it."

So Dorothy dried her eyes and said,

"I suppose we must try it; but I am sure I do not want to kill anybody, even to see Aunt Em again."

"I will go with you; but I'm too much of a coward to kill the Witch," said the Lion.

"I will go too," declared the Scarecrow; "but I shall not be of much help to you, I am such a fool."

"I haven't the heart to harm even a Witch," remarked the Tin Woodman; "but if you go I certainly shall go with you."

Therefore it was decided to start upon their journey the next morning, and the Woodman sharpened his axe on a green grindstone and had all his joints properly oiled. The Scarecrow stuffed himself with fresh straw and Dorothy put new paint on his eyes that he might see better. The green girl, who was very kind to them, filled Dorothy's basket with good things to eat, and fastened a little bell around Toto's neck with a green ribbon.

They went to bed quite early and slept soundly until daylight, when they were awakened by the crowing of a green cock that lived in the back yard of the palace, and the cackling of a hen that had laid a green egg.

CHAPTER 12

The Search for the Wicked Witch

The soldier with the green whiskers led them through the streets of the Emerald City until they reached the room where the Guardian of the Gates lived. This officer unlocked their spectacles to put them back in his great box, and then he politely opened the gate for our friends.

"Which road leads to the Wicked Witch of the West?" asked Dorothy.

"There is no road," answered the Guardian of the Gates; "no one ever wishes to go that way."

"How, then, are we to find her?" inquired the girl.

"That will be easy," replied the man; "for when she knows you are in the Country of the Winkies she will find you, and make you all her slaves."

"Perhaps not," said the Scarecrow, "for we mean to destroy her."

"Oh, that is different," said the Guardian of the Gates. "No one has ever destroyed her before, so I naturally thought she would make slaves of you, as she has of all the rest. But take care; for she is wicked and fierce, and may not allow you to destroy her. Keep to the West, where the sun sets, and you cannot fail to find her."

They thanked him and bade him good-bye, and turned toward the West, walking over fields of soft grass dotted here and there with daisies and buttercups. Dorothy still wore the pretty silk dress she had put on in the palace, but now, to her surprise, she found it was no longer green, but pure white. The ribbon around Toto's neck had also lost its green color and was as white as Dorothy's dress.

The Emerald City was soon left far behind. As they advanced the ground became rougher and hillier, for there were no farms nor houses in this country of the West, and the ground was untilled.

In the afternoon the sun shone hot in their faces, for there were no trees to offer them shade; so that before night Dorothy and Toto and the Lion were tired, and lay down upon the grass and fell asleep, with the Woodman and the Scarecrow keeping watch.

Now the Wicked Witch of the West had but one eye, yet that was as powerful as a telescope, and could see everywhere. So, as she sat in the door of her castle, she happened to look around and saw Dorothy lying asleep, with her friends all about her. They were a long distance off, but the Wicked Witch was angry to find them in her country; so she blew upon a silver whistle that hung around her neck.

At once there came running to her from all directions a pack of great wolves. They had long legs and fierce eyes and sharp teeth.

"Go to those people," said the Witch, "and tear them to pieces."

"Are you not going to make them your slaves?" asked the leader of the wolves.

"No," she answered, "one is of tin, and one of straw; one is a girl and another a Lion. None of them is fit to work, so you may tear them into small pieces."

"Very well," said the wolf, and he dashed away at full speed, followed by the others.

It was lucky the Scarecrow and the Woodman were wide awake
and heard the wolves coming.

"This is my fight," said the Woodman; "so get behind me and I
will meet them as they come."

He seized his axe, which he had made very sharp, and as the leader
of the wolves came on the Tin Woodman swung his arm and chopped
the wolf's head from its body, so that it immediately died. As soon as
he could raise his axe another wolf came up, and he also fell under the
sharp edge of the Tin Woodman's weapon. There were forty wolves,[1]
and forty times a wolf was killed; so that at last they all lay dead in a
heap before the Woodman.

Then he put down his axe and sat beside the Scarecrow, who said,
"It was a good fight, friend."

They waited until Dorothy awoke the next morning. The little girl
was quite frightened when she saw the great pile of shaggy wolves,
but the Tin Woodman told her all. She thanked him for saving them
and sat down to breakfast, after which they started again upon their
journey.

Now this same morning the Wicked Witch came to the door of her
castle and looked out with her one eye that could see afar off. She saw
all her wolves lying dead, and the strangers still traveling through her
country. This made her angrier than before, and she blew her silver
whistle twice.

Straightway a great flock of wild crows came flying toward her,
enough to darken the sky. And the Wicked Witch said to the King
Crow,

"Fly at once to the strangers; peck out their eyes and tear them to
pieces."

The wild crows flew in one great flock toward Dorothy and her
companions. When the little girl saw them coming she was afraid. But
the Scarecrow said,

"This is my battle; so lie down beside me and you will not be
harmed."

So they all lay upon the ground except the Scarecrow, and he stood
up and stretched out his arms. And when the crows saw him they
were frightened, as these birds always are by scarecrows, and did not
dare to come any nearer. But the King Crow said,

"It is only a stuffed man. I will peck his eyes out."

The King Crow flew at the Scarecrow, who caught it by the head
and twisted its neck until it died. And then another crow flew at him,
and the Scarecrow twisted its neck also. There were forty crows, and

forty times the Scarecrow twisted a neck, until at last all were lying dead beside him. Then he called to his companions to rise, and again they went upon their journey.

When the Wicked Witch looked out again and saw all her crows lying in a heap, she got into a terrible rage, and blew three times upon her silver whistle.

Forthwith there was heard a great buzzing in the air, and a swarm of black bees came flying towards her.

"Go to the strangers and sting them to death!" commanded the Witch, and the bees turned and flew rapidly until they came to where Dorothy and her friends were walking. But the Woodman had seen them coming and the Scarecrow had decided what to do.

"Take out my straw and scatter it over the little girl and the dog and the lion," he said to the Woodman, "and the bees cannot sting them." This the Woodman did, and as Dorothy lay close beside the Lion and held Toto in her arms, the straw covered them entirely.

The bees came and found no one but the Woodman to sting, so they flew at him and broke off all their stings against the tin, without hurting the Woodman at all. And as bees cannot live when their stings are broken that was the end of the black bees, and they lay scattered thick about the Woodman, like little heaps of fine coal.

Then Dorothy and the Lion got up, and the girl helped the Tin Woodman put the straw back into the Scarecrow again, until he was as good as ever. So they started upon their journey once more.

The Wicked Witch was so angry when she saw her black bees in little heaps like fine coal that she stamped her foot and tore her hair and gnashed her teeth. And then she called a dozen of her slaves, who were the Winkies, and gave them sharp spears, telling them to go to the strangers and destroy them.

The Winkies were not a brave people, but they had to do as they were told; so they marched away until they came near to Dorothy. Then the Lion gave a great roar and sprang toward them, and the poor Winkies were so frightened that they ran back as fast as they could.

When they returned to the castle the Wicked Witch beat them well with a strap, and sent them back to their work, after which she sat down to think what she should do next. She could not understand how all her plans to destroy these strangers had failed; but she was a powerful Witch, as well as a wicked one, and she soon made up her mind how to act.

There was, in her cupboard, a Golden Cap,[2] with a circle of diamonds and rubies running round it. This Golden Cap had a charm. Whoever owned it could call three times upon the Winged Monkeys,[3] who would obey any order they were given. But no person could command these strange creatures more than three times. Twice already the Wicked Witch had used the charm of the Cap. Once was when she had made the Winkies her slaves, and set herself to rule over their country. The Winged Monkeys had helped her to do this. The second time was when she had fought against the Great Oz himself, and driven him out of the land of the West. The Winged Monkeys had also helped her in doing this. Only once more could she use this Golden Cap, for which reason she did not like to do so until all her other powers were exhausted. But now that her fierce wolves and her wild crows and her stinging bees were gone, and her slaves had been scared away by the Cowardly Lion, she saw there was only one way left to destroy Dorothy and her friends.

So the Wicked Witch took the Golden Cap from her cupboard and placed it upon her head. Then she stood upon her left foot and said, slowly,

"Ep-pe, pep-pe, kak-ke!"

Next she stood upon her right foot and said,

"Hil-lo, hol-lo, hel-lo!"

After this she stood upon both feet and cried in a loud voice . . . "Ziz-zy, zuz-zy, zik!"

Now the charm began to work. The sky was darkened, and a low rumbling sound was heard in the air. There was a rushing of many wings; a great chattering and laughing; and the sun came out of the dark sky to show the Wicked Witch surrounded by a crowd of monkeys, each with a pair of immense and powerful wings on his shoulders.

One, much bigger than the others, seemed to be their leader. He flew close to the Witch and said,

"You have called us for the third and last time. What do you command?"

"Go to the strangers who are within my land and destroy them all except the Lion," said the Wicked Witch. "Bring that beast to me, for I have a mind to harness him like a horse, and make him work."

"Your commands shall be obeyed," said the leader; and then, with a great deal of chattering and noise, the Winged Monkeys flew away to the place where Dorothy and her friends were walking.

Some of the Monkeys seized the Tin Woodman and carried him

through the air until they were over a country thickly covered with sharp rocks. Here they dropped the poor Woodman, who fell a great distance to the rocks, where he lay so battered and dented that he could neither move nor groan.

Others of the Monkeys caught the Scarecrow, and with their long fingers pulled all of the straw out of his clothes and head. They made his hat and boots and clothes into a small bundle and threw it into the top branches of a tall tree.

The remaining Monkeys threw pieces of stout rope around the Lion and wound many coils about his body and head and legs, until he was unable to bite or scratch or struggle in any way. Then they lifted him up and flew away with him to the Witch's castle, where he was placed in a small yard with a high iron fence around it, so that he could not escape.

But Dorothy they did not harm at all. She stood, with Toto in her arms, watching the sad fate of her comrades and thinking it would soon be her turn. The leader of the Winged Monkeys flew up to her, his long, hairy arms stretched out and his ugly face grinning terribly; but he saw the mark of the Good Witch's kiss upon her forehead and stopped short, motioning the others not to touch her.

"We dare not harm this little girl," he said to them, "for she is protected by the Power of Good, and that is greater than the Power of Evil. All we can do is to carry her to the castle of the Wicked Witch, and leave her there."

So, carefully and gently, they lifted Dorothy in their arms and carried her swiftly through the air until they came to the castle, where they set her down upon the front doorstep. Then the leader said to the Witch,

"We have obeyed you as far as we were able. The Tin Woodman and the Scarecrow are destroyed, and the Lion is tied up in your yard. The little girl we dare not harm, nor the dog she carries in her arms. Your power over our band is now ended, and you will never see us again."

Then all the Winged Monkeys, with much laughing and chattering and noise, flew into the air and were soon out of sight.

The Wicked Witch was both surprised and worried when she saw the mark on Dorothy's forehead, for she knew well that neither the Winged Monkey nor she, herself, dare hurt the girl in any way. She looked down at Dorothy's feet, and seeing the Silver Shoes, began to tremble with fear, for she knew what a powerful charm belonged to them. At first the Witch was tempted to run away from Dorothy; but she happened to look into the child's eyes and saw how simple the soul behind them was, and that the little girl did not know of the wonderful power the Silver Shoes gave her. So the Wicked Witch laughed to herself, and thought, "I can still make her my slave, for she does not know how to use her power." Then she said to Dorothy, harshly and severely,

"Come with me; and see that you mind everything I tell you, for if you do not I will make an end of you, as I did of the Tin Woodman and the Scarecrow."

Dorothy followed her through many of the beautiful rooms in her castle until they came to the kitchen, where the Witch bade her clean the pots and kettles and sweep the floor and keep the fire fed with wood.[4]

Dorothy went to work meekly, with her mind made up to work as hard as she could; for she was glad the Wicked Witch had decided not to kill her.

With Dorothy hard at work, the Witch thought she would go into the courtyard and harness the Cowardly Lion like a horse; it would amuse her, she was sure, to make him draw her chariot whenever she wished to go to drive. But as she opened the gate the Lion gave a loud roar and bounded at her so fiercely that the Witch was afraid, and ran out and shut the gate again.

"If I cannot harness you," said the Witch to the Lion, speaking through the bars of the gate, "I can starve you. You shall have nothing to eat until you do as I wish."

So after that she took no food to the imprisoned Lion; but every day she came to the gate at noon and asked,

"Are you ready to be harnessed like a horse?"

And the Lion would answer,

"No. If you come in this yard I will bite you."

The reason the Lion did not have to do as the Witch wished was that every night, while the woman was asleep, Dorothy carried him food from the cupboard. After he had eaten he would lie down on his bed of straw, and Dorothy would lie beside him and put her head on his soft, shaggy mane, while they talked of their troubles and tried to plan some way to escape. But they could find no way to get out of the castle, for it was constantly guarded by the yellow Winkies, who were the slaves of the Wicked Witch and too afraid of her not to do as she told them.

The girl had to work hard during the day, and often the Witch threatened to beat her with the same old umbrella[5] she always carried in her hand. But, in truth, she did not dare to strike Dorothy, because of the mark upon her forehead. The child did not know this, and was full of fear for herself and Toto. Once the Witch struck Toto a blow with her umbrella and the brave little dog flew at her and bit her leg in return. The Witch did not bleed where she was bitten, for she was so wicked that the blood in her had dried up many years before.

Dorothy's life became very sad as she grew to understand that it would be harder than ever to get back to Kansas and Aunt Em again. Sometimes she would cry bitterly for hours, with Toto sitting at her feet and looking into her face, whining dismally to show how sorry he was for his little mistress. Toto did not really care whether he was in Kansas or the Land of Oz so long as Dorothy was with him; but he knew the little girl was unhappy, and that made him unhappy too.

Now the Wicked Witch had a great longing to have for her own the Silver Shoes which the girl always wore. Her Bees and her Crows and her Wolves were lying in heaps and drying up, and she had used up all the power of the Golden Cap; but if she could only get hold of the Silver Shoes they would give her more power than all the other things she had lost. She watched Dorothy carefully, to see if she ever took off her shoes, thinking she might steal them. But the child was so proud of her pretty shoes that she never took them off except at night and when she took her bath. The Witch was too much afraid of the dark to dare to go in Dorothy's room at night to take the shoes, and her dread of water was greater than her fear of the dark, so she never came near when Dorothy was bathing. Indeed, the old Witch never touched water, nor ever let water touch her in any way.

But the wicked creature was very cunning, and she finally thought of a trick that would give her what she wanted. She placed a bar of iron in the middle of the kitchen floor, and then by her magic arts made the iron invisible to human eyes. So that when Dorothy walked across the floor she stumbled over the bar, not being able to see it, and fell at full length. She was not much hurt, but in her fall one of the Silver Shoes came off, and before she could reach it the Witch snatched it away and put it on her own skinny foot.

The wicked woman was greatly pleased with the success of her trick, for as long as she had one of the shoes she owned half the power of their charm, and Dorothy could not use it against her, even had she known how to do so.

The little girl, seeing she had lost one of her pretty shoes, grew angry, and said to the Witch,

"Give me back my shoe!"

"I will not," retorted the Witch, "for it is now my shoe, and not yours."

"You are a wicked creature!" cried Dorothy. "You have no right to take my shoe from me."

"I shall keep it, just the same," said the Witch, laughing at her, "and some day I shall get the other one from you, too."

This made Dorothy so very angry that she picked up the bucket of water[6] that stood near and dashed it over the Witch, wetting her from head to foot.

Instantly the wicked woman gave a loud cry of fear; and then, as Dorothy looked at her in wonder, the Witch began to shrink and fall away.

"See what you have done!" she screamed. "In a minute I shall melt away."

"I'm very sorry, indeed," said Dorothy, who was truly frightened to see the Witch actually melting away like brown sugar before her very eyes.

"Didn't you know water would be the end of me?" asked the Witch, in a wailing, despairing voice.

"Of course not," answered Dorothy; "how should I?"

"Well, in a few minutes I shall be all melted, and you will have the castle to yourself. I have been wicked in my day, but I never thought a little girl like you would ever be able to melt me and end my wicked deeds. Look out—here I go!"

With these words the Witch fell down in a brown, melted, shapeless mass and began to spread over the clean boards of the kitchen floor. Seeing that she had really melted away to nothing, Dorothy drew another bucket of water and threw it over the mess. She then swept it all out the door. After picking out the silver shoe, which was all that was left of the old woman, she cleaned and dried it with a cloth, and put it on her foot again. Then, being at last free to do as she chose, she ran out to the courtyard to tell the Lion that the Wicked Witch of the West had come to an end, and that they were no longer prisoners in a strange land.

CHAPTER 13

The Rescue

The Cowardly Lion was much pleased to hear that the Wicked Witch had been melted by a bucket of water, and Dorothy at once unlocked the gate of his prison and set him free. They went in together to the castle, where Dorothy's first act was to call all the Winkies together and tell them that they were no longer slaves.

There was great rejoicing among the yellow Winkies, for they had been made to work hard during many years for the Wicked Witch, who had always treated them with great cruelty. They kept this day as a holiday, then and ever after, and spent the time in feasting and dancing.

"If our friends, the Scarecrow and the Tin Woodman, were only with us," said the Lion, "I would be happy."

"Don't you suppose we could rescue them?" asked the girl anxiously.

"We can try," answered the Lion.

So they called the yellow Winkies and asked them if they would help to rescue their friends, and the Winkies said they would be delighted to do all in their power for Dorothy, who had set them free from bondage. So she chose a number of the Winkies who looked as if they knew the most, and they all started away. They traveled that day and part of the next until they came to the rocky plain where the Tin Woodman lay, all battered and bent. His axe was near him, but the blade was rusted and the handle broken off short.

The Winkies lifted him tenderly in their arms, and carried him back to the yellow castle again, Dorothy shedding a few tears by the way at the sad plight of her old friend, and the Lion looking sober and sorry. When they reached the castle Dorothy said to the Winkies,

"Are any of your people tinsmiths?"

"Oh, yes; some of us are good tinsmiths," they told her.

"Then bring them to me," she said. And when the tinsmiths came, bringing with them all their tools in baskets, she inquired,

"Can you straighten out those dents in the Tin Woodman, and bend him back into shape again, and solder him together where he is broken?"

The tinsmiths looked the Woodman over carefully and then answered that they thought they could mend him so he would be as good as ever. So they set to work in one of the big yellow rooms of the castle and worked for three days and four nights, hammering and twisting and bending and soldering and polishing and pounding at the legs and body and head of the Tin Woodman, until at last he was straightened out into his old form, and his joints worked as well as ever. To be sure, there were several patches on him, but the tinsmiths did a good job, and as the Woodman was not a vain man he did not mind the patches at all.

When, at last, he walked into Dorothy's room and thanked her for rescuing him, he was so pleased that he wept tears of joy, and Dorothy had to wipe every tear carefully from his face with her apron, so his joints would not be rusted. At the same time her own tears fell thick and fast at the joy of meeting her old friend again, and these tears did not need to be wiped away. As for the Lion, he wiped his eyes so often with the tip of his tail that it became quite wet, and he was obliged to go out into the courtyard and hold it in the sun till it dried.

"If we only had the Scarecrow with us again," said the Tin Woodman, when Dorothy had finished telling him everything that had happened, "I should be quite happy."

"We must try to find him," said the girl.

So she called the Winkies to help her, and they walked all that day and part of the next until they came to the tall tree in the branches of which the Winged Monkeys had tossed the Scarecrow's clothes.

It was a very tall tree, and the trunk was so smooth that no one could climb it; but the Woodman said at once,

"I'll chop it down, and then we can get the Scarecrow's clothes."

Now while the tinsmiths had been at work mending the Woodman himself, another of the Winkies, who was a goldsmith, had made an axe-handle of solid gold and fitted it to the Woodman's axe, instead of the old broken handle. Others polished the blade until all the rust was removed and it glistened like burnished silver.

As soon as he had spoken, the Tin Woodman began to chop, and in a short time the tree fell over with a crash, when the Scarecrow's clothes fell out of the branches and rolled off on the ground.

Dorothy picked them up and had the Winkies carry them back to the castle, where they were stuffed with nice, clean straw; and, behold! here was the Scarecrow, as good as ever, thanking them over and over again for saving him.

Now they were reunited, Dorothy and her friends spent a few happy days at the Yellow Castle, where they found everything they needed to make them comfortable. But one day the girl thought of Aunt Em, and said,

"We must go back to Oz, and claim his promise."

"Yes," said the Woodman, "at last I shall get my heart."

"And I shall get my brains," added the Scarecrow.

"And I shall get my courage," said the Lion.

"And I shall get back to Kansas," cried Dorothy, joyfully. "Oh, let us start for the Emerald City tomorrow!"

This they decided to do. The next day they called the Winkies together and bade them good-bye. The Winkies were sorry to have them go, and they had grown so fond of the Tin Woodman that they begged him to stay and rule over them and the Yellow Land of the West. Finding they were determined to go, the Winkies gave Toto and the Lion each a golden collar; and to Dorothy they presented a beautiful bracelet, studded with diamonds;[1] and to the Scarecrow they gave a gold-headed walking stick, to keep him from stumbling; and to the Tin Woodman they offered a silver oil-can, inlaid with gold and set with jewels.

Every one of the travelers made the Winkies a pretty speech in return, and all shook hands with them until their arms ached.

Dorothy went to the Witch's cupboard to fill her basket with food for the journey, and there she saw the Golden Cap. She tried it on her own head and found that it fitted her exactly. She did not know anything about the charm of the Golden Cap, but she saw that it was pretty, so she made up her mind to wear it and carry her sunbonnet in the basket.

Then, being prepared for the journey, they all started for the Emerald City; and the Winkies gave them three cheers and many good wishes to carry with them.

CHAPTER 14

The Winged Monkeys

You will remember there was no road—not even a pathway—between the castle of the Wicked Witch and the Emerald City. When the four travelers went in search of the Witch she had seen them coming, and so sent the Winged Monkeys to bring them to her. It was much harder to find their way back through the big fields of buttercups and yellow daisies than it was being carried. They knew, of course, they must go straight east, toward the rising sun; and they started off in the right way. But at noon, when the sun was over their heads, they did not know which was east and which was west, and that was the reason they were lost in the great fields. They kept on walking, however, and at night the moon came out and shone brightly. So they lay down among the sweet-smelling yellow flowers and slept soundly until morning—all but the Scarecrow and the Tin Woodman.

The next morning the sun was behind a cloud, but they started on, as if they were quite sure which way they were going.

"If we walk far enough," said Dorothy, "we shall sometime come to some place, I am sure."

But day by day passed away, and they still saw nothing before them but the yellow fields. The Scarecrow began to grumble a bit.

"We have surely lost our way," he said, "and unless we find it again in time to reach the Emerald City I shall never get my brains."

"Nor I my heart," declared the Tin Woodman. "It seems to me I can scarcely wait till I get to Oz, and you must admit this is a very long journey."

"You see," said the Cowardly Lion, with a whimper, "I haven't the courage to keep tramping forever, without getting anywhere at all."

Then Dorothy lost heart. She sat down on the grass and looked at her companions, and they sat down and looked at her, and Toto found that for the first time in his life he was too tired to chase a butterfly that flew past his head; so he put out his tongue and panted and looked at Dorothy as if to ask what they should do next.

"Suppose we call the Field Mice," she suggested. "They could probably tell us the way to the Emerald City."

"To be sure they could," cried the Scarecrow; "why didn't we think of that before?"

Dorothy blew the little whistle she had always carried about her neck since the Queen of the Mice had given it to her. In a few minutes they heard the pattering of tiny feet, and many of the small gray mice came running up to her. Among them was the Queen herself, who asked, in her squeaky little voice,

"What can I do for my friends?"

"We have lost our way," said Dorothy. "Can you tell us where the Emerald City is?"

"Certainly," answered the Queen; "but it is a great way off, for you have had it at your back all this time." Then she noticed

Dorothy's Golden Cap, and said, "Why don't you use the charm of the Cap, and call the Winged Monkeys to you? They will carry you to the City of Oz in less than an hour."

"I didn't know there was a charm," answered Dorothy, in surprise. "What is it?"

"It is written inside the Golden Cap," replied the Queen of the Mice; "but if you are going to call the Winged Monkeys we must run away, for they are full of mischief and think it is great fun to plague us."

"Won't they hurt me?" asked the girl anxiously.

"Oh, no; they must obey the wearer of the Cap. Good-bye!" And she scampered out of sight, with all the mice hurrying after her.

Dorothy looked inside the Golden Cap and saw some words written upon the lining. These, she thought, must be the charm, so she read the directions carefully and put the cap upon her head.

"Ep-pe, pep-pe, kak-ke!" she said, standing on her left foot.

"What did you say?" asked the Scarecrow, who did not know what she was doing.

"Hil-lo, hol-lo, hel-lo!" Dorothy went on, standing this time on her right foot.

"Hello!" replied the Tin Woodman calmly.

"Ziz-zy, zuz-zy, zik!" said Dorothy, who was now standing on both feet. This ended the saying of the charm, and they heard a great chattering and flapping of wings, as the band of Winged Monkeys flew up to them. The King bowed low before Dorothy, and asked,

"What is your command?"

"We wish to go to the Emerald City," said the child, "and we have lost our way."

"We will carry you," replied the King, and no sooner had he spoken than two of the Monkeys caught Dorothy in their arms and flew away with her. Others took the Scarecrow and the Woodman and the Lion, and one little Monkey seized Toto and flew after them, although the dog tried hard to bite him.

The Scarecrow and the Tin Woodman were rather frightened at first, for they remembered how badly the Winged Monkeys had treated them before; but they saw that no harm was intended, so they rode through the air quite cheerfully, and had a fine time looking at the pretty gardens and woods far below them.

Dorothy found herself riding easily between two of the biggest Monkeys, one of them the King himself. They had made a chair of their hands and were careful not to hurt her.

"Why do you have to obey the charm of the Golden Cap?" she asked.

"That is a long story,"[1] answered the King, with a laugh; "but as we have a long journey before us I will pass the time by telling you about it, if you wish."

"I shall be glad to hear it," she replied.

"Once," began the leader, "we were a free people, living happily in the great forest, flying from tree to tree, eating nuts and fruit, and doing just as we pleased without calling anybody master. Perhaps some of us were rather too full of mischief at times, flying down to pull the tails of the animals that had no wings, chasing birds, and throwing nuts at the people who walked in the forest. But we were careless and happy and full of fun, and enjoyed every minute of the day. This was years ago, long before Oz came out of the clouds to rule over this land.

"There lived here then, away at the North, a beautiful princess, who was also a powerful sorceress. All her magic was used to help the people, and she was never known to hurt anyone who was good. Her name was Gayelette, and she lived in a handsome palace built from great blocks of ruby. Everyone loved her, but her greatest sorrow was that she could find no one to love in return, since all the men were much too stupid and ugly to mate with one so beautiful and wise. At last, however, she found a boy who was handsome and manly and wise beyond his years. Gayelete made up her mind that when he grew to be a man she would make him her husband, so she took him to her ruby palace and used all her magic powers to make him as strong and good and lovely as any woman could wish. When he grew to manhood, Quelala, as he was called, was said to be the best and wisest man in all the land, while his manly beauty was so great that Gayelette loved him dearly, and hastened to make everything ready for the wedding.

"My grandfather was at that time the King of the Winged Monkeys which lived in the forest near Gayelette's palace, and the old fellow loved a joke better than a good dinner. One day, just before the wedding, my grandfather was flying out with his band when he saw Quelala walking beside the river. He was dressed in a rich costume of pink silk and purple velvet, and my grandfather thought he would see what he could do. At his word the band flew down and seized Quelala, carried him in their arms until they were over the middle of the river, and then dropped him into the water.

" 'Swim out, my fine fellow,' cried my grandfather, 'and see if the water has spotted your clothes.' Quelala was much too wise not to swim, and he was not in the least spoiled by all his good fortune. He laughed, when he came to the top of the water, and swam in to shore. But when Gayelette came running out to him she found his silks and velvet all ruined by the river.

"The princess was very angry, and she knew, of course, who did it. She had all the Winged Monkeys brought before her, and she said at first that their wings should be tied and they should be treated as they had treated Quelala, and dropped in the river. But my grandfather pleaded hard, for he knew the Monkeys would drown in the river with their wings tied, and Quelala said a kind word for them also; so that Gayelette finally spared them, on condition that the Winged Monkeys should ever after do three times the bidding of the owner of the Golden Cap. This Cap had been made for a wedding present to Quelala, and it is said to have cost the princess half her kingdom. Of course my grandfather and all the other Monkeys at once agreed to the condition, and that is how it happens that we are three times the slaves of the owner of the Golden Cap, whomsoever he may be."

"And what became of them?" asked Dorothy.

"Quelala, being the first owner of the Golden Cap," replied the Monkey, "was the first to lay his wishes upon us. As his bride could not bear the sight of us, he called us all to him in the forest after he had married her and ordered us to always keep where she could never again set eyes on a Winged Monkey, which we were glad to do, for we were all afraid of her.

"This was all we ever had to do until the Golden Cap fell into the hands of the Wicked Witch of the West, who made us enslave the Winkies, and afterward drive Oz himself out of the Land of the West. Now the Golden Cap is yours, and three times you have the right to lay your wishes upon us."

As the Monkey King finished his story Dorothy looked down and saw the green, shining walls of the Emerald City before them. She wondered at the rapid flight of the Monkeys, but was glad the journey was over. The strange creatures set the travelers down carefully before the gate of the City, the King bowed low to Dorothy, and then flew swiftly away, followed by all his band.

"That was a good ride," said the little girl.

"Yes, and a quick way out of our troubles," replied the Lion. "How lucky it was you brought away that wonderful Cap!"

CHAPTER 15

The Discovery of Oz, the Terrible

The four travelers walked up to the great gate of the Emerald City and rang the bell. After ringing several times it was opened by the same Guardian of the Gate they had met before.

"What! are you back again?" he asked in surprise.

"Do you not see us?" answered the Scarecrow.

"But I thought you had gone to visit the Wicked Witch of the West."

"We did visit her," said the Scarecrow.

"And she let you go again?" asked the man in wonder.

"She could not help it, for she is melted," explained the Scarecrow.

"Melted! Well, that is good news, indeed," said the man. "Who melted her?"

"It was Dorothy," said the Lion gravely.

"Good gracious!" exclaimed the man, and he bowed very low indeed before her.

Then he led them into his little room and locked the spectacles from the great box on all their eyes, just as he had done before. Afterward they passed on through the gate into the Emerald City, and when the people heard from the Guardian of the Gate that they had melted the Wicked Witch of the West they all gathered around the travelers and followed them in a great crowd to the Palace of Oz.

The soldier with the green whiskers was still on guard before the door, but he let them in at once and they were again met by the beautiful green girl, who showed each of them to his old room at once, so they might rest until the Great Oz was ready to receive them.

The soldier had the news carried straight to Oz that Dorothy and the other travelers had come back again, after destroying the Wicked Witch; but Oz made no reply. They thought the Great Wizard would send for them at once, but he did not. They had no word from him the next day, nor the next, nor the next. The waiting was tiresome and wearing, and at last they grew vexed that Oz should treat them in so poor a fashion, after sending them to undergo hardships and slavery. So the Scarecrow at last asked the green girl to take another message to Oz, saying if he did not let them in to see him at once they would call the Winged Monkeys to help them, and find out whether he kept his promises or not. When the Wizard was given this message he was

so frightened that he sent word for them to come to the Throne Room
at four minutes after nine o'clock the next morning. He had once met
the Winged Monkeys in the Land of the West, and he did not wish to
meet them again.

The four travelers passed a sleepless night, each thinking of the gift
Oz had promised to bestow upon him. Dorothy fell asleep only once,
and then she dreamed she was in Kansas, where Aunt Em was telling
her how glad she was to have her little girl at home again.

Promptly at nine o'clock the next morning the green-whiskered soldier came to them, and four minutes later they all went into the
Throne Room of the Great Oz.

Of course each one of them expected to see the Wizard in the shape
he had taken before, and all were greatly surprised when they looked
about and saw no one at all in the room. They kept close to the door
and closer to one another, for the stillness of the empty room was
more dreadful than any of the forms they had seen Oz take.

Presently they heard a Voice, seeming to come from somewhere
near the top of the great dome, and it said solemnly,

"I am Oz, the Great and Terrible. Why do you seek me?"

They looked again in every part of the room, and then, seeing no
one, Dorothy asked,

"Where are you?"

"I am everywhere," answered the Voice, "but to the eyes of common mortals I am invisible. I will now seat myself upon my throne,
that you may converse with me." Indeed, the Voice seemed just then
to come straight from the throne itself; so they walked toward it and
stood in a row while Dorothy said:

"We have come to claim our promise, O Oz."

"What promise?" asked Oz.

"You promised to send me back to Kansas when the Wicked Witch
was destroyed," said the girl.

"You promised to give me brains," said the Scarecrow.

"And you promised to give me a heart," said the Tin Woodman.

"And you promised to give me courage," said the Cowardly Lion.

"Is the Wicked Witch really destroyed?" asked the Voice, and
Dorothy thought it trembled a little.

"Yes," she answered, "I melted her with a bucket of water."

"Dear me," said the Voice; "how sudden! Well, come to me tomorrow, for I must have time to think it over."

"You've had plenty of time already," said the Tin Woodman angrily.

"We shan't wait a day longer," said the Scarecrow.

"You must keep your promises to us!" exclaimed Dorothy.

The Lion thought it might be as well to frighten the Wizard, so he gave a large, loud roar, which was so fierce and dreadful that Toto jumped away from him in alarm and tipped over the screen that stood in a corner. As it fell with a crash they looked that way, and the next moment all of them were filled with wonder. For they saw, standing in just the spot the screen had hidden, a little, old man, with a bald head and a wrinkled face,[1] who seemed to be as much surprised as they were. The Tin Woodman, raising his axe, rushed toward the little man and cried out,

"Who are you?"

"I am Oz, the Great and Terrible," said the little man, in a trembling voice, "but don't strike me—please don't!—and I'll do anything you want me to."

Our friends looked at him in surprise and dismay.

"I thought Oz was a great Head," said Dorothy.

"I thought Oz was a lovely Lady," said the Scarecrow.

"And I thought Oz was a terrible Beast," said the Tin Woodman.

"And I thought Oz was a Ball of Fire," exclaimed the Lion.

"No; you are all wrong," said the little man meekly. "I have been making believe."

"Making believe!" cried Dorothy. "Are you not a great Wizard?"

"Hush, my dear," he said; "don't speak so loud, or you will be overheard—and I should be ruined. I'm supposed to be a great Wizard."

"And aren't you?" she asked.

"Not a bit of it, my dear; I'm just a common man."

"You're more than that," said the Scarecrow, in a grieved tone; "you're a humbug."

"Exactly so!" declared the little man, rubbing his hands together as if it pleased him; "I am a humbug."[2]

"But this is terrible," said the Tin Woodman; "how shall I ever get my heart?"

"Or I my courage?" asked the Lion.

"Or I my brains?" wailed the Scarecrow, wiping the tears from his eyes with his coat-sleeve.

"My dear friends," said Oz, "I pray you not to speak of these little things. Think of me, and the terrible trouble I'm in at being found out."

"Doesn't anyone else know you're a humbug?" asked Dorothy.

"No one knows it but you four—and myself," replied Oz. "I have fooled everyone so long that I thought I should never be found out. It was a great mistake my ever letting you into the Throne Room. Usually I will not see even my subjects, and so they believe I am something terrible."

"But I don't understand," said Dorothy, in bewilderment. "How was it that you appeared to me as a great Head?"

"That was one of my tricks," answered Oz. "Step this way, please, and I will tell you all about it."

He led the way to a small chamber in the rear of the Throne Room, and they all followed him. He pointed to one corner, in which lay the Great Head, made out of many thicknesses of paper, and with a carefully painted face.

"This I hung from the ceiling by a wire," said Oz; "I stood behind the screen and pulled a thread to make the eyes move and the mouth open."

"But how about the voice?" she inquired.

"Oh, I am a ventriloquist," said the little man, "and I can throw the sound of my voice wherever I wish; so that you thought it was coming out of the Head. Here are the other things I used to deceive you." He showed the Scarecrow the dress and the mask he had worn when he seemed to be the lovely Lady; and the Tin Woodman saw that his Terrible Beast was nothing but a lot of skins, sewn together, with slats to keep their sides out. As for the Ball of Fire, the false Wizard had hung that also from the ceiling. It was really a ball of cotton, but when oil was poured upon it the ball burned fiercely.

"Really," said the Scarecrow, "you ought to be ashamed of yourself for being such a humbug."

"I am—I certainly am," answered the little man sorrowfully; "but it was the only thing I could do. Sit down, please, there are plenty of chairs, and I will tell you my story."

So they sat down and listened while he told the following tale:

"I was born in Omaha—"[3]

"Why, that isn't very far from Kansas!" cried Dorothy.

"No; but it's farther from here," he said, shaking his head at her sadly. "When I grew up I became a ventriloquist, and at that I was very well trained by a great master. I can imitate any kind of a bird or beast." Here he mewed so like a kitten that Toto pricked up his ears and looked everywhere to see where she was. "After a time," continued Oz, "I tired of that, and became a balloonist."

"What is that?" asked Dorothy.

"A man who goes up in a balloon on circus day, so as to draw a crowd of people together and get them to pay to see the circus," he explained.

"Oh," she said; "I know."

"Well, one day I went up in a balloon and the ropes got twisted, so that I couldn't come down again. It went way up above the clouds, so far that a current of air struck it and carried it many, many miles away. For a day and a night I traveled through the air, and on the morning of the second day I awoke and found the balloon floating over a strange and beautiful country.

"It came down gradually, and I was not hurt a bit. But I found myself in the midst of a strange people, who, seeing me come from the clouds, thought I was a great Wizard. Of course I let them think so, because they were afraid of me, and promised to do anything I wished them to.

"Just to amuse myself, and keep the good people busy, I ordered them to build this City, and my palace; and they did it all willingly and well. Then I thought, as the country was so green and beautiful, I would call it the Emerald City, and to make the name fit better I put green spectacles on all the people, so that everything they saw was green."

"But isn't everything here green?" asked Dorothy.

"No more than in any other city,"[4] replied Oz; "but when you wear green spectacles, why of course everything you see looks green to you. The Emerald City was built a great many years ago, for I was a young man when the balloon brought me here, and I am a very old man now.[5] But my people have worn green glasses on their eyes so long that most of them think it really is an Emerald City, and it certainly is a beautiful place, abounding in jewels and precious metals, and every good thing that is needed to make one happy. I have been good to the people, and they like me; but ever since this Palace was built I have shut myself up and would not see any of them.

"One of my greatest fears was the Witches, for while I had no magical powers at all I soon found out that the Witches were really able to do wonderful things. There were four of them in this country, and they ruled the people who live in the North and South and East and West. Fortunately, the Witches of the North and South were good, and I knew they would do me no harm; but the Witches of the East and West were terribly wicked, and had they not thought I was more powerful than they themselves, they would surely have destroyed me. As it was, I lived in deadly fear of them for many years; so you can

imagine how pleased I was when I heard your house had fallen on the
Wicked Witch of the East. When you came to me I was willing to
promise anything if you would only do away with the other Witch;
but, now that you have melted her, I am ashamed to say that I cannot
keep my promises."

"I think you are a very bad man," said Dorothy.

"Oh, no, my dear; I'm really a very good man; but I'm a very bad
Wizard, I must admit."

"Can't you give me brains?" asked the Scarecrow.

"You don't need them. You are learning something every day. A
baby has brains, but it doesn't know much. Experience is the only
thing that brings knowledge, and the longer you are on earth the more
experience you are sure to get."

"That may all be true," said the Scarecrow, "but I shall be very
unhappy unless you give me brains."

The false Wizard looked at him carefully.

"Well," he said, with a sigh, "I'm not much of a magician, as I
said; but if you will come to me tomorrow morning, I will stuff your
head with brains. I cannot tell you how to use them, however; you
must find that out for yourself."

"Oh, thank you—thank you!" cried the Scarecrow. "I'll find a way
to use them, never fear!"

"But how about my courage?" asked the Lion anxiously.

"You have plenty of courage, I am sure," answered Oz. "All you
need is confidence in yourself. There is no living thing that is not
afraid when it faces danger. True courage is in facing danger when
you are afraid, and that kind of courage you have in plenty."

"Perhaps I have, but I'm scared just the same," said the Lion. "I
shall really be very unhappy unless you give me the sort of courage
that makes one forget he is afraid."

"Very well; I will give you that sort of courage tomorrow," replied
Oz.

"How about my heart?" asked the Tin Woodman.

"Why, as for that," answered Oz, "I think you are wrong to want
a heart. It makes most people unhappy. If you only knew it, you are in
luck not to have a heart."

"That must be a matter of opinion," said the Tin Woodman. "For
my part, I will bear all the unhappiness without a murmur, if you will
give me the heart."

"Very well," answered Oz, meekly. "Come to me tomorrow and

you shall have a heart. I have played Wizard for so many years that I may as well continue the part a little longer."

"And now," said Dorothy, "how am I going to get back to Kansas?"

"We shall have to think about that," replied the little man, "Give me two or three days to consider the matter and I'll try to find a way to carry you over the desert. In the meantime you shall all be treated as my guests, and while you live in the Palace my people will wait upon you and obey your slightest wish. There is only one thing I ask in return for my help—such as it is. You must keep my secret and tell no one I am a humbug."

They agreed to say nothing of what they had learned, and went back to their rooms in high spirits. Even Dorothy had hope that "The Great and Terrible Humbug," as she called him, would find a way to send her back to Kansas, and if he did that she was willing to forgive him everything.

CHAPTER 16

The Magic Art of the Great Humbug

Next morning the Scarecrow said to his friends:

"Congratulate me. I am going to Oz to get my brains at last. When I return I shall be as other men are."

"I have always liked you as you were," said Dorothy simply.

"It is kind of you to like a Scarecrow," he replied. "But surely you will think more of me when you hear the splendid thoughts my new brain is going to turn out." Then he said good-bye to them all in a cheerful voice and went to the Throne Room, where he rapped upon the door.

"Come in," said Oz.

The Scarecrow went in and found the little man sitting down by the window, engaged in deep thought.

"I have come for my brains," remarked the Scarecrow a little uneasily.

"Oh, yes; sit down in that chair, please," replied Oz. "You must excuse me for taking your head off, but I shall have to do it in order to put your brains in their proper place."

"That's all right," said the Scarecrow. "You are quite welcome to take my head off, as long as it will be a better one when you put it on again."

So the Wizard unfastened his head and emptied out the straw. Then he entered the back room and took up a measure of bran, which he mixed with a great many pins and needles. Having shaken them together thoroughly, he filled the top of the Scarecrow's head with the mixture and stuffed the rest of the space with straw, to hold it in place. When he had fastened the Scarecrow's head on his body again he said to him,

"Hereafter you will be a great man, for I have given you a lot of bran-new brains."

The Scarecrow was both pleased and proud at the fulfillment of his greatest wish, and having thanked Oz warmly he went back to his friends.

Dorothy looked at him curiously. His head was quite bulging out at the top with brains.

"How do you feel?" she asked.

"I feel wise, indeed," he answered earnestly. "When I get used to my brains I shall know everything."

"Why are those needles and pins sticking out of your head?" asked the Tin Woodman.

"That is proof that he is sharp," remarked the Lion.

"Well, I must go to Oz and get my heart," said the Woodman. So he walked to the Throne Room and knocked at the door.

"Come in," called Oz, and the Woodman entered and said,

"I have come for my heart."

"Very well," answered the little man. "But I shall have to cut a hole in your breast, so I can put your heart in the right place. I hope it won't hurt you."

"Oh, no," answered the Woodman. "I shall not feel it at all."

So Oz brought a pair of tinners' shears and cut a small, square hole in the left side of the Tin Woodman's breast. Then, going to a chest of drawers, he took out a pretty heart, made entirely of silk and stuffed with sawdust.

"Isn't it a beauty," he asked.

"It is, indeed!" replied the Woodman, who was greatly pleased. "But is it a kind heart?"

"Oh, very!" answered Oz. He put the heart in the Woodman's breast and then replaced the square of tin, soldering it neatly together where it had been cut.

"There," said he; "now you have a heart that any man might be proud of. I'm sorry I had to put a patch on your breast, but it really couldn't be helped."

"Never mind the patch," exclaimed the happy Woodman. "I am very grateful to you, and shall never forget your kindness."

"Don't speak of it," replied Oz.

Then the Tin Woodman went back to his friends, who wished him every joy on account of his good fortune.

The Lion now walked to the Throne Room and knocked at the door.

"Come in," said Oz.

"I have come for my courage," announced the Lion, entering the room.

"Very well," answered the little man; "I will get it for you."

He went to a cupboard and reaching up to a high shelf took down a square green bottle, the contents of which he poured into a green-gold dish, beautifully carved. Placing this before the Cowardly Lion, who sniffed at it as if he did not like it, the Wizard said,

"Drink."

"What is it?" asked the Lion.

"Well," answered Oz, "if it were inside of you, it would be courage. You know, of course, that courage is always inside one; so that this really cannot be called courage until you have swallowed it. Therefore I advise you to drink it as soon as possible."

The Lion hesitated no longer, but drank till the dish was empty.

"How do you feel now?" asked Oz.

"Full of courage," replied the Lion, who went joyfully back to his friends to tell them of his good fortune.

Oz, left to himself, smiled to think of his success in giving the Scarecrow and the Tin Woodman and the Lion exactly what they thought they wanted. "How can I help being a humbug," he said, "when all these people make me do things that everybody knows can't be done? It was easy to make the Scarecrow and the Lion and the Woodman happy, because they imagined I could do anything. But it will take more than imagination to carry Dorothy back to Kansas, and I'm sure I don't know how it can be done."

CHAPTER 17

How the Balloon Was Launched

For three days Dorothy heard nothing from Oz. These were sad days for the little girl, although her friends were all quite happy and contented. The Scarecrow told them there were wonderful thoughts in his head; but he would not say what they were because he knew no one could understand them but himself. When the Tin Woodman walked about he felt his heart rattling around in his breast; and he told Dorothy he had discovered it to be a kinder and more tender heart than the one he had owned when he was made of flesh. The Lion declared he was afraid of nothing on earth, and would gladly face an army of men or a dozen of the fierce Kalidahs.

Thus each of the little party was satisfied except Dorothy, who longed more than ever to get back to Kansas.

On the fourth day, to her great joy, Oz sent for her, and when she entered the Throne Room he said pleasantly:

"Sit down, my dear; I think I have found the way to get you out of this country."

"And back to Kansas?" she asked eagerly.

"Well, I'm not sure about Kansas," said Oz; "for I haven't the faintest notion which way it lies. But the first thing to do is to cross the desert, and then it should be easy to find your way home."

"How can I cross the desert?" she inquired.

"Well, I'll tell you what I think," said the little man. "You see, when I came to this country it was in a balloon. You also came through the air, being carried by a cyclone. So I believe the best way to get across the desert will be through the air. Now, it is quite beyond my powers to make a cyclone; but I've been thinking the matter over, and I believe I can make a balloon."

"How?" asked Dorothy.

"A balloon," said Oz, "is made of silk, which is coated with glue to keep the gas in it. I have plenty of silk in the Palace, so it will be no trouble for us to make the balloon. But in all this country there is no gas to fill the balloon with, to make it float."

"If it won't float," remarked Dorothy, "it will be of no use to us."

"True," answered Oz. "But there is another way to make it float, which is to fill it with hot air. Hot air isn't as good as gas, for if the air should get cold the balloon would come down in the desert, and we should be lost."

"We!" exclaimed the girl; "are you going with me?"

"Yes, of course," replied Oz. "I am tired of being such a humbug. If I should go out of this Palace my people would soon discover I am not a Wizard, and then they would be vexed with me for having deceived them. So I have to stay shut up in these rooms all day, and it gets tiresome. I'd much rather go back to Kansas with you and be in a circus again."

"I shall be glad to have your company," said Dorothy.

"Thank you," he answered. "Now if you will help me sew the silk together, we will begin to work on our balloon."

So Dorothy took a needle and thread, and as fast as Oz cut the strips of silk into proper shape the girl sewed them neatly together. First there was a strip of light green silk, then a strip of dark green and then a strip of emerald green; for Oz had a fancy to make the balloon in different shades of the color about them. It took three days to sew all the strips together, but when it was finished they had a big bag of green silk more than twenty feet long.

Then Oz painted it on the inside with a coat of thin glue, to make it airtight, after which he announced that the balloon was ready.

"But we must have a basket to ride in," he said. So he sent the soldier with the green whiskers for a big clothes basket, which he fastened with many ropes to the bottom of the balloon.

When it was all ready, Oz sent word to his people that he was going to make a visit to a great brother Wizard who lived in the clouds. The news spread rapidly throughout the city and everyone came to see the wonderful sight.

Oz ordered the balloon carried out in front of the Palace, and the people gazed upon it with much curiosity. The Tin Woodman had chopped a big pile of wood, and now he made a fire of it, and Oz held the bottom of the balloon over the fire so that the hot air that arose from it would be caught in the silken bag. Gradually the balloon swelled out and rose into the air, until finally the basket just touched the ground.

Then Oz got into the basket and said to all the people in a loud voice:

"I am now going away to make a visit. While I am gone the Scarecrow will rule over you. I command you to obey him as you would me."

The balloon was by this time tugging hard at the rope that held it to the ground, for the air within it was hot, and this made it so much lighter in weight than the air without that it pulled hard to rise into the sky.

"Come, Dorothy!" cried the Wizard; "hurry up, or the balloon will fly away."

"I can't find Toto anywhere," replied Dorothy, who did not wish to leave her little dog behind. Toto had run into the crowd to bark at a kitten, and Dorothy at last found him. She picked him up and ran toward the balloon.

She was within a few steps of it, and Oz was holding out his hands to help her into the basket, when, crack! went the ropes, and the balloon rose into the air without her.

"Come back!" she screamed; "I want to go, too!"

"I can't come back, my dear,"[1] called Oz from the basket. "Good-bye!"

"Good-bye!" shouted everyone, and all eyes were turned upward to where the Wizard was riding in the basket, rising every moment farther and farther into the sky.

And that was the last any of them ever saw of Oz,[2] the Wonderful Wizard, though he may have reached Omaha safely, and be there now, for all we know. But the people remembered him lovingly, and said to one another,

"Oz was always our friend. When he was here he built for us this beautiful Emerald City, and now he is gone he has left the Wise Scarecrow to rule over us."

Still, for many days they grieved over the loss of the Wonderful Wizard, and would not be comforted.

CHAPTER 18

Away to the South

Dorothy wept bitterly at the passing of her hope to get home to Kansas again; but when she thought it all over she was glad she had not gone up in a balloon. And she also felt sorry at losing Oz, and so did her companions.

The Tin Woodman came to her and said,

"Truly I should be ungrateful if I failed to mourn for the man who gave me my lovely heart. I should like to cry a little because Oz is gone, if you will kindly wipe away my tears, so that I shall not rust."

"With pleasure," she answered, and brought a towel at once. Then the Tin Woodman wept for several minutes, and she watched the tears carefully and wiped them away with the towel. When he had finished he thanked her kindly and oiled himself thoroughly with his jeweled oilcan, to guard against mishap.

The Scarecrow was now the ruler of the Emerald City, and although he was not a Wizard the people were proud of him. "For," they said, "there is not another city in all the world that is ruled by a stuffed man." And, so far as they knew, they were quite right.

The morning after the balloon had gone up with Oz the four travelers met in the Throne Room and talked matters over. The Scarecrow sat in the big throne and the others stood respectfully before him.

"We are not so unlucky," said the new ruler; "for this Palace and the Emerald City belong to us, and we can do just as we please. When I remember that a short time ago I was up on a pole in a farmer's cornfield, and that I am now the ruler of this beautiful City, I am quite satisfied with my lot."

"I also," said the Tin Woodman, "am well pleased with my new heart; and, really, that was the only thing I wished in all the world."

"For my part, I am content in knowing I am as brave as any beast that ever lived, if not braver," said the Lion modestly.

"If Dorothy would only be contented to live in the Emerald City," continued the Scarecrow, "we might all be happy together."

"But I don't want to live here," cried Dorothy. "I want to go to Kansas, and live with Aunt Em and Uncle Henry."

"Well, then, what can be done?" inquired the Woodman.

The Scarecrow decided to think, and he thought so hard that the pins and needles began to stick out of his brains. Finally he said:

"Why not call the Winged Monkeys, and ask them to carry you over the desert?"

"I never thought of that!" said Dorothy joyfully. "It's just the thing. I'll go at once for the Golden Cap."

When she brought it into the Throne Room she spoke the magic words, and soon the band of Winged Monkeys flew in through an open window and stood beside her.

"This is the second time you have called us," said the Monkey King, bowing before the little girl. "What do you wish?"

"I want you to fly with me to Kansas," said Dorothy.

But the Monkey King shook his head.

"That cannot be done," he said. "We belong to this country alone, and cannot leave it. There has never been a Winged Monkey in Kansas yet, and I suppose there never will be, for they don't belong there. We shall be glad to serve you in any way in our power, but we cannot cross the desert.[1] Good-bye."

And with another bow the Monkey King spread his wings and flew away through the window, followed by all his band.

Dorothy was almost ready to cry with disappointment.

"I have wasted the charm of the Golden Cap to no purpose," she said, "for the Winged Monkeys cannot help me."

"It is certainly too bad!" said the tenderhearted Woodman.

The Scarecrow was thinking again, and his head bulged out so horribly that Dorothy feared it would burst.

"Let us call in the soldier with the green whiskers," he said, "and ask his advice."

So the soldier was summoned and entered the Throne Room timidly, for while Oz was alive he never was allowed to come farther than the door.

"This little girl," said the Scarecrow to the soldier, "wishes to cross the desert. How can she do so?"

"I cannot tell," answered the soldier; "for nobody has ever crossed the desert, unless it is Oz himself."

"Is there no one who can help me?" asked Dorothy earnestly.

"Glinda[2] might," he suggested.

"Who is Glinda?" inquired the Scarecrow.

"The Witch of the South. She is the most powerful of all the Witches, and rules over the Quadlings. Besides, her castle stands on the edge of the desert, so she may know a way to cross it."

"Glinda is a good Witch, isn't she?" asked the child.

"The Quadlings think she is good," said the soldier, "and she is kind to everyone. I have heard that Glinda is a beautiful woman, who knows how to keep young in spite of the many years she has lived."[3]

"How can I get to her castle?" asked Dorothy.

"The road is straight to the South," he answered, "but it is said to be full of dangers to travelers. There are wild beasts in the woods, and a race of queer men who do not like strangers to cross their country. For this reason none of the Quadlings ever come to the Emerald City."

The soldier then left them and the Scarecrow said,

"It seems, in spite of dangers, that the best thing Dorothy can do is to travel to the Land of the South and ask Glinda to help her. For, of course, if Dorothy stays here she will never get back to Kansas."

"You must have been thinking again," remarked the Tin Woodman.

"I have," said the Scarecrow.

"I shall go with Dorothy," declared the Lion, "for I am tired of your city and long for the woods and the country again. I am really a wild beast, you know. Besides, Dorothy will need someone to protect her."

"That is true," agreed the Woodman. "My axe may be of service to her; so I, also, will go with her to the Land of the South."

"When shall we start?" asked the Scarecrow.

"Are you going?" they asked in surprise.

"Certainly. If it wasn't for Dorothy I should never have had brains. She lifted me from the pole in the cornfield and brought me to the Emerald City. So my good luck is all due to her, and I shall never leave her until she starts back to Kansas for good and all."

"Thank you," said Dorothy, gratefully. "You are all very kind to me. But I should like to start as soon as possible."

"We shall go tomorrow morning," returned the Scarecrow. "So now let us all get ready, for it will be a long journey."

CHAPTER 19

Attacked by the Fighting Trees

The next morning Dorothy kissed the pretty green girl good-bye, and they all shook hands with the soldier with the green whiskers, who had walked with them as far as the gate.

When the Guardian of the Gate saw them again he wondered greatly that they could leave the beautiful City to get into new trouble. But he at once unlocked their spectacles, which he put back into the green box, and gave them many good wishes to carry with them.

"You are now our ruler," he said to the Scarecrow; "so you must come back to us as soon as possible."

"I certainly shall if I am able," the Scarecrow replied; "but I must help Dorothy to get home, first."

As Dorothy bade the good-natured Guardian a last farewell she said,

"I have been very kindly treated in your lovely City, and everyone has been good to me. I cannot tell you how grateful I am."

"Don't try, my dear," he answered. "We should like to keep you with us, but if it is your wish to return to Kansas I hope you will find a way." He then opened the gate of the outer wall and they walked forth and started upon their journey.

The sun shone brightly as our friends turned their faces toward the Land of the South. They were all in the best of spirits, and laughed and chatted together. Dorothy was once more filled with the hope of getting home, and the Scarecrow and the Tin Woodman were glad to be of use to her. As for the Lion, he sniffed the fresh air with delight and whisked his tail from side to side in pure joy at being in the country again, while Toto ran around them and chased the moths and butterflies, barking merrily all the time.

"City life does not agree with me at all," remarked the Lion, as they walked along at a brisk pace. "I have lost much flesh since I lived there, and now I am anxious to show the other beasts how courageous I have grown."

They now turned and took a last look at the Emerald City. All they could see was a mass of towers and steeples behind the green walls, and high up above everything the spires and dome of the Palace of Oz.

"Oz was not such a bad Wizard, after all," said the Tin Woodman, as he felt his heart rattling around in his breast.

"He knew how to give me brains, and very good brains, too," said the Scarecrow.

"If Oz had taken a dose of the same courage he gave me," added the Lion, "he would have been a brave man."

Dorothy said nothing. Oz had not kept the promise he made her, but he had done his best, so she forgave him. As he said, he was a good man, even if he was a bad Wizard.

The first day's journey was through the green fields and bright flowers that stretched about the Emerald City on every side. They slept that night on the grass, with nothing but the stars over them; and they rested very well indeed.

In the morning they traveled on until they came to a thick wood. There was no way of going around it, for it seemed to extend to the right and left as far as they could see; and, besides, they did not dare change the direction of their journey for fear of getting lost. So they looked for the place where it would be easiest to get into the forest.

The Scarecrow, who was in the lead, finally discovered a big tree with such wide-spreading branches that there was room for the party to pass underneath. So he walked forward to the tree, but just as he came under the first branches they bent down and twined around him, and the next minute he was raised from the ground and flung headlong among his fellow travelers.

This did not hurt the Scarecrow, but it surprised him, and he looked rather dizzy when Dorothy picked him up.

"Here is another space between the trees," called the Lion.

"Let me try it first," said the Scarecrow, "for it doesn't hurt me to get thrown about." He walked up to another tree, as he spoke, but its branches immediately seized him and tossed him back again.

"This is strange," exclaimed Dorothy; "what shall we do?"

"The trees seem to have made up their minds to fight us, and stop our journey,"[1] remarked the Lion.

"I believe I will try it myself," said the Woodman, and shouldering his axe he marched up to the first tree that had handled the Scarecrow so roughly. When a big branch bent down to seize him the Woodman chopped at it so fiercely that he cut it in two. At once the tree began shaking all its branches as if in pain, and the Tin Woodman passed safely under it.

"Come on!" he shouted to the others; "be quick!"

They all ran forward and passed under the tree without injury, except Toto, who was caught by a small branch and shaken until he howled. But the Woodman promptly chopped off the branch and set the little dog free.

The other trees of the forest did nothing to keep them back, so they made up their minds that only the first row of trees could bend their branches, and that probably these were the policemen of the forest, and given this wonderful power in order to keep strangers out of it.

The four travelers walked with ease through the trees until they came to the farther edge of the wood. Then, to their surprise, they found before them a high wall, which seemed to be made of white china.[2] It was smooth, like the surface of a dish, and higher than their heads.

"What shall we do now?" asked Dorothy.

"I will make a ladder," said the Tin Woodman, "for we certainly must climb over the wall."

CHAPTER 20

The Dainty China Country

While the Tin Woodman was making a ladder from wood which he had found in the forest, Dorothy lay down and slept, for she was tired by the long walk.

The Lion also curled himself up to sleep and Toto lay beside him.

The Scarecrow watched the Woodman while he worked, and said to him:

"I cannot think why this wall is here, nor what it is made of."

"Rest your brains and do not worry about the wall," replied the Woodman; "When we have climbed over it we shall know what is on the other side."

After a time the ladder was finished. It looked clumsy, but the Tin Woodman was sure it was strong and would answer their purpose. The Scarecrow waked Dorothy and the Lion and Toto, and told them that the ladder was ready. The Scarecrow climbed up the ladder first, but he was so awkward that Dorothy had to follow close behind and keep him from falling off. When he got his head over the top of the wall the Scarecrow said,

"Oh, my!"

"Go on," exclaimed Dorothy.

So the Scarecrow climbed farther up and sat down on the top of the wall, and Dorothy put her head over and cried,

"Oh, my!" just as the Scarecrow had done.

Then Toto came up, and immediately began to bark, but Dorothy made him be still.

The Lion climbed the ladder next, and the Tin Woodman came last; but both of them cried, "Oh, my!" as soon as they looked over the wall. When they were all sitting in a row on the top of the wall they looked down and saw a strange sight.

Before them was a great stretch of country having a floor as smooth and shining and white as the bottom of a big platter. Scattered around were many houses made entirely of china and painted in the brightest colors. These houses were quite small, the biggest of them reaching only as high as Dorothy's waist. There were also pretty little barns, with china fences around them, and many cows and sheep and horses and pigs and chickens, all made of china, standing about in groups.

But the strangest of all were the people who lived in this queer country. There were milkmaids and shepherdesses, with bright-colored bodices and golden spots all over their gowns; and princesses with most gorgeous frocks of silver and gold and purple; and shepherds dressed in knee-breeches with pink and yellow and blue stripes down them, and golden buckles on their shoes; and princes with jeweled crowns upon their heads, wearing ermine robes and satin doublets; and funny clowns in ruffled gowns, with round red spots upon their cheeks and tall, pointed caps. And, strangest of all, these people were all made of china, even to their clothes, and were so small that the tallest of them was no higher than Dorothy's knee.

No one did so much as look at the travelers at first, except one little purple china dog with an extra-large head, which came to the wall and barked at them in a tiny voice, afterwards running away again.

"How shall we get down?" asked Dorothy.

They found the ladder so heavy they could not pull it up, so the Scarecrow fell off the wall and the others jumped down upon him so that the hard floor would not hurt their feet. Of course they took pains not to light on his head and get the pins in their feet. When all were safely down they picked up the Scarecrow, whose body was quite flattened out, and patted his straw into shape again.

"We must cross this strange place in order to get to the other side," said Dorothy; "for it would be unwise for us to go any other way except due South."

They began walking through the country of the china people, and the first thing they came to was a china milkmaid milking a china cow. As they drew near the cow suddenly gave a kick and kicked over the stool, the pail, and even the milkmaid herself, all falling on the china ground with a great clatter.

Dorothy was shocked to see that the cow had broken her leg short off, and that the pail was lying in several small pieces, while the poor milkmaid had a nick in her left elbow.

"There," cried the milkmaid angrily; "see what you have done! My cow had broken her leg, and I must take her to the mender's shop and have it glued on again. What do you mean by coming here and frightening my cow?"

"I'm very sorry," returned Dorothy; "please forgive us."

But the pretty milkmaid was much too vexed to make any answer. She picked up the leg sulkily and led her cow away, the poor animal limping on three legs. As she left them the milkmaid cast many reproachful glances over her shoulder at the clumsy strangers, holding her nicked elbow close to her side.

Dorothy was quite grieved at this mishap.

"We must be very careful here," said the kind-hearted Woodman, "or we may hurt these pretty little people so they will never get over it."

A little farther on Dorothy met a most beautiful-dressed young princess, who stopped short as she saw the strangers and started to run away.

Dorothy wanted to see more of the Princess, so she ran after her; but the china girl cried out:

"Don't chase me! don't chase me!"

She had such a frightened little voice that Dorothy stopped and said,

"Why not?"

"Because," answered the princess, also stopping, a safe distance away, "if I run I may fall down and break myself."

"But couldn't you be mended?" asked the girl.

"Oh, yes; but one is never so pretty after being mended, you know," replied the princess.

"I suppose not," said Dorothy.

"Now there is Mr. Joker,[1] one of our clowns," continued the china lady, "who is always trying to stand upon his head. He has broken himself so often that he is mended in a hundred places, and doesn't look at all pretty. Here he comes now, so you can see for yourself."

Indeed a jolly little Clown now came walking toward them, and Dorothy could see that in spite of his pretty clothes of red and yellow and green he was completely covered with cracks, running every which way and showing plainly that he had been mended in many places.

The Clown put his hands in his pockets, and after puffing out his cheeks and nodding his head at them saucily he said,

> "My lady fair,
> Why do you stare
> At poor old Mr. Joker?
> You're quite as stiff
> And prim as if
> You'd eaten up a poker!"[2]

"Be quiet, sir!" said the princess; "can't you see these are strangers, and should be treated with respect?"

"Well, that's respect, I expect," declared the Clown, and immediately stood upon his head.

"Don't mind Mr. Joker," said the princess to Dorothy; "he is considerably cracked in his head, and that makes him foolish."

"Oh, I don't mind him a bit," said Dorothy. "But you are so beautiful," she continued, "that I am sure I could love you dearly. Won't you let me carry you back to Kansas and stand you on Aunt Em's mantel-shelf? I could carry you in my basket."

"That would make me very unhappy," answered the china princess. "You see, here in our own country we live contentedly, and can talk and move around as we please. But whenever any of us are taken away our joints at once stiffen, and we can only stand straight and look pretty. Of course that is all that is expected of us when we are on mantel-shelves and cabinets and drawing-room tables, but our lives are much pleasanter here in our own country."

"I would not make you unhappy for all the world!" exclaimed Dorothy; "so I'll just say good-bye."

"Good-bye," replied the princess.

They walked carefully through the china country. The little animals and all the people scampered out of their way, fearing the strangers would break them, and after an hour or so the travelers reached the other side of the country and came to another china wall.

It was not as high as the first, however, and by standing upon the Lion's back they all managed to scramble to the top. Then the Lion gathered his legs under him and jumped on the wall; but just as he jumped he upset a china church[3] with his tail and smashed it all to pieces.

"That was too bad," said Dorothy, "but really I think we were lucky in not doing these little people more harm than breaking a cow's leg and a church. They are all so brittle!"

"They are, indeed," said the Scarecrow, "and I am thankful I am made of straw and cannot be easily damaged. There are worse things in the world than being a Scarecrow."

CHAPTER 21

The Lion Becomes the King of Beasts

After climbing down from the china wall the travelers found themselves in a disagreeable country, full of bogs and marshes and covered with tall, rank grass. It was difficult to walk far without falling into muddy holes, for the grass was so thick that it hid them from sight. However, by carefully picking their way, they got safely along until they reached solid ground. But here the country seemed wilder than ever, and after a long tiresome walk through the underbrush they entered another forest, where the trees were bigger and older than any they had ever seen.

"This forest is perfectly delightful," declared the Lion, looking around him with joy; "never have I seen a more beautiful place."

"It seems gloomy," said the Scarecrow.

"Not a bit of it," answered the Lion; "I should like to live here all my life. See how soft the dried leaves are under your feet and how rich and green the moss is that clings to these old trees. Surely no wild beast could wish a pleasanter home."

"Perhaps there are wild beasts in the forest now," said Dorothy.

"I suppose there are," returned the Lion; "but I do not see any of them about."

They walked through the forest until it became too dark to go any farther. Dorothy and Toto and the Lion lay down to sleep, while the Woodman and the Scarecrow kept watch over them as usual.

When morning came they started again. Before they had gone far they heard a low rumble, as of the growling of many wild animals. Toto whimpered a little but none of the others was frightened and they kept along the well-trodden path until they came to an opening in the wood, in which were gathered hundreds of beasts of every variety. There were tigers and elephants and bears and wolves and foxes and all the others in the natural history, and for a moment Dorothy was afraid. But the Lion explained that the animals were holding a meeting, and he judged by their snarling and growling that they were in great trouble.

As he spoke several of the beasts caught sight of him, and at once the great assemblage hushed as if by magic. The biggest of the tigers[1] came up to the Lion and bowed, saying,

"Welcome, O King of Beasts! You have come in good time to fight our enemy and bring peace to all the animals of the forest once more."

"What is your trouble?" asked the Lion quietly.

"We are all threatened," answered the tiger, "by a fierce enemy which has lately come into this forest. It is a most tremendous monster, like a great spider, with a body as big as an elephant and legs as long as a tree trunk. It has eight of these long legs, and as the monster crawls through the forest he seizes an animal with a leg and drags it to his mouth, where he eats it as a spider does a fly. Not one of us is safe while this fierce creature is alive, and we had called a meeting to decide how to take care of ourselves when you came among us."

The Lion thought for a moment.

"Are there any other lions in this forest?" he asked.

"No; there were some, but the monster has eaten them all. And, besides, they were none of them nearly so large and brave as you."

"If I put an end to your enemy will you bow down to me and obey me as King of the Forest?" inquired the Lion.

"We will do that gladly," returned the tiger; and all the other beasts roared with a mighty roar: "We will!"

"Where is this great spider of yours now?" asked the Lion.

"Yonder, among the oak trees," said the tiger, pointing with his forefoot.

"Take good care of these friends of mine," said the Lion, "and I will go at once to fight the monster."

He bade his comrades good-bye and marched proudly away to do battle with the enemy.

The great spider[2] was lying asleep when the Lion found him, and it looked so ugly that its foe turned up his nose in disgust. Its legs were quite as long as the tiger had said, and its body covered with coarse, black hair. It had a great mouth, with a row of sharp teeth a foot long; but its head was joined to the pudgy body by a neck as slender as a wasp's waist. This gave the Lion a hint of the best way to attack the creature, and as he knew it was easier to fight it asleep than awake, he gave a great spring and landed directly upon the monster's back. Then, with one blow of his heavy paw, all armed with sharp claws, he knocked the spider's head from its body. Jumping down, he watched it until the long legs stopped wiggling, when he knew it was quite dead.

The Lion went back to the opening where the beasts of the forest were waiting for him and said proudly,

"You need fear your enemy no longer."

Then the beasts bowed down to the Lion as their King, and he promised to come back and rule over them as soon as Dorothy was safely on her way to Kansas.

CHAPTER 22

The Country of the Quadlings

The four travelers passed through the rest of the forest in safety, and when they came out from its gloom saw before them a steep hill, covered from top to bottom with great pieces of rock.

"That will be a hard climb," said the Scarecrow, "but we must get over the hill, nevertheless."

So he led the way and the others followed. They had nearly reached the first rock when they heard a rough voice cry out,

"Keep back!"

"Who are you?" asked the Scarecrow. Then a head showed itself over the rock and the same voice said,

"This hill belongs to us, and we don't allow anyone to cross it."

"But we must cross it," said the Scarecrow. "We're going to the country of the Quadlings."

"But you shall not!" replied the voice, and there stepped from behind the rock the strangest man the travelers had ever seen.

He was quite short and stout and had a big head, which was flat at the top and supported by a thick neck full of wrinkles. But he had no arms at all, and, seeing this, the Scarecrow did not fear that so helpless a creature could prevent them from climbing the hill. So he said,

"I'm sorry not to do as you wish, but we must pass over your hill whether you like it or not," and he walked boldly forward.

As quick as lightning the man's head shot forward and his neck stretched out until the top of the head, where it was flat, struck the Scarecrow in the middle, and sent him tumbling, over and over, down the hill. Almost as quickly as it came the head went back to the body, and the man laughed harshly as he said,

"It isn't as easy as you think!"

A chorus of boisterous laughter came from the other rocks, and Dorothy saw hundreds of the armless Hammer-Heads[1] upon the hillside, one behind every rock.

The Lion became quite angry at the laughter caused by the Scarecrow's mishap, and giving a loud roar that echoed like thunder he dashed up the hill.

Again a head shot swiftly out, and the great Lion went rolling down the hill as if he had been struck by a cannon ball.

Dorothy ran down and helped the Scarecrow to his feet, and the Lion came up to her, feeling rather bruised and sore, and said,

"It is useless to fight people with shooting heads; no one can withstand them."

"What can we do, then?" she asked.

"Call the Winged Monkeys," suggested the Tin Woodman; "you have still the right to command them once more."

"Very well," she answered, and putting on the Golden Cap she uttered the magic words. The Monkeys were as prompt as ever, and in a few moments the entire band stood before her.

"What are your commands?" inquired the King of the Monkeys, bowing low.

"Carry us over the hill to the country of the Quadlings,"[2] answered the girl.

"It shall be done," said the King, and at once the Winged Monkeys caught the four travelers and Toto up in their arms and flew away with them. As they passed over the hill the Hammer-Heads yelled with vexation, and shot their heads high in the air; but they could not reach the Winged Monkeys, which carried Dorothy and her comrades safely over the hill and set them down in the beautiful country of the Quadlings.

"This is the last time you can summon us," said the leader to Dorothy; "so good-bye and good luck to you."

"Good-bye, and thank you very much," returned the girl; and the Monkeys rose into the air and were out of sight in a twinkling.

The country of the Quadlings seemed rich and happy. There was field upon field of ripening grain, with well-paved roads running between, and pretty rippling brooks with strong bridges across them. The fences and houses and bridges were all painted bright red, just as they had been painted yellow in the country of the Winkies and blue in the country of the Munchkins. The Quadlings themselves, who were short and fat and looked chubby and good-natured, were dressed all in red, which showed bright against the green grass and the yellowing grain.

The Monkeys had set them down near a farm house, and the four travelers walked up to it and knocked at the door. It was opened by the farmer's wife, and when Dorothy asked for something to eat the woman gave them all a good dinner, with three kinds of cake and four kinds of cookies, and a bowl of milk for Toto.

"How far is it to the Castle of Glinda?" asked the child.

"It is not a great way," answered the farmer's wife. "Take the road to the South and you will soon reach it."

Thanking the good woman, they started afresh and walked by the fields and across the pretty bridges until they saw before them a very beautiful Castle. Before the gates were three young girls, dressed in handsome red uniforms trimmed with gold braid; and as Dorothy approached one of them said to her,

"Why have you come to the South Country?"

"To see the Good Witch who rules here," she answered. "Will you take me to her?"

"Let me have your name and I will ask Glinda if she will receive you." They told who they were, and the girl soldier went into the Castle. After a few moments she came back to say that Dorothy and the others were to be admitted at once.

CHAPTER 23

Glinda Grants Dorothy's Wish

Before they went to see Glinda, however, they were taken to a room of the Castle, where Dorothy washed her face and combed her hair, and the Lion shook the dust out of his mane, and the Scarecrow patted himself into his best shape, and the Woodman polished his tin and oiled his joints.

When they were all quite presentable they followed the soldier girl into a big room where the Witch Glinda sat upon a throne of rubies.

She was both beautiful and young to their eyes. Her hair was a rich red in color and fell in flowing ringlets over her shoulders. Her dress was pure white; but her eyes were blue, and they looked kindly upon the little girl.

"What can I do for you, my child?" she asked.

Dorothy told the Witch all her story; how the cyclone had brought her to the Land of Oz, how she had found her companions, and of the wonderful adventures they had met with.

"My greatest wish now," she added, "is to get back to Kansas, for Aunt Em will surely think something dreadful has happened to me, and that will make her put on mourning; and unless the crops are better this year than they were last I am sure Uncle Henry cannot afford it."

Glinda leaned forward and kissed the sweet, upturned face of the loving little girl.

"Bless your dear heart," she said, "I am sure I can tell you of a way to get back to Kansas." Then she added:

"But, if I do, you must give me the Golden Cap."

"Willingly!" exclaimed Dorothy; "indeed, it is of no use to me now, and when you have it you can command the Winged Monkeys three times."

"And I think I shall need their service just those three times," answered Glinda, smiling.

Dorothy then gave her the Golden Cap, and the Witch said to the Scarecrow,

"What will you do when Dorothy has left us?"

"I will return to the Emerald City," he replied, "for Oz has made me its ruler and the people like me. The only thing that worries me is how to cross the hill of the Hammer-Heads."

"By means of the Golden Cap I shall command the Winged Monkeys to carry you to the gates of the Emerald City," said Glinda, "for it would be a shame to deprive the people of so wonderful a ruler."

"Am I really wonderful?" asked the Scarecrow.

"You are unusual," replied Glinda.

Turning to the Tin Woodman, she asked;

"What will become of you when Dorothy leaves this country?"

He leaned on his axe and thought a moment. Then he said,

"The Winkies were very kind to me, and wanted me to rule over them after the Wicked Witch died. I am fond of the Winkies, and if I could get back again to the country of the West I should like nothing better than to rule over them forever."

"My second command to the Winged Monkeys," said Glinda, "will be that they carry you safely to the land of the Winkies. Your brains may not be so large to look at as those of the Scarecrow, but you are really brighter than he is—when you are well-polished—and I am sure you will rule the Winkies wisely and well."

Then the Witch looked at the big, shaggy lion and asked,

"When Dorothy has returned to her own home, what will become of you?"

"Over the hill of the Hammer-Heads," he answered, "lies a grand old forest, and all the beasts that live there have made me their King. If I could only get back to this forest I would pass my life very happily there."

"My third command to the Winged Monkeys," said Glinda, "shall

be to carry you to your forest. Then, having used up the powers of the
Golden Cap, I shall give it to the King of the Monkeys, that he and his
band may thereafter be free for evermore."

The Scarecrow and the Tin Woodman and the Lion now thanked
the Good Witch earnestly for her kindness, and Dorothy exclaimed,

"You are certainly as good as you are beautiful! But you have not
yet told me how to get back to Kansas."

"Your Silver Shoes will carry you over the desert,"[1] replied Glinda.
"If you had known their power[2] you could have gone back to your
Aunt Em the very first day you came to this country."

"But then I should not have had my wonderful brains!" cried the
Scarecrow. "I might have passed my whole life in the farmer's cornfield."

"And I should not have had my lovely heart," said the Tin Woodman. "I might have stood rusted in the forest till the end of the
world."

"And I should have lived a coward forever," declared the Lion,
"and no beast in all the forest would have had a good word to say
to me."

"This is all true," said Dorothy, "and I am glad I was of use to
these good friends. But now that each of them has had what he most
desired, and each is happy in having a kingdom to rule besides, I think
I should like to go back to Kansas."

"The Silver Shoes," said the Good Witch, "have wonderful powers.
And one of the most curious things about them is that they can carry
you to any place in the world in three steps, and each step will be
made in the wink of an eye. All you have to do is to knock the heels
together three times and command the shoes to carry you wherever
you wish to go."

"If that is so," said the child joyfully, "I will ask them to carry me
back to Kansas at once."

She threw her arms around the Lion's neck and kissed him, patting
his big head tenderly. Then she kissed the Tin Woodman, who was
weeping in a way most dangerous to his joints. But she hugged the
soft, stuffed body of the Scarecrow in her arms instead of kissing his
painted face, and found she was crying herself at this sorrowful parting from her loving comrades.

Glinda the Good stepped down from her ruby throne to give the
little girl a good-bye kiss, and Dorothy thanked her for all the kindness she had shown to her friends and herself.

Dorothy now took Toto up solemnly in her arms, and having said one last good-bye she clapped the heels of her shoes together three times, saying,

"Take me home to Aunt Em!"

Instantly she was whirling through the air, so swiftly that all she could see or feel was the wind whistling past her ears.

The Silver Shoes took but three steps, and then she stopped so suddenly that she rolled over upon the grass several times before she knew where she was.

At length, however, she sat up and looked about her.

"Good gracious!" she cried.

For she was sitting on the broad Kansas prairie, and just before her was the new farmhouse[3] Uncle Henry built after the cyclone had carried away the old one. Uncle Henry was milking the cows in the barnyard, and Toto had jumped out of her arms and was running toward the barn, barking joyously.

Dorothy stood up and found she was in her stocking-feet. For the Silver Shoes had fallen off[4] in her flight through the air, and were lost forever in the desert.

CHAPTER 24

Home Again

Aunt Em had just come out of the house to water the cabbages when she looked up and saw Dorothy running toward her.

"My darling child!" she cried, folding the little girl in her arms and covering her face with kisses; "where in the world did you come from?"

"From the Land of Oz," said Dorothy gravely. "And here is Toto, too. And oh, Aunt Em! I'm so glad to be at home again!"[1]

THE EMERALD CITY OF OZ

To Her Royal Highness Cynthia II of Syracuse;
and to each and every one of the children
whose loyal appreciation has encouraged me
to write the Oz books
this volume is affectionately dedicated.

Perhaps I should admit on the title page that this book is "By L. Frank Baum and his correspondents," for I have used many suggestions conveyed to me in letters from children. Once on a time I really imagined myself "an author of fairy tales," but now I am merely an editor or private secretary[1] for a host of youngsters whose ideas I am requested to weave into the thread of my stories.

These ideas are often clever. They are also logical and interesting. So I have used them whenever I could find an opportunity, and it is but just that I acknowledge my indebtedness to my little friends.

My, what imaginations these children have developed! Sometimes I am fairly astounded by their daring and genius. There will be no lack of fairy-tale authors in the future, I am sure. My readers have told me what to do with Dorothy, and Aunt Em and Uncle Henry, and I have obeyed their mandates. They have also given me a variety of subjects to write about in the future: enough, in fact, to keep me busy for some time. I am very proud of this alliance. Children love these stories because children have helped to create them. My readers know what they want and realize that I try to please them. The result is very satisfactory to the publishers, to me, and (I am quite sure) to the children.

I hope, my dears, it will be a long time before we are obliged to dissolve partnership.[2]

L. Frank Baum
Coronado, 1910

LIST OF CHAPTERS

CHAPTER 1

How the Nome King Became Angry

The Nome King[1] was in an angry mood, and at such times he was very disagreeable. Every one kept away from him, even his Chief Steward Kaliko.[2]

Therefore the King stormed and raved all by himself, walking up and down in his jewel-studded cavern and getting angrier all the time. Then he remembered that it was no fun being angry unless he had some one to frighten and make miserable, and he rushed to his big gong and made it clatter as loud as he could.

In came the Chief Steward, trying not to show the Nome King how frightened he was.

"Send the Chief Counselor here!" shouted the angry monarch.

Kaliko ran out as fast as his spindle legs could carry his fat round body, and soon the Chief Counselor entered the cavern. The King scowled and said to him:

"I'm in great trouble over the loss of my Magic Belt.[3] Every little while I want to do something magical, and find I can't because the Belt is gone. That makes me angry, and when I'm angry I can't have a good time. Now, what do you advise?"

"Some people," said the Chief Counselor, "enjoy getting angry."

"But not all the time," declared the King. "To be angry once in a while is really good fun, because it makes others so miserable. But to be angry morning, noon and night, as I am, grows monotonous and prevents my gaining any other pleasure in life. Now, what do you advise?"

"Why, if you are angry because you want to do magical things and can't, and if you don't want to get angry at all, my advice is not to want to do magical things."

Hearing this, the King glared at his Counselor with a furious expression and tugged at his own long white whiskers until he pulled them so hard that he yelled with pain.

"You are a fool!" he exclaimed.

"I share that honor with your Majesty," said the Chief Counselor.

The King roared with rage and stamped his foot.

"Ho, there, my guards!" he cried. "Ho" is a royal way of saying, "Come here." So, when the guards had hoed, the King said to them:

"Take this Chief Counselor and throw him away."

Then the guards took the Chief Counselor, and bound him with chains to prevent his struggling, and threw him away. And the King paced up and down his cavern more angry than before.

Finally he rushed to his big gong and made it clatter like a fire-alarm. Kaliko appeared again, trembling and white with fear.

"Fetch my pipe!" yelled the King.

"Your pipe is already here, your Majesty," replied Kaliko.

"Then get my tobacco!" roared the King.

"The tobacco is in your pipe, your Majesty," returned the Steward.

"Then bring a live coal from the furnace!" commanded the King.

"The tobacco is lighted, and your Majesty is already smoking your pipe," answered the Steward.

"Why, so I am!" said the King, who had forgotten this fact; "but you are very rude to remind me of it."

"I am a lowborn, miserable villain," declared the Chief Steward, humbly.

The Nome King could think of nothing to say next, so he puffed away at his pipe and paced up and down the room. Finally he remembered how angry he was, and cried out:

"What do you mean, Kaliko, by being so contented when your monarch is unhappy?"

"What makes you unhappy?" asked the Steward.

"I've lost my Magic Belt. A little girl named Dorothy, who was here with Ozma[4] of Oz, stole my Belt and carried it away with her," said the King, grinding his teeth with rage.

"She captured it in a fair fight," Kaliko ventured to say.

"But I want it! I must have it! Half my power is gone with that Belt!" roared the King.

"You will have to go to the Land of Oz to recover it, and your Majesty can't get to the Land of Oz in any possible way," said the Steward, yawning because he had been on duty ninety-six hours, and was sleepy.

"Why not?" asked the King.

"Because there is a deadly desert all around that fairy country, which no one is able to cross. You know that fact as well as I do, your Majesty. Never mind the lost Belt. You have plenty of power left, for you rule this underground kingdom like a tyrant, and thousands of Nomes obey your commands. I advise you to drink a glass of melted silver, to quiet your nerves, and then go to bed."

The King grabbed a big ruby and threw it at Kaliko's head. The Steward ducked to escape the heavy jewel, which crashed against the door just over his left ear.

"Get out of my sight! Vanish! Go away—and send General Blug here," screamed the Nome King.

Kaliko hastily withdrew, and the Nome King stamped up and down until the General of his armies appeared.

This Nome was known far and wide as a terrible fighter and a cruel, desperate commander. He had fifty thousand Nome soldiers, all well drilled, who feared nothing but their stern master. Yet General Blug was a trifle uneasy when he arrived and saw how angry the Nome King was.

"Ha! So you're here!" cried the King.

"So I am," said the General.

"March your army at once to the Land of Oz, capture and destroy the Emerald City, and bring back to me my Magic Belt!" roared the King.

"You're crazy," calmly remarked the General.

"What's that? What's that? What's that?" And the Nome King danced around on his pointed toes, he was so enraged.

"You don't know what you're talking about," continued the General, seating himself upon a large cut diamond. "I advise you to stand in a corner and count sixty before you speak again. By that time you may be more sensible."

The King looked around for something to throw at General Blug, but as nothing was handy he began to consider that perhaps the man was right and he had been talking foolishly. So he merely threw himself into his glittering throne and tipped his crown over his ear and curled his feet up under him and glared wickedly at Blug.

"In the first place," said the General, "we cannot march across the deadly desert to the Land of Oz; and, if we could, the Ruler of that country, Princess Ozma, has certain fairy powers that would render my army helpless. Had you not lost your Magic Belt we might have some chance of defeating Ozma; but the Belt is gone."

"I want it!" screamed the King. "I must have it."

"Well, then, let us try in a sensible way to get it," replied the General. "The Belt was captured by a little girl named Dorothy, who lives in Kansas, in the United States of America."

"But she left it in the Emerald City, with Ozma," declared the King.

"How do you know that?" asked the General.

"One of my spies, who is a Blackbird, flew over the desert to the Land of Oz, and saw the Magic Belt in Ozma's palace," replied the King with a groan.

"Now, that gives me an idea," said General Blug, thoughtfully. "There are two ways to get to the Land of Oz without traveling across the sandy desert."

"What are they?" demanded the King, eagerly.

"One way is *over* the desert, through the air; and the other way is *under* the desert, through the earth."

Hearing this the Nome King uttered a yell of joy and leaped from his throne, to resume his wild walk up and down the cavern.

"That's it, Blug!" he shouted. "That's the idea, General! I'm King of the Under World, and my subjects are all miners. I'll make a secret tunnel[5] under the desert to the Land of Oz—yes! right up to the Emerald City—and you will march your armies there and capture the whole country!"

"Softly, softly, your Majesty. Don't go too fast," warned the General. "My Nomes are good fighters, but they are not strong enough to conquer the Emerald City."

"Are you sure?" asked the King.

"Absolutely certain, your Majesty."

"Then what am I to do?"

"Give up the idea and mind your own business," advised the General. "You have plenty to do trying to rule your underground kingdom."

"But I want that Magic Belt—and I'm going to have it!" roared the Nome King.

"I'd like to see you get it," replied the General, laughing maliciously.

The King was by this time so exasperated that he picked up his scepter, which had a heavy ball, made from a sapphire, at the end of it, and threw it with all his force at General Blug. The sapphire hit the General upon his forehead and knocked him flat upon the ground, where he lay motionless. Then the King rang his gong and told his guards to drag out the General and throw him away; which they did.

This Nome King was named Roquat the Red, and no one loved him. He was a bad man and a powerful monarch, and he had resolved to destroy the Land of Oz and its magnificent Emerald City, to enslave Princess Ozma and little Dorothy and all the Oz people, and recover his Magic Belt. This same Belt had once enabled Roquat the Red to carry out many wicked plans; but that was before Ozma and her people marched to the underground cavern and captured it. The Nome King could not forgive Dorothy or Princess Ozma, and he had determined to be revenged upon them.

But they, for their part, did not know they had so dangerous an enemy. Indeed, Ozma and Dorothy had both almost forgotten that such a person as the Nome King yet lived under the mountains of the Land of Ev[6]—which lay just across the deadly desert to the south of the Land of Oz.

An unsuspected enemy is doubly dangerous.

CHAPTER 2

How Uncle Henry Got Into Trouble

Dorothy Gale lived on a farm in Kansas, with her Aunt Em and her Uncle Henry. It was not a big farm, nor a very good one, because sometimes the rain did not come when the crops needed it, and then

everything withered and dried up. Once a cyclone had carried away
Uncle Henry's house, so that he was obliged to build another; and as
he was a poor man he had to mortgage his farm[1] to get the money to
pay for the new house. Then his health became bad and he was too
feeble to work. The doctor ordered him to take a sea voyage and
he went to Australia and took Dorothy with him. That cost a lot of
money, too.

Uncle Henry grew poorer every year, and the crops raised on the
farm only bought food for the family. Therefore the mortgage could
not be paid. At last the banker[2] who had loaned him the money said
that if he did not pay on a certain day, his farm would be taken away
from him.

This worried Uncle Henry a good deal, for without the farm he
would have no way to earn a living. He was a good man, and worked
in the fields as hard as he could; and Aunt Em did all the housework,
with Dorothy's help. Yet they did not seem to get along.

This little girl, Dorothy, was like dozens of little girls you know.
She was loving and usually sweet-tempered, and had a round rosy face
and earnest eyes. Life was a serious thing to Dorothy, and a wonderful thing, too, for she had encountered more strange adventures in her
short life than many other girls of her age.[3]

Aunt Em once said she thought the fairies must have marked
Dorothy at her birth, because she had wandered into strange places
and had always been protected by some unseen power. As for Uncle
Henry, he thought his little niece merely a dreamer, as her dead mother had been, for he could not quite believe all the curious stories
Dorothy told them of the Land of Oz, which she had several times visited. He did not think that she tried to deceive her uncle and aunt, but
he imagined that she had dreamed all of those astonishing adventures,
and that the dreams had been so real to her that she had come to
believe them true.

Whatever the explanation might be, it was certain that Dorothy
had been absent from her Kansas home for several long periods,
always disappearing unexpectedly, yet always coming back safe and
sound, with amazing tales of where she had been and the unusual people she had met. Her uncle and aunt listened to her stories eagerly and
in spite of their doubts began to feel that the little girl had gained a lot
of experience and wisdom that were unaccountable in this age, when
fairies are supposed no longer to exist.

Most of Dorothy's stories were about the Land of Oz, with its beautiful Emerald City and a lovely girl Ruler named Ozma, who was the most faithful friend of the little Kansas girl. When Dorothy told about the riches of this fairy country Uncle Henry would sigh, for he knew that a single one of the great emeralds that were so common there would pay all his debts and leave his farm free. But Dorothy never brought any jewels home with her, so their poverty became greater every year.

When the banker told Uncle Henry that he must pay the money in thirty days or leave the farm, the poor man was in despair, as he knew he could not possibly get the money. So he told his wife, Aunt Em, of his trouble, and she first cried a little and then said that they must be brave and do the best they could, and go away somewhere and try to earn an honest living. But they were getting old and feeble and she feared that they could not take care of Dorothy as well as they had formerly done. Probably the little girl would also be obliged to go to work.

They did not tell their niece the sad news for several days, not wishing to make her unhappy; but one morning the little girl found Aunt Em softly crying while Uncle Henry tried to comfort her. Then Dorothy asked them to tell her what was the matter.

"We must give up the farm, my dear," replied her uncle, sadly, "and wander away into the world to work for our living."

The girl listened quite seriously, for she had not known before how desperately poor they were.

"We don't mind for ourselves," said her aunt, stroking the little girl's head tenderly; "but we love you as if you were our own child, and we are heart-broken to think that you must also endure poverty, and work for a living before you have grown big and strong."

"What could I do to earn money?" asked Dorothy.

"You might do housework for some one, dear, you are so handy; or perhaps you could be a nurse-maid to little children. I'm sure I don't know exactly what you *can* do to earn money, but if your uncle and I are able to support you we will do it willingly, and send you to school. We fear, though, that we shall have much trouble in earning a living for ourselves. No one wants to employ old people who are broken down in health, as we are."[4]

Dorothy smiled.

"Wouldn't it be funny," she said, "for me to do housework in Kansas, when I'm a Princess in the Land of Oz?"

"A Princess!" they both exclaimed, astonished.

"Yes; Ozma made me a Princess some time ago, and she has often begged me to come and live always in the Emerald City," said the child.

Her uncle and aunt looked at each other in amazement. Then the man said:

"Do you suppose you could manage to return to your fairyland, my dear?"

"Oh, yes," replied Dorothy; "I could do that easily."

"How?" asked Aunt Em.

"Ozma sees me every day at four o'clock, in her Magic Picture.[5] She can see me wherever I am, no matter what I am doing. And at that time, if I make a certain secret sign, she will send for me by means of the Magic Belt, which I once captured from the Nome King. Then, in the wink of an eye, I shall be with Ozma in her palace."

The elder people remained silent for some time after Dorothy had spoken. Finally Aunt Em said, with another sigh of regret:

"If that is the case, Dorothy, perhaps you'd better go and live in the Emerald City. It will break our hearts to lose you from our lives, but you will be so much better off with your fairy friends that it seems wisest and best for you to go."

"I'm not so sure about that," remarked Uncle Henry, shaking his gray head doubtfully. "These things all seem real to Dorothy, I know; but I'm afraid our little girl won't find her fairyland just what she has dreamed it to be. It would make me very unhappy to think that she was wandering among strangers who might be unkind to her."

Dorothy laughed merrily at this speech, and then she became very sober again, for she could see how all this trouble was worrying her aunt and uncle, and knew that unless she found a way to help them their future lives would be quite miserable and unhappy. She knew that she *could* help them. She had thought of a way already. Yet she did not tell them at once what it was, because she must ask Ozma's consent before she would be able to carry out her plans.

So she only said:

"If you will promise not to worry a bit about me, I'll go to the Land of Oz this very afternoon. And I'll make a promise, too; that you shall both see me again before the day comes when you must leave this farm."

"The day isn't far away, now," her uncle sadly replied. "I did not tell you of our trouble until I was obliged to, dear Dorothy, so the evil time is near at hand. But if you are quite sure your fairy friends will give you a home, it will be best for you to go to them, as your aunt says."

That was why Dorothy went to her little room in the attic that afternoon, taking with her a small dog named Toto. The dog had curly black hair and big brown eyes and loved Dorothy very dearly.

The child had kissed her uncle and aunt affectionately before she went upstairs, and now she looked around her little room rather wistfully, gazing at the simple trinkets and worn calico and gingham dresses, as if they were old friends. She was tempted at first to make a bundle of them, yet she knew very well that they would be of no use to her in her future life.

She sat down upon a broken-backed chair—the only one the room contained—and holding Toto in her arms waited patiently until the clock struck four.

Then she made the secret signal that had been agreed upon between her and Ozma.

Uncle Henry and Aunt Em waited downstairs. They were uneasy and a good deal excited, for this is a practical humdrum world, and it seemed to them quite impossible that their little niece could vanish from her home and travel instantly to fairyland.

So they watched the stairs, which seemed to be the only way that Dorothy could get out of the farmhouse, and they watched them a long time. They heard the clock strike four but there was no sound from above.

Half-past four came, and now they were too impatient to wait any longer. Softly they crept up the stairs to the door of the little girl's room.

"Dorothy! Dorothy!" they called.

There was no answer.

They opened the door and looked in.

The room was empty.

CHAPTER 3

How Ozma Granted Dorothy's Request

I suppose you have read so much about the magnificent Emerald City that there is little need for me to describe it here. It is the Capital City of the Land of Oz, which is justly considered the most attractive and delightful fairyland in all the world.

The Emerald City is built all of beautiful marbles in which are set a profusion of emeralds, every one exquisitely cut and of very great size. There are other jewels used in the decorations inside the houses and palaces, such as rubies, diamonds, sapphires, amethysts and turquoises. But in the streets and upon the outside of the buildings only emeralds appear, from which circumstance the place is named the Emerald City of Oz. It has nine thousand, six hundred and fifty-four buildings, in which lived fifty-seven thousand three hundred and eighteen people, up to the time my story opens.

All the surrounding country, extending to the borders of the desert which enclosed it upon every side, was full of pretty and comfortable farmhouses, in which resided those inhabitants of Oz who preferred country to city life.

Altogether there were more than half a million people in the Land of Oz—although some of them, as you will soon learn, were not made of flesh and blood as we are—and every inhabitant of that favored country was happy and prosperous.

No disease of any sort was ever known among the Ozites, and so no one ever died unless he met with an accident that prevented him from living. This happened very seldom, indeed. There were no poor people in the Land of Oz, because there was no such thing as money, and all property of every sort belonged to the Ruler. The people were her children, and she cared for them. Each person was given freely by his neighbors whatever he required for his use, which is as much as any one may reasonably desire. Some tilled the lands and raised great crops of grain, which was divided equally among the entire population, so that all had enough. There were many tailors and dressmakers and shoemakers and the like, who made things that any who desired them might wear. Likewise there were jewelers who made ornaments for the person, which pleased and beautified the people, and these ornaments also were free to those who asked for them. Each man and woman, no matter what he or she produced for the good of the community, was supplied by the neighbors with food and clothing and a house and furniture and ornaments and games. If by chance the supply ever ran short, more was taken from the great storehouses of the Ruler, which were afterward filled up again when there was more of any article than the people needed.

Every one worked half the time and played half the time, and the people enjoyed the work as much as they did the play, because it is good to be occupied and to have something to do. There were no cruel overseers set to watch them, and no one to rebuke them or to find fault with them. So each one was proud to do all he could for his friends and neighbors, and was glad when they would accept the things he produced.

You will know, by what I have here told you, that the Land of Oz was a remarkable country. I do not suppose such an arrangement would be practical with us, but Dorothy assures me that it works finely with the Oz people.

Oz being a fairy country, the people were, of course, fairy people; but that does not mean that all of them were very unlike the people of our own world. There were all sorts of queer characters among them, but not a single one who was evil, or who possessed a selfish or violent nature. They were peaceful, kind-hearted, loving and merry, and every inhabitant adored the beautiful girl who ruled them, and delighted to obey her every command.

In spite of all I have said in a general way, there were some parts of the Land of Oz not quite so pleasant as the farming country and the Emerald City which was its center. Far away in the South Country there lived in the mountains a band of strange people called Hammer-Heads, because they had no arms and used their flat heads to pound any one who came near them. Their necks were like rubber, so that they could shoot out their heads to quite a distance, and afterward draw them back again to their shoulders. The Hammer-Heads were called the "Wild People," but never harmed any but those who disturbed them in the mountains where they lived.

In some of the dense forests there lived great beasts of every sort; yet these were for the most part harmless and even sociable, and conversed agreeably with those who visited their haunts. The Kalidahs— beasts with bodies like bears and heads like tigers—had once been fierce and bloodthirsty, but even they were now nearly all tamed, although at times one or another of them would get cross and disagreeable.

Not so tame were the Fighting Trees, which had a forest of their own. If any one approached them these curious trees would bend down their branches, twine them around the intruders, and hurl them away.

But these unpleasant things existed only in a few remote parts of the Land of Oz. I suppose every country has some drawbacks, so even this almost perfect fairyland could not be quite perfect. Once there had been wicked witches in the land, too; but now these had all been destroyed; so, as I said, only peace and happiness reigned in Oz.

For some time Ozma has ruled over this fair country, and never was Ruler more popular or beloved. She is said to be the most beautiful girl the world has ever known, and her heart and mind are as lovely as her person.

Dorothy Gale[1] had several times visited the Emerald City and experienced adventures in the Land of Oz, so that she and Ozma had now become firm friends. The girl Ruler had even made Dorothy a Princess of Oz, and had often implored her to come to Ozma's stately palace and live there always; but Dorothy had been loyal to her Aunt Em and Uncle Henry, who had cared for her since she was a baby, and she had refused to leave them because she knew they would be lonely without her.

However, Dorothy now realized that things were going to be different with her uncle and aunt from this time forth, so after giving the matter deep thought she decided to ask Ozma to grant her a very great favor.

A few seconds after she had made the secret signal in her little bedchamber, the Kansas girl was seated in a lovely room in Ozma's palace in the Emerald City of Oz. When the first loving kisses and embraces had been exchanged, the fair Ruler inquired:

"What is the matter, dear? I know something unpleasant has happened to you, for your face was very sober when I saw it in my Magic Picture. And whenever you signal me to transport you to this safe place, where you are always welcome, I know you are in danger or in trouble."

Dorothy sighed.

"This time, Ozma, it isn't I," she replied. "But it's worse, I guess, for Uncle Henry and Aunt Em are in a heap of trouble, and there seems no way for them to get out of it—anyhow, not while they live in Kansas."

"Tell me about it, Dorothy," said Ozma, with ready sympathy.

"Why, you see Uncle Henry is poor; for the farm in Kansas doesn't 'mount to much, as farms go. So one day Uncle Henry borrowed some money, and wrote a letter saying that if he didn't pay the money back they could take his farm for pay. Course he 'spected to pay by making money from the farm, but he just couldn't. An' so they're going to take the farm, and Uncle Henry and Aunt Em won't have any place to live. They're pretty old to do much hard work, Ozma; so I'll have to work for them, unless—"

Ozma had been thoughtful during the story, but now she smiled and pressed her little friend's hand.

"Unless what, dear?" she asked.

Dorothy hesitated, because her request meant so much to them all.

"Well," said she, "I'd like to live here in the Land of Oz,[2] where you've often 'vited me to live. But I can't, you know, unless Uncle Henry and Aunt Em could live here too."

"Of course not," exclaimed the Ruler of Oz, laughing gaily. "So, in order to get you, little friend, we must invite your Uncle and Aunt to live in Oz, also."

"Oh, will you, Ozma?" cried Dorothy, clasping her chubby little hands eagerly. "Will you bring them here with the Magic Belt, and give them a nice little farm in the Munchkin Country, or the Winkie Country—or some other place?"

"To be sure," answered Ozma, full of joy at the chance to please her little friend. "I have long been thinking of this very thing, Dorothy dear, and often I have had it in my mind to propose it to you. I am sure your uncle and aunt must be good and worthy people, or you would not love them so much; and for *your* friends, Princess, there is always room in the Land of Oz."

Dorothy was delighted, yet not altogether surprised, for she had clung to the hope that Ozma would be kind enough to grant her request. When, indeed, had her powerful and faithful friend refused her anything?

"But you must not call me 'Princess,' " she said; "for after this I shall live on the little farm with Uncle Henry and Aunt Em, and princesses ought not to live on farms."

"Princess Dorothy will not," replied Ozma, with her sweet smile. "You are going to live in your own rooms in this palace, and be my constant companion."

"But Uncle Henry—" began Dorothy.

"Oh, he is old, and has worked enough in his lifetime," interrupted the girl Ruler; "so we must find a place for your uncle and aunt where they will be comfortable and happy and need not work more than they care to. When shall we transport them here, Dorothy?"

"I promised to go and see them again before they were turned out of the farmhouse," answered Dorothy; "so—perhaps next Saturday—"

"But why wait so long?" asked Ozma. "And why make the journey back to Kansas again? Let us surprise them, and bring them here without any warning."

"I'm not sure that they believe in the Land of Oz," said Dorothy, "though I've told 'em 'bout it lots of times."

"They'll believe when they see it," declared Ozma; "and if they are told they are to make a magical journey to our fairyland, it may make them nervous. I think the best way will be to use the Magic Belt without warning them, and when they have arrived you can explain to them whatever they do not understand."

"Perhaps that's best," decided Dorothy. "There isn't much use in their staying at the farm until they are put out, 'cause it's much nicer here."

"Then to-morrow morning they shall come here," said Princess Ozma. "I will order Jellia Jamb,[3] who is the palace housekeeper, to have rooms all prepared for them, and after breakfast we will get the Magic Belt and by its aid transport your uncle and aunt to the Emerald City."

"Thank you, Ozma!" cried Dorothy, kissing her friend gratefully.

"And now," Ozma proposed, "let us take a walk in the gardens before we dress for dinner. Come, Dorothy dear!"

CHAPTER 4

How the Nome King Planned Revenge

The reason most people are bad is because they do not try to be good. Now, the Nome King had never tried to be good, so he was very bad indeed. Having decided to conquer the Land of Oz and to destroy the Emerald City and enslave all its people, King Roquat the Red kept planning ways to do this dreadful thing, and the more he planned the more he believed he would be able to accomplish it.

About the time Dorothy went to Ozma the Nome King called his Chief Steward to him and said:

"Kaliko, I think I shall make you the General of my armies."

"I think you won't," replied Kaliko, positively.

"Why not?" inquired the King, reaching for his scepter with the big sapphire.

"Because I'm your Chief Steward, and know nothing of warfare," said Kaliko, preparing to dodge if anything were thrown at him. "I manage all the affairs of your kingdom better than you could yourself, and you'll never find another Steward as good as I am. But there are a hundred Nomes better fitted to command your army, and your Generals get thrown away so often that I have no desire to be one of them."

"Ah, there is some truth in your remarks, Kaliko," remarked the King, deciding not to throw the scepter. "Summon my army to assemble in the Great Cavern."

Kaliko bowed and retired, and in a few minutes returned to say that the army was assembled. So the King went out upon a balcony that overlooked the Great Cavern, where fifty thousand Nomes, all armed with swords and pikes, stood marshaled in military array.

When they were not required as soldiers all these Nomes were metal workers and miners, and they had hammered so much at the forges and dug so hard with pick and shovel that they had acquired great muscular strength. They were strangely formed creatures, rather round and not very tall. Their toes were curly and their ears broad and flat.

In time of war every Nome left his forge or mine and became part of the great army of King Roquat. The soldiers wore rock-colored uniforms and were excellently drilled.

The King looked upon this tremendous army, which stood silently arrayed before him, and a cruel smile curled the corners of his mouth, for he saw that his legions were very powerful. Then he addressed them from the balcony, saying:

"I have thrown away General Blug, because he did not please me. So I want another General to command this army. Who is next in command?"

"I am," replied Colonel Crinkle, a dapper-looking Nome, as he stepped forward to salute his monarch.

The King looked at him carefully and said:

"I want you to march this army through an underground tunnel, which I am going to bore, to the Emerald City of Oz. When you get there I want you to conquer the Oz people, destroy them and their city, and bring all their gold and silver and precious stones back to my cavern. Also you are to recapture my Magic Belt and return it to me. Will you do this, General Crinkle?"

"No, your Majesty," replied the Nome; "for it can't be done."

"Oh, indeed!" exclaimed the King. Then he turned to his servants and said: "Please take General Crinkle to the torture chamber.[1] There you will kindly slice him into thin slices. Afterward you may feed him to the seven-headed dogs."

"Anything to oblige your Majesty," replied the servants, politely, and led the condemned man away.

When they had gone the King addressed the army again.

"Listen!" said he. "The General who is to command my armies

must promise to carry out my orders. If he fails he will share the fate of poor Crinkle. Now, then, who will volunteer to lead my hosts to the Emerald City?"

For a time no one moved and all were silent. Then an old Nome with white whiskers so long that they were tied around his waist to prevent their tripping him up, stepped out of the ranks and saluted the King.

"I'd like to ask a few questions, your Majesty," he said.

"Go ahead," replied the King.

"These Oz people are quite good, are they not?"

"As good as apple pie," said the King.

"And they are happy, I suppose?" continued the old Nome.

"Happy as the day is long," said the King.

"And contented and prosperous?" inquired the Nome.

"Very much so," said the King.

"Well, your Majesty," remarked he of the white whiskers, "I think I should like to undertake the job, so I'll be your General. I hate good people; I detest happy people; I'm opposed to any one who is contented and prosperous. That is why I am so fond of your Majesty. Make me your General and I'll promise to conquer and destroy the Oz people. If I fail I'm ready to be sliced thin and fed to the seven-headed dogs."

"Very good! Very good, indeed! That's the way to talk!" cried Roquat the Red, who was greatly pleased. "What is your name, General?"

"I'm called Guph,[2] your Majesty."

"Well, Guph, come with me to my private cave and we'll talk it over." Then he turned to the army. "Nomes and soldiers," said he, "you are to obey the commands of General Guph until he becomes dog-feed. Any man who fails to obey his new General will be promptly thrown away. You are now dismissed."

Guph went to the King's private cave and sat down upon an amethyst chair and put his feet on the arm of the King's ruby throne. Then he lighted his pipe and threw the live coal he had taken from his pocket upon the King's left foot and puffed the smoke into the King's eyes and made himself comfortable. For he was a wise old Nome, and he knew that the best way to get along with Roquat the Red was to show that he was not afraid of him.

"I'm ready for the talk, your Majesty," he said.

The King coughed and looked at his new General fiercely.

"Do you not tremble to take such liberties with your monarch?" he asked.

"Oh, no," said Guph, calmly, and he blew a wreath of smoke that curled around the King's nose and made him sneeze. "You want to conquer the Emerald City, and I'm the only Nome in your dominions who can conquer it. So you will be very careful not to hurt me until I have carried out your wishes. After that—"

"Well, what then?" inquired the King.

"Then you will be so grateful to me that you won't care to hurt me," replied the General.

"That is a very good argument," said Roquat. "But suppose you fail?"

"Then it's the slicing machine. I agree to that," announced Guph. "But if you do as I tell you there will be no failure. The trouble with you, Roquat, is that you don't think carefully enough. I do. You would go ahead and march through your tunnel into Oz, and get defeated and driven back. I won't. And the reason I won't is because when I march I'll have all my plans made, and a host of allies to assist my Nomes."

"What do you mean by that?" asked the King.

"I'll explain, King Roquat. You're going to attack a fair country, and a mighty fairy country, too. They haven't much of an army in Oz, but the Princess who rules them has a fairy wand; and the little girl Dorothy has your Magic Belt; and at the North of the Emerald City lives a clever sorceress called Glinda the Good, who commands the spirits of the air. Also I have heard that there is a wonderful Wizard in Ozma's palace, who is so skillful that people used to pay him money in America to see him perform. So you see it will be no easy thing to overcome all this magic."

"We have fifty thousand soldiers!" cried the King, proudly.

"Yes; but they are Nomes," remarked Guph, taking a silk handkerchief from the King's pocket and wiping his own pointed shoes with it. "Nomes are immortals, but they are not strong on magic. When you lost your famous Belt the greater part of your own power was gone from you. Against Ozma you and your Nomes would have no show at all."

Roquat's eyes flashed angrily.

"Then away you go to the slicing machine!" he cried.

"Not yet," said the General, filling his pipe from the King's private tobacco pouch.

"What do you propose to do?" asked the monarch.

"I propose to obtain the power we need," answered Guph. "There are a good many evil creatures who have magic powers sufficient to destroy and conquer the Land of Oz. We will get them on our side, band them all together, and then take Ozma and her people by surprise. It's all very simple and easy when you know how. Alone we should be helpless to injure the Ruler of Oz, but with the aid of the evil powers we can summon we shall easily succeed."

King Roquat was delighted with this idea, for he realized how clever it was.

"Surely, Guph, you are the greatest General I have ever had!" he exclaimed, his eyes sparkling with joy. "You must go at once and make arrangements with the evil powers to assist us, and meantime I'll begin to dig the tunnel."

"I thought you'd agree with me, Roquat," replied the new General. "I'll start this very afternoon to visit the Chief of the Whimsies."[3]

CHAPTER 5

How Dorothy Became a Princess

When the people of the Emerald City heard that Dorothy had returned to them every one was eager to see her, for the little girl was a general favorite in the Land of Oz. From time to time some of the folk from the great outside world had found their way into this fairyland, but all except one had been companions of Dorothy and had turned out to be very agreeable people. The exception I speak of was the wonderful Wizard of Oz, a sleight-of-hand performer from Omaha who went up in a balloon and was carried by a current of air to the Emerald City. His queer and puzzling tricks made the people of Oz believe him a great wizard for a time, and he ruled over them until Dorothy arrived on her first visit and showed the Wizard to be a mere humbug. He was a gentle, kindly-hearted little man, and Dorothy grew to like him afterward. When, after an absence, the Wizard returned to the Land of Oz, Ozma received him graciously and gave him a home in a part of the palace.

In addition to the Wizard two other personages from the outside world had been allowed to make their home in the Emerald City. The first was a quaint Shaggy Man,[1] whom Ozma had made the Governor of the Royal Storehouses, and the second a Yellow Hen named Billina,[2] who had a fine house in the gardens back of the palace, where she looked after a large family. Both these had been old comrades of Dorothy, so you see the little girl was quite an important personage in Oz, and the people thought she had brought them good luck, and loved her next best to Ozma. During her several visits this little girl had been the means of destroying two wicked witches who oppressed the people, and she had discovered a live scarecrow who was now one of the most popular personages in all the fairy country. With the Scarecrow's help she had rescued Nick Chopper, a Tin Woodman, who had rusted in a lonely forest, and the tin man was now the Emperor of the Country of the Winkies and much beloved because of his kind heart. No wonder the people thought Dorothy had brought them good luck! Yet, strange as it may seem, she had accomplished all these wonders not because she was a fairy or had any magical powers whatever, but because she was a simple, sweet and true little girl who was honest to herself and to all whom she met. In this world in which we live simplicity and kindness are the only magic wands that work wonders, and in the Land of Oz Dorothy found these same qualities had won for her the love and admiration of the people. Indeed, the little girl had made many warm friends in the fairy country, and the only real grief the Ozites had ever experienced was when Dorothy left them and returned to her Kansas home.

Now she received a joyful welcome, although no one except Ozma knew at first that she had finally come to stay for good and all.

That evening Dorothy had many callers, and among them were such important people as Tiktok,[3] a machine man who thought and spoke and moved by clockwork; her old companion the genial Shaggy Man; Jack Pumpkinhead,[4] whose body was brush-wood and whose head was a ripe pumpkin with a face carved upon it; the Cowardly Lion and the Hungry Tiger,[5] two great beasts from the forest, who served Princess Ozma, and Professor H. M. Wogglebug, T. E.[6] This wogglebug was a remarkable creature. He had once been a tiny little bug, crawling around in a school-room, but he was discovered and highly magnified so that he could be seen more plainly, and while in this magnified condition he had escaped. He had always remained big, and he dressed like a dandy and was so full of knowledge and information (which are distinct acquirements), that he had been made a Professor and the head of the Royal College.

Dorothy had a nice visit with these old friends, and also talked a long time with the Wizard, who was little and old and withered and dried up, but as merry and active as a child. Afterward she went to see Billina's fast growing family of chicks.

Toto, Dorothy's little black dog, also met with a cordial reception. Toto was an especial friend of the Shaggy Man, and he knew every one else. Being the only dog in the Land of Oz, he was highly respected by the people, who believed animals entitled to every consideration if they behaved themselves properly.

Dorothy had four lovely rooms in the palace, which were always reserved for her use and were called "Dorothy's rooms." These consisted of a beautiful sitting room, a dressing room, a dainty bedchamber and a big marble bathroom. And in these rooms were everything that heart could desire, placed there with loving thoughtfulness by Ozma for her little friend's use. The royal dressmakers had the little girl's measure, so they kept the closets in her dressing room filled with lovely dresses of every description and suitable for every occasion. No wonder Dorothy had refrained from bringing with her her old calico and gingham dresses! Here everything that was dear to a little girl's heart was supplied in profusion, and nothing so rich and beautiful could ever have been found in the biggest department stores in America. Of course Dorothy enjoyed all these luxuries, and the only reason she had heretofore preferred to live in Kansas was because her uncle and aunt loved her and needed her with them.

Now, however, all was to be changed, and Dorothy was really more delighted to know that her dear relatives were to share in her good fortune and enjoy the delights of the Land of Oz, than she was to possess such luxury for herself.

Next morning, at Ozma's request, Dorothy dressed herself in a pretty sky-blue gown of rich silk, trimmed with real pearls. The buckles of her shoes were set with pearls, too, and more of these priceless gems were on a lovely coronet which she wore upon her forehead.

"For," said her friend Ozma, "from this time forth, my dear, you must assume your rightful rank as a Princess of Oz, and being my chosen companion you must dress in a way befitting the dignity of your position."

Dorothy agreed to this, although she knew that neither gowns nor jewels could make her anything else than the simple, unaffected little girl she had always been.

As soon as they had breakfasted—the girls eating together in Ozma's pretty boudoir—the Ruler of Oz said:

"Now, dear friend, we will use the Magic Belt to transport your uncle and aunt from Kansas to the Emerald City. But I think it would be fitting, in receiving such distinguished guests, for us to sit in my Throne Room."

"Oh, they're not very 'stinguished, Ozma," said Dorothy. "They're just plain people, like me."

"Being your friends and relatives, Princess Dorothy, they are certainly distinguished," replied the Ruler, with a smile.

"They—they won't hardly know what to make of all your splendid furniture and things," protested Dorothy, gravely. "It may scare 'em to see your grand Throne Room, an' p'raps we'd better go into the back yard, Ozma, where the cabbages grow an' the chickens are playing. Then it would seem more natural to Uncle Henry and Aunt Em."

"No; they shall first see me in my Throne Room," replied Ozma, decidedly; and when she spoke in that tone Dorothy knew it was not wise to oppose her, for Ozma was accustomed to having her own way.

So together they went to the Throne Room, an immense domed chamber in the center of the palace. Here stood the royal throne, made of solid gold and encrusted with enough precious stones to stock a dozen jewelry stores in our country.

Ozma, who was wearing the Magic Belt, seated herself in the throne, and Dorothy sat at her feet. In the room were assembled many ladies and gentlemen of the court, clothed in rich apparel and wearing fine jewelry. Two immense animals squatted, one on each side of the throne—the Cowardly Lion and the Hungry Tiger. In a balcony high up in the dome an orchestra played sweet music, and beneath the dome two electric fountains sent sprays of colored perfumed water shooting up nearly as high as the arched ceiling.

"Are you ready, Dorothy?" asked the Ruler.

"I am," replied Dorothy; "but I don't know whether Aunt Em and Uncle Henry are ready."

"That won't matter," declared Ozma. "The old life can have very little to interest them, and the sooner they begin the new life here the happier they will be. Here they come, my dear!"

As she spoke, there before the throne appeared Uncle Henry and Aunt Em, who for a moment stood motionless, glaring with white and startled faces at the scene that confronted them. If the ladies and gentlemen present had not been so polite I am sure they would have laughed at the two strangers.

Aunt Em had her calico dress skirt "tucked up," and she wore a faded blue-checked apron. Her hair was rather straggly and she had on a pair of Uncle Henry's old slippers. In one hand she held a dish-towel and in the other a cracked earthenware plate, which she had been engaged in wiping when so suddenly transported to the Land of Oz.

Uncle Henry, when the summons came, had been out in the barn "doin' chores." He wore a ragged and much soiled straw hat, a checked shirt without any collar and blue overalls tucked into the tops of his old cowhide boots.

"By gum!" gasped Uncle Henry, looking around as if bewildered.

"Well, I swan!" gurgled Aunt Em, in a hoarse, frightened voice. Then her eyes fell upon Dorothy, and she said: "D-d-d-don't that look like our little girl—our Dorothy, Henry?"

"Hi, there—look out, Em!" exclaimed the old man, as Aunt Em advanced a step; "take care o' the wild beastses, or you're a goner!"

But now Dorothy sprang forward and embraced and kissed her aunt and uncle affectionately, afterward taking their hands in her own.

"Don't be afraid," she said to them. "You are now in the Land of Oz, where you are to live always, and be comfer'ble an' happy. You'll never have to worry over anything again, 'cause there won't be any-thing to worry about. And you owe it all to the kindness of my friend Princess Ozma."

Here she led them before the throne and continued:

"Your Highness, this is Uncle Henry. And this is Aunt Em. They want to thank you for bringing them here from Kansas."

Aunt Em tried to "slick" her hair, and she hid the dishtowel and dish under her apron while she bowed to the lovely Ozma. Uncle Henry took off his straw hat and held it awkwardly in his hands.

But the Ruler of Oz rose and came from her throne to greet her newly arrived guests, and she smiled as sweetly upon them as if they had been a king and a queen.

"You are very welcome here, where I have brought you for Princess Dorothy's sake," she said, graciously, "and I hope you will be quite happy in your new home." Then she turned to her courtiers, who were silently and gravely regarding the scene, and added: "I pre-sent to my people our Princess Dorothy's beloved Uncle Henry and Aunt Em, who will hereafter be subjects of our kingdom. It will please me to have you show them every kindness and honor in your power, and to join me in making them happy and contented."

Hearing this, all those assembled bowed low and respectfully to the old farmer and his wife, who bobbed their own heads in return.

"And now," said Ozma to them, "Dorothy will show you the rooms prepared for you. I hope you will like them, and shall expect you to join me at luncheon."

So Dorothy led her relatives away, and as soon as they were out of the Throne Room and alone in the corridor Aunt Em squeezed Dorothy's hand and said:

"Child, child! How in the world did we ever get here so quick? And is it all real? And are we to stay here, as she says? And what does it all mean, anyhow?"

Dorothy laughed.

"Why didn't you tell us what you were goin' to do?" inquired Uncle Henry, reproachfully. "If I'd known about it I'd 'a put on my Sunday clothes."

"I'll 'splain ever'thing as soon as we get to your rooms," promised Dorothy. "You're in great luck, Uncle Henry and Aunt Em; an' so am I! And oh! I'm so happy to have got you here, at last!"

As he walked by the little girl's side Uncle Henry stroked his whiskers thoughtfully.

" 'Pears to me, Dorothy, we won't make bang-up fairies," he remarked.

"An' my back hair looks like a fright!" wailed Aunt Em.

"Never mind," returned the little girl, reassuringly. "You won't have anything to do now but to look pretty, Aunt Em; an' Uncle Henry won't have to work till his back aches, that's certain."

"Sure?" they asked, wonderingly, and in the same breath.

"Course I'm sure," said Dorothy. "You're in the Fairyland of Oz, now; an' what's more, you belong to it!"

CHAPTER 6

How Guph Visited the Whimsies

The new General of the Nome King's army knew perfectly well that to fail in his plans meant death for him. Yet he was not at all anxious or worried. He hated every one who was good and longed to make all who were happy unhappy. Therefore he had accepted this dangerous posi-

tion as General quite willingly, feeling sure in his evil mind that he would
be able to do a lot of mischief and finally conquer the Land of Oz.

Yet Guph determined to be careful, and to lay his plans well, so as
not to fail. He argued that only careless people fail in what they
attempt to do.

The mountains underneath which the Nome King's extensive caverns were located lay grouped just north of the Land of Ev, which lay
directly across the deadly desert to the east of the Land of Oz. As the
mountains were also on the edge of the desert the Nome King found
that he had only to tunnel underneath the desert to reach Ozma's
dominions. He did not wish his armies to appear above ground in the
Country of the Winkies, which was the part of the Land of Oz nearest
to King Roquat's own country, as then the people would give the
alarm and enable Ozma to fortify the Emerald City and assemble an
army. He wanted to take all the Oz people by surprise; so he decided
to run the tunnel clear through to the Emerald City, where he and his
hosts could break through the ground without warning and conquer
the people before they had time to defend themselves.

Roquat the Red began work at once upon his tunnel, setting a
thousand miners at the task and building it high and broad enough for
his armies to march through it with ease. The Nomes were used to
making tunnels, as all the kingdom in which they lived was under
ground; so they made rapid progress.

While this work was going on General Guph started out alone to
visit the Chief of the Whimsies.

These Whimsies were curious people who lived in a retired country
of their own. They had large, strong bodies, but heads so small that
they were no bigger than door-knobs. Of course, such tiny heads
could not contain any great amount of brains, and the Whimsies were
so ashamed of their personal appearance and lack of commonsense
that they wore big heads, made of pasteboard, which they fastened
over their own little heads. On these pasteboard heads they sewed
sheep's wool for hair, and the wool was colored many tints—pink,
green and lavender being the favorite colors.

The faces of these false heads were painted in many ridiculous
ways, according to the whims of the owners, and these big, burly creatures looked so whimsical and absurd in their queer masks that they
were called "Whimsies." They foolishly imagined that no one would
suspect the little heads that were inside the imitation ones, not knowing that it is folly to try to appear otherwise than as nature has
made us.

The Chief of the Whimsies had as little wisdom as the others, and had been chosen chief merely because none among them was any wiser or more capable of ruling. The Whimsies were evil spirits and could not be killed. They were hated and feared by every one and were known as terrible fighters because they were so strong and muscular and had not sense enough to know when they were defeated.

General Guph thought the Whimsies would be a great help to the Nomes in the conquest of Oz, for under his leadership they could be induced to fight as long as they could stand up. So he traveled to their country and asked to see the Chief, who lived in a house that had a picture of his grotesque false head painted over the doorway.

The Chief's false head had blue hair, a turned-up nose, and a mouth that stretched half across the face. Big green eyes had been painted upon it, but in the center of the chin were two small holes made in the pasteboard, so that the Chief could see through them with his own tiny eyes; for when the big head was fastened upon his shoulders the eyes in his own natural head were on a level with the false chin.

Said General Guph to the Chief of the Whimsies:

"We Nomes are going to conquer the Land of Oz and capture our King's Magic Belt, which the Oz people stole from him. Then we are going to plunder and destroy the whole country. And we want the Whimsies to help us."

"Will there be any fighting?" asked the Chief.

"Plenty," replied Guph.

That must have pleased the Chief, for he got up and danced around the room three times. Then he seated himself again, adjusted his false head, and said:

"We have no quarrel with Ozma of Oz."

"But you Whimsies love to fight, and here is a splendid chance to do so," urged Guph.

"Wait till I sing a song," said the Chief. Then he lay back in his chair and sang a foolish song that did not seem to the General to mean anything, although he listened carefully. When he had finished, the Chief Whimsie looked at him through the holes in his chin and asked:

"What reward will you give us if we help you?"

The General was prepared for this question, for he had been thinking the matter over on his journey. People often do a good deed without hope of reward, but for an evil deed they always demand payment.

"When we get our Magic Belt," he made reply, "our King, Roquat the Red, will use its power to give every Whimsie a natural head as big and fine as the false head he now wears. Then you will no longer be ashamed because your big strong bodies have such teenty-weenty heads."

"Oh! Will you do that?" asked the Chief, eagerly.

"We surely will," promised the General.

"I'll talk to my people," said the Chief.

So he called a meeting of all the Whimsies and told them of the offer made by the Nomes. The creatures were delighted with the bargain, and at once agreed to fight for the Nome King and help him to conquer Oz.

One Whimsie alone seemed to have a glimmer of sense, for he asked:

"Suppose we fail to capture the Magic Belt? What will happen then, and what good will all our fighting do?"

But they threw him into the river for asking foolish questions, and laughed when the water ruined his pasteboard head before he could swim out again.

So the compact was made and General Guph was delighted with his success in gaining such powerful allies.

But there were other people, too, just as important as the Whimsies, whom the clever old Nome had determined to win to his side.

CHAPTER 7

How Aunt Em Conquered the Lion

"These are your rooms," said Dorothy, opening a door.

Aunt Em drew back at sight of the splendid furniture and draperies.

"Ain't there any place to wipe my feet?" she asked.

"You will soon change your slippers for new shoes," replied Dorothy. "Don't be afraid, Aunt Em. Here is where you are to live, so walk right in and make yourself at home."

Aunt Em advanced hesitatingly.

"It beats the Topeka Hotel!"[1] she cried, admiringly. "But this place is too grand for us, child. Can't we have some back room in the attic, that's more in our class?"

"No," said Dorothy. "You've got to live here, 'cause Ozma says so. And all the rooms in this palace are just as fine as these, and some are better. It won't do any good to fuss, Aunt Em. You've got to be swell and high-toned in the Land of Oz, whether you want to or not; so you may as well make up your mind to it."

"It's hard luck," replied her aunt, looking around with an awed expression; "but folks can get used to anything, if they try. Eh, Henry?"

"Why, as to that," said Uncle Henry, slowly, "I b'lieve in takin' what's pervided us, an' askin' no questions. I've traveled some, Em, in my time, an' you hain't; an' that makes a difference atween us."

Then Dorothy showed them through the rooms. The first was a handsome sitting-room, with windows opening upon the rose gardens. Then came separate bedrooms for Aunt Em and Uncle Henry, with a fine bathroom between them. Aunt Em had a pretty dressing room, besides, and Dorothy opened the closets and showed several exquisite costumes that had been provided for her aunt by the royal dressmakers, who had worked all night to get them ready. Everything that Aunt Em could possibly need was in the drawers and closets, and her dressing-table was covered with engraved gold toilet articles.

Uncle Henry had nine suits of clothes, cut in the popular Munchkin fashion, with knee-breeches, silk stockings and low shoes with jeweled buckles. The hats to match these costumes had painted tops and wide brims with small gold bells around the edges. His shirts were of fine linen with frilled bosoms, and his vests were richly embroidered with colored silks.

Uncle Henry decided that he would first take a bath and then dress himself in a blue satin suit that had caught his fancy. He accepted his good fortune with calm composure and refused to have a servant to assist him. But Aunt Em was "all of a flutter," as she said, and it took Dorothy and Jellia Jamb, the housekeeper, and two maids a long time to dress her and do up her hair and get her "rigged like a popinjay," as she quaintly expressed it. She wanted to stop and admire everything that caught her eye, and she sighed continually and declared that such finery was too good for an old country woman, and that she never thought she would have to "put on airs" at her time of life.

Finally she was dressed, and when they went into the sitting-room there was Uncle Henry in his blue satin, walking gravely up and down the room. He had trimmed his beard and mustache and looked very dignified and respectable.

"Tell me, Dorothy," he said; "do all the men here wear duds like these?"

"Yes," she replied; "all 'cept the Scarecrow and the Shaggy Man— and of course the Tin Woodman and Tiktok, who are made of metal. You'll find all the men at Ozma's court dressed just as you are—only perhaps a little finer."

"Henry, you look like a play-actor," announced Aunt Em, looking at her husband critically.

"An' you, Em, look more highfalutin' than a peacock," he replied.

"I guess you're right," she said, regretfully; "but we're helpless victims of high-toned royalty."

Dorothy was much amused.

"Come with me," she said, "and I'll show you 'round the palace."

She took them through the beautiful rooms and introduced them to all the people they chanced to meet. Also she showed them her own pretty rooms, which were not far from their own.

"So it's all true," said Aunt Em, wide-eyed with amazement, "and what Dorothy told us of this fairy country was plain facts instead of dreams! But where are all the strange creatures you used to know here?"

"Yes; where's the Scarecrow?" inquired Uncle Henry.

"Why, he's just now away on a visit to the Tin Woodman, who is Emp'ror of the Winkie Country," answered the little girl. "You'll see him when he comes back, and you're sure to like him."

"And where's the Wonderful Wizard?" asked Aunt Em.

"You'll see him at Ozma's luncheon, for he lives in this palace," was the reply.

"And Jack Pumpkinhead?"

"Oh, he lives a little way out of town, in his own pumpkin field. We'll go there some time and see him, and we'll call on Professor Wogglebug, too. The Shaggy Man will be at the luncheon, I guess, and Tiktok. And now I'll take you out to see Billina, who has a house of her own."

So they went into the back yard, and after walking along winding paths some distance through the beautiful gardens they came to an attractive little house where the Yellow Hen sat on the front porch sunning herself.

"Good morning, my dear Mistress," called Billina, fluttering down to meet them. "I was expecting you to call, for I heard you had come back and brought your uncle and aunt with you."

"We're here for good and all, this time, Billina," cried Dorothy, joyfully. "Uncle Henry and Aunt Em belong in Oz now as much as I do!"

"Then they are very lucky people," declared Billina; "for there couldn't be a nicer place to live. But come, my dear; I must show you all my Dorothys. Nine are living and have grown up to be very respectable hens; but one took cold at Ozma's birthday party and died of the pip,[2] and the other two turned out to be horrid roosters, so I had to change their names from Dorothy to Daniel. They all had the letter 'D' engraved upon their gold lockets, you remember, with your picture inside, and 'D' stands for Daniel as well as for Dorothy."

"Did you call both the roosters Daniel?" asked Uncle Henry.

"Yes, indeed. I've nine Dorothys and two Daniels; and the nine Dorothys have eighty-six sons and daughters and over three hundred grandchildren," said Billina, proudly.

"What names do you give 'em all, dear?" inquired the little girl.

"Oh, they are all Dorothys and Daniels, some being Juniors and some Double-Juniors. Dorothy and Daniel are two good names, and I see no object in hunting for others," declared the Yellow Hen. "But just think, Dorothy, what a big chicken family we've grown to be, and our numbers increase nearly every day! Ozma doesn't know what to do with all the eggs we lay, and we are never eaten or harmed in any way, as chickens are in your country. They give us everything to make us contented and happy, and I, my dear, am the acknowledged Queen and Governor of every chicken in Oz, because I'm the eldest and started the whole colony."

"You ought to be very proud, ma'am," said Uncle Henry, who was astonished to hear a hen talk so sensibly.

"Oh, I am," she replied. "I've the loveliest pearl necklace you ever saw. Come in the house and I'll show it to you. And I've nine leg bracelets and a diamond pin for each wing. But I only wear them on state occasions."

They followed the Yellow Hen into the house, which Aunt Em declared was neat as a pin. They could not sit down, because all Billina's chairs were roosting-poles made of silver; so they had to stand while the hen fussily showed them her treasures.

Then they had to go into the back rooms occupied by Billina's nine Dorothys and two Daniels, who were all plump yellow chickens and greeted the visitors very politely. It was easy to see that they were well bred and that Billina had looked after their education.

In the yards were all the children and grandchildren of these eleven elders and they were of all sizes, from well-grown hens to tiny chickens just out of the shell. About fifty fluffy yellow youngsters were at school, being taught good manners and good grammar by a young hen who wore spectacles. They sang in chorus a patriotic song of the Land of Oz, in honor of their visitors, and Aunt Em was much impressed by these talking chickens.

Dorothy wanted to stay and play with the young chickens for a while, but Uncle Henry and Aunt Em had not seen the palace grounds and gardens yet and were eager to get better acquainted with the marvelous and delightful land in which they were to live.

"I'll stay here, and you can go for a walk," said Dorothy. "You'll be perfec'ly safe anywhere, and may do whatever you want to. When you get tired, go back to the palace and find your rooms, and I'll come to you before luncheon is ready."

So Uncle Henry and Aunt Em started out alone to explore the grounds, and Dorothy knew that they couldn't get lost, because all the palace grounds were enclosed by a high wall of green marble set with emeralds.

It was a rare treat to these simple folk, who had lived in the country all their lives and known little enjoyment of any sort, to wear beautiful clothes and live in a palace and be treated with respect and consideration by all around them. They were very happy indeed as they strolled up the shady walks and looked upon the gorgeous flowers and shrubs, feeling that their new home was more beautiful than any tongue could describe.

Suddenly, as they turned a corner and walked through a gap in a high hedge, they came face to face with an enormous Lion, which crouched upon the green lawn and seemed surprised by their appearance.

They stopped short, Uncle Henry trembling with horror and Aunt Em too terrified to scream. Next moment the poor woman clasped her husband around the neck and cried:

"Save me, Henry, save me!"

"Can't even save myself, Em," he returned, in a husky voice, "for the animile looks as if it could eat both of us, an' lick its chops for more! If I only had a gun—"

"Haven't you, Henry? Haven't you?" she asked anxiously.

"Nary gun, Em. So let's die as brave an' graceful as we can. I knew our luck couldn't last!"

"I won't die. I won't be eaten by a lion!" wailed Aunt Em, glaring upon the huge beast. Then a thought struck her, and she whispered: "Henry, I've heard as savage beastses can be conquered by the human eye. I'll eye that lion out o' countenance an' save our lives."

"Try it, Em," he returned, also in a whisper. "Look at him as you do at me when I'm late to dinner."

Aunt Em turned upon the Lion a determined countenance and a wild dilated eye. She glared at the immense beast steadily, and the Lion, who had been quietly blinking at them, began to appear uneasy and disturbed.

"Is anything the matter, ma'am?" he asked, in a mild voice.

At this speech from the terrible beast Aunt Em and Uncle Henry both were startled, and then Uncle Henry remembered that this must be the Lion they had seen in Ozma's Throne Room.

"Hold on, Em!" he exclaimed. "Quit the eagle eye conquest an' take courage. I guess this is the same Cowardly Lion Dorothy has told us about."

"Oh, is it?" she asked, much relieved.

"When he spoke, I got the idea; and when he looked so 'shamed like, I was sure of it," Uncle Henry continued.

Aunt Em regarded the animal with new interest.

"Are you the Cowardly Lion?" she inquired. "Are you Dorothy's friend?"

"Yes'm," answered the Lion, meekly. "Dorothy and I are old chums and are very fond of each other. I'm the King of Beasts, you know, and the Hungry Tiger and I serve Princess Ozma as her body guards."

"To be sure," said Aunt Em, nodding. "But the King of Beasts shouldn't be cowardly."

"I've heard that said before," remarked the Lion, yawning till he showed his two great rows of sharp white teeth; "but that does not keep me from being frightened whenever I go into battle."

"What do you do, run?" asked Uncle Henry.

"No; that would be foolish, for the enemy would run after me," declared the Lion. "So I tremble with fear and pitch in as hard as I can; and so far I have always won my fight."

"Ah, I begin to understand," said Uncle Henry.

"Were you scared when I looked at you just now?" inquired Aunt Em.

"Terribly scared, madam," answered the Lion, "for at first I thought you were going to have a fit. Then I noticed you were trying to overcome me by the power of your eye, and your glance was so fierce and penetrating that I shook with fear."

This greatly pleased the lady, and she said quite cheerfully:

"Well, I won't hurt you, so don't be scared any more. I just wanted to see what the human eye was good for."

"The human eye is a fearful weapon," remarked the Lion, scratching his nose softly with his paw to hide a smile. "Had I not known you were Dorothy's friends I might have torn you both into shreds in order to escape your terrible gaze."

Aunt Em shuddered at hearing this, and Uncle Henry said hastily:

"I'm glad you knew us. Good morning, Mr. Lion; we'll hope to see you again—by and by—some time in the future."

"Good morning," replied the Lion, squatting down upon the lawn again. "You are likely to see a good deal of me, if you live in the Land of Oz."

CHAPTER 8

How the Grand Gallipoot Joined the Nomes

After leaving the Whimsies, Guph continued on his journey and penetrated far into the Northwest. He wanted to get to the Country of the Growleywogs,[1] and in order to do that he must cross the Ripple Land,[2] which was a hard thing to do. For the Ripple Land was a succession of hills and valleys, all very steep and rocky, and they changed places constantly by rippling. While Guph was climbing a hill it sank down under him and became a valley, and while he was descending into a valley it rose up and carried him to the top of a hill. This was very perplexing to the traveler, and a stranger might have thought he could never cross the Ripple Land at all. But Guph knew that if he kept steadily on he would get to the end at last; so he paid no attention to the changing hills and valleys and plodded along as calmly as if walking upon the level ground.

The result of this wise persistence was that the General finally reached firmer soil and, after penetrating a dense forest, came to the Dominion of the Growleywogs.

No sooner had he crossed the border of this domain when two guards seized him and carried him before the Grand Gallipoot[3] of the Growleywogs, who scowled upon him ferociously and asked him why he dared intrude upon his territory.

"I'm the Lord High General of the Invincible Army of the Nomes, and my name is Guph," was the reply. "All the world trembles when that name is mentioned."

The Growleywogs gave a shout of jeering laughter at this, and one of them caught the Nome in his strong arms and tossed him high into the air. Guph was considerably shaken when he fell upon the hard ground, but he appeared to take no notice of the impertinence and composed himself to speak again to the Grand Gallipoot.

"My master, King Roquat the Red, has sent me here to confer with you. He wishes your assistance to conquer the Land of Oz."

Here the General paused, and the Grand Gallipoot scowled upon him more terribly than ever and said:

"Go on!"

The voice of the Grand Gallipoot was partly a roar and partly a growl. He mumbled his words badly and Guph had to listen carefully in order to understand him.

These Growleywogs were certainly remarkable creatures. They were of gigantic size, yet were all bone and skin and muscle, there being no meat or fat upon their bodies at all. Their powerful muscles lay just underneath their skins, like bunches of tough rope, and the weakest Growleywog was so strong that he could pick up an elephant and toss it seven miles away.

It seems unfortunate that strong people are usually so disagreeable and overbearing that no one cares for them. In fact, to be different from your fellow creatures is always a misfortune. The Growleywogs knew that they were disliked and avoided by every one, so they had

become surly and unsociable even among themselves. Guph knew that they hated all people, including the Nomes; but he hoped to win them over, nevertheless, and knew that if he succeeded they would afford him very powerful assistance.

"The Land of Oz is ruled by a namby-pamby girl who is disgustingly kind and good," he continued. "Her people are all happy and contented and have no care or worries whatever."

"Go on!" growled the Grand Gallipoot.

"Once the Nome King enslaved the Royal Family of Ev—another goody-goody lot that we detest," said the General. "But Ozma interfered, although it was none of her business, and marched her army against us. With her was a Kansas girl named Dorothy, and a Yellow Hen, and they marched directly into the Nome King's cavern. There they liberated our slaves from Ev and stole King Roquat's Magic Belt, which they carried away with them. So now our King is making a tunnel under the deadly desert, so we can march through it to the Emerald City. When we get there we mean to conquer and destroy all the land and recapture the Magic Belt."

Again he paused, and again the Grand Gallipoot growled:

"Go on!"

Guph tried to think what to say next, and a happy thought soon occurred to him.

"We want you to help us in this conquest," he announced, "for we need the mighty aid of the Growleywogs in order to make sure that we shall not be defeated. You are the strongest people in all the world, and you hate good and happy creatures as much as we Nomes do. I am sure it will be a real pleasure to you to tear down the beautiful Emerald City, and in return for your valuable assistance we will allow you to bring back to your country ten thousand people of Oz, to be your slaves."

"Twenty thousand!" growled the Grand Gallipoot.

"All right, we promise you twenty thousand," agreed the General.

The Gallipoot made a signal and at once his attendants picked up General Guph and carried him away to a prison, where the jailor amused himself by sticking pins in the round fat body of the old Nome, to see him jump and hear him yell.

But while this was going on the Grand Gallipoot was talking with his counselors, who were the most important officials of the Growleywogs. When he had stated to them the proposition of the Nome King he said:

"My advice is to offer to help them. Then, when we have conquered the Land of Oz, we will take not only our twenty thousand prisoners but all the gold and jewels we want."

"Let us take the Magic Belt, too," suggested one counselor.

"And rob the Nome King and make him our slave," said another.

"That is a good idea," declared the Grand Gallipoot. "I'd like King Roquat for my own slave. He could black my boots and bring me my porridge every morning while I am in bed."

"There is a famous Scarecrow in Oz. I'll take him for my slave," said a counselor.

"I'll take Tiktok, the machine man," said another.

"Give me the Tin Woodman," said a third.

They went on for some time, dividing up the people and the treasure of Oz in advance of the conquest. For they had no doubt at all that they would be able to destroy Ozma's domain. Were they not the strongest people in all the world?

"The deadly desert has kept us out of Oz before," remarked the Grand Gallipoot, "but now that the Nome King is building a tunnel we shall get into the Emerald City very easily. So let us send the little fat General back to his King with our promise to assist him. We will not say that we intend to conquer the Nomes after we have conquered Oz, but we will do so, just the same."

This plan being agreed upon, they all went home to dinner, leaving General Guph still in prison. The Nome had no idea that he had succeeded in his mission, for finding himself in prison he feared the Growleywogs intended to put him to death.

By this time the jailor had tired of sticking pins in the General, and was amusing himself by carefully pulling the Nome's whiskers out by the roots, one at a time. This enjoyment was interrupted by the Grand Gallipoot sending for the prisoner.

"Wait a few hours," begged the jailor. "I haven't pulled out a quarter of his whiskers yet."

"If you keep the Grand Gallipoot waiting he'll break your back," declared the messenger.

"Perhaps you're right," sighed the jailor. "Take the prisoner away, if you will, but I advise you to kick him at every step he takes. It will be good fun, for he is as soft as a ripe peach."

So Guph was led away to the royal castle, where the Grand Gallipoot told him that the Growleywogs had decided to assist the Nomes in conquering the Land of Oz.

"Whenever you are ready," he added, "send me word and I will march with eighteen thousand of my most powerful warriors to your aid."

Guph was so delighted that he forgot all the smarting caused by the pins and the pulling of whiskers. He did not even complain of the treatment he had received, but thanked the Grand Gallipoot and hurried away upon his journey.

He had now secured the assistance of the Whimsies and the Growleywogs; but his success made him long for still more allies. His own life depended upon his conquering Oz, and he said to himself:

"I'll take no chances. I'll be certain of success. Then, when Oz is destroyed, perhaps I shall be a greater man than old Roquat, and I can throw him away and be King of the Nomes myself. Why not? The Whimsies are stronger than the Nomes, and they are my friends. The Growleywogs are stronger than the Whimsies, and they also are my friends. There are some people still stronger than the Growleywogs, and if I can but induce them to aid me I shall have nothing more to fear."

CHAPTER 9

How the Wogglebug Taught Athletics

It did not take Dorothy long to establish herself in her new home, for she knew the people and the manners and customs of the Emerald City just as well as she knew the old Kansas farm.

But Uncle Henry and Aunt Em had some trouble in getting used to the finery and pomp and ceremony of Ozma's palace, and felt uneasy because they were obliged to be "dressed up" all the time. Yet every one was very courteous and kind to them and endeavored to make them happy. Ozma, especially, made much of Dorothy's relatives, for her little friend's sake, and she well knew that the awkwardness and strangeness of their new mode of life would all wear off in time.

The old people were chiefly troubled by the fact that there was no work for them to do.[1]

"Ev'ry day is like Sunday, now," declared Aunt Em, solemnly, "and I can't say I like it. If they'd only let me do up the dishes after meals, or even sweep an' dust my own rooms, I'd be a deal happier. Henry don't know what to do with himself either, and once when he stole out an' fed the chickens Billina scolded him for letting 'em eat between meals. I never knew before what a hardship it is to be rich and have everything you want."

These complaints began to worry Dorothy; so she had a long talk with Ozma upon the subject.

"I see I must find them something to do," said the girlish Ruler of Oz, seriously. "I have been watching your uncle and aunt, and I believe they will be more contented if occupied with some light tasks. While I am considering this matter, Dorothy, you might make a trip with them through the Land of Oz, visiting some of the odd corners and introducing your relatives to some of our curious people."

"Oh, that would be fine!" exclaimed Dorothy, eagerly.

"I will give you an escort befitting your rank as a Princess," continued Ozma; "and you may go to some of the places you have not yet visited yourself, as well as some others that you know. I will mark out a plan of the trip for you and have everything in readiness for you to start tomorrow morning. Take your time, dear, and be gone as long as you wish. By the time you return I shall have found some occupation for Uncle Henry and Aunt Em that will keep them from being restless and dissatisfied."

Dorothy thanked her good friend and kissed the lovely Ruler gratefully. Then she ran to tell the joyful news to her uncle and aunt.

Next morning, after breakfast, everything was found ready for their departure.

The escort included Omby Amby,[2] the Captain General of Ozma's army, which consisted merely of twenty-seven officers besides the Captain General. Once Omby Amby had been a private soldier— the only private in the army—but as there was never any fight to do Ozma saw no need of a private, so she made Omby Amby the highest officer of them all. He was very tall and slim and wore a gay uniform and a fierce mustache. Yet the mustache was the only fierce thing about Omby Amby, whose nature was as gentle as that of a child.

The wonderful Wizard had asked to join the party, and with him came his friend the Shaggy Man, who was shaggy but not ragged, being dressed in fine silks with satin shags and bobtails. The Shaggy Man had shaggy whiskers and hair, but a sweet disposition and a soft, pleasant voice.

There was an open wagon, with three seats for the passengers, and the wagon was drawn by the famous wooden Sawhorse[3] which had once been brought to life by Ozma by means of a magic powder. The

Sawhorse wore golden shoes to keep his wooden legs from wearing away, and he was strong and swift. As this curious creature was Ozma's own favorite steed, and very popular with all the people of the Emerald City, Dorothy knew that she had been highly favored by being permitted to use the Sawhorse on her journey.

In the front seat of the wagon sat Dorothy and the Wizard. Uncle Henry and Aunt Em sat in the next seat and the Shaggy Man and Omby Amby in the third seat. Of course Toto was with the party, curled up at Dorothy's feet, and just as they were about to start Billina came fluttering along the path and begged to be taken with them. Dorothy readily agreed, so the Yellow Hen flew up and perched herself upon the dashboard. She wore her pearl necklace and three bracelets upon each leg, in honor of the occasion.

Dorothy kissed Ozma good-bye, and all the people standing around waved their handkerchiefs, and the band in an upper balcony struck up a military march. Then the Wizard clucked to the Sawhorse and said: "Gid-dap!" and the wooden animal pranced away and drew behind him the big red wagon and all the passengers, without any effort at all. A servant threw open a gate of the palace enclosure, that they might pass out; and so, with music and shouts following them, the journey was begun.

"It's almost like a circus," said Aunt Em, proudly. "I can't help feelin' high an' mighty in this kind of a turn-out."

Indeed, as they passed down the street, all the people cheered them lustily, and the Shaggy Man and the Wizard and the Captain General all took off their hats and bowed politely in acknowledgment.

When they came to the great wall of the Emerald City the gates were opened by the Guardian who always tended them. Over the gateway hung a dull-colored metal magnet shaped like a horse-shoe, placed against a shield of polished gold.

"That," said the Shaggy Man, impressively, "is the wonderful Love Magnet. I brought it to the Emerald City myself, and all who pass beneath this gateway are both loving and beloved."

"It's a fine thing," declared Aunt Em, admiringly. "If we'd had it in Kansas I guess the man who held a mortgage on the farm wouldn't have turned us out."

"Then I'm glad we didn't have it," returned Uncle Henry. "I like Oz better than Kansas, even; an' this little wood Sawhorse beats all the critters I ever saw. He don't have to be curried, or fed, or watered, an' he's strong as an ox. Can he talk, Dorothy?"

"Yes, Uncle," replied the child. "But the Sawhorse never says much. He told me once that he can't talk and think at the same time, so he prefers to think."

"Which is very sensible," declared the Wizard, nodding approvingly. "Which way do we go, Dorothy?"

"Straight ahead into the Quadling Country," she answered. "I've got a letter of interduction to Miss Cuttenclip."

"Oh!" exclaimed the Wizard, much interested. "Are we going there? Then I'm glad I came, for I've always wanted to meet the Cuttenclips."[4]

"Who are they?" inquired Aunt Em.

"Wait till we get there," replied Dorothy, with a laugh; "then you'll see for yourself. I've never seen the Cuttenclips, you know, so I can't 'zactly 'splain 'em to you."

Once free of the Emerald City the Sawhorse dashed away at tremendous speed. Indeed, he went so fast that Aunt Em had hard work to catch her breath, and Uncle Henry held fast to the seat of the red wagon.

"Gently—gently, my boy!" called the Wizard, and at this the Sawhorse slackened his speed.

"What's wrong?" asked the animal, slightly turning his wooden head to look at the party with one eye, which was a knot of wood.

"Why, we wish to admire the scenery, that's all," answered the Wizard.

"Some of your passengers," added the Shaggy Man, "have never been out of the Emerald City before, and the country is all new to them."

"If you go too fast you'll spoil all the fun," said Dorothy. "There's no hurry."

"Very well; it is all the same to me," observed the Sawhorse; and after that he went at a more moderate pace.

Uncle Henry was astonished.

"How can a wooden thing be so intelligent?" he asked.

"Why, I gave him some sawdust brains the last time I fitted his head with new ears," explained the Wizard. "The sawdust was made from hard knots, and now the Sawhorse is able to think out any knotty problem he meets with."

"I see," said Uncle Henry.

"I don't," remarked Aunt Em; but no one paid any attention to this statement.

Before long they came to a stately building that stood upon a green plain with handsome shade trees grouped here and there.

"What is that?" asked Uncle Henry.

"That," replied the Wizard, "is the Royal Athletic College of Oz, which is directed by Professor H. M. Wogglebug, T. E."

"Let's stop and make a call," suggested Dorothy.

So the Sawhorse drew up in front of the great building and they were met at the door by the learned Wogglebug himself. He seemed fully as tall as the Wizard, and was dressed in a red and white checked vest and a blue swallow-tailed coat, and had yellow knee breeches and purple silk stockings upon his slender legs. A tall hat was jauntily set upon his head and he wore spectacles over his big bright eyes.

"Welcome, Dorothy," said the Wogglebug; "and welcome to all your friends. We are indeed pleased to receive you at this great Temple of Learning."

"I thought it was an Athletic College," said the Shaggy Man.

"It is, my dear sir," answered the Wogglebug proudly. "Here it is that we teach the youth of our great land scientific College Athletics[5]—in all their purity."

"Don't you teach them anything else?" asked Dorothy. "Don't they get any reading, writing and 'rithmetic?"

"Oh, yes; of course. They get all those, and more," returned the Professor. "But such things occupy little of their time. Please follow me and I will show you how my scholars are usually occupied. This is a class hour and they are all busy."

They followed him to a big field back of the college building, where several hundred young Ozites were at their classes. In one place they played football, in another baseball. Some played tennis, some golf; some were swimming in a big pool. Upon a river which wound through the grounds several crews in racing boats were rowing with great enthusiasm. Other groups of students played basketball and cricket, while in one place a ring was roped in to permit boxing and wrestling by the energetic youths. All the collegians seemed busy and there was much laughter and shouting.

"This college," said Professor Wogglebug, complacently, "is a great success. Its educational value is undisputed, and we are turning out many great and valuable citizens every year."

"But when do they study?" asked Dorothy.

"Study?" said the Wogglebug, looking perplexed at the question.

"Yes; when do they get their 'rithmetic, and jogerfy, and such things?"

"Oh, they take doses of those every night and morning," was the reply.

"What do you mean by doses?" Dorothy inquired, wonderingly.

"Why, we use the newly invented School Pills, made by your friend the Wizard. These pills we have found to be very effective, and they save a lot of time. Please step this way and I will show you our Laboratory of Learning."

He led them to a room in the building where many large bottles were standing in rows upon shelves.

"These are the Algebra Pills," said the Professor, taking down one of the bottles. "One at night, on retiring, is equal to four hours of study. Here are the Geography Pills—one at night and one in the morning. In this next bottle are the Latin Pills—one three times a day. Then we have the Grammar Pills—one before each meal—and the Spelling Pills, which are taken whenever needed."

"Your scholars must have to take a lot of pills," remarked Dorothy, thoughtfully. "How do they take 'em, in applesauce?"

"No, my dear. They are sugar-coated and are quickly and easily swallowed. I believe the students would rather take the pills than study, and certainly the pills are a more effective method. You see, until these School Pills were invented we wasted a lot of time in study that may now be better employed in practising athletics."

"Seems to me the pills are a good thing," said Omby Amby, who remembered how it used to make his head ache as a boy to study arithmetic.

"They are, sir," declared the Wogglebug, earnestly. "They give us an advantage over all other colleges, because at no loss of time our boys become thoroughly conversant with Greek and Latin, Mathematics and Geography, Grammar and Literature. You see they are never obliged to interrupt their games to acquire the lesser branches of learning."

"It's a great invention, I'm sure," said Dorothy, looking admiringly at the Wizard, who blushed modestly at this praise.

"We live in an age of progress," announced Professor Wogglebug, pompously. "It is easier to swallow knowledge than to acquire it laboriously from books. Is it not so, my friends?"

"Some folks can swallow anything," said Aunt Em, "but to me this seems too much like taking medicine."

"Young men in college always have to take their medicine, one way or another," observed the Wizard, with a smile; "and, as our Professor says, these School Pills have proved to be a great success. One day while I was making them I happened to drop one of them, and one of Billina's chickens gobbled it up. A few minutes afterward this chick got upon a roost and recited 'The Boy Stood on the Burning Deck' without making a single mistake. Then it recited 'The Charge of the Light Brigade' and afterwards 'Excelsior.' You see, the chicken had eaten an Elocution Pill."

They now bade good bye to the Professor, and thanking him for his kind reception mounted again into the red wagon and continued their journey.

CHAPTER 10

How the Cuttenclips Lived

The travelers had taken no provisions with them because they knew that they would be welcomed wherever they might go in the Land of Oz, and that the people would feed and lodge them with genuine hospitality. So about noon they stopped at a farmhouse and were given a delicious luncheon of bread and milk, fruits and wheat cakes with maple syrup. After resting a while and strolling through the orchards with their host—a round, jolly farmer—they got into the wagon and again started the Sawhorse along the pretty, winding road.

There were sign-posts at all the corners, and finally they came to one which read:

TAKE THIS ROAD TO THE CUTTENCLIPS

There was also a hand pointing in the right direction, so they turned the Sawhorse that way and found it a very good road, but seemingly little traveled.

"I've never been to see the Cuttenclips before," remarked Dorothy.

"Nor I," said the Captain General.

"Nor I," said the Wizard.

"Nor I," said Billina.

"I've hardly been out of the Emerald City since I arrived in this country," added the Shaggy Man.

"Why, none of us has been there, then," exclaimed the little girl. "I wonder what the Cuttenclips are like."

"We shall soon find out," said the Wizard, with a sly laugh. "I've heard they are rather flimsy things."

The farmhouses became fewer as they proceeded, and the path was at times so faint that the Sawhorse had hard work to keep in the road. The wagon began to jounce, too; so they were obliged to go slowly.

After a somewhat wearisome journey they came in sight of a high wall, painted blue with pink ornaments. This wall was circular, and seemed to enclose a large space. It was so high that only the tops of the trees could be seen above it.

The path led up to a small door in the wall, which was closed and latched. Upon the door was a sign in gold letters reading as follows:

VISITORS ARE REQUESTED TO MOVE SLOWLY AND CARE-FULLY, AND TO AVOID COUGHING OR MAKING ANY BREEZE OR DRAUGHT

"That's strange," said the Shaggy Man, reading the sign aloud. "Who *are* the Cuttenclips, anyhow?"

"Why, they're paper dolls," answered Dorothy. "Didn't you know that?"

"Paper dolls! Then let's go somewhere else," said Uncle Henry. "We're all too old to play with dolls, Dorothy."

"But these are different," declared the girl. "They're alive."

"Alive!" gasped Aunt Em, in amazement.

"Yes. Let's go in," said Dorothy.

So they all got out of the wagon, since the door in the wall was not big enough for them to drive the Sawhorse and wagon through it.

"You stay here, Toto!" commanded Dorothy, shaking her finger at the little dog. "You're so careless that you might make a breeze if I let you inside."

Toto wagged his tail as if disappointed at being left behind; but he made no effort to follow them. The Wizard unlatched the door, which opened outward, and they all looked eagerly inside.

Just before the entrance was drawn up a line of tiny soldiers, with uniforms brightly painted and paper guns upon their shoulders. They were exactly alike, from one end of the line to the other, and all were cut out of paper and joined together in the centers of their bodies.

As the visitors entered the enclosure the Wizard let the door swing back into place, and at once the line of soldiers tumbled over, fell flat upon their backs, and lay fluttering upon the ground.

"Hi, there!" called one of them; "what do you mean by slamming the door and blowing us over?"

"I beg your pardon, I'm sure," said the Wizand, regretfully. "I didn't know you were so delicate."

"We're not delicate!" retorted another soldier, raising his head from the ground. "We are strong and healthy; but we can't stand draughts."

"May I help you up?" asked Dorothy.

"If you please," replied the end soldier. "But do it gently, little girl."

Dorothy carefully stood up the line of soldiers, who first dusted their painted clothes and then saluted the visitors with their paper muskets. From the end it was easy to see that the entire line had been cut out of paper, although from the front the soldiers looked rather solid and imposing.

"I've a letter of introduction from Princess Ozma to Miss Cuttenclip," announced Dorothy.

"Very well," said the end soldier, and blew upon a paper whistle that hung around his neck. At once a paper soldier in a Captain's uniform came out of a paper house nearby and approached the group at the entrance. He was not very big, and he walked rather stiffly and uncertainly on his paper legs; but he had a pleasant face, with very red cheeks and very blue eyes, and he bowed so low to the strangers that Dorothy laughed, and the breeze from her mouth nearly blew the Captain over. He wavered and struggled and finally managed to remain upon his feet.

"Take care, Miss!" he said, warningly. "You're breaking the rules, you know, by laughing."

"Oh, I didn't know that," she replied.

"To laugh in this place is nearly as dangerous as to cough," said the Captain. "You'll have to breathe very quietly, I assure you."

"We'll try to," promised the girl. "May we see Miss Cuttenclip, please?"

"You may," promptly returned the Captain. "This is one of her reception days. Be good enough to follow me."

He turned and led the way up a path, and as they followed slowly, because the paper Captain did not move very swiftly, they took the opportunity to gaze around them at this strange paper country.

Beside the path were paper trees, all cut out very neatly and painted a brilliant green color. And back of the trees were rows of cardboard houses, painted in various colors but most of them having green blinds. Some were large and some small, and in the front yards were beds of paper flowers quite natural in appearance. Over some of the porches paper vines were twined, giving them a cosy and shady look.

As the visitors passed along the street a good many paper dolls came to the doors and windows of their houses to look at them curiously. These dolls were nearly all the same height, but were cut into various shapes, some being fat and some lean. The girl dolls wore many beautiful costumes of tissue paper, making them quite fluffy; but their heads and hands were no thicker than the paper of which they were made.

Some of the paper people were on the street, walking along or congregated in groups and talking together; but as soon as they saw the strangers they all fluttered into the houses as fast as they could go, so as to be out of danger.

"Excuse me if I go edgewise," remarked the Captain, as they came to a slight hill. "I can get along faster that way and not flutter so much."

"That's all right," said Dorothy. "We don't mind how you go, I'm sure."

At one side of the street was a paper pump, and a paper boy was pumping paper water into a paper pail. The Yellow Hen happened to brush against this boy with her wing, and he flew into the air and fell into a paper tree, where he stuck until the Wizard gently pulled him out. At the same time the pail went soaring into the air, spilling the paper water, while the paper pump bent nearly double.

"Goodness me!" said the Hen. "If I should flop my wings I believe I'd knock over the whole village!"

"Then don't flop them—please don't!" entreated the Captain. "Miss Cuttenclip would be very much distressed if her village was spoiled."

"Oh, I'll be careful," promised Billina.

"Are not all these paper girls and women named Miss Cuttenclips?" inquired Omby Amby.

"No, indeed," answered the Captain, who was walking better since he began to move edgewise. "There is but one Miss Cuttenclip, who is our Queen, because she made us all. These girls are Cuttenclips, to be sure, but their names are Emily and Polly and Sue and Betty and such things. Only the Queen is called Miss Cuttenclip."

"I must say that this place beats anything I ever heard of," observed Aunt Em. "I used to play with paper dolls myself, an' cut 'em out; but I never thought I'd ever see such things alive."

"I don't see as it's any more curious than hearing hens talk," returned Uncle Henry.

"You're likely to see many queer things in the Land of Oz, sir," said the Wizard. "But a fairy country is extremely interesting when you get used to being surprised."

"Here we are!" called the Captain, stopping before a cottage.

This house was made of wood, and was remarkably pretty in design. In the Emerald City it would have been considered a tiny dwelling, indeed; but in the midst of this paper village it seemed immense. Real flowers were in the garden and real trees grew beside it. Upon the front door was a sign reading:

MISS CUTTENCLIP

Just as they reached the porch the front door opened and a little girl stood before them. She appeared to be about the same age as Dorothy, and smiling upon her visitors she said, sweetly:

"You are welcome."

All the party seemed relieved to find that here was a real girl, of flesh and blood. She was very dainty and pretty as she stood there welcoming them. Her hair was a golden blonde and her eyes turquoise blue. She had rosy cheeks and lovely white teeth. Over her simple white lawn dress she wore an apron with pink and white checks, and in one hand she held a pair of scissors.

"May we see Miss Cuttenclip, please?" asked Dorothy.

"I am Miss Cuttenclip," was the reply. "Won't you come in?"

She held the door open while they all entered a pretty sitting-room that was littered with all sorts of paper—some stiff, some thin, and some tissue. The sheets and scraps were of all colors. Upon a table were paints and brushes, while several pair of scissors, of different sizes, were lying about.

"Sit down, please," said Miss Cuttenclip, clearing the paper scraps off some of the chairs. "It is so long since I have had any visitors that I am not properly prepared to receive them. But I'm sure you will pardon my untidy room, for this is my workshop."

"Do you make all the paper dolls?" inquired Dorothy.

"Yes; I cut them out with my scissors, and paint the faces and some of the costumes. It is very pleasant work, and I am happy making my paper village grow."

"But how do the paper dolls happen to be alive?" asked Aunt Em.

"The first dolls I made were not alive," said Miss Cuttenclip. "I used to live near the castle of a great Sorceress named Glinda the

Good, and she saw my dolls and said they were very pretty. I told her I thought I would like them better if they were alive, and the next day the Sorceress brought me a lot of magic paper. 'This is live paper,' she said, 'and all the dolls you cut out of it will be alive, and able to think and to talk. When you have used it all up, come to me and I will give you more.'

"Of course I was delighted with this present," continued Miss Cuttenclip, "and at once set to work and made several paper dolls, which, as soon as they were cut out, began to walk around and talk to me. But they were so thin that I found that any breeze would blow them over and scatter them dreadfully; so Glinda found this lonely place for me, where few people ever come. She built the wall to keep any wind from blowing away my people, and told me I could build a paper village here and be its Queen. That is why I came here and settled down to work and started the village you now see. It was many years ago that I built the first houses, and I've kept pretty busy and made my village grow finely; and I need not tell you that I am very happy in my work."

"Many years ago!" exclaimed Aunt Em. "Why, how old are you, child?"

"I never keep track of the years," said Miss Cuttenclip, laughing. "You see, I don't grow up at all, but stay just the same as I was when first I came here. Perhaps I'm older even than you are, madam; but I couldn't say for sure."

They looked at the lovely little girl wonderingly, and the Wizard asked:

"What happens to your paper village when it rains?"

"It does not rain here," replied Miss Cuttenclip. "Glinda keeps all the rain storms away; so I never worry about my dolls getting wet. But now, if you will come with me, it will give me pleasure to show you over my paper kingdom. Of course you must go slowly and carefully, and avoid making any breeze."

They left the cottage and followed their guide through the various streets of the village. It was indeed an amazing place, when one considered that it was all made with scissors, and the visitors were not only greatly interested but full of admiration for the skill of little Miss Cuttenclip.

In one place a large group of especially nice paper dolls assembled to greet their Queen, whom it was easy to see they loved dearly. These dolls marched and danced before the visitors, and then they all waved their paper handkerchiefs and sang in a sweet chorus a song called "The Flag of Our Native Land."

At the conclusion of the song they ran up a handsome paper flag on a tall flagpole, and all of the people of the village gathered around to cheer as loudly as they could—although, of course, their voices were not especially strong.

Miss Cuttenclip was about to make her subjects a speech in reply to this patriotic song, when the Shaggy Man happened to sneeze.

He was a very loud and powerful sneezer at any time, and he had tried so hard to hold in this sneeze that when it suddenly exploded the result was terrible.

The paper dolls were mowed down by dozens, and flew and fluttered in wild confusion in every direction, tumbling this way and that and getting more or less wrinkled and bent.

A wail of terror and grief came from the scattered throng, and Miss Cuttenclip exclaimed:

"Dear me! dear me!" and hurried at once to the rescue of her overturned people.

"Oh, Shaggy Man! How could you?" asked Dorothy, reproachfully.

"I couldn't help it—really I couldn't," protested the Shaggy Man, looking quite ashamed. "And I had no idea it took so little to upset these paper dolls."

"So little!" said Dorothy. "Why, it was 'most as bad as a Kansas cyclone." And then she helped Miss Cuttenclip rescue the paper folk and stand them on their feet again. Two of the cardboard houses had also tumbled over, and the little Queen said she would have to repair them and paste them together before they could be lived in again.

And now, fearing they might do more damage to the flimsy paper people, they decided to go away. But first they thanked Miss Cuttenclip very warmly for her courtesy and kindness to them.

"Any friend of Princess Ozma is always welcome here—unless he sneezes," said the Queen, with a rather severe look at the Shaggy Man, who hung his head. "I like to have visitors admire my wonderful village, and I hope you will call again."

Miss Cuttenclip herself led them to the door in the wall, and as they passed along the street the paper dolls peeped at them half fearfully from the doors and windows. Perhaps they will never forget the Shaggy Man's awful sneeze, and I am sure they were all glad to see the meat people go away.

CHAPTER 11

How the General Met the First and Foremost

On leaving the Growleywogs General Guph had to recross the Ripple Lands, and he did not find it a pleasant thing to do. Perhaps having his whiskers pulled out one by one and being used as a pin-cushion for the innocent amusement of a good natured jailor had not improved the quality of Guph's temper, for the old Nome raved and raged at the recollection of the wrongs he had suffered, and vowed to take vengeance upon the Growleywogs after he had used them for his purposes and Oz had been conquered. He went on in this furious way until he was half across the Ripple Land. Then he became seasick, and the rest of the way this naughty Nome was almost as miserable as he deserved to be.

But when he reached the plains again and the ground was firm under his feet he began to feel better, and instead of going back home he turned directly west. A squirrel, perched in a tree, saw him take this road and called to him warningly: "Look out!" But he paid no attention. An eagle paused in its flight through the air to look at him wonderingly and say: "Look out!" But on he went.

No one can say that Guph was not brave, for he had determined to visit those dangerous creatures the Phanfasms,[1] who resided upon the very top of the dread Mountain of Phantastico. The Phanfasms were Erbs, and so dreaded by mortals and immortals alike that no one had been near their mountain home for several thousand years. Yet General Guph hoped to induce them to join in his proposed warfare against the good and happy Oz people.

Guph knew very well that the Phanfasms would be almost as dangerous to the Nomes as they would to the Ozites, but he thought himself so clever that he believed that he could manage these strange creatures and make them obey him. And there was no doubt at all that if he could enlist the services of the Phanfasms their tremendous power, united to the strength of the Growleywogs and the cunning of the Whimsies would doom the Land of Oz to absolute destruction.

So the old Nome climbed the foothills and trudged along the wild mountain paths until he came to a big gully that encircled the Mountain of Phantastico and marked the boundary line of the dominion of the Phanfasms. This gully was about a third of the way up the mountain, and it was filled to the brim with red-hot molten lava, in which swam fire-serpents and poisonous salamanders. The heat from this mass and its poisonous smell were both so unbearable that even birds hesitated to fly over the gully, but circled around it. All living things kept away from the mountain.

Now Guph had heard, during his long lifetime, many tales of these dreaded Phanfasms; so he had heard of this barrier of melted lava, and also he had been told that there was a narrow bridge that spanned it in one place. So he walked along the edge until he found the bridge. It was a single arch of gray stone, and lying flat upon this bridge was a scarlet alligator, seemingly fast asleep.

When Guph stumbled over the rocks in approaching the bridge the creature opened its eyes, from which tiny flames shot in all directions, and after looking at the intruder very wickedly the scarlet alligator closed its eyelids again and lay still.

Guph saw there was no room for him to pass the alligator on the narrow bridge, so he called out to it:

"Good morning, friend. I don't wish to hurry you, but please tell me if you are coming down, or going up?"

"Neither," snapped the alligator, clicking its cruel jaws together. The General hesitated.

"Are you likely to stay there long?" he asked.

"A few hundred years or so," said the alligator.

Guph softly rubbed the end of his nose and tried to think what to do.

"Do you know whether the First and Foremost Phanfasm of Phantastico is at home or not?" he presently inquired.

"I expect he is, seeing he is always at home," replied the alligator.

"Ah; who is that coming down the mountain?" asked the Nome, gazing upward.

The alligator turned to look over its shoulder, and at once Guph ran to the bridge and leaped over the sentinel's back before it could turn back again. The scarlet monster made a snap at the Nome's left foot, but missed it by fully an inch.

"Ah ha!" laughed the General, who was now on the mountain path. "I fooled you that time."

"So you did; and perhaps you fooled yourself," retorted the alligator. "Go up the mountain, if you dare, and find out what the First and Foremost will do to you!"

"I will," declared Guph, boldly; and on he went up the path.

At first the scene was wild enough, but gradually it grew more and more awful in appearance. All the rocks had the shapes of frightful beings and even the tree trunks were gnarled and twisted like serpents.

Suddenly there appeared before the Nome a man with the head of an owl. His body was hairy, like that of an ape, and his only clothing was a scarlet scarf twisted around his waist. He bore a huge club in his hand and his round owl eyes blinked fiercely upon the intruder.

"What are you doing here?" he demanded, threatening Guph with his club.

"I've come to see the First and Foremost Phanfasm of Phantastico," replied the General, who did not like the way this creature looked at him, but still was not afraid.

"Ah; you shall see him!" the man said, with a sneering laugh. "The First and Foremost shall decide upon the best way to punish you."

"He will not punish me," returned Guph, calmly, "for I have come here to do him and his people a rare favor. Lead on, fellow, and take me directly to your master."

The owl-man raised his club with a threatening gesture.

"If you try to escape," he said, "beware—"

But here the General interrupted him.

"Spare your threats," said he, "and do not be impertinent, or I will have you severely punished. Lead on, and keep silent!"

This Guph was really a clever rascal, and it seems a pity he was so bad, for in a good cause he might have accomplished much. He realized that he had put himself into a dangerous position by coming to this dreadful mountain, but he also knew that if he showed fear he was lost. So he adopted a bold manner as his best defense. The wisdom of this plan was soon evident, for the Phanfasm with the owl's head turned and led the way up the mountain.

At the very top was a level plain, upon which were heaps of rock that at first glance seemed solid. But on looking closer Guph discovered that these rock heaps were dwellings, for each had an opening.

Not a person was to be seen outside the rock huts. All was silent.

The owl-man led the way among the groups of dwellings to one standing in the center. It seemed no better and no worse than any of the others. Outside the entrance to this rock heap the guide gave a low wail that sounded like "Lee-ow-ah!"

Suddenly there bounded from the opening another hairy man. This one wore the head of a bear. In his hand he bore a brass hoop. He glared at the stranger in evident surprise.

"Why have you captured this foolish wanderer and brought him here?" he demanded, addressing the owl-man.

"I did not capture him," was the answer. "He passed the scarlet alligator and came here of his own free will and accord."

The First and Foremost looked at the General.

"Have you tired of life, then?" he asked.

"No, indeed," answered Guph. "I am a Nome, and the Chief General of King Roquat the Red's great army of Nomes. I come of a long-lived race, and I may say that I expect to live a long time yet. Sit down, you Phanfasms—if you can find a seat in this wild haunt—and listen to what I have to say."

With all his knowledge and bravery General Guph did not know that the steady glare from the bear eyes was reading his inmost thoughts as surely as if they had been put into words. He did not know that these despised rock heaps of the Phanfasms were merely deceptions to his own eyes, nor could he guess that he was standing in the midst of one of the most splendid and luxurious cities ever built by magic power. All that he saw was a barren waste of rock heaps, a hairy man with an owl's head and another with a bear's head. The sorcery of the Phanfasms permitted him to see no more.

Suddenly the First and Foremost swung his brass hoop and caught Guph around the neck with it. The next instant, before the General could think what had happened to him, he was dragged inside the rock hut. Here, his eyes still blinded to realities, he perceived only a dim light, by which the hut seemed as rough and rude inside as it was outside. Yet he had a strange feeling that many bright eyes were fastened upon him and that he stood in a vast and extensive hall.

The First and Foremost now laughed grimly and released his prisoner.

"If you have anything to say that is interesting," he remarked, "speak out, before I strangle you."

So Guph spoke out. He tried not to pay any attention to a strange rustling sound that he heard, as of an unseen multitude drawing near to listen to his words. His eyes could see only the fierce bear-man, and to him he addressed his speech. First he told of his plan to conquer the Land of Oz and plunder the country of its riches and enslave its people, who, being fairies, could not be killed. After relating all this, and telling of the tunnel the Nome King was building, he said he had come to ask the First and Foremost to join the Nomes, with his band of terrible warriors, and help them to defeat the Oz people.

The General spoke very earnestly and impressively, but when he had finished the bear-man began to laugh as if much amused, and his laughter seemed to be echoed by a chorus of merriment from an unseen multitude. Then, for the first time, Guph began to feel a trifle worried.

"Who else has promised to help you?" finally asked the First and Foremost.

"The Whimsies," replied the General.

Again the bear-headed Phanfasm laughed.

"Any others?" he inquired.

"Only the Growleywogs," said Guph.

This answer set the First and Foremost laughing anew.

"What share of the spoils am I to have?" was the next question.

"Anything you like, except King Roquat's Magic Belt," replied Guph.

At this the Phanfasm set up a roar of laughter, which had its echo in the unseen chorus, and the bear-man seemed so amused that he actually rolled upon the ground and shouted with merriment.

"Oh, these blind and foolish Nomes!" he said. "How big they seem to themselves and how small they really are!"

Suddenly he arose and seized Guph's neck with one hairy paw, dragging him out of the hut into the open.

Here he gave a curious wailing cry, and, as if in answer, from all the rocky huts on the mountain-top came flocking a horde of Phanfasms, all with hairy bodies, but wearing heads of various animals, birds and reptiles. All were ferocious and repulsive-looking to the deceived eyes of the Nome, and Guph could not repress a shudder of disgust as he looked upon them.

The First and Foremost slowly raised his arms, and in a twinkling his hairy skin fell from him and he appeared before the astonished Nome as a beautiful woman, clothed in a flowing gown of pink gauze. In her dark hair flowers were entwined, and her face was noble and calm.

At the same instant the entire band of Phanfasms was transformed into a pack of howling wolves, running here and there as they snarled and showed their ugly yellow fangs.

The woman now raised her arms, even as the man-bear had done, and in a twinkling the wolves became crawling lizards, while she herself changed into a huge butterfly.

Guph had only time to cry out in fear and take a step backward to avoid the lizards when another transformation occurred, and all returned instantly to the forms they had originally worn.

Then the First and Foremost, who had resumed his hairy body and bear head, turned to the Nome and asked:

"Do you still demand our assistance?"

"More than ever," answered the General, firmly.

"Then tell me: what can you offer the Phanfasms that they have not already?" inquired the First and Foremost.

Guph hesitated. He really did not know what to say. The Nome King's vaunted Magic Belt seemed a poor thing compared to the astonishing magical powers of these people. Gold, jewels and slaves they might secure in any quantity without especial effort. He felt that he was dealing with powers greatly beyond him. There was but one argument that might influence the Phanfasms, who were creatures of evil.

"Permit me to call your attention to the exquisite joy of making the happy unhappy," said he at last. "Consider the pleasure of destroying innocent and harmless people."

"Ah! you have answered me," cried the First and Foremost. "For that reason alone we will aid you. Go home, and tell your bandy-legged king that as soon as his tunnel is finished the Phanfasms will be with him and lead his legions to the conquest of Oz. The deadly desert alone has kept us from destroying Oz long ago, and your underground tunnel is a clever thought. Go home, and prepare for our coming!"

Guph was very glad to be permitted to go with this promise. The owl-man led him back down the mountain path and ordered the scarlet alligator to crawl away and allow the Nome to cross the bridge in safety.

After the visitor had gone a brilliant and gorgeous city appeared upon the mountain top, clearly visible to the eyes of the gaily dressed multitude of Phanfasms that lived there. And the First and Foremost, beautifully arrayed, addressed the others in these words:

"It is time we went into the world and brought sorrow and dismay to its people. Too long have we remained by ourselves upon this mountain top, for while we are thus secluded many nations have grown happy and prosperous, and the chief joy of the race of Phanfasms is to destroy happiness. So I think it is lucky that this messenger from the Nomes arrived among us just now, to remind us that the opportunity has come for us to make trouble. We will use King Roquat's tunnel to conquer the Land of Oz. Then we will destroy the Whimsies, the Growleywogs and the Nomes, and afterward go out to ravage and annoy and grieve the whole world."

The multitude of evil Phanfasms eagerly applauded this plan, which they fully approved.

I am told that the Erbs are the most powerful and merciless of all the evil spirits, and the Phanfasms of Phantastico belong to the race of Erbs.

CHAPTER 12

How They Matched the Fuddles

Dorothy and her fellow travelers rode away from the Cuttenclip village and followed the indistinct path as far as the sign-post. Here they took the main road again and proceeded pleasantly through the pretty farming country. When evening came they stopped at a dwelling and were joyfully welcomed and given plenty to eat and good beds for the night.

Early next morning, however, they were up and eager to start, and after a good breakfast they bade their host good-bye and climbed into the red wagon, to which the Sawhorse had been hitched all night. Being made of wood, this horse never got tired nor cared to lie down. Dorothy was not quite sure whether he ever slept or not, but it was certain that he never did when anybody was around.

The weather is always beautiful in Oz, and this morning the air was cool and refreshing and the sunshine brilliant and delightful.

In about an hour they came to a place where another road branched off. There was a sign-post here which read:

THIS WAY TO FUDDLECUMJIG

"Oh, here is where we turn," said Dorothy, observing the sign.

"What! Are we going to Fuddlecumjig?" asked the Captain General.

"Yes; Ozma thought we would enjoy the Fuddles.[1] They are said to be very interesting," she replied.

"No one would suspect it from their name," said Aunt Em. "Who are they, anyhow? More paper things?"

"I think not," answered Dorothy, laughing; "but I can't say 'zactly, Aunt Em, what they are. We'll find out when we get there."

"Perhaps the Wizard knows," suggested Uncle Henry.

"No; I've never been there before," said the Wizard. "But I've often heard of Fuddlecumjig and the Fuddles, who are said to be the most peculiar people in all the Land of Oz."

"In what way?" asked the Shaggy Man.

"I don't know, I'm sure," said the Wizard.

Just then, as they rode along the pretty green lane toward Fuddle-cumjig, they espied a kangaroo sitting by the roadside. The poor animal had its face covered with both its front paws and was crying so bitterly that the tears coursed down its cheeks in two tiny streams and trickled across the road, where they formed a pool in a small hollow.

The Sawhorse stopped short at this pitiful sight, and Dorothy cried out, with ready sympathy:

"What's the matter, Kangaroo?"

"Boo-hoo! Boo-hoo!" wailed the kangaroo; "I've lost my mi—mi—mi—Oh, boo-hoo! Boo-hoo!"—

"Poor thing," said the Wizard, "she's lost her mister. It's probably her husband, and he's dead."

"No, no, no!" sobbed the kangaroo. "It—it isn't that. I've lost my mi—mi— Oh, boo, boo-hoo!"

"I know," said the Shaggy Man; "she's lost her mirror."

"No; it's my mi—mi—mi—Boo-hoo! My mi—Oh, Boo-hoo!" and the kangaroo cried harder than ever.

"It must be her mince-pie," suggested Aunt Em.

"Or her milk-toast," proposed Uncle Henry.

"I've lost my mi—mi—mittens!" said the kangaroo, getting it out at last.

"Oh!" cried the Yellow Hen, with a cackle of relief. "Why didn't you say so before?"

"Boo-hoo! I—I—couldn't," answered the kangaroo.

"But, see here," said Dorothy, "you don't need mittens in this warm weather."

"Yes, indeed I do," replied the animal, stopping her sobs and removing her paws from her face to look at the little girl reproachfully. "My hands will get all sunburned and tanned without my mittens, and I've worn them so long that I'll probably catch cold without them."

"Nonsense!" said Dorothy. "I never heard before of any kangaroo wearing mittens."

"Didn't you?" asked the animal, as if surprised.

"Never!" repeated the girl. "And you'll probably make yourself sick if you don't stop crying. Where do you live?"

"About two miles beyond Fuddlecumjig," was the answer. "Grandmother Gnit[2] made me the mittens, and she's one of the Fuddles."

"Well, you'd better go home now, and perhaps the old lady will make you another pair," suggested Dorothy. "We're on our way to Fuddlecumjig, and you may hop along beside us."

So they rode on, and the kangaroo hopped beside the red wagon and seemed quickly to have forgotten her loss. By and by the Wizard said to the animal:

"Are the Fuddles nice people?"

"Oh, very nice," answered the kangaroo; "that is, when they're properly put together. But they get dreadfully scattered and mixed up, at times, and then you can't do anything with them."

"What do you mean by their getting scattered?" inquired Dorothy.

"Why, they're made in a good many small pieces," explained the kangaroo; "and whenever any stranger comes near them they have a habit of falling apart and scattering themselves around. That's when they get so dreadfully mixed, and it's a hard puzzle to put them together again."

"Who usually puts them together?" asked Omby Amby.

"Any one who is able to match the pieces. I sometimes put Grandmother Gnit together myself, because I know her so well I can tell every piece that belongs to her. Then, when she's all matched, she knits for me, and that's how she made my mittens. But it took a good many days hard knitting, and I had to put Grandmother together a good many times, because every time I came near she'd scatter herself."

"I should think she would get used to your coming, and not be afraid," said Dorothy.

"It isn't that," replied the kangaroo. "They're not a bit afraid, when they're put together, and usually they're very jolly and pleasant. It's just a habit they have, to scatter themselves, and if they didn't do it they wouldn't be Fuddles."

The travelers thought upon this quite seriously for a time, while the Sawhorse continued to carry them rapidly forward. Then Aunt Em remarked:

"I don't see much use our visitin' these Fuddles. If we find them scattered, all we can do is to sweep 'em up, and then go about our business."

"Oh, I b'lieve we'd better go on," replied Dorothy. "I'm getting hungry, and we must try to get some luncheon at Fuddlecumjig. Perhaps the food won't be scattered as badly as the people."

"You'll find plenty to eat there," declared the kangaroo, hopping along in big bounds because the Sawhorse was going so fast; "and they have a fine cook, too, if you can manage to put him together. There's the town now—just ahead of us!"

They looked ahead and saw a group of very pretty houses standing in a green field a little apart from the main road.

"Some Munchkins came here a few days ago and matched a lot of people together," said the kangaroo. "I think they are together yet, and if you go softly, without making any noise, perhaps they won't scatter."

"Let's try it," suggested the Wizard.

So they stopped the Sawhorse and got out of the wagon, and, after bidding good bye to the kangaroo, who hopped away home, they entered the field and very cautiously approached the group of houses.

So silently did they move that soon they saw through the windows of the houses, people moving around, while others were passing to and fro in the yards between the buildings. They seemed much like other people, from a distance, and apparently they did not notice the little party so quietly approaching.

They had almost reached the nearest house when Toto saw a large beetle crossing the path and barked loudly at it. Instantly a wild clatter was heard from the houses and yards. Dorothy thought it sounded like a sudden hailstorm, and the visitors, knowing that caution was no longer necessary, hurried forward to see what had happened.

After the clatter an intense stillness reigned in the town. The strangers entered the first house they came to, which was also the largest, and found the floor strewn with pieces of the people who lived there. They looked much like fragments of wood neatly painted, and were of all sorts of curious and fantastic shapes, no two pieces being in any way alike.

They picked up some of these pieces and looked at them carefully. On one which Dorothy held was an eye, which looked at her pleasantly but with an interested expression, as if it wondered what she was going to do with it. Quite near by she discovered and picked up a nose, and by matching the two pieces together found that they were part of a face.

"If I could find the mouth," she said, "this Fuddle might be able to talk, and tell us what to do next."

"Then let us find it," replied the Wizard, and so all got down on their hands and knees and began examining the scattered pieces.

"I've found it!" cried the Shaggy Man, and ran to Dorothy with a queer-shaped piece that had a mouth on it. But when they tried to fit it to the eye and nose they found the parts wouldn't match together.

"That mouth belongs to some other person," said Dorothy. "You see we need a curve here and a point there, to make it fit the face."

"Well, it must be here some place," declared the Wizard; "so if we search long enough we shall find it."

Dorothy fitted an ear on next, and the ear had a little patch of red hair above it. So while the others were searching for the mouth she hunted for pieces with red hair, and found several of them which, when matched to the other pieces, formed the top of a man's head. She had also found the other eye and the ear by the time Omby Amby in a far corner discovered the mouth. When the face was thus completed all parts joined together with a nicety that was astonishing.

"Why, it's like a picture puzzle!" exclaimed the little girl. "Let's find the rest of him, and get him all together."

"What's the rest of him like?" asked the Wizard. "Here are some pieces of blue legs and green arms, but I don't know whether they are his or not."

"Look for a white shirt and a white apron," said the head which had been put together, speaking in a rather faint voice. "I'm the cook."

"Oh, thank you," said Dorothy. "It's lucky we started you first, for I'm hungry, and you can be cooking something for us to eat while we match the other folks together."

It was not so very difficult, now that they had a hint as to how the man was dressed, to find the other pieces belonging to him, and as all of them now worked on the cook, trying piece after piece to see if it would fit, they finally had the cook set up complete.

When he was finished he made them a low bow and said:

"I will go at once to the kitchen and prepare your dinner. You will find it something of a job to get all the Fuddles together, so I advise you to begin on the Lord High Chigglewitz, whose first name is Larry. He's a bald-headed fat man and is dressed in a blue coat with brass buttons, a pink vest and drab breeches. A piece of his left knee is missing, having been lost years ago when he scattered himself too carelessly. That makes him limp a little, but he gets along very well with half a knee. As he is the chief personage in this town of Fuddlecumjig, he will be able to welcome you and assist you with the others. So it will be best to work on him while I'm getting your dinner."

"We will," said the Wizard; "and thank you very much, cook, for the suggestion."

Aunt Em was the first to discover a piece of the Lord High Chigglewitz.

"It seems to me like a fool business, this matching folks together," she remarked; "but as we haven't anything to do till dinner's ready we may as well get rid of some of this rubbish. Here, Henry, get busy and look for Larry's bald head. I've got his pink vest, all right."

They worked with eager interest, and Billina proved a great help to them. The Yellow Hen had sharp eyes and could put her head close to the various pieces that lay scattered around. She would examine the Lord High Chigglewitz and see which piece of him was next needed, and then hunt around until she found it. So before an hour had passed old Larry was standing complete before them.

"I congratulate you, my friends," he said, speaking in a cheerful voice. "You are certainly the cleverest people who ever visited us. I was never matched together so quickly in my life. I'm considered a great puzzle, usually."

"Well," said Dorothy, "there used to be a picture puzzle craze in Kansas, and so I've had some 'sperience matching puzzles. But the pictures were flat, while you are round, and that makes you harder to figure out."

"Thank you, my dear," replied old Larry, greatly pleased. "I feel highly complimented. Were I not a really good puzzle there would be no object in my scattering myself."

"Why do you do it?" asked Aunt Em, severely. "Why don't you behave yourself, and stay put together?"

The Lord High Chigglewitz seemed annoyed by this speech; but he replied, politely:

"Madam, you have perhaps noticed that every person has some peculiarity. Mine is to scatter myself. What your own peculiarity is I will not venture to say; but I shall never find fault with you, whatever you do."

"Now, you've got your diploma, Em," said Uncle Henry, with a laugh, "and I'm glad of it. This is a queer country, and we may as well take people as we find them."

"If we did, we'd leave these folks scattered," she returned, and this retort made everybody laugh good-naturedly.

Just then Omby Amby found a hand with a knitting needle in it, and they decided to put Grandmother Gnit together. She proved an easier puzzle than old Larry, and when she was completed they found her a pleasant old lady who welcomed them cordially. Dorothy told her how the kangaroo had lost her mittens, and Grandmother Gnit promised to set to work at once and make the poor animal another pair.

Then the cook came to call them to dinner, and they found an inviting meal prepared for them. The Lord High Chigglewitz sat at the head of the table and Grandmother Gnit at the foot, and the guests had a merry time and thoroughly enjoyed themselves.

After dinner they went out into the yard and matched several other people together, and this work was so interesting that they might have spent the entire day at Fuddlecumjig had not the Wizard suggested that they resume their journey.

"But I don't like to leave all these poor people scattered," said Dorothy, undecided what to do.

"Oh, don't mind us, my dear," returned old Larry. "Every day or so some of the Gillikins, or Munchkins, or Winkies come here to amuse themselves by matching us together, so there will be no harm in leaving these pieces where they are for a time. But I hope you will visit us again, and if you do you will always be welcome, I assure you."

"Don't you ever match each other?" she inquired.

"Never; for we are no puzzles to ourselves, and so there wouldn't be any fun in it."

They now said goodbye to the queer Fuddles and got into their wagon to continue their journey.

"Those are certainly strange people," remarked Aunt Em, thoughtfully, as they drove away from Fuddlecumjig, "but I really can't see what use they are, at all."

"Why, they amused us all for several hours," replied the Wizard. "That is being of use to us, I'm sure."

"I think they're more fun than playing solitaire or mumbletypeg," declared Uncle Henry, soberly. "For my part, I'm glad we visited the Fuddles."

CHAPTER 13

How the General Talked to the King

When General Guph returned to the cavern of the Nome King his Majesty asked:

"Well, what luck? Will the Whimsies join us?"

"They will," answered the General. "They will fight for us with all their strength and cunning."

"Good!" exclaimed the King. "What reward did you promise them?"

"Your Majesty is to use the Magic Belt to give each Whimsie a large, fine head, in place of the small one he is now obliged to wear."

"I agree to that," said the King. "This is good news, Guph, and it makes me feel more certain of the conquest of Oz."

"But I have other news for you," announced the General.

"Good or bad?"

"Good, your Majesty."

"Then I will hear it," said the King, with interest.

"The Growleywogs will join us."

"No!" cried the astonished King.

"Yes, indeed," said the General. "I have their promise."

"But what reward do they demand?" inquired the King, suspiciously, for he knew how greedy the Growleywogs were.

"They are to take a few of the Oz people for their slaves," replied Guph. He did not think it necessary to tell Roquat that the Growleywogs demanded twenty thousand slaves. It would be time enough for that when Oz was conquered.

"A very reasonable request, I'm sure," remarked the King. "I must congratulate you, Guph, upon the wonderful success of your journey."

"But that is not all," said the General, proudly.

The King seemed astonished.

"Speak out, sir!" he commanded.

"I have seen the First and Foremost Phanfasm of the Mountain of Phantastico, and he will bring his people to assist us."

"What!" cried the King. "The Phanfasms! You don't mean it, Guph!"

"It is true," declared the General, proudly.

The King became thoughtful, and his brows wrinkled.

"I'm afraid, Guph," he said rather anxiously, "that the First and Foremost may prove as dangerous to us as to the Oz people. If he and his terrible band come down from the mountain they may take the notion to conquer the Nomes!"

"Pah! That is a foolish idea," retorted Guph, irritably, but he knew in his heart that the King was right. "The First and Foremost is a particular friend of mine, and will do us no harm. Why, when I was there, he even invited me into his house."

The General neglected to tell the King how he had been jerked into the hut of the First and Foremost by means of the brass hoop. So Roquat the Red looked at his General admiringly and said:

"You are a wonderful Nome, Guph. I'm sorry I did not make you my General before. But what reward did the First and Foremost demand?"

"Nothing at all," answered Guph. "Even the Magic Belt itself could not add to his powers of sorcery. All the Phanfasms wish is to destroy the Oz people, who are good and happy. This pleasure will amply repay them for assisting us."

"When will they come?" asked Roquat, half fearfully.

"When the tunnel is completed," said the General.

"We are nearly half way under the desert now," announced the King; "and that is fast work, because the tunnel has to be drilled through solid rock. But after we have passed the desert it will not take us long to extend the tunnel to the walls of the Emerald City."

"Well, whenever you are ready, we shall be joined by the Whimsies, the Growleywogs and the Phanfasms," said Guph; "so the conquest of Oz is assured without a doubt."

Again the King seemed thoughtful.

"I'm almost sorry we did not undertake the conquest alone," said he. "All of these allies are dangerous people, and they may demand more than you have promised them. It might have been better to have conquered Oz without any outside assistance."

"We could not do it," said the General, positively.

"Why not, Guph?"

"You know very well. You have had one experience with the Oz people, and they defeated you."

"That was because they rolled eggs at us," replied the King, with a shudder. "My Nomes cannot stand eggs, any more than I can myself. They are poison to all who live underground."

"That is true enough," agreed Guph.

"But we might have taken the Oz people by surprise, and conquered them before they had a chance to get any eggs. Our former defeat was due to the fact that the girl Dorothy had a Yellow Hen with her. I do not know what ever became of that hen, but I believe there are no hens at all in the Land of Oz, and so there could be no eggs there."

"On the contrary," said Guph, "there are now hundreds of chickens in Oz, and they lay heaps of those dangerous eggs. I met a goshawk on my way home, and the bird informed me that he had lately been to Oz to capture and devour some of the young chickens. But they are protected by magic, so the hawk did not get a single one of them."

"That is a very bad report," said the King, nervously. "Very bad, indeed. My Nomes are willing to fight, but they simply can't face hen's eggs—and I don't blame them."

"They won't need to face them," replied Guph. "I'm afraid of eggs myself, and don't propose to take any chances of being poisoned by them. My plan is to send the Whimsies through the tunnel first, and then the Growleywogs and the Phanfasms. By the time we Nomes get there the eggs will all be used up, and we may then pursue and capture the inhabitants at our leisure."

"Perhaps you are right," returned the King, with a dismal sigh. "But I want it distinctly understood that I claim Ozma and Dorothy as my own prisoners. They are rather nice girls, and I do not intend to let any of those dreadful creatures hurt them, or make them their slaves. When I have captured them I will bring them here and transform them into china ornaments[1] to stand on my mantle. They will look very pretty—Dorothy on one end of the mantle and Ozma on the other—and I shall take great care to see they are not broken when the maids dust them."

"Very well, your Majesty. Do what you will with the girls, for all I care. Now that our plans are arranged, and we have the three most powerful bands of evil spirits in the world to assist us, let us make haste to get the tunnel finished as soon as possible."

"It will be ready in three days," promised the King, and hurried away to inspect the work and see that the Nomes kept busy.

CHAPTER 14

How the Wizard Practiced Sorcery

"Where next?" asked the Wizard, when they had left the town of Fuddlecumjig and the Sawhorse had started back along the road.

"Why, Ozma laid out this trip," replied Dorothy, "and she 'vised us to see the Rigmaroles[1] next, and then visit the Tin Woodman."

"That sounds good," said the Wizard. "But what road do we take to get to the Rigmaroles?"

"I don't know, 'zactly," returned the little girl; "but it must be somewhere just southwest from here."

"Then why need we go back to the crossroads?" asked the Shaggy Man. "We might save a lot of time by branching off here."

"There isn't any path," asserted Uncle Henry.

"Then we'd better go back to the signposts, and make sure of our way," decided Dorothy.

But after they had gone a short distance farther the Sawhorse, who had overheard their conversation, stopped and said:

"Here is a path."

Sure enough, a dim path seemed to branch off from the road they were on, and it led across pretty green meadows and past leafy groves, straight toward the southwest.

"That looks like a good path," said Omby Amby. "Why not try it?"

"All right," answered Dorothy. "I'm anxious to see what the Rigmaroles are like, and this path ought to take us there the quickest way."

No one made any objection to the plan, so the Sawhorse turned into the path, which proved to be nearly as good as the one they had taken to get to the Fuddles.

At first they passed a few retired farmhouses, but soon these scattered dwellings were left behind and only the meadows and the trees were before them. But they rode along in cheerful contentment, and Aunt Em got into an argument with Billina about the proper way to raise chickens.

"I do not care to contradict you," said the Yellow Hen, with dignity, "but I have an idea I know more about chickens than human beings do."

"Pshaw!" replied Aunt Em, "I've raised chickens for nearly forty years, Billina, and I know you've got to starve 'em to make 'em lay lots of eggs, and stuff 'em if you want good broilers."

"Broilers!" exclaimed Billina, in horror. "Broil my chickens!"

"Why, that's what they're for, ain't it?" asked Aunt Em, astonished.

"No, Aunt, not in Oz," said Dorothy. "People do not eat chickens here. You see, Billina was the first hen that was ever seen in this country, and I brought her here myself. Everybody liked her an' respected her, so the Oz people wouldn't any more eat her chickens than they would eat Billina."

"Well, I declare," gasped Aunt Em. "How about the eggs?"

"Oh, if we have more eggs than we want to hatch, we allow people to eat them," said Billina. "Indeed, I am very glad the Oz folks like our eggs, for otherwise they would spoil."

"This certainly is a queer country," sighed Aunt Em.

"Excuse me," called the Sawhorse, "the path has ended and I'd like to know which way to go."

They looked around and, sure enough, there was no path to be seen.

"Well," said Dorothy, "we're going southwest, and it seems just as easy to follow that direction without a path as with one."

"Certainly," answered the Sawhorse. "It is not hard to draw the wagon over the meadow. I only want to know where to go."

"There's a forest over there across the prairie," said the Wizard, "and it lies in the direction we are going. Make straight for the forest, Sawhorse, and you're bound to go right."

So the wooden animal trotted on again and the meadow grass was so soft under the wheels that it made easy riding. But Dorothy was a little uneasy at losing the path, because now there was nothing to guide them.

No houses were to be seen at all, so they could not ask their way of any farmer; and although the Land of Oz was always beautiful, wherever one might go, this part of the country was strange to all the party.

"Perhaps we're lost," suggested Aunt Em, after they had proceeded quite a way in silence.

"Never mind," said the Shaggy Man; "I've been lost many a time—and so has Dorothy—and we've always been found again."

"But we may get hungry," remarked Omby Amby. "That is the worst of getting lost in a place where there are no houses near."

"We had a good dinner at the Fuddle town," said Uncle Henry, "and that will keep us from starving to death for a long time."

"No one ever starved to death in Oz," declared Dorothy, positively; "but people may get pretty hungry sometimes."

The Wizard said nothing, and he did not seem especially anxious. The Sawhorse was trotting along briskly, yet the forest seemed farther away than they had thought when they first saw it. So it was nearly sundown when they finally came to the trees; but now they found themselves in a most beautiful spot, the wide-spreading trees being covered with flowering vines and having soft mosses underneath them.

"This will be a good place to camp," said the Wizard, as the Sawhorse stopped for further instructions.

"Camp!" they all echoed.

"Certainly," asserted the Wizard. "It will be dark before very long and we cannot travel through this forest at night. So let us make a camp here, and have some supper, and sleep until daylight comes again."

They all looked at the little man in astonishment, and Aunt Em said, with a sniff:

"A pretty camp we'll have, I must say! I suppose you intend us to sleep under the wagon."

"And chew grass for our supper," added the Shaggy Man, laughing.

But Dorothy seemed to have no doubts and was quite cheerful.

"It's lucky we have the wonderful Wizard with us," she said; "because he can do 'most anything he wants to."

"Oh, yes; I forgot we had a Wizard," said Uncle Henry, looking at the little man curiously.

"I didn't," chirped Billina, contentedly.

The Wizard smiled and climbed out of the wagon, and all the others followed him.

"In order to camp," said he, "the first thing we need is tents. Will some one please lend me a handkerchief?"

The Shaggy Man offered him one, and Aunt Em another. He took them both and laid them carefully upon the grass near to the edge of the forest. Then he laid his own handkerchief down, too, and standing a little back from them he waved his left hand toward the handkerchiefs and said:

> "Tents of canvas, white as snow,
> Let me see how fast you grow!"

Then, lo and behold! the handkerchiefs became tiny tents, and as the travelers looked at them the tents grew bigger and bigger until in a few minutes each one was large enough to contain the entire party.

"This," said the Wizard, pointing to the first tent, "is for the accommodation of the ladies. Dorothy, you and your Aunt may step inside and take off your things."

Every one ran to look inside the tent, and they saw two pretty white beds, all ready for Dorothy and Aunt Em, and a silver roost for Billina. Rugs were spread upon the grassy floor and some camp chairs and a table completed the furniture.

"Well, well, well! This beats anything I ever saw or heard of!" exclaimed Aunt Em, and she glanced at the Wizard almost fearfully, as if he might be dangerous because of his great powers.

"Oh, Mr. Wizard! How did you manage to do it?" asked Dorothy.

"It's a trick Glinda the Sorceress taught me, and it is much better magic than I used to practise in Omaha, or when I first came to Oz," he answered. "When the Good Glinda found I was to live in the Emerald City always, she promised to help me, because she said the Wizard of Oz ought really to be a clever Wizard, and not a humbug. So we have been much together and I am learning so fast that I expect to be able to accomplish some really wonderful things in time."

"You've done it now!" declared Dorothy. "These tents are just wonderful!"

"But come and see the men's tent," said the Wizard. So they went to the second tent, which had shaggy edges because it had been made from the Shaggy Man's handkerchief, and found that completely furnished also. It contained four neat beds for Uncle Henry, Omby Amby, the Shaggy Man and the Wizard. Also there was a soft rug for Toto to lie upon.

"The third tent," explained the Wizard, "is our dining room and kitchen."

They visited that next, and found a table and dishes in the dining tent, with plenty of those things necessary to use in cooking. The Wizard carried out a big kettle and set it swinging on a crossbar before the tent. While he was doing this Omby Amby and the Shaggy Man brought a supply of twigs from the forest and then they built a fire underneath the kettle.

"Now, Dorothy," said the Wizard, smiling, "I expect you to cook our supper."

"But there is nothing in the kettle," she cried.

"Are you sure?" inquired the Wizard.

"I didn't see anything put in, and I'm almost sure it was empty when you brought it out," she replied.

"Nevertheless," said the little man, winking slyly at Uncle Henry, "you will do well to watch our supper, my dear, and see that it doesn't boil over."

Then the men took some pails and went into the forest to search for a spring of water, and while they were gone Aunt Em said to Dorothy:

"I believe the Wizard is fooling us. I saw the kettle myself, and when he hung it over the fire there wasn't a thing in it but air."

"Don't worry," remarked Billina, confidently, as she nestled in the grass before the fire. "You'll find something in the kettle when it's taken off—and it won't be poor, innocent chickens, either."

"Your hen has very bad manners, Dorothy," said Aunt Em, looking somewhat disdainfully at Billina. "It seems too bad she ever learned how to talk."

There might have been another unpleasant quarrel between Aunt Em and Billina had not the men returned just then with their pails filled with clear, sparkling water. The Wizard told Dorothy that she was a good cook and he believed their supper was ready.

So Uncle Henry lifted the kettle from the fire and poured its contents into a big platter which the Wizard held for him. The platter was fairly heaped with a fine stew, smoking hot, with many kinds of vegetables and dumplings and a rich, delicious gravy.

The Wizard triumphantly placed the platter upon the table in the dining tent and then they all sat down in camp chairs to the feast.

There were several other dishes on the table, all carefully covered, and when the time came to remove these covers they found bread and butter, cakes, cheese, pickles and fruits—including some of the luscious strawberries of Oz.

No one ventured to ask a question as to how these things came there. They contented themselves by eating heartily the good things provided, and Toto and Billina had their full share, you may be sure. After the meal was over Aunt Em whispered to Dorothy:

"That may have been magic food, my dear, and for that reason perhaps it won't be very nourishing; but I'm willing to say it tasted as good as anything I ever et." Then she added, in a louder tone: "Who's going to do the dishes?"

"No one, madam," answered the Wizard. "The dishes have 'done' themselves."

"La sakes!" ejaculated the good lady, holding up her hands in amazement. For, sure enough, when she looked at the dishes they had a moment before left upon the table, she found them all washed and dried and piled up into neat stacks.

CHAPTER 15

How Dorothy Happened to Get Lost

It was a beautiful evening, so they drew their camp chairs in a circle before one of the tents and began to tell stories to amuse themselves and pass away the time before they went to bed.

Pretty soon a zebra was seen coming out of the forest, and he trotted straight up to them and said politely:

"Good evening, people."

The zebra was a sleek little animal and had a slender head, a stubby mane and a paint-brush tail—very like a donkey's. His neatly shaped white body was covered with regular bars of dark brown, and his hoofs were delicate as those of a deer.

"Good evening, friend Zebra," said Omby Amby, in reply to the creature's greeting. "Can we do anything for you?"

"Yes," answered the zebra. "I should like you to settle a dispute that has long been a bother to me, as to whether there is more water or land in the world."

"Who are you disputing with?" asked the Wizard.

"With a soft-shell crab," said the zebra. "He lives in a pool where I go to drink every day, and he is a very impertinent crab, I assure you. I have told him many times that the land is much greater in extent than the water, but he will not be convinced. Even this very evening, when I told him he was an insignificant creature who lived in a small pool, he asserted that the water was greater and more important than the land. So, seeing your camp, I decided to ask you to settle the dispute for once and all, that I may not be further annoyed by this ignorant crab."

When they had listened to this explanation Dorothy inquired:

"Where is the soft-shell crab?"

"Not far away," replied the zebra. "If you will agree to judge between us I will run and get him."

"Run along, then," said the little girl.

So the animal pranced into the forest and soon came trotting back to them. When he drew near they found a soft-shell crab clinging fast to the stiff hair of the zebra's head, where it held on by one claw.

"Now then, Mr. Crab," said the zebra, "here are the people I told you about; and they know more than you do, who live in a pool, and more than I do, who live in a forest. For they have been travelers all over the world, and know every part of it."

"There's more of the world than Oz," declared the crab, in a stubborn voice.

"That is true," said Dorothy; "but I used to live in Kansas, in the United States, and I've been to California and to Australia—and so has Uncle Henry."

"For my part," added the Shaggy Man, "I've been to Mexico and Boston and many other foreign countries."

"And I," said the Wizard, "have been to Europe and Ireland."

"So you see," continued the zebra, addressing the crab, "here are people of real consequence, who know what they are talking about."

"Then they know there's more water in the world than there is land," asserted the crab, in a shrill, petulant voice.

"They know you are wrong to make such an absurd statement, and they will probably think you are a lobster instead of a crab," retorted the animal.

At this taunt the crab reached out its other claw and seized the zebra's ear, and the creature gave a cry of pain and began prancing up and down, trying to shake off the crab, which clung fast.

"Stop pinching!" cried the zebra. "You promised not to pinch if I would carry you here!"

"And you promised to treat me respectfully," said the crab, letting go the ear.

"Well, haven't I?" demanded the zebra.

"No; you called me a lobster," said the crab.

"Ladies and gentlemen," continued the zebra, "please pardon my poor friend, because he is ignorant and stupid, and does not understand. Also the pinch of his claw is very annoying. So pray tell him that the world contains more land than water, and when he has heard your judgment I will carry him back and dump him into his pool, where I hope he will be more modest in the future."

"But we cannot tell him that," said Dorothy, gravely, "because it would not be true."

"What!" exclaimed the zebra, in astonishment; "do I hear you aright?"

"The soft-shell crab is correct," declared the Wizard. "There is considerably more water than there is land in the world."

"Impossible!" protested the zebra. "Why, I can run for days upon the land, and find but little water."

"Did you ever see an ocean?" asked Dorothy.

"Never," admitted the zebra. "There is no such thing as an ocean in the Land of Oz."

"Well, there are several oceans in the world," said Dorothy, "and people sail in ships upon these oceans for weeks and weeks, and never see a bit of land at all. And the joggerfys will tell you that all the oceans put together are bigger than all the land put together."

At this the crab began laughing in queer chuckles that reminded Dorothy of the way Billina sometimes cackled.

"*Now* will you give up, Mr. Zebra?" it cried, jeeringly; "now will you give up?"

The zebra seemed much humbled.

"Of course I cannot read geographys," he said.

"You could take one of the Wizard's School Pills," suggested Billina, "and that would make you learned and wise without studying."

The crab began laughing again, which so provoked the zebra that he tried to shake the little creature off. This resulted in more ear-pinching, and finally Dorothy told them that if they could not behave they must go back to the forest.

"I'm sorry I asked you to decide this question," said the zebra, crossly. "So long as neither of us could prove we were right we quite enjoyed the dispute; but now I can never drink at that pool again without the soft-shell crab laughing at me. So I must find another drinking place."

"Do! Do, you ignoramus!" shouted the crab, as loudly as his little voice would carry. "Rile some other pool with your clumsy hoofs, and let your betters alone after this!"

Then the zebra trotted back to the forest, bearing the crab with him, and disappeared amid the gloom of the trees. And as it was now getting dark the travelers said good night to one another and went to bed.

Dorothy awoke just as the light was beginning to get strong next morning, and not caring to sleep any later she quietly got out of bed, dressed herself, and left the tent where Aunt Em was yet peacefully slumbering.

Outside she noticed Billina busily pecking around to secure bugs or other food for breakfast, but none of the men in the other tent seemed awake. So the little girl decided to take a walk in the woods and try to discover some path or road that they might follow when they again started upon their journey.

She had reached the edge of the forest when the Yellow Hen came fluttering along and asked where she was going.

"Just to take a walk, Billina; and maybe I'll find some path," said Dorothy.

"Then I'll go along," decided Billina, and scarcely had she spoken when Toto ran up and joined them.

Toto and the Yellow Hen had become quite friendly by this time, although at first they did not get along well together. Billina had been rather suspicious of dogs, and Toto had had an idea that it was every dog's duty to chase a hen on sight. But Dorothy had talked to them and scolded them for not being agreeable to one another until they grew better acquainted and became friends.

I won't say they loved each other dearly, but at least they had stopped quarreling and now managed to get on together very well.

The day was growing lighter every minute and driving the black shadows out of the forest; so Dorothy found it very pleasant walking under the trees. She went some distance in one direction, but not finding a path, presently turned in a different direction. There was no path here, either, although she advanced quite a way into the forest, winding here and there among the trees and peering through the bushes in an endeavor to find some beaten track.

"I think we'd better go back," suggested the Yellow Hen, after a time. "The people will all be up by this time and breakfast will be ready."

"Very well," agreed Dorothy. "Let's see—the camp must be over this way."

She had probably made a mistake about that, for after they had gone far enough to have reached the camp they still found themselves in the thick of the woods. So the little girl stopped short and looked around her, and Toto glanced up into her face with his bright little eyes and wagged his tail as if he knew something was wrong. He couldn't tell much about direction himself, because he had spent his time prowling among the bushes and running here and there; nor had Billina paid much attention to where they were going, being interested in picking bugs from the moss as they passed along. The Yellow Hen now turned one eye up toward the little girl and asked:

"Have you forgotten where the camp is, Dorothy?"

"Yes," she admitted; "have you, Billina?"

"I didn't try to remember," returned Billina. "I'd no idea you would get lost, Dorothy."

"It's the thing we don't expect, Billina, that usually happens," observed the girl, thoughtfully. "But it's no use standing here. Let's go in that direction," pointing a finger at random. "It may be we'll get out of the forest over there."

So on they went again, but this way the trees were closer together, and the vines were so tangled that often they tripped Dorothy up.

Suddenly a voice cried sharply:

"Halt!"

At first Dorothy could see nothing, although she looked around very carefully. But Billina exclaimed:

"Well, I declare!"

"What is it?" asked the little girl: for Toto began barking at something, and following his gaze she discovered what it was.

A row of spoons had surrounded the three, and these spoons stood straight up on their handles and carried swords and muskets. Their faces were outlined in the polished bowls and they looked very stern and severe.

Dorothy laughed at the queer things.

"Who are you?" she asked.

"We're the Spoon Brigade," said one.

"In the service of his Majesty King Kleaver," said another.

"And you are our prisoners," said a third.

Dorothy sat down on an old stump and looked at them, her eyes twinkling with amusement.

"What would happen," she inquired, "if I should set my dog on your Brigade?"

"He would die," replied one of the spoons, sharply. "One shot from our deadly muskets would kill him, big as he is."

"Don't risk it, Dorothy," advised the Yellow Hen. "Remember this is a fairy country, yet none of us three happens to be a fairy."

Dorothy grew sober at this.

"P'raps you're right, Billina," she answered. "But how funny it is, to be captured by a lot of spoons!"

"I do not see anything very funny about it," declared a spoon. "We're the regular military brigade of the kingdom."

"What kingdom?" she asked.

"Utensia,"[1] said he.

"I never heard of it before," asserted Dorothy. Then she added, thoughtfully, "I don't believe Ozma ever heard of Utensia, either. Tell me, are you not subjects of Ozma of Oz?"

"We never have heard of her," retorted a spoon. "We are subjects of King Kleaver, and obey only his orders, which are to bring all prisoners to him as soon as they are captured. So step lively, my girl, and march with us, or we may be tempted to cut off a few of your toes with our swords."

This threat made Dorothy laugh again. She did not believe she was in any danger; but here was a new and interesting adventure, so she was willing to be taken to Utensia that she might see what King Kleaver's kingdom was like.

CHAPTER 16

How Dorothy Visited Utensia

There must have been from six to eight dozen spoons in the Brigade, and they marched away in the shape of a hollow square, with Dorothy, Billina and Toto in the center of the square. Before they had gone very far Toto knocked over one of the spoons by wagging his tail, and then the Captain of the Spoons told the little dog to be more careful, or he would be punished. So Toto was careful, and the Spoon Brigade moved along with astonishing swiftness, while Dorothy really had to walk fast to keep up with it.

By and by they left the woods and entered a big clearing, in which was the Kingdom of Utensia.

Standing all around the clearing were a good many cookstoves, ranges and grills, of all sizes and shapes, and besides these there were several kitchen cabinets and cupboards and a few kitchen tables. These things were crowded with utensils of all sorts: frying pans, sauce pans, kettles, forks, knives, basting and soup spoons, nutmeg graters, sifters, colenders, meat saws, flat irons, rolling pins and many other things of a like nature.

When the Spoon Brigade appeared with the prisoners a wild

shout arose and many of the utensils hopped off their stoves or their benches and ran crowding around Dorothy and the hen and the dog.

"Stand back!" cried the Captain, sternly, and he led his captives through the curious throng until they came before a big range that stood in the center of the clearing. Beside this range was a butcher's block upon which lay a great cleaver with a keen edge. It rested upon the flat of its back, its legs were crossed and it was smoking a long pipe.

"Wake up, your Majesty," said the Captain. "Here are prisoners."

Hearing this, King Kleaver sat up and looked at Dorothy sharply.

"Gristle and fat!" he cried. "Where did this girl come from?"

"I found her in the forest and brought her here a prisoner," replied the Captain.

"Why did you do that?" inquired the King, puffing his pipe lazily.

"To create some excitement," the Captain answered. "It is so quiet here that we are all getting rusty for want of amusement. For my part, I prefer to see stirring times."

"Naturally," returned the cleaver, with a nod. "I have always said, Captain, without a bit of irony, that you are a sterling officer and a solid citizen, bowled and polished to a degree. But what do you expect me to do with these prisoners?"

"That is for you to decide," declared the Captain. "You are the King."

"To be sure; to be sure," muttered the cleaver, musingly. "As you say, we have had dull times since the steel and grindstone eloped and left us. Command my Counselors and the Royal Courtiers to attend me, as well as the High Priest and the Judge. We'll then decide what can be done."

The Captain saluted and retired and Dorothy sat down on an overturned kettle and asked:

"Have you anything to eat in your kingdom?"

"Here! Get up! Get off from me!" cried a faint voice, at which his Majesty the cleaver said:

"Excuse me, but you're sitting on my friend the Ten-quart Kettle."

Dorothy at once arose, and the kettle turned right side up and looked at her reproachfully.

"I'm a friend of the King, so no one dares sit on me," said he.

"I'd prefer a chair, anyway," she replied.

"Sit on that hearth," commanded the King.

So Dorothy sat on the hearth-shelf of the big range, and the subjects of Utensia began to gather around in a large and inquisitive throng. Toto lay at Dorothy's feet and Billina flew upon the range, which had no fire in it, and perched there as comfortably as she could.

When all the Counselors and Courtiers had assembled—and these seemed to include most of the inhabitants of the kingdom—the King rapped on the block for order and said:

"Friends and Fellow Utensils! Our worthy Commander of the Spoon Brigade, Captain Dipp, has captured the three prisoners you see before you and brought them here for—for—I don't know what for. So I ask your advice how to act in this matter, and what fate I should mete out to these captives. Judge Sifter, stand on my right. It is your business to sift this affair to the bottom. High Priest Colender, stand on my left and see that no one testifies falsely in this matter."

As these two officials took their places Dorothy asked:

"Why is the colender the High Priest?"

"He's the holiest thing we have in the kingdom," replied King Kleaver.

"Except me," said a sieve. "I'm the whole thing when it comes to holes."

"What we need," remarked the King, rebukingly, "is a wireless sieve. I must speak to Marconi about it. These old fashioned sieves talk too much. Now, it is the duty of the King's Counselors to counsel the King at all times of emergency, so I beg you to speak out and advise me what to do with these prisoners."

"I demand that they be killed several times, until they are dead!" shouted a pepperbox, hopping around very excitedly.

"Compose yourself, Mr. Paprica," advised the King. "Your remarks are piquant and highly-seasoned, but you need a scattering of commonsense. It is only necessary to kill a person once to make him dead; but I do not see that it is necessary to kill this little girl at all."

"I don't, either," said Dorothy.

"Pardon me, but you are not expected to advise me in this matter," replied King Kleaver.

"Why not?" asked Dorothy.

"You might be prejudiced in your own favor, and so mislead us," he said. "Now then, good subjects, who speaks next?"

"I'd like to smooth this thing over, in some way," said a flatiron, earnestly. "We are supposed to be useful to mankind, you know."

"But the girl isn't mankind! She's womankind!" yelled a corkscrew.

"What do you know about it?" inquired the King.

"I'm a lawyer," said the corkscrew, proudly. "I am accustomed to appear at the bar."

"But you're crooked," retorted the King, "and that debars you. You may be a corking good lawyer, Mr. Popp, but I must ask you to withdraw your remarks."

"Very well," said the corkscrew, sadly; "I see I haven't any pull at this court."

"Permit me," continued the flatiron, "to press my suit, your Majesty. I do not wish to gloss over any fault the prisoner may have committed, if such a fault exists; but we owe her some consideration, and that's flat!"

"I'd like to hear from Prince Karver," said the King.

At this a stately carvingknife stepped forward and bowed.

"The Captain was wrong to bring this girl here, and she was wrong to come," he said. "But now that the foolish deed is done let us all prove our mettle and have a slashing good time."

"That's it! that's it!" screamed a fat chopping-knife. "We'll make mincemeat of the girl and hash of the chicken and sausage of the dog!"

There was a shout of approval at this and the King had to rap again for order.

"Gentlemen, gentlemen!" he said, "your remarks are somewhat cutting and rather disjointed, as might be expected from such acute intellects. But you give no reasons for your demands."

"See here, Kleaver; you make me tired," exclaimed a saucepan, strutting before the King very impudently. "You're about the worst King that ever reigned in Utensia, and that's saying a good deal. Why don't you run things yourself, instead of asking everybody's advice, like the big, clumsy idiot you are?"

The King sighed.

"I wish there wasn't a saucepan in my kingdom," he said. "You fellows are always stewing over something, and every once in a while you slop over and make a mess of it. Go hang yourself, sir—by the handle—and don't let me hear from you again."

Dorothy was much shocked by the dreadful language the utensils employed, and she thought that they must have had very little proper training. So she said, addressing the King, who seemed very unfit to rule his turbulent subjects:

"I wish you'd decide my fate right away. I can't stay here all day, trying to find out what you're going to do with me."

"This thing is becoming a regular broil, and it's time I took part in it," observed a big grid-iron, coming forward.

"What I'd like to know," said a can-opener, in a shrill voice, "is why the girl came to our forest, anyhow, and why she intruded upon Captain Dipp—who ought to be called Dippy—and who she is, and where she came from, and where she is going, and why and wherefore and therefore and when."

"I'm sorry to see, Sir Jabber," remarked the King to the can-opener, "that you have such a prying disposition. As a matter of fact, all the things you mention are none of our business."

Having said this the King relighted his pipe, which had gone out.

"Tell me, please, what *is* our business?" inquired a potato-masher, winking at Dorothy somewhat impertinently. "I'm fond of little girls, myself, and it seems to me she has as much right to wander in the forest as we have."

"Who accuses the little girl, anyway?" inquired a rolling-pin. "What has she done?"

"I don't know," said the King. "What has she done, Captain Dipp?"

"That's the trouble, your Majesty. She hasn't done anything," replied the Captain.

"What do you want me to do?" asked Dorothy.

This question seemed to puzzle them all. Finally a chafingdish exclaimed, irritably:

"If no one can throw any light on this subject you must excuse me if I go out."

At this a big kitchen fork pricked up its ears and said in a tiny voice:

"Let's hear from Judge Sifter."

"That's proper," returned the King.

So Judge Sifter turned around slowly several times and then said:

"We have nothing against the girl except the stove-hearth upon which she sits. Therefore I order her instantly discharged."

"Discharged!" cried Dorothy. "Why, I never was discharged in my life, and I don't intend to be. If it's all the same to you, I'll resign."

"It's all the same," declared the King. "You are free—you and your companions—and may go wherever you like."

"Thank you," said the little girl. "But haven't you anything to eat in your kingdom? I'm hungry."

"Go into the woods and pick blackberries," advised the King, lying down upon his back again and preparing to go to sleep. "There isn't a morsel to eat in all Utensia, that I know of."

So Dorothy jumped up and said:

"Come on, Toto and Billina. If we can't find the camp we may find some blackberries."

The utensils drew back and allowed them to pass without protest, although Captain Dipp marched the Spoon Brigade in close order after them until they had reached the edge of the clearing.

There the spoons halted; but Dorothy and her companions entered the forest again and began searching diligently for a way back to the camp, that they might rejoin their party.

CHAPTER 17

How They Came to Bunbury

Wandering through the woods, without knowing where you are going or what adventure you are about to meet next, is not as pleasant as one might think. The woods are always beautiful and impressive, and if you are not worried or hungry you may enjoy them immensely; but Dorothy was worried and hungry that morning, so she paid little attention to the beauties of the forest, and hurried along as fast as she could go. She tried to keep in one direction and not circle around, but she was not at all sure that the direction she had chosen would lead her to the camp.

By and by, to her great joy, she came upon a path. It ran to the right and to the left, being lost in the trees in both directions, and just before her, upon a big oak, were fastened two signs, with arms pointing both ways. One sign read:

TAKE THE OTHER ROAD TO BUNBURY

and the second sign read:

TAKE THE OTHER ROAD TO BUNNYBURY

"Well!" exclaimed Billina, eyeing the signs, "this looks as if we were getting back to civilization again."

"I'm not sure about the civil'zation, dear," replied the little girl; "but it looks as if we might get *somewhere*, and that's a big relief, anyhow."

"Which path shall we take?" inquired the Yellow Hen.

Dorothy stared at the signs thoughtfully.

"Bunbury sounds like something to eat," she said. "Let's go there."

"It's all the same to me," replied Billina. She had picked up enough bugs and insects from the moss as she went along to satisfy her own hunger, but the hen knew Dorothy could not eat bugs; nor could Toto.

The path to Bunbury seemed little traveled, but it was distinct enough and ran through the trees in a zigzag course until it finally led them to an open space filled with the queerest houses Dorothy had ever seen. They were all made of crackers, laid out in tiny squares, and were of many pretty and ornamental shapes, having balconies and porches with posts of bread-sticks and roofs shingled with wafer-crackers.

There were walks of bread-crusts leading from house to house and forming streets, and the place seemed to have many inhabitants.

When Dorothy, followed by Billina and Toto, entered the place, they found people walking the streets or assembled in groups talking together, or sitting upon the porches and balconies.

And what funny people they were!

Men, women and children were all made of buns and bread. Some were thin and others fat; some were white, some light brown and some very dark of complexion. A few of the buns, which seemed to form the more important class of the people, were neatly frosted. Some had raisins for eyes and currant buttons on their clothes; others had eyes of cloves and legs of stick cinnamon, and many wore hats and bonnets frosted pink and green.

There was something of a commotion in Bunbury when the strangers suddenly appeared among them. Women caught up their children and hurried into their houses, shutting the cracker doors carefully behind them. Some men ran so hastily that they tumbled over one another, while others, more brave, assembled in a group and faced the intruders defiantly.

Dorothy at once realized that she must act with caution in order not to frighten these shy people, who were evidently unused to the presence of strangers. There was a delightful fragrant odor of fresh bread in the town, and this made the little girl more hungry than ever. She told Toto and Billina to stay back while she slowly advanced toward the group that stood silently awaiting her.

"You must 'scuse me for coming unexpected," she said, softly, "but I really didn't know I was coming here until I arrived. I was lost in the woods, you know, and I'm as hungry as anything."

"Hungry!" they murmured, in a horrified chorus.

"Yes; I haven't had anything to eat since last night's supper," she explained. "Are there any eatables in Bunbury?"

They looked at one another undecidedly, and then one portly bun man, who seemed a person of consequence, stepped forward and said:

"Little girl, to be frank with you, we are all eatables. Everything in Bunbury is eatable to ravenous human creatures like you. But it is to escape being eaten and destroyed that we have secluded ourselves in this out-of-the-way place, and there is neither right nor justice in your coming here to feed upon us."

Dorothy looked at him longingly.

"You're bread, aren't you?" she asked.

"Yes; bread and butter. The butter is inside me, so it won't melt and run. I do the running myself."

At this joke all the others burst into a chorus of laughter, and Dorothy thought they couldn't be much afraid if they could laugh like that.

"Couldn't I eat something besides people?" she asked. "Couldn't I eat just one house, or a side-walk, or something? I wouldn't mind much what it was, you know."

"This is not a public bakery, child," replied the man, sternly. "It's private property."

"I know Mr.—Mr.—"

"My name is C. Bunn, Esquire," said the man. "C stands for Cinnamon, and this place is called after my family, which is the most aristocratic in the town."

"Oh, I don't know about that," objected another of the queer people. "The Grahams and the Browns and Whites are all excellent families, and there are none better of their kind. I'm a Boston Brown, myself."

"I admit you are all desirable citizens," said Mr. Bunn, rather stiffly; "but the fact remains that our town is called Bunbury."

" 'Scuse me," interrupted Dorothy; "but I'm getting hungrier every minute. Now, if you're polite and kind, as I'm sure you ought to be, you'll let me eat *something*. There's so much to eat here that you never will miss it."

Then a big, puffed-up man, of a delicate brown color, stepped forward and said:

"I think it would be a shame to send this child away hungry, especially as she agrees to eat whatever we can spare and not touch our people."

"So do I, Pop," replied a Roll who stood near.

"What, then, do you suggest, Mr. Over?" inquired Mr. Bunn.

"Why, I'll let her eat my back fence, if she wants to. It's made of waffles, and they're very crisp and nice."

"She may also eat my wheelbarrow," added a pleasant looking Muffin. "It's made of nabiscos with a zuzu wheel."

"Very good; very good," remarked Mr. Bunn. "That is certainly very kind of you. Go with Pop Over and Mr. Muffin, little girl, and they will feed you."

"Thank you very much," said Dorothy, gratefully. "May I bring my dog Toto, and the Yellow Hen? They're hungry, too."

"Will you make them behave?" asked the Muffin.

"Of course," promised Dorothy.

"Then come along," said Pop Over.

So Dorothy and Billina and Toto walked up the street and the people seemed no longer to be at all afraid of them. Mr. Muffin's house came first, and as his wheelbarrow stood in the front yard the little girl ate that first. It didn't seem very fresh, but she was so hungry that she was not particular. Toto ate some, too, while Billina picked up the crumbs.

While the strangers were engaged in eating, many of the people came and stood in the street curiously watching them. Dorothy noticed six roguish looking brown children standing all in a row, and she asked:

"Who are you, little ones?"

"We're the Graham Gems," replied one; "and we're all twins."

"I wonder if your mother could spare one or two of you?" asked Billina, who decided that they were fresh baked; but at this dangerous question the six little gems ran away as fast as they could go.

"You mustn't say such things, Billina," said Dorothy, reprovingly. "Now let's go into Pop Over's back yard and get the waffles."

"I sort of hate to let that fence go," remarked Mr. Over, nervously, as they walked toward his house. "The neighbors back of us are Soda Biscuits, and I don't care to mix with them."

"But I'm hungry yet," declared the girl. "That wheelbarrow wasn't very big."

"I've got a shortcake piano, but none of my family can play on it," he said, reflectively. "Suppose you eat that."

"All right," said Dorothy; "I don't mind. Anything to be accommodating."

So Mr. Over led her into the house, where she ate the piano, which was of an excellent flavor.

"Is there anything to drink here?" she asked.

"Yes; I've a milk pump and a water pump; which will you have?" he asked.

"I guess I'll try 'em both," said Dorothy.

So Mr. Over called to his wife, who brought into the yard a pail made of some kind of baked dough, and Dorothy pumped the pail full of cool, sweet milk and drank it eagerly.

The wife of Pop Over was several shades darker than her husband.

"Aren't you overdone?" the little girl asked her.

"No indeed," answered the woman. "I'm neither overdone nor done over; I'm just Mrs. Over, and I'm the President of the Bunbury Breakfast Band."

Dorothy thanked them for their hospitality and went away. At the gate Mr. Cinnamon Bunn met her and said he would show her around the town.

"We have some very interesting inhabitants," he remarked, walking stiffly beside her on his stick-cinnamon legs; "and all of us who are in good health are well bred. If you are no longer hungry we will call upon a few of the most important citizens."

Toto and Billina followed behind them, behaving very well, and a little way down the street they came to a handsome residence where Aunt Sally Lunn lived. The old lady was glad to meet the little girl and gave her a slice of white bread and butter which had been used as a door-mat. It was almost fresh and tasted better than anything Dorothy had eaten in the town.

"Where do you get the butter?" she inquired.

"We dig it out of the ground, which, as you may have observed, is all flour and meal," replied Mr. Bunn. "There is a butter mine just at the opposite side of the village. The trees which you see here are all doughleanders and doughderas, and in the season we get quite a crop of dough-nuts off them."

"I should think the flour would blow around and get into your eyes," said Dorothy.

"No," said he; "we are bothered with cracker dust sometimes, but never with flour."

Then he took her to see Johnny Cake, a cheerful old gentleman who lived near by.

"I suppose you've heard of me," said old Johnny, with an air of pride. "I'm a great favorite all over the world."

"Aren't you rather yellow?" asked Dorothy, looking at him critically.

"Maybe, child. But don't think I'm bilious, for I was never in better health in my life," replied the old gentleman. "If anything ailed me, I'd willingly acknowledge the corn."

"Johnny's a trifle stale," said Mr. Bunn, as they went away; "but he's a good mixer and never gets cross-grained. I will now take you to call upon some of my own relatives."

They visited the Sugar Bunns, the Currant Bunns and the Spanish Bunns, the latter having a decidedly foreign appearance. Then they saw the French Rolls, who were very polite to them, and made a brief call upon the Parker H. Rolls, who seemed a bit proud and overbearing.

"But they're not as stuck up as the Frosted Jumbles," declared Mr. Bunn, "who are people I really can't abide. I don't like to be suspicious or talk scandal, but sometimes I think the Jumbles have too much baking powder in them."

Just then a dreadful scream was heard, and Dorothy turned hastily around to find a scene of great excitement a little way down the street. The people were crowding around Toto and throwing at him everything they could find at hand. They pelted the little dog with hardtack, crackers, and even articles of furniture which were hard baked and heavy enough for missiles.

Toto howled a little as the assortment of bake stuff struck him; but he stood still, with head bowed and tail between his legs, until Dorothy ran up and inquired what the matter was.

"Matter!" cried a rye loafer, indignantly, "why the horrid beast has eaten three of our dear Crumpets, and is now devouring a Salt-rising Biscuit!"

"Oh, Toto! How could you?" exclaimed Dorothy, much distressed.

Toto's mouth was full of his salt-rising victim; so he only whined and wagged his tail. But Billina, who had flown to the top of a cracker house to be in a safe place, called out:

"Don't blame him, Dorothy; the Crumpets dared him to do it."

"Yes, and you pecked out the eyes of a Raisin Bunn—one of our best citizens!" shouted a bread pudding, shaking its fist at the Yellow Hen.

"What's that! What's that?" wailed Mr. Cinnamon Bunn, who had now joined them. "Oh, what a misfortune—what a terrible misfortune!"

"See here," said Dorothy, determined to defend her pets, "I think we've treated you all pretty well, seeing you're eatables, an' reg'lar food for us. I've been kind to you, and eaten your old wheelbarrows and pianos and rubbish, an' not said a word. But Toto and Billina can't be 'spected to go hungry when the town's full of good things they like to eat, 'cause they can't understand your stingy ways as I do."

"You must leave here at once!" said Mr. Bunn, sternly.

"Suppose we won't go?" asked Dorothy, who was now much provoked.

"Then," said he, "we will put you into the great ovens where we are made, and bake you."

Dorothy gazed around and saw threatening looks upon the faces of all. She had not noticed any ovens in the town, but they might be there, nevertheless, for some of the inhabitants seemed very fresh. So she decided to go, and calling to Toto and Billina to follow her she marched up the street with as much dignity as possible, considering that she was followed by the hoots and cries of the buns and biscuits and other bake stuff.

CHAPTER 18

How Ozma Looked into the Magic Picture

Princess Ozma was a very busy little ruler, for she looked carefully after the comfort and welfare of her people and tried to make them happy. If any quarrels arose she decided them justly; if any one needed counsel or advice she was ready and willing to listen to them.

For a day or two after Dorothy and her companions had started on their trip, Ozma was occupied with the affairs of her kingdom. Then she began to think of some manner of occupation for Uncle Henry and Aunt Em that would be light and easy and yet give the old people something to do.

She soon decided to make Uncle Henry the Keeper of the Jewels, for some one really was needed to count and look after the bins and barrels of emeralds, diamonds, rubies and other precious stones that were in the Royal Storehouses. That would keep Uncle Henry busy enough, but it was harder to find something for Aunt Em to do. The palace was full of servants, so there was no detail of housework that Aunt Em could look after.

While Ozma sat in her pretty room engaged in thought she happened to glance at her Magic Picture.

This was one of the most important treasures in all the Land of Oz. It was a large picture, set in a beautiful gold frame, and it hung in a prominent place upon a wall of Ozma's private room.

Usually this picture seemed merely a country scene, but whenever Ozma looked at it and wished to know what any of her friends or acquaintances were doing, the magic of this wonderful picture was straightway disclosed. For the country scene would gradually fade away and in its place would appear the likeness of the person or persons Ozma might wish to see, surrounded by the actual scenes in which they were then placed. In this way the Princess could view any part of the world she wished, and watch the actions of any one in whom she was interested.

Ozma had often seen Dorothy in her Kansas home by this means, and now, having a little leisure, she expressed a desire to see her little friend again. It was while the travelers were at Fuddlecumjig, and Ozma laughed merrily as she watched in the picture her friends trying to match the pieces of Grandmother Gnit.

"They seem happy and are doubtless having a good time," the girl Ruler said to herself; and then she began to think of the many adventures she herself had encountered with Dorothy.

The images of her friends now faded from the Magic Picture and the old landscape slowly reappeared.

Ozma was thinking of the time when with Dorothy and her army she marched to the Nome King's underground cavern, beyond the Land of Ev, and forced the old monarch to liberate his captives, who belonged to the Royal Family of Ev. That was the time when the Scarecrow nearly frightened the Nome King into fits by throwing one of Billina's eggs at him, and Dorothy had captured King Roquat's Magic Belt and brought it away with her to the Land of Oz.

The pretty Princess smiled at the recollection of this adventure, and then she wondered what had become of the Nome King since then. Merely because she was curious and had nothing better to do, Ozma glanced at the Magic Picture and wished to see in it the King of the Nomes.

Roquat the Red went every day into his tunnel to see how the work was getting along and to hurry his workmen as much as possible. He was there now, and Ozma saw him plainly in the Magic Picture.

She saw the underground tunnel, reaching far underneath the Deadly Desert which separated the Land of Oz from the mountains beneath which the Nome King had his extensive caverns. She saw that the tunnel was being made in the direction of the Emerald City, and knew at once it was being dug so that the army of Nomes could march through it and attack her own beautiful and peaceful country.

"I suppose King Roquat is planning revenge against us," she said, musingly, "and thinks he can surprise us and make us his captives and slaves. How sad it is that any one can have such wicked thoughts! But I must not blame King Roquat too severely, for he is a Nome, and his nature is not so gentle as my own."

Then she dismissed from her mind further thought of the tunnel, for that time, and began to wonder if Aunt Em would not be happy as Royal Mender of the Stockings of the Ruler of Oz. Ozma wore few holes in her stockings; still, they sometimes needed mending. Aunt Em ought to be able to do that very nicely.

Next day the Princess watched the tunnel again in her Magic Picture, and every day afterward she devoted a few minutes to inspecting the work. It was not especially interesting, but she felt that it was her duty.

Slowly but surely the big arched hole crept through the rocks underneath the deadly desert, and day by day it drew nearer and nearer to the Emerald City.

CHAPTER 19

How Bunnybury Welcomed the Strangers

Dorothy left Bunbury the same way she had entered it and when they were in the forest again she said to Billina:

"I never thought that things good to eat could be so dis'gree'ble."

"Often I've eaten things that tasted good but were disagreeable afterward," returned the Yellow Hen. "I think, Dorothy, if eatables are going to act badly, it's better before than after you eat them."

"P'raps you're right," said the little girl, with a sigh. "But what shall we do now?"

"Let us follow the path back to the signpost," suggested Billina. "That will be better than getting lost again."

"Why, we're lost anyhow," declared Dorothy; "but I guess you're right about going back to that signpost, Billina."

They returned along the path to the place where they had first found it, and at once took "the other road" to Bunnybury. This road was a mere narrow strip, worn hard and smooth but not wide enough for Dorothy's feet to tread. Still it was a guide, and the walking through the forest was not at all difficult.

Before long they reached a high wall of solid white marble, and the path came to an end at this wall.

At first Dorothy thought there was no opening at all in the marble, but on looking closely she discovered a small square door about on a level with her head, and underneath this closed door was a bell-push. Near the bell-push a sign was painted in neat letters upon the marble, and the sign read:

No Admittance
Except on Business

This did not discourage Dorothy, however, and she rang the bell.

Pretty soon a bolt was cautiously withdrawn and the marble door swung slowly open. Then she saw it was not really a door, but a window, for several brass bars were placed across it, being set fast in the marble and so close together that the little girl's fingers might barely go between them. Back of the bars appeared the face of a white rabbit—a very sober and sedate face—with an eye-glass held in his left eye and attached to a cord in his button-hole.

"Well! what is it?" asked the rabbit, sharply.

"I'm Dorothy," said the girl, "and I'm lost, and—"

"State your business, please," interrupted the rabbit.

"My business," she replied, "is to find out where I am, and to—"

"No one is allowed in Bunnybury without an order or a letter of introduction from either Ozma of Oz or Glinda the Good," announced the rabbit; "so that that settles the matter," and he started to close the window.

"Wait a minute!" cried Dorothy. "I've got a letter from Ozma."

"From the Ruler of Oz?" asked the rabbit, doubtingly.

"Of course. Ozma's my best friend, you know; and I'm a Princess myself," she announced, earnestly.

"Hum—ha! Let me see your letter," returned the rabbit, as if he still doubted her.

So she hunted in her pocket and found the letter Ozma had given her. Then she handed it through the bars to the rabbit, who took it in his paws and opened it. He read it aloud in a pompous voice, as if to let Dorothy and Billina see that he was educated and could read writing. The letter was as follows:

"It will please me to have my subjects greet Princess Dorothy, the bearer of this royal missive, with the same courtesy and consideration they would extend to me."

"Ha—hum! It is signed 'Ozma of Oz,' " continued the rabbit, "and is sealed with the Great Seal of the Emerald City. Well, well, well! How strange! How remarkable!"

"What are you going to do about it?" inquired Dorothy, impatiently.

"We must obey the royal mandate," replied the rabbit. "We are subjects of Ozma of Oz, and we live in her country. Also we are under the protection of the great Sorceress Glinda the Good, who made us promise to respect Ozma's commands."

"Then may I come in?" she asked.

"I'll open the door," said the rabbit. He shut the window and disappeared, but a moment afterward a big door in the wall opened and admitted Dorothy to a small room, which seemed to be a part of the wall and built into it.

Here stood the rabbit she had been talking with, and now that she could see all of him she gazed at the creature in surprise. He was a good sized white rabbit with pink eyes, much like all other white rabbits. But the astonishing thing about him was the manner in which he was dressed. He wore a white satin jacket embroidered with gold, and having diamond buttons. His vest was rose-colored satin, with tourmaline buttons. His trousers were white, to correspond with the jacket, and they were baggy at the knees—like those of a zouave— being tied with knots of rose ribbons. His shoes were of white plush with diamond buckles, and his stockings were rose silk.

The richness and even magnificence of the rabbit's clothing made Dorothy stare at the little creature wonderingly. Toto and Billina had followed her into the room and when he saw them the rabbit ran to a table and sprang upon it nimbly. Then he looked at the three through his monocle and said:

"These companions, Princess, cannot enter Bunnybury with you."

"Why not?" asked Dorothy.

"In the first place they would frighten our people, who dislike dogs above all things on earth; and, secondly, the letter of the Royal Ozma does not mention them."

"But they're my friends," persisted Dorothy, "and go wherever I go."

"Not this time," said the rabbit, decidedly. "You, yourself, Princess, are a welcome visitor, since you come so highly recommended; but unless you consent to leave the dog and the hen in this room I cannot permit you to enter the town."

"Never mind us, Dorothy," said Billina. "Go inside and see what the place is like. You can tell us about it afterward, and Toto and I will rest comfortably here until you return."

This seemed the best thing to do, for Dorothy was curious to see how the rabbit people lived and she was aware of the fact that her friends might frighten the timid little creatures. She had not forgotten how Toto and Billina had misbehaved in Bunbury, and perhaps the rabbit was wise to insist on their staying outside the town.

"Very well," she said, "I'll go in alone. I s'pose you're the King of this town, aren't you?"

"No," answered the rabbit, "I'm merely the Keeper of the Wicket, and a person of little importance, although I try to do my duty. I must now inform you, Princess, that before you enter our town you must consent to reduce."

"Reduce what?" asked Dorothy.

"Your size.[1] You must become the size of the rabbits, although you may retain your own form."

"Wouldn't my clothes be too big for me?" she inquired.

"No; they will reduce when your body does."

"Can *you* make me smaller?" asked the girl.

"Easily," returned the rabbit.

"And will you make me big again, when I'm ready to go away?"

"I will," said he.

"All right, then; I'm willing," she announced.

The rabbit jumped from the table and ran—or rather hopped—to the further wall, where he opened a door so tiny that even Toto could scarcely have crawled through it.

"Follow me," he said.

Now, almost any other little girl would have declared that she could not get through so small a door; but Dorothy had already encountered so many fairy adventures that she believed nothing was impossible in the Land of Oz. So she quietly walked toward the door, and at every step she grew smaller and smaller until, by the time the opening was reached, she could pass through it with ease. Indeed, as she stood beside the rabbit, who sat upon his hind legs and used his paws as hands, her head was just about as high as his own.

Then the Keeper of the Wicket passed through and she followed, after which the door swung shut and locked itself with a sharp click.

Dorothy now found herself in a city so strange and beautiful that she gave a gasp of surprise. The high marble wall extended all around the place and shut out all the rest of the world. And here were marble houses of curious forms, most of them resembling overturned kettles but with delicate slender spires and minarets running far up into the sky. The streets were paved with white marble and in front of each house was a lawn of rich green clover. Everything was as neat as wax, the green and white contrasting prettily together.

But the rabbit people were, after all, the most amazing things Dorothy saw. The streets were full of them, and their costumes were so splendid that the rich dress of the Keeper of the Wicket was commonplace when compared with the others. Silks and satins of delicate hues seemed always used for material, and nearly every costume sparkled with exquisite gems.

But the lady rabbits outshone the gentlemen rabbits in splendor, and the cut of their gowns was really wonderful. They wore bonnets, too, with feathers and jewels in them, and some wheeled baby carriages in which the girl could see wee bunnies. Some were lying asleep while others lay sucking their paws and looking around them with big pink eyes.

As Dorothy was no bigger in size than the grown-up rabbits she had a chance to observe them closely before they noticed her presence. Then they did not seem at all alarmed, although the little girl naturally became the center of attraction and all regarded her with great curiosity.

"Make way!" cried the Keeper of the Wicket, in a pompous voice; "make way for Princess Dorothy, who comes from Ozma of Oz."

Hearing this announcement, the throng of rabbits gave place to them on the walks, and as Dorothy passed along they all bowed their heads respectfully.

Walking thus through several handsome streets they came to a square in the center of the City. In this square were some pretty trees and a statue in bronze of Glinda the Good, while beyond it were the portals of the Royal Palace—an extensive and imposing building of white marble covered with a filigree of frosted gold.

CHAPTER 20

How Dorothy Lunched With a King

A line of rabbit soldiers was drawn up before the palace entrance, and they wore green and gold uniforms with high shakos upon their heads and held tiny spears in their hands. The Captain had a sword and a white plume in his shako.

"Salute!" cried the Keeper of the Wicket. "Salute Princess Dorothy, who comes from Ozma of Oz!"

"Salute!" yelled the Captain, and all the soldiers promptly saluted.

They now entered the great hall of the palace, where they met a gaily dressed attendant, from whom the Keeper of the Wicket inquired if the King were at leisure.

"I think so," was the reply. "I heard his Majesty blubbering and wailing as usual only a few minutes ago. If he doesn't stop acting like a cry-baby I'm going to resign my position here and go to work."

"What's the matter with your King?" asked Dorothy, surprised to hear the rabbit attendant speak so disrespectfully of his monarch.

"Oh, he doesn't want to be King, that's all; and he simply *has* to," was the reply.

"Come!" said the Keeper of the Wicket, sternly; "lead us to his Majesty; and do not air our troubles before strangers, I beg of you."

"Why, if this girl is going to see the King, he'll air his own troubles," returned the attendant.

"That is his royal privilege," declared the Keeper.

So the attendant led them into a room all draped with cloth-of-gold and furnished with satin-covered gold furniture. There was a throne in this room, set on a dais and having a big cushioned seat, and on this seat reclined the Rabbit King. He was lying on his back, with his paws in the air, and whining very like a puppy-dog.

"Your Majesty! your Majesty! Get up. Here's a visitor," called out the attendant.

The King rolled over and looked at Dorothy with one watery pink eye. Then he sat up and wiped his eyes carefully with a silk handkerchief and put on his jeweled crown, which had fallen off.

"Excuse my grief, fair stranger," he said, in a sad voice. "You behold in me the most miserable monarch in all the world. What time is it, Blinkem?"

"One o'clock, your Majesty," replied the attendant to whom the question was addressed.

"Serve luncheon at once!" commanded the King. "Luncheon for two—that's for my visitor and me—and see that the human has some sort of food she's accustomed to."

"Yes, your Majesty," answered the attendant, and went away.

"Tie my shoe, Bristle," said the King to the Keeper of the Wicket. "Ah, me! how unhappy I am!"

"What seems to be worrying your Majesty?" asked Dorothy.

"Why, it's this king business, of course," he returned, while the Keeper tied his shoe. "I didn't want to be King of Bunnybury at all, and the rabbits all knew it. So they elected me—to save themselves from such a dreadful fate, I suppose—and here I am, shut up in a palace, when I might be free and happy."

"Seems to me," said Dorothy, "it's a great thing to be a King."

"Were you ever a King?" inquired the monarch.

"No," she answered, laughing.

"Then you know nothing about it," he said. "I haven't inquired who you are, but it doesn't matter. While we're at luncheon, I'll tell you all my troubles. They're a great deal more interesting than anything you can say about yourself."

"Perhaps they are, to you," replied Dorothy.

"Luncheon is served!" cried Blinkem, throwing open the door, and in came a dozen rabbits in livery, all bearing trays which they placed upon the table, where they arranged the dishes in an orderly manner.

"Now clear out—all of you!" exclaimed the King. "Bristle, you may wait outside, in case I want you."

When they had gone and the King was alone with Dorothy he came down from his throne, tossed his crown into a corner and kicked his ermine robe under the table.

"Sit down," he said, "and try to be happy. It's useless for me to try, because I'm always wretched and miserable. But I'm hungry, and I hope you are."

"I am," said Dorothy. "I've only eaten a wheelbarrow and a piano to-day—oh, yes! and a slice of bread and butter that used to be a door-mat."

"That sounds like a square meal," remarked the King, seating himself opposite her; "but perhaps it wasn't a square piano. Eh?"

Dorothy laughed.

"You don't seem so very unhappy now," she said.

"But I am," protested the King, fresh tears gathering in his eyes. "Even my jokes are miserable. I'm wretched, woeful, afflicted, distressed and dismal as an individual can be. Are you not sorry for me?"

"No," answered Dorothy, honestly, "I can't say I am. Seems to me that for a rabbit you're right in clover. This is the prettiest little city I ever saw."

"Oh, the city is good enough," he admitted. "Glinda, the Good Sorceress, made it for us because she was fond of rabbits. I don't mind the City so much, although I wouldn't live here if I had my choice. It is being King that has absolutely ruined my happiness."

"Why wouldn't you live here by choice?" she asked.

"Because it is all unnatural, my dear. Rabbits are out of place in such luxury. When I was young I lived in a burrow in the forest. I was surrounded by enemies and often had to run for my life. It was hard getting enough to eat, at times, and when I found a bunch of clover I had to listen and look for danger while I ate it. Wolves prowled around the hole in which I lived and sometimes I didn't dare stir out for days at a time. Oh, how happy and contented I was then! I was a real rabbit, as nature made me—wild and free!—and I even enjoyed listening to the startled throbbing of my own heart!"

"I've often thought," said Dorothy, who was busily eating, "that it would be fun to be a rabbit."

"It *is* fun—when you're the genuine article," agreed his Majesty. "But look at me now! I live in a marble palace instead of a hole in the ground. I have all I want to eat, without the joy of hunting for it. Every day I must dress in fine clothes and wear that horrible crown till it makes my head ache. Rabbits come to me with all sorts of troubles, when my own troubles are the only ones I care about. When I walk out I can't hop and run; I must strut on my rear legs and wear an ermine robe! And the soldiers salute me and the band plays and the other rabbits laugh and clap their paws and cry out: 'Hail to the King!' Now let me ask you, as a friend and a young lady of good judgment: isn't all this pomp and foolishness enough to make a decent rabbit miserable?"

"Once," said Dorothy, reflectively, "men were wild and unclothed and lived in caves and hunted for food as wild beasts do. But they got civ'lized, in time, and now they'd hate to go back to the old days."

"That is an entirely different case," replied the King. "None of you Humans were civilized in one lifetime. It came to you by degrees. But I have known the forest and the free life, and that is why I resent being civilized all at once, against my will, and being made a King with a crown and an ermine robe. Pah!"

"If you don't like it, why don't you resign?" she asked.

"Impossible!" wailed the Rabbit, wiping his eyes again with his handkerchief. "There's a beastly law in this town that forbids it. When one is elected a King there's no getting out of it."

"Who made the laws?" inquired Dorothy.

"The same Sorceress who made the town—Glinda the Good. She built the wall, and fixed up the City, and gave us several valuable enchantments, and made the laws. Then she invited all the pink-eyed white rabbits of the forest to come here, after which she left us to our fate."

"What made you 'cept the invitation, and come here?" asked the child.

"I didn't know how dreadful city life was, and I'd no idea I would be elected King," said he, sobbing bitterly. "And—and—now I'm It—with a capital I—and can't escape!"

"I know Glinda," remarked Dorothy, eating for dessert a dish of charlotte russe, "and when I see her again I'll ask her to put another King in your place."

"Will you? Will you, indeed?" asked the King, joyfully.

"I will if you want me to," she replied.

"Hurroo—hurray!" shouted the King; and then he jumped up from the table and danced wildly about the room, waving his napkin like a flag and laughing with glee.

After a time he managed to control his delight and returned to the table.

"When are you likely to see Glinda?" he inquired.

"Oh, p'raps in a few days," said Dorothy.

"And you won't forget to ask her?"

"Of course not."

"Princess," said the Rabbit King, earnestly, "you have relieved me of a great unhappiness, and I am very grateful. Therefore I propose to entertain you, since you are my guest and I am the King, as a slight mark of my appreciation. Come with me to my reception hall."

He then summoned Bristle and said to him: "Assemble all the nobility in the great reception hall, and also tell Blinkem that I want him immediately."

The Keeper of the Wicket bowed and hurried away, and his Majesty turned to Dorothy and continued: "We'll have time for a walk in the gardens before the people get here."

The gardens were back of the palace and were filled with beautiful flowers and fragrant shrubs, with many shade and fruit trees and marble paved walks running in every direction. As they entered this place Blinkem came running to the King, who gave him several orders in a low voice. Then his Majesty rejoined Dorothy and led her through the gardens, which she admired very much.

"What lovely clothes your Majesty wears!" she said, glancing at the rich blue satin costume, embroidered with pearls, in which the King was dressed.

"Yes," he returned, with an air of pride, "this is one of my favorite suits; but I have a good many that are even more elaborate. We have excellent tailors in Bunnybury, and Glinda supplies all the material. By the way, you might ask the Sorceress, when you see her, to permit me to keep my wardrobe."

"But if you go back to the forest you will not need clothes," she said.

"N—o!" he faltered; "that may be so. But I've dressed up so long that I'm used to it, and I don't imagine I'd care to run around naked again. So perhaps the Good Glinda will let me keep the costumes."

"I'll ask her," agreed Dorothy.

Then they left the gardens and went into a fine big reception hall, where rich rugs were spread upon the tiled floors and the furniture was exquisitely carved and studded with jewels. The King's chair was an especially pretty piece of furniture, being in the shape of a silver lily with one leaf bent over to form the seat. The silver was everywhere thickly encrusted with diamonds and the seat was upholstered in white satin.

"Oh, what a splendid chair!" cried Dorothy, clasping her hands admiringly.

"Isn't it?" answered the King, proudly. "It is my favorite seat, and I think it especially becoming to my complexion. While I think of it, I wish you'd ask Glinda to let me keep this lily chair when I go away."

"It wouldn't look very well in a hole in the ground, would it?" she suggested.

"Maybe not; but I'm used to sitting in it and I'd like to take it with me," he answered. "But here come the ladies and gentlemen of the court; so please sit beside me and be presented."

CHAPTER 21

How the King Changed His Mind

Just then a rabbit band of nearly fifty pieces marched in, playing upon golden instruments and dressed in neat uniforms. Following the band came the nobility of Bunnybury, all richly dressed and hopping along on their rear legs. Both the ladies and the gentlemen wore white gloves upon their paws, with their rings on the outside of the gloves, as this seemed to be the fashion here. Some of the lady rabbits carried lorgnettes, while many of the gentlemen rabbits wore monocles in their left eyes.

The courtiers and their ladies paraded past the King, who introduced Princess Dorothy to each couple in a very graceful manner. Then the company seated themselves in chairs and on sofas and looked expectantly at their monarch.

"It is our royal duty, as well as our royal pleasure," he said, "to provide fitting entertainment for our distinguished guest. We will now present the Royal Band of Whiskered Friskers."

As he spoke the musicians, who had arranged themselves in a corner, struck up a dance melody while into the room pranced the Whiskered Friskers. They were eight pretty rabbits dressed only in gauzy purple skirts fastened around their waists with diamond bands. Their whiskers were colored a rich purple, but otherwise they were pure white.

After bowing before the King and Dorothy the Friskers began their pranks, and these were so comical that Dorothy laughed with real enjoyment. They not only danced together, whirling and gyrating around the room, but they leaped over one another, stood upon their heads and hopped and skipped here and there so nimbly that it was hard work to keep track of them. Finally they all made double somersaults and turned handsprings out of the room.

The nobility enthusiastically applauded, and Dorothy applauded with them.

"They're fine!" she said to the King.

"Yes, the Whiskered Friskers are really very clever," he replied. "I shall hate to part with them when I go away, for they have often amused me when I was very miserable. I wonder if you would ask Glinda—"

"No, it wouldn't do at all," declared Dorothy, positively. "There wouldn't be room in your hole in the ground for so many rabbits, 'spec'ly when you get the lily chair and your clothes there. Don't think of such a thing, your Majesty."

The King sighed. Then he stood up and announced to the company:

"We will now behold a military drill by my picked Bodyguard of Royal Pikemen."

Now the band played a march and a company of rabbit soldiers came in. They wore green and gold uniforms and marched very stiffly but in perfect time. Their spears, or pikes, had slender shafts of polished silver with golden heads, and during the drill they handled these weapons with wonderful dexterity.

"I should think you'd feel pretty safe with such a fine Bodyguard," remarked Dorothy.

"I do," said the King. "They protect me from every harm. I suppose Glinda wouldn't—"

"No," interrupted the girl; "I'm sure she wouldn't. It's the King's own Bodyguard, and when you are no longer King you can't have 'em."

The King did not reply, but he looked rather sorrowful for a time.

When the soldiers had marched out he said to the company:

"The Royal Jugglers will now appear."

Dorothy had seen many jugglers in her lifetime, but never any so interesting as these. There were six of them, dressed in black satin embroidered with queer symbols in silver—a costume which contrasted strongly with their snow-white fur.

First they pushed in a big red ball and three of the rabbit jugglers stood upon its top and made it roll. Then two of them caught up a third and tossed him into the air, all vanishing, until only the two were left. Then one of these tossed the other upward and remained alone of all his fellows. This last juggler now touched the red ball, which fell apart, being hollow, and the five rabbits who had disappeared in the air scrambled out of the hollow ball.

Next they all clung together and rolled swiftly upon the floor. When they came to a stop only one fat rabbit juggler was seen, the others seeming to be inside him. This one leaped lightly into the air and when he came down he exploded and separated into the original six. Then four of them rolled themselves into round balls and the other two tossed them around and played ball with them.

These were but a few of the tricks the rabbit jugglers performed, and they were so skillful that all the nobility and even the King applauded as loudly as did Dorothy.

"I suppose there are no rabbit jugglers in all the world to compare with these," remarked the King. "And since I may not have the Whiskered Friskers or my Bodyguard, you might ask Glinda to let me take away just two or three of these jugglers. Will you?"

"I'll ask her," replied Dorothy, doubtfully.

"Thank you," said the King; "thank you very much. And now you shall listen to the Winsome Waggish Warblers, who have often cheered me in my moments of anguish."

The Winsome Waggish Warblers proved to be a quartette of rabbit singers, two gentlemen and two lady rabbits. The gentlemen Warblers wore full-dress swallow-tailed suits of white satin, with pearls for buttons, while the lady Warblers were gowned in white satin dresses with long trails.

The first song they sang began in this way:

> "When a rabbit gets a habit
>   Of living in a city
> And wearing clothes and furbelows
>   And jewels rare and pretty,
> He scorns the Bun who has to run
>   And burrow in the ground
> And pities those whose watchful foes
>   Are man and gun and hound."

Dorothy looked at the King when she heard this song and noticed that he seemed disturbed and ill at ease.

"I don't like that song," he said to the Warblers. "Give us something jolly and rollicking."

So they sang to a joyous, tinkling melody as follows:

> "Bunnies gay
>   Delight to play
> In their fairy town secure;

Ev'ry frisker
Flirts his whisker
At a pink-eyed girl demure.
Ev'ry maid
In silk arrayed
At her partner shyly glances,
Paws are grasped,
Waists are clasped
As they whirl in giddy dances.
Then together
Through the heather
'Neath the moonlight soft they stroll;
Each is very
Blithe and merry,
Gamboling with laughter droll.
Life is fun
To ev'ry one
Guarded by our magic charm
For to dangers
We are strangers,
Safe from any thought of harm."

"You see," said Dorothy to the King, when the song ended, "the rabbits all seem to like Bunnybury except you. And I guess you're the only one that ever has cried or was unhappy and wanted to get back to your muddy hole in the ground."

His Majesty seemed thoughtful, and while the servants passed around glasses of nectar and plates of frosted cakes their King was silent and a bit nervous.

When the refreshments had been enjoyed by all and the servants had retired Dorothy said:

"I must go now, for it's getting late and I'm lost. I've got to find the Wizard and Aunt Em and Uncle Henry and all the rest sometime before night comes, if I poss'bly can."

"Won't you stay with us?" asked the King. "You will be very welcome."

"No, thank you," she replied. "I must get back to my friends. And I want to see Glinda just as soon as I can, you know."

So the King dismissed his court and said he would himself walk with Dorothy to the gate. He did not weep nor groan any more, but his long face was quite solemn and his big ears hung dejectedly on each side of it. He still wore his crown and his ermine and walked with a handsome gold-headed cane.

When they arrived at the room in the wall the little girl found Toto and Billina waiting for her very patiently. They had been liberally fed by some of the attendants and were in no hurry to leave such comfortable quarters.

The Keeper of the Wicket was by this time back in his old place, but he kept a safe distance from Toto. Dorothy bade good-bye to the King as they stood just inside the wall.

"You've been good to me," she said, "and I thank you ever so much. As soon as poss'ble I'll see Glinda and ask her to put another King in your place and send you back into the wild forest. And I'll ask her to let you keep some of your clothes and the lily chair and one or two jugglers to amuse you. I'm sure she will do it, 'cause she's so kind she doesn't like any one to be unhappy."

"Ahem!" said the King, looking rather downcast. "I don't like to trouble you with my misery; so you needn't see Glinda."

"Oh, yes I will," she replied. "It won't be any trouble at all."

"But, my dear," continued the King, in an embarrassed way, "I've been thinking the subject over carefully, and I find there are a lot of pleasant things here in Bunnybury that I would miss if I went away. So perhaps I'd better stay."

Dorothy laughed. Then she looked grave.

"It won't do for you to be a King and a cry-baby at the same time," she said. "You've been making all the other rabbits unhappy and discontented with your howls about being so miserable. So I guess it's better to have another King."

"Oh, no indeed!" exclaimed the King, earnestly. "If you won't say anything to Glinda I'll promise to be merry and gay all the time, and never cry or wail again."

"Honor bright?" she asked.

"On the royal word of a King I promise it!" he answered.

"All right," said Dorothy. "You'd be a reg'lar lunatic to want to leave Bunnybury for a wild life in the forest, and I'm sure any rabbit outside the city would be glad to take your place."

"Forget it, my dear; forget all my foolishness," pleaded the King, earnestly. "Hereafter I'll try to enjoy myself and do my duty by my subjects."

So then she left him and entered through the little door into the room in the wall, where she grew gradually bigger and bigger until she had resumed her natural size.

The Keeper of the Wicket let them out into the forest and told Dorothy that she had been of great service to Bunnybury because she had brought their dismal King to a realization of the pleasure of ruling so beautiful a city.

"I shall start a petition to have your statue erected beside Glinda's in the public square," said the Keeper. "I hope you will come again, some day, and see it."

"Perhaps I shall," she replied.

Then, followed by Toto and Billina, she walked away from the high marble wall and started back along the narrow path toward the signpost.

CHAPTER 22

How the Wizard Found Dorothy

When they came to the signpost, there, to their joy, were the tents of the Wizard pitched beside the path and the kettle bubbling merrily over a fire. The Shaggy Man and Omby Amby were gathering firewood while Uncle Henry and Aunt Em sat in their camp chairs talking with the Wizard.

They all ran forward to greet Dorothy, as she approached, and Aunt Em exclaimed: "Goodness gracious, child! Where have you been?"

"You've played hookey the whole day," added the Shaggy Man, reproachfully.

"Well, you see, I've been lost," explained the little girl, "and I've tried awful hard to find the way back to you, but just couldn't do it."

"Did you wander in the forest all day?" asked Uncle Henry.

"You must be a'most starved!" said Aunt Em.

"No," said Dorothy, "I'm not hungry. I had a wheelbarrow and a piano for breakfast, and lunched with a King."

"Ah!" exclaimed the Wizard, nodding with a bright smile. "So you've been having adventures again."

"She's stark crazy!" cried Aunt Em. "Whoever heard of eating a wheelbarrow?"

"It wasn't very big," said Dorothy; "and it had a zuzu wheel."

"And I ate the crumbs," added Billina, soberly.

"Sit down and tell us about it," begged the Wizard. "We've hunted for you all day, and at last I noticed your footsteps in this path—and the tracks of Billina. We found the path by accident, and seeing it only led to two places I decided you were at either one or the other of those places. So we made camp and waited for you to return. And now, Dorothy, tell us where you have been—to Bunbury or to Bunnybury?"

"Why, I've been to both," she replied; "but first I went to Utensia, which isn't on any path at all."

She then sat down and related the day's adventures, and you may be sure Aunt Em and Uncle Henry were much astonished at the story.

"But after seeing the Cuttenclips and the Fuddles," remarked her uncle, "we ought not to wonder at anything in this strange country."

"Seems like the only common and ordinary folks here are ourselves," rejoined Aunt Em, diffidently.

"Now that we're together again, and one reunited party," observed the Shaggy Man, "what are we to do next?"

"Have some supper and a night's rest," answered the Wizard promptly, "and then proceed upon our journey."

"Where to?" asked the Captain General.

"We haven't visited the Rigmaroles or the Flutterbudgets[1] yet," said Dorothy. "I'd like to see them—wouldn't you?"

"They don't sound very interesting," objected Aunt Em. "But perhaps they are."

"And then," continued the little Wizard, "we will call upon the Tin Woodman and Jack Pumpkinhead and our old friend the Scarecrow, on our way home."

"That will be nice!" cried Dorothy, eagerly.

"Can't say they sound very interesting, either," remarked Aunt Em.

"Why, they're the best friends I have!" asserted the little girl, "and you're sure to like them, Aunt Em, 'cause ever'-body likes them."

By this time twilight was approaching, so they ate the fine supper which the Wizard magically produced from the kettle and then went to bed in the cosy tents.

They were all up bright and early next morning, but Dorothy didn't venture to wander from the camp again for fear of more accidents.

"Do you know where there's a road?" she asked the little man.

"No, my dear," replied the Wizard; "but I'll find one."

After breakfast he waved his hand toward the tents and they became handkerchiefs again, which were at once returned to the pockets of their owners. Then they all climbed into the red wagon and the Sawhorse inquired:

"Which way?"

"Never mind which way," replied the Wizard. "Just go as you please and you're sure to be right. I've enchanted the wheels of the wagon, and they will roll in the right direction, never fear."

As the Sawhorse started away through the trees Dorothy said:

"If we had one of those new-fashioned airships we could float away over the top of the forest, and look down and find just the places we want."

"Airship? Pah!" retorted the little man, scornfully. "I hate those things, Dorothy, although they are nothing new to either you or me. I was a balloonist for many years, and once my balloon carried me to the Land of Oz, and once to the Vegetable Kingdom. And once Ozma had a Gump[2] that flew all over this kingdom and had sense enough to go where it was told to—which airships won't do. The house which the cyclone brought to Oz all the way from Kansas, with you and Toto in it—was a real airship at the time; so you see we've had plenty of experience flying with the birds."

"Airships are not so bad, after all," declared Dorothy. "Some day they'll fly all over the world, and perhaps bring people even to the Land of Oz."

"I must speak to Ozma about that," said the Wizard, with a slight frown. "It wouldn't do at all, you know, for the Emerald City to become a way-station on an airship line."

"No," said Dorothy, "I don't s'pose it would. But what can we do to prevent it?"

"I'm working out a magic recipe to fuddle men's brains, so they'll never make an airship that will go where they want it to go," the Wizard confided to her. "That won't keep the things from flying, now and then, but it'll keep them from flying to the Land of Oz."

Just then the Sawhorse drew the wagon out of the forest and a beautiful landscape lay spread before the travelers' eyes. Moreover, right before them was a good road that wound away through the hills and valleys.

"Now," said the Wizard, with evident delight, "we are on the right track again, and there is nothing more to worry about."

"It's a foolish thing to take chances in a strange country," observed the Shaggy Man. "Had we kept to the roads we never would have been lost. Roads always lead to some place, else they wouldn't be roads."

"This road," added the Wizard, "leads to Rigmarole Town. I'm sure of that because I enchanted the wagon wheels."

Sure enough, after riding along the road for an hour or two they entered a pretty valley where a village was nestled among the hills. The houses were Munchkin shaped, for they were all domes, with windows wider than they were high, and pretty balconies over the front doors.

Aunt Em was greatly relieved to find this town "neither paper nor patch-work," and the only surprising thing about it was that it was so far distant from all other towns.

As the Sawhorse drew the wagon into the main street the travelers noticed that the place was filled with people, standing in groups and seeming to be engaged in earnest conversation. So occupied with themselves were the inhabitants that they scarcely noticed the strangers at all. So the Wizard stopped a boy and asked:

"Is this Rigmarole Town?"

"Sir," replied the boy, "if you have traveled very much you will have noticed that every town differs from every other town in one way or another and so by observing the methods of the people and the way they live as well as the style of their dwelling places it ought not to be a difficult thing to make up your mind without the trouble of asking questions whether the town bears the appearance of the one you intended to visit or whether perhaps having taken a different road from the one you should have taken you have made an error in your way and arrived at some point where—"

"Land sakes!" cried Aunt Em, impatiently; "what's all this rigmarole about?"

"That's it!" said the Wizard, laughing merrily. "It's a rigmarole because the boy is a Rigmarole and we've come to Rigmarole Town."

"Do they all talk like that?" asked Dorothy, wonderingly.

"He might have said 'yes' or 'no' and settled the question," observed Uncle Henry.

"Not here," said Omby Amby. "I don't believe the Rigmaroles know what 'yes' or 'no' means."

While the boy had been talking several other people had approached the wagon and listened intently to his speech. Then they began talking to one another in long, deliberate speeches, where many words were used but little was said. But when the strangers criticised them so frankly one of the women, who had no one else to talk to, began an address to them, saying:

"It is the easiest thing in the world for a person to say 'yes' or 'no' when a question that is asked for the purpose of gaining information or satisfying the curiosity of the one who has given expression to the inquiry has attracted the attention of an individual who may be competent either from personal experience or the experience of others to answer it with more or less correctness or at least an attempt to satisfy the desire for information on the part of the one who has made the inquiry by—"

"Dear me!" exclaimed Dorothy, interrupting the speech. "I've lost all track of what you are saying."

"Don't let her begin over again, for goodness sake!" cried Aunt Em.

But the woman did not begin again. She did not even stop talking, but went right on as she had begun, the words flowing from her mouth in a stream.

"I'm quite sure that if we waited long enough and listened carefully, some of these people might be able to tell us something, in time," said the Wizard.

"Don't let's wait," returned Dorothy. "I've heard of the Rigmaroles, and wondered what they were like; but now I know, and I'm ready to move on."

"So am I," declared Uncle Henry; "we're wasting time here."

"Why, we're all ready to go," added the Shaggy Man, putting his fingers to his ears to shut out the monotonous babble of those around the wagon.

So the Wizard spoke to the Sawhorse, who trotted nimbly through the village and soon gained the open country on the other side of it. Dorothy looked back, as they rode away, and noticed that the woman had not yet finished her speech but was talking as glibly as ever, although no one was near to hear her.

"If those people wrote books," Omby Amby remarked with a smile, "it would take a whole library to say the cow jumped over the moon."

"Perhaps some of 'em do write books," asserted the little Wizard. "I've read a few rigmaroles that might have come from this very town."

"Some of the college lecturers and ministers are certainly related to these people," observed the Shaggy Man; "and it seems to me the Land of Oz is a little ahead of the United States in some of its laws. For here, if one can't talk clearly, and straight to the point, they send him to Rigmarole Town; while Uncle Sam lets him roam around wild and free, to torture innocent people."

Dorothy was thoughtful. The Rigmaroles had made a strong

impression upon her. She decided that whenever she spoke, after this, she would use only enough words to express what she wanted to say.

CHAPTER 23

How They Encountered the Flutterbudgets

They were soon among the pretty hills and valleys again, and the Sawhorse sped up hill and down at a fast and easy pace, the roads being hard and smooth. Mile after mile was speedily covered, and before the ride had grown at all tiresome they sighted another village. The place seemed even larger than Rigmarole Town, but was not so attractive in appearance.

"This must be Flutterbudget Center," declared the Wizard. "You see, it's no trouble at all to find places if you keep to the right road."

"What are the Flutterbudgets like?" inquired Dorothy.

"I do not know, my dear. But Ozma has given them a town all their own, and I've heard that whenever one of the people becomes a Flutterbudget he is sent to this place to live."

"That is true," Omby Amby added; "Flutterbudget Center and Rigmarole Town are called 'the Defensive Settlements of Oz.' "

The village they now approached was not built in a valley, but on top of a hill, and the road they followed wound around the hill like a corkscrew, ascending the hill easily until it came to the town.

"Look out!" screamed a voice. "Look out, or you'll run over my child!"

They gazed around and saw a woman standing upon the sidewalk nervously wringing her hands as she gazed at them appealingly.

"Where is your child?" asked the Sawhorse.

"In the house," said the woman, bursting into tears; "but if it should happen to be in the road, and you ran over it, those great wheels would crush my darling to jelly. Oh, dear! oh dear! Think of my darling child being crushed to jelly by those great wheels!"

"Gid-dap!" said the Wizard, sharply, and the Sawhorse started on.

They had not gone far before a man ran out of a house shouting wildly: "Help! Help!"

The Sawhorse stopped short and the Wizard and Uncle Henry and the Shaggy Man and Omby Amby jumped out of the wagon and ran to the poor man's assistance. Dorothy followed them as quickly as she could.

"What's the matter?" asked the Wizard.

"Help! help!" screamed the man; "my wife has cut her finger off and she's bleeding to death!"

Then he turned and rushed back to the house, and all the party went with him. They found a woman in the front dooryard moaning and groaning as if in great pain.

"Be brave, madam!" said the Wizard, consolingly. "You won't die just because you have cut off a finger, you may be sure."

"But I haven't cut off a finger!" she sobbed.

"Then what *has* happened?" asked Dorothy.

"I—I pricked my finger with a needle while I was sewing, and—and the blood came!" she replied. "And now I'll have blood-poisoning, and the doctors will cut off my finger, and that will give me a fever and I shall die!"

"Pshaw!" said Dorothy; "I've pricked my finger many a time, and nothing happened."

"Really?" asked the woman, brightening and wiping her eyes upon her apron.

"Why, it's nothing at all," declared the girl. "You're more scared than hurt."

"Ah, that's because she's a Flutterbudget," said the Wizard, nodding wisely. "I think I know now what these people are like."

"So do I," announced Dorothy.

"Oh, boo-hoo-hoo!" sobbed the woman, giving way to a fresh burst of grief.

"What's wrong now?" asked the Shaggy Man.

"Oh, suppose I had pricked my foot!" she wailed. "Then the doctors would have cut my foot off, and I'd be lamed for life!"

"Surely, ma'am," replied the Wizard, "and if you'd pricked your nose they might cut your head off. But you see you didn't."

"But I might have!" she exclaimed, and began to cry again. So they left her and drove away in their wagon. And her husband came out and began calling "Help!" as he had before; but no one seemed to pay any attention to him.

As the travelers turned into another street they found a man walking excitedly up and down the pavement. He appeared to be in a very nervous condition and the Wizard stopped him to ask:

"Is anything wrong, sir?"

"Everything is wrong," answered the man, dismally. "I can't sleep."

"Why not?" inquired Omby Amby.

"If I go to sleep I'll have to shut my eyes," he explained; "and if I shut my eyes they may grow together, and then I'd be blind for life!"

"Did you ever hear of any one's eyes growing together?" asked Dorothy.

"No," said the man, "I never did. But it would be a dreadful thing, wouldn't it? And the thought of it makes me so nervous I'm afraid to go to sleep."

"There's no help for this case," declared the Wizard; and they went on.

At the next street corner a woman rushed up to them crying:

"Save my baby! Oh, good, kind people, save my baby!"

"Is it in danger?" asked Dorothy, noticing that the child was clasped in her arms and seemed sleeping peacefully.

"Yes, indeed," said the woman, nervously. "If I should go into the house and throw my child out of the window, it would roll way down to the bottom of the hill; and then if there were a lot of tigers and bears down there, they would tear my darling babe to pieces and eat it up!"

"Are there any tigers and bears in this neighborhood?" the Wizard asked.

"I've never heard of any," admitted the woman; "but if there were—"

"Have you any idea of throwing your baby out of the window?" questioned the little man.

"None at all," she said; "but if—"

"All your troubles are due to those 'ifs'," declared the Wizard. "If you were not a Flutterbudget you wouldn't worry."

"There's another 'if'," replied the woman. "Are you a Flutterbudget, too?"

"I will be, if I stay here long," exclaimed the Wizard, nervously.

"Another 'if'!" cried the woman.

But the Wizard did not stop to argue with her. He made the Sawhorse canter all the way down the hill, and only breathed easily when they were miles away from the village.

After they had ridden in silence for a while Dorothy turned to the little man and asked:

"Do 'ifs' really make Flutterbudgets?"

"I think the 'ifs' help," he answered seriously. "Foolish fears, and worries over nothing, with a mixture of nerves and ifs, will soon make a Flutterbudget of any one."

Then there was another long silence, for all the travelers were thinking over this statement, and nearly all decided it must be true.

The country they were now passing through was everywhere tinted purple, the prevailing color of the Gillikin Country; but as the Sawhorse ascended a hill they found that upon the other side everything was of a rich yellow hue.

"Aha!" cried the Captain General; "here is the Country of the Winkies. We are just crossing the boundary line."

"Then we may be able to lunch with the Tin Woodman," announced the Wizard, joyfully.

"Must we lunch on tin?" asked Aunt Em.

"Oh, no," replied Dorothy. "Nick Chopper knows how to feed meat people, and he will give us plenty of good things to eat, never fear. I've been to his castle before."

"Is Nick Chopper the Tin Woodman's name?" asked Uncle Henry.

"Yes; that's one of his names," answered the little girl; "and another of his names is 'Em'pror of the Winkies.' He's the King of this country, you know, but Ozma rules over all the countries of Oz."

"Does the Tin Woodman keep any Flutterbudgets or Rigmaroles at his castle?" inquired Aunt Em, uneasily.

"No, indeed," said Dorothy, positively. "He lives in a new tin castle, all full of lovely things."

"I should think it would rust," said Uncle Henry.

"He has thousands of Winkies to keep it polished for him," explained the Wizard. "His people love to do anything in their power for their beloved Emperor, so there isn't a particle of rust on all the big castle."

"I suppose they polish their Emperor, too," said Aunt Em.

"Why, some time ago he had himself nickel-plated," the Wizard answered; "so he only needs rubbing up once in a while. He's the brightest man in all the world, is dear Nick Chopper; and the kindest-hearted."

"I helped find him," said Dorothy, reflectively. "Once the Scarecrow and I found the Tin Woodman in the woods, and he was just rusted still, that time, an' no mistake. But we oiled his joints, an' got 'em good and slippery, and after that he went with us to visit the Wizard at the Em'rald City."

"Was that the time the Wizard scared you?" asked Aunt Em.

"He didn't treat us well, at first," acknowledged Dorothy; "for he made us go away and destroy the Wicked Witch. But after we found out he was only a humbug wizard we were not afraid of him."

The Wizard sighed and looked a little ashamed.

"When we try to deceive people we always make mistakes," he said. "But I'm getting to be a real wizard now, and Glinda the Good's magic, that I am trying to practice, can never harm any one."

"You were always a good man," declared Dorothy, "even when you were a bad wizard."

"He's a good wizard now," asserted Aunt Em, looking at the little man admiringly. "The way he made those tents grow out of handkerchiefs was just wonderful! And didn't he enchant the wagon wheels so they'd find the road?"

"All the people of Oz," said the Captain General, "are very proud of their Wizard. He once made some soap-bubbles that astonished the world."

The Wizard blushed at this praise, yet it pleased him. He no longer looked sad, but seemed to have recovered his usual good humor.

The country through which they now rode was thickly dotted with farmhouses, and yellow grain waved in all the fields. Many of the Winkies could be seen working on their farms and the wild and unsettled parts of Oz were by this time left far behind.

These Winkies appeared to be happy, lighthearted folk, and all removed their caps and bowed low when the red wagon with its load of travelers passed by.

It was not long before they saw something glittering in the sunshine far ahead.

"See!" cried Dorothy; "that's the Tin Castle, Aunt Em!"

And the Sawhorse, knowing his passengers were eager to arrive, broke into a swift trot that soon brought them to their destination.

CHAPTER 24

How the Tin Woodman Told the Sad News

The Tin Woodman received Princess Dorothy's party with much grace and cordiality, yet the little girl decided that something must be worrying her old friend, because he was not so merry as usual.

But at first she said nothing about this, for Uncle Henry and Aunt Em were fairly bubbling over with admiration for the beautiful tin castle and its polished tin owner. So her suspicion that something unpleasant had happened was for a time forgotten.

"Where is the Scarecrow?" she asked, when they had all been ushered into the big tin drawing-room of the castle, the Sawhorse being led around to the tin stable in the rear.

"Why, our old friend has just moved into his new mansion," explained the Tin Woodman. "It has been a long time in building, although my Winkies and many other people from all parts of the country have been busily working upon it. At last, however, it is completed, and the Scarecrow took possession of his new home just two days ago."

"I hadn't heard that he wanted a home of his own," said Dorothy. "Why doesn't he live with Ozma in the Emerald City? He used to, you know; and I thought he was happy there."

"It seems," said the Tin Woodman, "that our dear Scarecrow cannot be contented with city life, however beautiful his surroundings might be. Originally he was a farmer, for he passed his early life in a cornfield, where he was supposed to frighten away the crows."

"I know," said Dorothy, nodding. "I found him, and lifted him down from his pole."

"So now, after a long residence in the Emerald City, his tastes have turned to farm life again," continued the Tin Man. "He feels that he cannot be happy without a farm of his own, so Ozma gave him some land and every one helped him build his mansion, and now he is settled there for good."

"Who designed his house?" asked the Shaggy Man.

"I believe it was Jack Pumpkinhead, who is also a farmer," was the reply.

They were now invited to enter the tin dining room, where luncheon was served.

Aunt Em found, to her satisfaction, that Dorothy's promise was more than fulfilled; for, although the Tin Woodman had no appetite of his own, he respected the appetites of his guests and saw that they were bountifully fed.

They passed the afternoon in wandering through the beautiful gardens and grounds of the palace. The walks were all paved with sheets of tin, brightly polished, and there were tin fountains and tin statues here and there among the trees. The flowers were mostly natural flowers and grew in the regular way; but their host showed them one flower bed which was his especial pride.

"You see, all common flowers fade and die in time," he explained, "and so there are seasons when the pretty blooms are scarce. Therefore I decided to make one tin flower bed all of tin flowers, and my workmen have created them with rare skill. Here you see tin camelias, tin marigolds, tin carnations, tin poppies and tin hollyhocks growing as naturally as if they were real."

Indeed, they were a pretty sight, and glistened under the sunlight like spun silver.

"Isn't this tin hollyhock going to seed?" asked the Wizard, bending over the flowers.

"Why, I believe it is!" exclaimed the Tin Woodman, as if surprised. "I hadn't noticed that before. But I shall plant the tin seeds and raise another bed of tin hollyhocks."

In one corner of the gardens Nick Chopper had established a fishpond, in which they saw swimming and disporting themselves many pretty tin fishes.

"Would they bite on hooks?" asked Aunt Em, curiously.

The Tin Woodman seemed hurt at this question.

"Madam," said he, "do you suppose I would allow anyone to catch my beautiful fishes, even if they were foolish enough to bite on hooks? No, indeed! Every created thing is safe from harm in my domain, and I would as soon think of killing my little friend Dorothy as killing one of my tin fishes."

"The Emperor is very kind-hearted, ma'am," explained the Wizard. "If a fly happens to light upon his tin body he doesn't rudely brush it off, as some people might do; he asks it politely to find some other resting place."

"What does the fly do then?" enquired Aunt Em.

"Usually it begs his pardon and goes away," said the Wizard, gravely. "Flies like to be treated politely as well as other creatures, and here in Oz they understand what we say to them, and behave very nicely."

"Well," said Aunt Em, "the flies in Kansas, where I came from, don't understand anything but a swat. You have to smash 'em to make 'em behave; and it's the same way with 'skeeters. Do you have 'skeeters in Oz?"

"We have some very large mosquitoes here, which sing as beautifully as song birds," replied the Tin Woodman. "But they never bite or annoy our people, because they are well fed and taken care of. The reason they bite people in your country is because they are hungry—poor things!"

"Yes," agreed Aunt Em; "they're hungry, all right. An' they ain't very particular who they feed on. I'm glad you've got the 'skeeters educated in Oz."

That evening after dinner they were entertained by the Emperor's Tin Cornet Band, which played for them several sweet melodies. Also the Wizard did a few sleight-of-hand tricks to amuse the company; after which they all retired to their cosy tin bedrooms and slept soundly until morning.

After breakfast Dorothy said to the Tin Woodman:

"If you'll tell us which way to go we'll visit the Scarecrow on our way home."

"I will go with you, and show you the way," replied the Emperor; "for I must journey to-day to the Emerald City."

He looked so anxious, as he said this, that the little girl asked:

"There isn't anything wrong with Ozma, is there?"

He shook his tin head.

"Not yet," said he; "but I'm afraid the time has come when I must tell you some very bad news, little friend."

"Oh, what is it?" cried Dorothy.

"Do you remember the Nome King?" asked the Tin Woodman.

"I remember him very well," she replied.

"The Nome King has not a kind heart," said the Emperor, sadly, "and he has been harboring wicked thoughts of revenge, because we once defeated him and liberated his slaves and you took away his Magic Belt. So he has ordered his Nomes to dig a long tunnel underneath the deadly desert, so that he may march his hosts right into the Emerald City. When he gets there he intends to destroy our beautiful country."

Dorothy was much surprised to hear this.

"How did Ozma find out about the tunnel?" she asked.

"She saw it in her Magic Picture."

"Of course," said Dorothy; "I might have known that. And what is she going to do?"

"I cannot tell," was the reply.

"Pooh!" cried the Yellow Hen. "We're not afraid of the Nomes. If we roll a few of our eggs down the tunnel they'll run away back home as fast as they can go."

"Why, that's true enough!" exclaimed Dorothy. "The Scarecrow once conquered all the Nome King's army with some of Billina's eggs."

"But you do not understand all of the dreadful plot," continued the Tin Woodman. "The Nome King is clever, and he knows his Nomes would run from eggs; so he has bargained with many terrible creatures to help him. These evil spirits are not afraid of eggs or anything else, and they are very powerful. So the Nome King will send them through the tunnel first, to conquer and destroy, and then the Nomes will follow after to get their share of the plunder and slaves."

They were all startled to hear this, and every face wore a troubled look.

"Is the tunnel all ready?" asked Dorothy.

"Ozma sent me word yesterday that the tunnel was all completed except for a thin crust of earth at the end. When our enemies break through this crust they will be in the gardens of the royal palace, in the heart of the Emerald City. I offered to arm all my Winkies and march to Ozma's assistance; but she said no."

"I wonder why?" asked Dorothy.

"She answered that all the inhabitants of Oz, gathered together, were not powerful enough to fight and overcome the evil forces of the Nome King. Therefore she refuses to fight at all."

"But they will capture and enslave us, and plunder and ruin all our lovely land!" exclaimed the Wizard, greatly disturbed by this statement.

"I fear they will," said the Tin Woodman, sorrowfully. "And I also fear that those who are not fairies, such as the Wizard, and Dorothy, and her uncle and aunt, as well as Toto and Billina, will be speedily put to death by the conquerors."

"What can be done?" asked Dorothy, shuddering a little at the prospect of this awful fate.

"Nothing can be done!" gloomily replied the Emperor of the Winkies. "But since Ozma refuses my army I will go myself to the Emerald City. The least I may do is to perish beside my beloved Ruler."

CHAPTER 25

How the Scarecrow Displayed His Wisdom

This amazing news had saddened every heart and all were now anxious to return to the Emerald City and share Ozma's fate. So they started without loss of time, and as the road led past the Scarecrow's new mansion they determined to make a brief halt there and confer with him.

"The Scarecrow is probably the wisest man in all Oz," remarked the Tin Woodman, when they had started upon their journey. "His brains are plentiful and of excellent quality, and often he has told me things I might never have thought of myself. I must say I rely a good deal upon the Scarecrow's brains in this emergency."

The Tin Woodman rode on the front seat of the wagon, where Dorothy sat between him and the Wizard.

"Has the Scarecrow heard of Ozma's trouble?" asked the Captain General.

"I do not know, sir," was the reply.

"When I was a private," said Omby Amby, "I was an excellent army, as I fully proved in our war against the Nomes. But now there is not a single private left in our army, since Ozma made me the Captain General, so there is no one to fight and defend our lovely Ruler."

"True," said the Wizard. "The present army is composed only of officers, and the business of an officer is to order his men to fight. Since there are no men there can be no fighting."

"Poor Ozma!" whispered Dorothy, with tears in her sweet eyes. "It's dreadful to think of all her lovely fairy country being destroyed. I wonder if we couldn't manage to escape and get back to Kansas by means of the Magic Belt? And we might take Ozma with us and all work hard to get money for her, so she wouldn't be so *very* lonely and unhappy about the loss of her fairyland."

"Do you think there would be any work for *me* in Kansas?" asked the Tin Woodman.

"If you are hollow, they might use you in a canning factory," suggested Uncle Henry. "But I can't see the use of your working for a living. You never eat or sleep or need a new suit of clothes."

"I was not thinking of myself," replied the Emperor, with dignity. "I merely wondered if I could not help to support Dorothy and Ozma."

As they indulged in these sad plans for the future they journeyed in sight of the Scarecrow's new mansion, and even though filled with care and worry over the impending fate of Oz, Dorothy could not help a feeling of wonder at the sight she saw.

The Scarecrow's new house was shaped like an immense ear of corn. The rows of kernels were made of solid gold, and the green upon which the ear stood upright was a mass of sparkling emeralds.

Upon the very top of the structure was perched a figure representing the Scarecrow himself, and upon his extended arms, as well as upon his head, were several crows carved out of ebony and having ruby eyes. You may imagine how big this ear of corn was when I tell you that a single gold kernel formed a window, swinging outward upon hinges, while a row of four kernels opened to make the front entrance. Inside there were five stories, each story being a single room.

The gardens around the mansion consisted of cornfields, and Dorothy acknowledged that the place was in all respects a very appropriate home for her good friend the Scarecrow.

"He would have been very happy here, I'm sure," she said, "if only the Nome King had left us alone. But if Oz is destroyed of course this place will be destroyed too."

"Yes," replied the Tin Woodman, "and also my beautiful tin castle, that has been my joy and pride."

"Jack Pumpkinhead's house will go too," remarked the Wizard, "as well as Professor Wogglebug's Athletic College, and Ozma's royal palace, and all our other handsome buildings."

"Yes, Oz will indeed become a desert when the Nome King gets through with it," sighed Omby Amby.

The Scarecrow came out to meet them and gave them all a hearty welcome.

"I hear you have decided always to live in the Land of Oz, after this," he said to Dorothy; "and that will delight my heart, for I have greatly disliked our frequent partings. But why are you all so downcast?"

"Have you heard the news?" asked the Tin Woodman.

"No news to make me sad," replied the Scarecrow.

Then Nick Chopper told his friend of the Nome King's tunnel, and how the evil creatures of the North had allied themselves with the underground monarch for the purpose of conquering and destroying Oz. "Well," said the Scarecrow, "it certainly looks bad for Ozma, and all of us. But I believe it is wrong to worry over anything before it happens. It is surely time enough to be sad when our country is despoiled and our people made slaves. So let us not deprive ourselves of the few happy hours remaining to us."

"Ah! that is real wisdom," declared the Shaggy Man, approvingly. "After we become really unhappy we shall regret these few hours that are left to us, unless we enjoy them to the utmost."

"Nevertheless," said the Scarecrow, "I shall go with you to the Emerald City and offer Ozma my services."

"She says we can do nothing to oppose our enemies," announced the Tin Woodman.

"And doubtless she is right, sir," answered the Scarecrow. "Still, she will appreciate our sympathy, and it is the duty of Ozma's friends to stand by her side when the final disaster occurs."

He then led them into his queer mansion and showed them the beautiful rooms in all the five stories. The lower room was a grand reception hall, with a hand-organ in one corner. This instrument the Scarecrow, when alone, could turn to amuse himself, as he was very fond of music. The walls were hung with white silk, upon which flocks of black crows were embroidered in black diamonds. Some of the chairs were made in the shape of big crows and upholstered with cushions of corn-colored silk.

The second story contained a fine banquet room, where the Scarecrow might entertain his guests, and the three stories above that were bedchambers exquisitely furnished and decorated.

"From these rooms," said the Scarecrow, proudly, "one may obtain fine views of the surrounding cornfields. The corn I grow is always husky, and I call the ears my regiments, because they have so many kernels. Of course I cannot ride my cobs, but I really don't care shucks about that. Taken altogether, my farm will stack up with any in the neighborhood."

The visitors partook of some light refreshment and then hurried away to resume the road to the Emerald City. The Scarecrow found a seat in the wagon between Omby Amby and the Shaggy Man, and his weight did not add much to the load because he was stuffed with straw.

"You will notice I have one oat-field on my property," he remarked, as they drove away. "Oat-straw is, I have found, the best of all straws to re-stuff myself with when my interior gets musty or out of shape."

"Are you able to re-stuff yourself without help?" asked Aunt Em. "I should think that after the straw was taken out of you there wouldn't be anything left but your clothes."

"You are almost correct, madam," he answered. "My servants do the stuffing, under my direction. For my head, in which are my excellent brains, is a bag tied at the bottom. My face is neatly painted upon one side of the bag, as you may see. My head does not need restuffing, as my body does, for all that it requires is to have the face touched up with fresh paint occasionally."

It was not far from the Scarecrow's mansion to the farm of Jack

Pumpkinhead, and when they arrived there both Uncle Henry and Aunt Em were much impressed. The farm was one vast pumpkin field, and some of the pumpkins were of enormous size. In one of them, which had been neatly hollowed out, Jack himself lived, and he declared that it was a very comfortable residence. The reason he grew so many pumpkins was in order that he might change his head as often as it became wrinkled or threatened to spoil.

The pumpkin-headed man welcomed his visitors joyfully and offered them several delicious pumpkin pies to eat.

"I don't indulge in pumpkin pies myself, for two reasons," he said. "One reason is that were I to eat pumpkins I would become a cannibal, and the other reason is that I never eat, not being hollow inside."

"Very good reasons," agreed the Scarecrow.

They told Jack Pumpkinhead the dreadful news about the Nome King, and he decided to go with them to the Emerald City and help comfort Ozma.

"I had expected to live here in ease and comfort for many centuries," said Jack, dolefully; "but of course if the Nome King destroys everything in Oz I shall be destroyed too. Really, it seems too bad, doesn't it?"

They were soon on their journey again, and so swiftly did the Sawhorse draw the wagon over the smooth roads that before twilight fell they had reached the royal palace in the Emerald City, and were at their journey's end.

CHAPTER 26

How Ozma Refused to Fight for Her Kingdom

Ozma was in her rose garden picking a bouquet when the party arrived, and she greeted all her old and new friends as smilingly and sweetly as ever.

Dorothy's eyes were full of tears as she kissed the lovely Ruler of Oz, and she whispered to her:

"Oh, Ozma, Ozma! I'm so sorry!"

Ozma seemed surprised.

"Sorry for what, Dorothy?" she asked.

"For all your trouble about the Nome King," was the reply.

Ozma laughed with genuine amusement.

"Why, that has not troubled me a bit, dear Princess," she replied. Then, looking around at the sad faces of her friends, she added: "Have you all been worrying about this tunnel?"

"We have!" they exclaimed in a chorus.

"Well, perhaps it is more serious than I imagined," admitted the fair Ruler; "but I haven't given the matter much thought. After dinner we will all meet together and talk it over."

So they went to their rooms and prepared for dinner, and Dorothy dressed herself in her prettiest gown and put on her coronet, for she thought that this might be the last time she would ever appear as a Princess of Oz.

The Scarecrow, the Tin Woodman and Jack Pumpkinhead all sat at the dinner table, although none of them was made so he could eat. Usually they served to enliven the meal with their merry talk, but to-night all seemed strangely silent and uneasy.

As soon as the dinner was finished Ozma led the company to her own private room in which hung the Magic Picture. When they had seated themselves the Scarecrow was the first to speak.

"Is the Nome King's tunnel finished, Ozma?" he asked.

"It was completed to-day," she replied. "They have built it right under my palace grounds, and it ends in front of the Forbidden Fountain. Nothing but a crust of earth remains to separate our enemies from us, and when they march here they will easily break through this crust and rush upon us."

"Who will assist the Nome King?" inquired the Scarecrow.

"The Whimsies, the Growleywogs and the Phanfasms," she replied. "I watched to-day in my Magic Picture the messengers whom the Nome King sent to all these people to summon them to assemble in his great caverns."

"Let us see what they are doing now," suggested the Tin Woodman.

So Ozma wished to see the Nome King's cavern, and at once the landscape faded from the Magic Picture and was replaced by the scene then being enacted in the jeweled cavern of King Roquat.

A wild and startling scene it was which the Oz people beheld.

Before the Nome King stood the Chief of the Whimsies and the Grand Gallipoot of the Growleywogs, surrounded by their most skillful generals. Very fierce and powerful they looked, so that even the Nome King and General Guph, who stood beside his master, seemed a bit fearful in the presence of their allies.

Now a still more formidable creature entered the cavern. It was the

First and Foremost of the Phanfasms and he proudly sat down in King Roquat's own throne and demanded the right to lead his forces through the tunnel in advance of all the others. The First and Foremost now appeared to all eyes in his hairy skin and the bear's head. What his real form was even Roquat did not know.

Through the arches leading into the vast series of caverns that lay beyond the throne room of King Roquat, could be seen ranks upon ranks of the invaders—thousands of Phanfasms, Growleywogs and Whimsies standing in serried lines, while behind them were massed the thousands upon thousands of General Guph's own army of Nomes.

"Listen!" whispered Ozma. "I think we can hear what they are saying."

So they kept still and listened.

"Is all ready?" demanded the First and Foremost, haughtily.

"The tunnel is finally completed," replied General Guph.

"How long will it take us to march to the Emerald City?" asked the Grand Gallipoot of the Growleywogs.

"If we start at midnight," replied the Nome King, "we shall arrive at the Emerald City by daybreak. Then, while all the Oz people are sleeping, we will capture them and make them our slaves. After that we will destroy the city itself and march through the Land of Oz, burning and devastating as we go."

"Good!" cried the First and Foremost. "When we get through with Oz it will be a desert wilderness. Ozma shall be my slave."

"She shall be *my* slave!" shouted the Grand Gallipoot, angrily.

"We'll decide that by and by," said King Roquat, hastily. "Don't let us quarrel now, friends. First let us conquer Oz, and then we will divide the spoils of war in a satisfactory manner."

The First and Foremost smiled wickedly; but he only said:

"I and my Phanfasms go first, for nothing on earth can oppose our power."

They all agreed to that, knowing the Phanfasms to be the mightiest of the combined forces. King Roquat now invited them to attend a banquet he had prepared, where they might occupy themselves in eating and drinking until midnight arrived.

As they had now seen and heard all of the plot against them that they cared to, Ozma allowed her Magic Picture to fade away. Then she turned to her friends and said:

"Our enemies will be here sooner than I expected. What do you advise me to do?"

"It is now too late to assemble our people," said the Tin Woodman, despondently. "If you had allowed me to arm and drill my Winkies we might have put up a good fight and destroyed many of our enemies before we were conquered."

"The Munchkins are good fighters, too," said Omby Amby; "and so are the Gillikins."

"But I do not wish to fight," declared Ozma, firmly. "No one has the right to destroy any living creatures, however evil they may be, or to hurt them or make them unhappy. I will not fight—even to save my kingdom."[1]

"The Nome King is not so particular," remarked the Scarecrow. "He intends to destroy us all and ruin our beautiful country."

"Because the Nome King intends to do evil is no excuse for my doing the same," replied Ozma.

"Self-preservation is the first law of nature," quoted the Shaggy Man.

"True," she said, readily. "I would like to discover a plan to save ourselves without fighting."

That seemed a hopeless task to them, but realizing that Ozma was determined not to fight, they tried to think of some means that might promise escape.

"Couldn't we bribe our enemies, by giving them a lot of emeralds and gold?" asked Jack Pumpkinhead.

"No, because they believe they are able to take everything we have," replied the Ruler.

"I have thought of something," said Dorothy.

"What is it, dear?" asked Ozma.

"Let us use the Magic Belt to wish all of us in Kansas. We will put some emeralds in our pockets, and can sell them in Topeka for enough to pay off the mortgage on Uncle Henry's farm. Then we can all live together and be happy."

"A clever idea!" exclaimed the Scarecrow.

"Kansas is a very good country. I've been there," said the Shaggy Man.

"That seems to me an excellent plan," approved the Tin Woodman.

"No!" said Ozma, decidedly. "Never will I desert my people and leave them to so cruel a fate. I will use the Magic Belt to send the rest of you to Kansas, if you wish, but if my beloved country must be destroyed and my people enslaved I will remain and share their fate."

"Quite right," asserted the Scarecrow, sighing. "I will remain with you."

"And so will I," declared the Tin Woodman and the Shaggy Man and Jack Pumpkinhead, in turn. Tiktok, the machine man, also said he intended to stand by Ozma. "For," said he, "I should be of no use at all in Kansas."

"For my part," announced Dorothy, gravely, "if the Ruler of Oz must not desert her people, a Princess of Oz has no right to run away, either. I'm willing to become a slave with the rest of you; so all we can do with the Magic Belt is to use it to send Uncle Henry and Aunt Em back to Kansas."

"I've been a slave all my life,"[2] Aunt Em replied, with considerable cheerfulness, "and so has Henry. I guess we won't go back to Kansas, anyway. I'd rather take my chances with the rest of you."

Ozma smiled upon them all gratefully.

"There is no need to despair just yet," she said. "I'll get up early tomorrow morning and be at the Forbidden Fountain[3] when the fierce warriors break through the crust of earth. I will speak to them pleasantly and perhaps they won't be so very bad, after all."

"Why do they call it the Forbidden Fountain?" asked Dorothy, thoughtfully.

"Don't you know, dear?" returned Ozma, surprised.

"No," said Dorothy. "Of course I've seen the fountain in the palace grounds, ever since I first came to Oz; and I've read the sign which says: 'All Persons are Forbidden to Drink at this Fountain.' But I never knew *why* they were forbidden. The water seems clear and sparkling and it bubbles up in a golden basin all the time."

"That water," declared Ozma, gravely, "is the most dangerous thing in all the Land of Oz. It is the Water of Oblivion."

"What does that mean?" asked Dorothy.

"Whoever drinks at the Forbidden Fountain at once forgets everything he has ever known," Ozma asserted.

"It wouldn't be a bad way to forget our troubles," suggested Uncle Henry.

"That is true; but you would forget everything else, and become as ignorant as a baby," returned Ozma.

"Does it make one crazy?" asked Dorothy.

"No; it only makes one forget," replied the girl Ruler. "It is said that once—long, long ago—a wicked King ruled Oz, and made himself and all his people very miserable and unhappy. So Glinda, the Good Sorceress, placed this fountain here, and the King drank of its water and forgot all his wickedness. His mind became innocent and vacant, and when he learned the things of life again they were all good things. But the people remembered how wicked their King had been, and were still afraid of him. Therefore he made them all drink of the Water of Oblivion and forget everything they had known, so that they became as simple and innocent as their King. After that they all grew wise together, and their wisdom was good, so that peace and happiness reigned in the land. But for fear some one might drink of the water again, and in an instant forget all he had learned, the King put that sign upon the fountain, where it has remained for many centuries up to this very day."

They had all listened intently to Ozma's story, and when she finished speaking there was a long period of silence while all thought upon the curious magical power of the Water of Oblivion.

Finally the Scarecrow's painted face took on a broad smile that stretched the cloth as far as it would go.

"How thankful I am," he said, "that I have such an excellent assortment of brains!"

"I gave you the best brains I ever mixed," declared the Wizard, with an air of pride.

"You did, indeed!" agreed the Scarecrow, "and they work so splendidly that they have found a way to save Oz—to save us all!"

"I'm glad to hear that," said the Wizard. "We never needed saving more than we do just now."

"Do you mean to say you can save us from those awful Phanfasms, and Growleywogs and Whimsies?" asked Dorothy eagerly.

"I'm sure of it, my dear," asserted the Scarecrow, still smiling genially.

"Tell us how!" cried the Tin Woodman.

"Not now," said the Scarecrow. "You may all go to bed, and I advise you to forget your worries just as completely as if you had drunk of the Water of Oblivion in the Forbidden Fountain. I'm going to stay here and tell my plan to Ozma alone, but if you will all be at the Forbidden Fountain at daybreak, you'll see how easily we will save the kingdom when our enemies break through the crust of earth and come from the tunnel."

So they went away and left the Scarecrow and Ozma alone; but Dorothy could not sleep a wink all night.

"He is only a Scarecrow," she said to herself, "and I'm not sure that his mixed brains are as clever as he thinks they are."

But she knew that if the Scarecrow's plan failed they were all lost; so she tried to have faith in him.

CHAPTER 27

How the Fierce Warriors Invaded Oz

The Nome King and his terrible allies sat at the banquet table until midnight. There was much quarreling between the Growleywogs and Phanfasms, and one of the wee-headed Whimsies got angry at General Guph and choked him until he nearly stopped breathing. Yet no one was seriously hurt, and the Nome King felt much relieved when the clock struck twelve and they all sprang up and seized their weapons.

"Aha!" shouted the First and Foremost. "Now to conquer the Land of Oz!"

He marshaled his Phanfasms in battle array and at his word of command they marched into the tunnel and began the long journey through it to the Emerald City. The First and Foremost intended to take all the treasures in Oz for himself; to kill all who could be killed and enslave the rest; to destroy and lay waste the whole country, and afterward to conquer and enslave the Nomes, the Growleywogs and the Whimsies. And he knew his power was sufficient to enable him to do all these things easily.

Next marched into the tunnel the army of gigantic Growleywogs, with their Grand Gallipoot at their head. They were dreadful beings, indeed, and longed to get to Oz that they might begin to pilfer and destroy. The Grand Gallipoot was a little afraid of the First and Foremost, but had a cunning plan to murder or destroy that powerful being and secure the wealth of Oz for himself. Mighty little of the plunder would the Nome King get, thought the Grand Gallipoot.

The Chief of the Whimsies now marched his false-headed forces into the tunnel. In his wicked little head was a plot to destroy both the First and Foremost and the Grand Gallipoot. He intended to let them conquer Oz, since they insisted on going first; but he would afterward treacherously destroy them, as well as King Roquat, and keep all the slaves and treasure of Ozma's kingdom for himself.

After all his dangerous allies had marched into the tunnel the Nome King and General Guph started to follow them, at the head of fifty thousand Nomes, all fully armed.

"Guph," said the King, "those creatures ahead of us mean mischief. They intend to get everything for themselves and leave us nothing."

"I know," replied the General; "but they are not as clever as they think they are. When you get the Magic Belt you must at once wish the Whimsies and Growleywogs and the Phanfasms all back into their own countries—and the Belt will surely take them there."

"Good!" cried the King. "An excellent plan, Guph. I'll do it. While they are conquering Oz I'll get the Magic Belt, and then only the Nomes will remain to ravage the country."

So you see there was only one thing that all were agreed upon—that Oz should be destroyed.

On, on, on the vast ranks of invaders marched, filling the tunnel from side to side. With a steady tramp, tramp, they advanced, every step taking them nearer to the beautiful Emerald City.

"Nothing can save the Land of Oz!" thought the First and Foremost, scowling until his bear face was as black as the tunnel.

"The Emerald City is as good as destroyed already!" muttered the Grand Gallipoot, shaking his war club fiercely.

"In a few hours Oz will be a desert!" said the Chief of the Whimsies, with an evil laugh.

"My dear Guph," remarked the Nome King to his General, "at last my vengeance upon Ozma of Oz and her people is about to be accomplished."

"You are right!" declared the General. "Ozma is surely lost."

And now the First and Foremost, who was in advance and nearing the Emerald City, began to cough and to sneeze.

"This tunnel is terribly dusty," he growled, angrily. "I'll punish that Nome King for not having it swept clean. My throat and eyes are getting full of dust and I'm as thirsty as a fish!"

The Grand Gallipoot was coughing too, and his throat was parched and dry.

"What a dusty place!" he cried. "I'll be glad when we reach Oz, where we can get a drink."

"Who has any water?" asked the Whimsie Chief, gasping and choking. But none of his followers carried a drop of water, so he hastened on to get through the dusty tunnel to the Land of Oz.

"Where did all this dust come from?" demanded General Guph, trying hard to swallow but finding his throat so dry he couldn't.

"I don't know," answered the Nome King. "I've been in the tunnel every day while it was being built, but I never noticed any dust before."

"Let's hurry!" cried the General. "I'd give half the gold in Oz for a drink of water."

The dust grew thicker and thicker, and the throats and eyes and noses of the invaders were filled with it. But not one halted or turned back. They hurried forward more fierce and vengeful than ever.

CHAPTER 28

How They Drank at the Forbidden Fountain

The Scarecrow had no need to sleep; neither had the Tin Woodman or Tiktok or Jack Pumpkinhead. So they all wandered out into the palace grounds and stood beside the sparkling water of the Forbidden Fountain until daybreak. During this time they indulged in occasional conversation.

"Nothing could make me forget what I know," remarked the Scarecrow, gazing into the fountain, "for I cannot drink the Water of Oblivion or water of any kind. And I am glad that this is so, for I consider my wisdom unexcelled."

"You are cer-tain-ly ve-ry wise," agreed Tiktok. "For my part, I can on-ly think by ma-chin-er-y, so I do not pre-tend to know as much as you do."

"My tin brains are very bright, but that is all I claim for them," said Nick Chopper, modestly. "Yet I do not aspire to being very wise, for I have noticed that the happiest people are those who do not let their brains oppress them."

"Mine never worry me," Jack Pumpkinhead acknowledged. "There are many seeds of thought in my head, but they do not sprout easily. I am glad that it is so, for if I occupied my days in thinking I should have no time for anything else."

In this cheery mood they passed the hours until the first golden streaks of dawn appeared in the sky. Then Ozma joined them, as fresh and lovely as ever and robed in one of her prettiest gowns.

"Our enemies have not yet arrived," said the Scarecrow, after greeting affectionately the sweet and girlish Ruler.

"They will soon be here," she said, "for I have just glanced at my Magic Picture, and have seen them coughing and choking with the dust in the tunnel."

"Oh, is there dust in the tunnel?" asked the Tin Woodman.

"Yes; Ozma placed it there by means of the Magic Belt," explained the Scarecrow, with one of his broad smiles.

Then Dorothy came to them, Uncle Henry and Aunt Em following close after her. The little girl's eyes were heavy because she had had a sleepless and anxious night. Toto walked by her side, but the little dog's spirits were very much subdued. Billina, who was always up by daybreak, was not long in joining the group by the fountain.

The Wizard and the Shaggy Man next arrived, and soon after appeared Omby Amby, dressed in his best uniform.

"There lies the tunnel," said Ozma, pointing to a part of the ground just before the Forbidden Fountain, "and in a few moments the dreadful invaders will break through the earth and swarm over the land. Let us all stand on the other side of the Fountain and watch to see what happens."

At once they followed her suggestion and moved around the fountain of the Water of Oblivion. There they stood silent and expectant until the earth beyond gave way with a sudden crash and up leaped the powerful form of the First and Foremost, followed by all his grim warriors.

As the leader sprang forward his gleaming eyes caught the play of the fountain and he rushed toward it and drank eagerly of the sparkling water. Many of the other Phanfasms drank, too, in order to clear their dry and dusty throats. Then they stood around and looked at one another with simple, wondering smiles.

The First and Foremost saw Ozma and her companions beyond the fountain, but instead of making an effort to capture her he merely stared at her in pleased admiration of her beauty—for he had forgotten where he was and why he had come there.

But now the Grand Gallipoot arrived, rushing from the tunnel with a hoarse cry of mingled rage and thirst. He too saw the fountain and hastened to drink of its forbidden waters. The other Growleywogs were not slow to follow suit, and even before they had finished drinking the Chief of the Whimsies and his people came to push them away, while they one and all cast off their false heads that they might slake their thirst at the fountain.

When the Nome King and General Guph arrived they both made a dash to drink, but the General was so mad with thirst that he knocked his King over, and while Roquat lay sprawling upon the ground the General drank heartily of the Water of Oblivion.

This rude act of his General made the Nome King so angry that for a moment he forgot he was thirsty and rose to his feet to glare upon the group of terrible warriors he had brought here to assist him. He saw Ozma and her people, too, and yelled out:

"Why don't you capture them? Why don't you conquer Oz, you idiots? Why do you stand there like a lot of dummies?"

But the great warriors had become like little children. They had forgotten all their enmity against Ozma and against Oz. They had even forgotten who they themselves were, or why they were in this strange and beautiful country. As for the Nome King, they did not recognize him, and wondered who he was.

The sun came up and sent its flood of silver rays to light the faces of the invaders. The frowns and scowls and evil looks were all gone. Even the most monstrous of the creatures there assembled smiled innocently and seemed lighthearted and content merely to be alive.

Not so with Roquat, the Nome King. He had not drunk from the Forbidden Fountain and all his former rage against Ozma and Dorothy now inflamed him as fiercely as ever. The sight of General Guph babbling like a happy child and playing with his hands in the cool waters of the fountain astonished and maddened Red Roquat. Seeing that his terrible allies and his own General refused to act, the Nome King turned to order his great army of Nomes to advance from the tunnel and seize the helpless Oz people.

But the Scarecrow suspected what was in the King's mind and spoke a word to the Tin Woodman. Together they ran at Roquat and grabbing him up tossed him into the great basin of the fountain.

The Nome King's body was round as a ball, and it bobbed up and down in the Water of Oblivion while he spluttered and screamed with fear lest he should drown. And when he cried out his mouth filled with water, which ran down his throat, so that straightway he forgot all he had formerly known just as completely as had all the other invaders.

Ozma and Dorothy could not refrain from laughing to see their dreaded enemies become as harmless as babes. There was no danger now that Oz would be destroyed. The only question remaining to solve was how to get rid of this horde of intruders.

The Shaggy Man kindly pulled the Nome King out of the fountain and set him upon his thin legs. Roquat was dripping wet, but he chat-

tered and laughed and wanted to drink more of the water. No thought
of injuring any person was now in his mind.

Before he left the tunnel he had commanded his fifty thousand
Nomes to remain there until he ordered them to advance, as he
wished to give his allies time to conquer Oz before he appeared with
his own army. Ozma did not wish all these Nomes to overrun her
land, so she advanced to King Roquat and taking his hand in her own
said gently:

"Who are you? What is your name?"

"I don't know," he replied, smiling at her. "Who are you, my
dear?"

"My name is Ozma," she said; "and your name is Roquat."

"Oh, is it?" he replied, seeming pleased.

"Yes; you are King of the Nomes," she said.

"Ah; I wonder what the Nomes are!" returned the King, as if puzzled.

"They are underground elves, and that tunnel over there is full of
them," she answered. "You have a beautiful cavern at the other end
of the tunnel, so you must go to your Nomes and say: 'March home!'
Then follow after them and in time you will reach the pretty cavern
where you live."

The Nome King was much pleased to learn this, for he had forgotten he had a cavern. So he went to the tunnel and said to his army:
"March home!" At once the Nomes turned and marched back
through the tunnel, and the King followed after them, laughing with
delight to find his orders so readily obeyed.

The Wizard went to General Guph, who was trying to count his
fingers, and told him to follow the Nome King, who was his master.
Guph meekly obeyed, and so all the Nomes quitted the Land of Oz
forever.

But there were still the Phanfasms and Whimsies and Growleywogs
standing around in groups, and they were so many that they filled the
gardens and trampled upon the flowers and grass because they did not
know that the tender plants would be injured by their clumsy feet. But
in all other respects they were perfectly harmless and played together
like children or gazed with pleasure upon the pretty sights of the
royal gardens.

After counseling with the Scarecrow Ozma sent Omby Amby to the
palace for the Magic Belt, and when the Captain General returned
with it the Ruler of Oz at once clasped the precious Belt around her
waist.

"I wish all these strange people—the Whimsies and the Growley-wogs and the Phanfasms—safe back in their own homes!" she said.

It all happened in a twinkling, for of course the wish was no sooner spoken than it was granted.

All the hosts of the invaders were gone, and only the trampled grass showed that they had ever been in the Land of Oz.

CHAPTER 29

How Glinda Worked a Magic Spell

"That was better than fighting," said Ozma, when all our friends were assembled in the palace after the exciting events of the morning; and each and every one agreed with her.

"No one was hurt," said the Wizard delightedly.

"And no one hurt us," added Aunt Em.

"But, best of all," said Dorothy, "the wicked people have all forgotten their wickedness, and will not wish to hurt any one after this."

"True, Princess," declared the Shaggy Man. "It seems to me that to have reformed all those evil characters is more important than to have saved Oz."

"Nevertheless," remarked the Scarecrow, "I am glad Oz is saved. I can now go back to my new mansion and live happily."

"And I am glad and grateful that my pumpkin farm is saved," said Jack.

"For my part," added the Tin Woodman, "I cannot express my joy that my lovely tin castle is not to be demolished by wicked enemies."

"Still," said Tiktok, "o-ther en-e-mies may come to Oz some day."

"Why do you allow your clock-work brains to interrupt our joy?" asked Omby Amby, frowning at the machine man.

"I say what I am wound up to say," answered Tiktok.

"And you are right," declared Ozma. "I myself have been thinking of this very idea, and it seems to me there are entirely too many ways for people to get to the Land of Oz. We used to think the deadly desert that surrounds us was enough protection; but that is no longer the case. The Wizard and Dorothy have both come here through the air, and I am told the earth people have invented airships that can fly anywhere they wish them to go."

"Why, sometimes they do, and sometimes they don't," asserted Dorothy.

"But in time the airships may cause us trouble," continued Ozma, "for if the earth folk learn how to manage them we would be overrun with visitors who would ruin our lovely, secluded fairyland."[1]

"That is true enough," agreed the Wizard.

"Also the desert fails to protect us in other ways," Ozma went on, thoughtfully. "Johnny Dooit[2] once made a sandboat that sailed across it, and the Nome King made a tunnel under it. So I believe something ought to be done to cut us off from the rest of the world entirely, so that no one in the future will ever be able to intrude upon us."

"How will you do that?" asked the Scarecrow.

"I do not know; but in some way I am sure it can be accomplished. To-morrow I will make a journey to the castle of Glinda the Good, and ask her advice."

"May I go with you?" asked Dorothy, eagerly.

"Of course, my dear Princess; and also I invite any of our friends here who would like to undertake the journey."

They all declared they wished to accompany their girl Ruler, for this was indeed an important mission, since the future of the Land of Oz to a great extent depended upon it. So Ozma gave orders to her servants to prepare for the journey on the morrow.

That day she watched her Magic Picture, and when it showed her that all the Nomes had returned through the tunnel to their underground caverns, Ozma used the Magic Belt to close up the tunnel, so that the earth underneath the desert sands became as solid as it was before the Nomes began to dig.

Early the following morning a gay cavalcade set out to visit the famous Sorceress, Glinda the Good. Ozma and Dorothy rode in a chariot drawn by the Cowardly Lion and the Hungry Tiger, while the Sawhorse drew the red wagon in which rode the rest of the party.

With hearts light and free from care they traveled merrily along through the lovely and fascinating Land of Oz, and in good season reached the stately castle in which resided the Sorceress.

Glinda knew that they were coming.

"I have been reading about you in my Magic Book," she said, as she greeted them in her gracious way.

"What is your Magic Book like?" inquired Aunt Em, curiously.

"It is a record of everything that happens," replied the Sorceress. "As soon as an event takes place, anywhere in the world, it is immediately found printed in my Magic Book. So when I read its pages I am well informed."

"Did it tell how our enemies drank the Water of 'Blivion?" asked Dorothy.

"Yes, my dear; it told all about it. And also it told me you were all coming to my castle, and why."

"Then," said Ozma, "I suppose you know what is in my mind, and that I am seeking a way to prevent any one in the future from discovering the Land of Oz."

"Yes; I know that. And while you were on your journey I have thought of a way to accomplish your desire. For it seems to me unwise to allow too many outside people to come here. Dorothy, with her uncle and aunt, has now returned to Oz to live always, and there is no reason why we should leave any way open for others to travel uninvited to our fairyland. Let us make it impossible for any one ever to communicate with us in any way, after this. Then we may live peacefully and contentedly."

"Your advice is wise," returned Ozma. "I thank you, Glinda, for your promise to assist me."

"But how can you do it?" asked Dorothy. "How can you keep every one from ever finding Oz?"

"By making our country invisible to all eyes but our own," replied the Sorceress, smiling. "I have a magic charm powerful enough to accomplish that wonderful feat, and now that we have been warned of our danger by the Nome King's invasion, I believe we must not hesitate to separate ourselves forever from all the rest of the world."[3]

"I agree with you," said the Ruler of Oz.

"Won't it make any difference to us?" asked Dorothy, doubtfully.

"No, my dear," Glinda answered, assuringly. "We shall still be able to see each other and everything in the Land of Oz. It won't affect us at all; but those who fly through the air over our country will look down and see nothing at all. Those who come to the edge of the desert, or try to cross it, will catch no glimpse of Oz, or know in what direction it lies. No one will try to tunnel to us again because we cannot be seen and therefore cannot be found. In other words, the Land of Oz will entirely disappear from the knowledge of the rest of the world."

"That's all right," said Dorothy, cheerfully. "You may make Oz invis'ble as soon as you please, for all I care."

"It is already invisible," Glinda stated. "I knew Ozma's wishes, and performed the Magic Spell before you arrived."

Ozma seized the hand of the Sorceress and pressed it gratefully.
"Thank you!" she said.

CHAPTER 30

How the Story of Oz Came to an End

The writer of these Oz stories has received a little note from Princess
Dorothy of Oz which, for a time, has made him feel rather discontented. The note was written on a broad white feather from a stork's
wing, and it said:

> "You will never hear anything more about Oz,[1] because we are now
> cut off forever from all the rest of the world. But Toto and I will always
> love you and all the other children who love us.
>   "DOROTHY GALE."

This seemed to me too bad, at first, for Oz is a very interesting
fairyland. Still, we have no right to feel grieved, for we have had
enough of the history of the Land of Oz to fill six story books, and
from its quaint people and their strange adventures we have been able
to learn many useful and amusing things.

So good luck to little Dorothy and her companions. May they live
long in their invisible country and be very happy!

THE END

GLINDA OF OZ

This Book is Dedicated to
My Son
Robert Stanton Baum

TO OUR READERS

Glinda the Good, lovely Sorceress of the Land of Oz and friend of Princess Ozma and Dorothy, has lots of personal acquaintances who want to know more about her. So, in the new Oz story, Mr. L. Frank Baum, Royal Historian of Oz, has written a whole book about how Glinda and the Wizard worked with all their might to save the Princess and Dorothy from the dire dangers which threatened them when they went among the warring tribes of the Flatheads and Skeezers.

The wicked Queen Coo-ee-oh, a vain and evil witch, was really to blame for all the trouble. She surely succeeded in getting every one on the magic, glass-domed island of the Skeezers into amazing difficulties. When Mr. Baum tells you how worried everybody in the Land of Oz felt about the Princess Ozma and Dorothy and what wonderful sorcery Glinda had to perform to save them, you'll be thrilled with excitement and admiration. He reveals the most hidden mysteries of magic.

Mr. Baum did his best to answer all the letters[1] from his small earth-friends before he had to leave them, but he couldn't answer quite all, for there were very many. In May, nineteen hundred nineteen, he went away[2] to take his stories to the little child-souls who had lived here too long ago to read the Oz stories for themselves.

We are sorry he could not stay here and we are sad to tell you this is his last complete story. But he left some unfinished notes about the Princess Ozma and Dorothy and the Oz people and we promise that some day we will put them all together like a picture puzzle and give you more stories of the wonderful Land of Oz.

Cordially, your friends,
The Publishers.

LIST OF CHAPTERS

CHAPTER 1

The Call to Duty

Glinda, the good Sorceress of Oz, sat in the grand court of her palace, surrounded by her maids of honor—a hundred of the most beautiful girls of the Fairyland of Oz. The palace court was built of rare marbles, exquisitely polished. Fountains tinkled musically here and there; the vast colonnade, open to the south, allowed the maidens, as they raised their heads from their embroideries, to gaze upon a vista of rose-hued fields and groves of trees bearing fruits or laden with sweet-scented flowers. At times one of the girls would start a song, the others joining in the chorus, or one would rise and dance, gracefully swaying to the music of a harp played by a companion. And then Glinda smiled, glad to see her maids mixing play with work.

Presently among the fields an object was seen moving, threading the broad path that led to the castle gate. Some of the girls looked upon this object enviously; the Sorceress merely gave it a glance and nodded her stately head as if pleased, for it meant the coming of her friend and mistress—the only one in all the land that Glinda bowed to.

Then up the path trotted a wooden animal attached to a red wagon, and as the quaint steed halted at the gate there descended from the wagon two young girls, Ozma, Ruler of Oz, and her companion, Princess Dorothy. Both were dressed in simple white muslin gowns, and as they ran up the marble steps of the palace they laughed and chatted as gaily as if they were not the most important persons in the world's loveliest fairyland.

The maids of honor had risen and stood with bowed heads to greet the royal Ozma, while Glinda came forward with outstretched arms to greet her guests.

"We've just come on a visit, you know," said Ozma. "Both Dorothy and I were wondering how we should pass the day when we happened to think we'd not been to your Quadling Country for weeks, so we took the Sawhorse and rode straight here."

"And we came so fast," added Dorothy, "that our hair is blown all fuzzy, for the Sawhorse makes a wind of his own. Usually it's a day's journey from the Em'rald City, but I don't s'pose we were two hours on the way."

"You are most welcome," said Glinda the Sorceress, and led them through the court to her magnificent reception hall. Ozma took the arm of her hostess, but Dorothy lagged behind, kissing some of the maids she knew best, talking with others, and making them all feel that she was their friend. When at last she joined Glinda and Ozma in the reception hall, she found them talking earnestly about the condition of the people, and how to make them more happy and contented—although they were already the happiest and most contented folks in all the world.

This interested Ozma, of course, but it didn't interest Dorothy very much, so the little girl ran over to a big table on which was lying open Glinda's Great Book of Records.

This Book is one of the greatest treasures in Oz, and the Sorceress prizes it more highly than any of her magical possessions. That is the reason it is firmly attached to the big marble table by means of golden chains, and whenever Glinda leaves home she locks the Great Book together with five jeweled padlocks, and carries the keys safely hidden in her bosom.

I do not suppose there is any magical thing in any fairyland to compare with the Record Book, on the pages of which are constantly being printed a record of every event that happens in any part of the world, at exactly the moment it happens. And the records are always truthful, although sometimes they do not give as many details as one could wish. But then, lots of things happen, and so the records have to be brief or even Glinda's Great Book could not hold them all.

Glinda looked at the records several times each day, and Dorothy, whenever she visited the Sorceress, loved to look in the Book and see what was happening everywhere. Not much was recorded about the Land of Oz, which is usually peaceful and uneventful, but today Dorothy found something which interested her. Indeed, the printed letters were appearing on the page even while she looked.

"This is funny!" she exclaimed. "Did you know, Ozma, that there were people in your Land of Oz called Skeezers?"

"Yes," replied Ozma, coming to her side, "I know that on Professor Wogglebug's Map of the Land of Oz there is a place marked 'Skeezer,' but what the Skeezers are like I do not know. No one I know has ever seen them or heard of them. The Skeezer Country is 'way at the upper edge of the Gillikin Country, with the sandy, impassable desert on one side and the mountains of Oogaboo on another side. That is a part of the Land of Oz of which I know very little."

"I guess no one else knows much about it either, unless it's the Skeezers themselves," remarked Dorothy. "But the Book says: 'The Skeezers of Oz have declared war on the Flatheads of Oz, and there is likely to be fighting and much trouble as the result.' "

"Is that all the Book says?" asked Ozma.

"Every word," said Dorothy, and Ozma and Glinda both looked at the Record and seemed surprised and perplexed.

"Tell me, Glinda," said Ozma, "who are the Flatheads?"

"I cannot, your Majesty," confessed the Sorceress. "Until now I never have heard of them, nor have I ever heard the Skeezers mentioned. In the faraway corners of Oz are hidden many curious tribes of people, and those who never leave their own countries and never are visited by those from our favored part of Oz, naturally are unknown to me. However, if you so desire, I can learn through my arts of sorcery something of the Skeezers and the Flatheads."

"I wish you would," answered Ozma seriously. "You see, Glinda, if these are Oz people they are my subjects and I cannot allow any wars or troubles in the Land I rule, if I can possibly help it."

"Very well, your Majesty," said the Sorceress, "I will try to get some information to guide you. Please excuse me for a time, while I retire to my Room of Magic and Sorcery."

"May I go with you?" asked Dorothy, eagerly.

"No, Princess," was the reply. "It would spoil the charm to have anyone present."

So Glinda locked herself in her own Room of Magic and Dorothy and Ozma waited patiently for her to come out again.

In about an hour Glinda appeared, looking grave and thoughtful.

"Your Majesty," she said to Ozma, "the Skeezers live on a Magic Isle in a great lake. For that reason—because the Skeezers deal in magic—I can learn little about them."

"Why, I didn't know there was a lake in that part of Oz," exclaimed Ozma. "The map shows a river running through the Skeezer Country, but no lake."

"That is because the person who made the map never had visited that part of the country," explained the Sorceress. "The lake surely is there, and in the lake is an island—a Magic Isle—and on that island live the people called the Skeezers."

"What are they like?" inquired the Ruler of Oz.

"My magic cannot tell me that," confessed Glinda, "for the magic of the Skeezers prevents anyone outside of their domain knowing anything about them."

"The Flatheads must know, if they're going to fight the Skeezers," suggested Dorothy.

"Perhaps so," Glinda replied, "but I can get little information concerning the Flatheads, either. They are people who inhabit a mountain just south of the Lake of the Skeezers. The mountain has steep sides and a broad, hollow top, like a basin, and in this basin the Flatheads have their dwellings. They also are magic-workers and usually keep to themselves and allow no one from outside to visit them. I have learned that the Flatheads number about one hundred people—men, women and children—while the Skeezers number just one hundred and one."

"What did they quarrel about, and why do they wish to fight one another?" was Ozma's next question.

"I cannot tell your Majesty that," said Glinda.

"But see here!" cried Dorothy, "it's against the law for anyone but Glinda and the Wizard to work magic in the Land of Oz,[1] so if these two strange people are magic-makers they are breaking the law and ought to be punished!"

Ozma smiled upon her little friend.

"Those who do not know me or my laws," she said, "cannot be expected to obey my laws. If we know nothing of the Skeezers or the Flatheads, it is likely that they know nothing of us."

"But they *ought* to know, Ozma, and *we* ought to know. Who's going to tell them, and how are we going to make them behave?"

"That," returned Ozma, "is what I am now considering. What would you advise, Glinda?"

The Sorceress took a little time to consider this question, before she made reply. Then she said:

"Had you not learned of the existence of the Flatheads and the Skeezers, through my Book of Records, you would never have worried about them or their quarrels. So, if you pay no attention to these peoples, you may never hear of them again."

"But that wouldn't be right," declared Ozma. "I am Ruler of all the Land of Oz, which includes the Gillikin Country, the Quadling Country, the Winkie Country and the Munchkin Country, as well as the Emerald City, and being the Princess of this fairyland it is my duty to make all my people—wherever they may be—happy and content and to settle their disputes and keep them from quarreling. So, while the Skeezers and Flatheads may not know me or that I am their lawful Ruler, I now know that they inhabit my kingdom and are my subjects, so I would not be doing my duty if I kept away from them and allowed them to fight."

"That's a fact, Ozma," commented Dorothy. "You've got to go up to the Gillikin Country and make these people behave themselves and make up their quarrels. But how are you going to do it?"

"That is what is puzzling me also, your Majesty," said the Sorceress. "It may be dangerous for you to go into those strange countries, where the people are possibly fierce and warlike."

"I am not afraid," said Ozma, with a smile.

" 'Tisn't a question of being 'fraid," argued Dorothy. "Of course we know you're a fairy, and can't be killed or hurt, and we know you've a lot of magic of your own to help you. But, Ozma dear, in spite of all this you've been in trouble before, on account of wicked enemies, and it isn't right for the Ruler of all Oz to put herself in danger."

"Perhaps I shall be in no danger at all," returned Ozma, with a little laugh. "You mustn't *imagine* danger, Dorothy, for one should only imagine nice things, and we do not know that the Skeezers and Flatheads are wicked people or my enemies. Perhaps they would be good and listen to reason."

"Dorothy is right, your Majesty," asserted the Sorceress. "It is true we know nothing of these faraway subjects, except that they intend to fight one another, and have a certain amount of magic power at their command. Such folks do not like to submit to interference and they are more likely to resent your coming among them than to receive you kindly and graciously as is your due."

"If you had an army to take with you," added Dorothy, "it wouldn't be so bad; but there isn't such a thing as an army in all Oz."

"I have one soldier," said Ozma.

"Yes, the soldier with the green whiskers; but he's dreadful 'fraid of his gun and never loads it. I'm sure he'd run rather than fight. And one soldier, even if he were brave, couldn't do much against two hundred and one Flatheads and Skeezers."

"What then, my friends, would you suggest?" inquired Ozma.

"I advise you to send the Wizard of Oz to them, and let him inform them that it is against the laws of Oz to fight, and that you command them to settle their differences and become friends," proposed Glinda. "Let the Wizard tell them they will be punished if they refuse to obey the commands of the Princess of all the Land of Oz."

Ozma shook her head, to indicate that the advice was not to her satisfaction.

"If they refuse, what then?" she asked. "I should be obliged to carry out my threat and punish them, and that would be an unpleasant and difficult thing to do. I am sure it would be better for me to go peacefully, without an army and armed only with my authority as Ruler, and plead with them to obey me. Then, if they prove obstinate I could resort to other means to win their obedience."

"It's a ticklish thing, anyhow you look at it," sighed Dorothy. "I'm sorry now that I noticed the Record in the Great Book."

"But can't you realize, my dear, that I must do my duty, now that I am aware of this trouble?" asked Ozma. "I am fully determined to go at once to the Magic Isle of the Skeezers and to the enchanted mountain of the Flatheads, and prevent war and strife between their inhabitants. The only question to decide is whether it is better for me to go alone, or to assemble a party of my friends and loyal supporters to accompany me."

"If you go I want to go, too," declared Dorothy. "Whatever happens it's going to be fun—'cause all excitement is fun—and I wouldn't miss it for the world!"

Neither Ozma nor Glinda paid any attention to this statement, for they were gravely considering the serious aspect of this proposed adventure.

"There are plenty of friends who would like to go with you," said the Sorceress, "but none of them would afford your Majesty any protection in case you were in danger. You are yourself the most powerful fairy in Oz, although both I and the Wizard have more varied arts of magic at our command. However, you have one art that no other in all the world can equal—the art of winning hearts and making people love to bow to your gracious presence. For that reason I believe you can accomplish more good alone than with a large number of subjects in your train."

"I believe that also," agreed the Princess. "I shall be quite able to take care of myself, you know, but might not be able to protect others so well. I do not look for opposition, however. I shall speak to these people in kindly words and settle their dispute—whatever it may be—in a just manner."

"Aren't you going to take *me?*" pleaded Dorothy. "You'll need *some* companion, Ozma."

The Princess smiled upon her little friend.

"I see no reason why you should not accompany me," was her reply. "Two girls are not very warlike and they will not suspect us of being on any errand but a kindly and peaceful one. But, in order to prevent war and strife between these angry peoples, we must go to them at once. Let us return immediately to the Emerald City and prepare to start on our journey early tomorrow morning."

Glinda was not quite satisfied with this plan, but could not think of any better way to meet the problem. She knew that Ozma, with all her gentleness and sweet disposition, was accustomed to abide by any decision she had made and could not easily be turned from her purpose. Moreover she could see no great danger to the fairy Ruler of Oz in the undertaking, even though the unknown people she was to visit proved obstinate. But Dorothy was not a fairy; she was a little girl who had come from Kansas to live in the Land of Oz. Dorothy might encounter dangers that to Ozma would be as nothing but to an "Earth child" would be very serious.

The very fact that Dorothy lived in Oz, and had been made a Princess by her friend Ozma, prevented her from being killed or suffering any great bodily pain as long as she lived in that fairyland. She could not grow big, either, and would always remain the same little girl who had come to Oz, unless in some way she left that fairyland or was spirited away from it. But Dorothy was a mortal, nevertheless, and might possibly be destroyed, or hidden where none of her friends could ever find her. She could, for instance, be cut into pieces, and the pieces, while still alive and free from pain, could be widely scattered; or she might be buried deep underground, or "destroyed" in other ways by evil magicians, were she not properly protected. These facts Glinda was considering while she paced with stately tread her marble hall.

Finally the good Sorceress paused and drew a ring from her finger, handing it to Dorothy.

"Wear this ring constantly until your return," she said to the girl. "If serious danger threatens you, turn the ring around on your finger once to the right and another turn to the left. That will ring the alarm bell in my palace and I will at once come to your rescue. But do not use the ring unless you are actually in danger of destruction. While you remain with Princess Ozma I believe she will be able to protect you from all lesser ills."

"Thank you, Glinda," responded Dorothy gratefully, as she placed the ring on her finger. "I'm going to wear my Magic Belt which I took from the Nome King, too, so I guess I'll be safe from anything the Skeezers and Flatheads try to do to me."

Ozma had many arrangements to make before she could leave her throne and her palace in the Emerald City, even for a trip of a few

days, so she bade goodbye to Glinda and with Dorothy climbed into the Red Wagon. A word to the wooden Sawhorse started that astonishing creature on the return journey, and so swiftly did he run that Dorothy was unable to talk or do anything but hold tight to her seat all the way back to the Emerald City.

CHAPTER 2

Ozma and Dorothy

Residing in Ozma's palace at this time was a live Scarecrow, a most remarkable and intelligent creature who had once ruled the Land of Oz for a brief period and was much loved and respected by all the people. Once a Munchkin farmer had stuffed an old suit of clothes with straw and put stuffed boots on the feet and used a pair of stuffed cotton gloves for hands. The head of the Scarecrow was a stuffed sack fastened to the body, with eyes, nose, mouth and ears painted on the sack. When a hat had been put on the head, the thing was a good imitation of a man. The farmer placed the Scarecrow on a pole in his cornfield and it came to life in a curious manner. Dorothy, who was passing by the field, was hailed by the live Scarecrow and lifted him off his pole. He then went with her to the Emerald City, where the Wizard of Oz gave him some excellent brains, and the Scarecrow soon became an important personage.

Ozma considered the Scarecrow one of her best friends and most loyal subjects, so the morning after her visit to Glinda she asked him to take her place as Ruler of the Land of Oz while she was absent on a journey, and the Scarecrow at once consented without asking any questions.

Ozma had warned Dorothy to keep their journey a secret and say nothing to anyone about the Skeezers and Flatheads until their return, and Dorothy promised to obey. She longed to tell her girl friends, tiny Trot[1] and Betsy Bobbin,[2] of the adventure they were undertaking, but refrained from saying a word on the subject although both these girls lived with her in Ozma's palace.

Indeed, only Glinda the Sorceress knew they were going, until after they had gone, and even the Sorceress didn't know what their errand might be.

Princess Ozma took the Sawhorse and the Red Wagon, although

she was not sure there was a wagon road all the way to the Lake of the Skeezers. The Land of Oz is a pretty big place, surrounded on all sides by a Deadly Desert which it is impossible to cross, and the Skeezer Country, according to the map, was in the farthest northwestern part of Oz, bordering on the north desert. As the Emerald City was exactly in the center of Oz, it was no small journey from there to the Skeezers.

Around the Emerald City the country is thickly settled in every direction, but the farther away you get from the city the fewer people there are, until those parts that border on the desert have small populations. Also those faraway sections are little known to the Oz people, except in the south, where Glinda lives and where Dorothy has often wandered on trips of exploration.

The least known of all is the Gillikin Country, which harbors many strange bands of people among its mountains and valleys and forests and streams, and Ozma was now bound for the most distant part of the Gillikin Country.

"I am really sorry," said Ozma to Dorothy, as they rode away in the Red Wagon, "not to know more about the wonderful Land I rule. It is my duty to be acquainted with every tribe of people and every strange and hidden country in all Oz, but I am kept so busy at my palace making laws and planning for the comforts of those who live near the Emerald City, that I do not often find time to make long journeys."

"Well," replied Dorothy, "we'll prob'bly find out a lot on this trip, and we'll learn all about the Skeezers and Flatheads, anyhow. Time doesn't make much diff'rence in the Land of Oz, 'cause we don't grow up, or get old, or become sick and die, as they do other places; so, if we explore one place at a time, we'll by-an'-by know all about every nook and corner in Oz."

Dorothy wore around her waist the Nome King's Magic Belt, which protected her from harm, and the Magic Ring which Glinda had given her was on her finger. Ozma had merely slipped a small silver wand into the bosom of her gown, for fairies do not use chemicals and herbs and the tools of wizards and sorcerers to perform their magic. The Silver Wand was Ozma's one weapon of offense and defense and by its use she could accomplish many things.

They had left the Emerald City just at sunrise and the Sawhorse traveled very swiftly over the roads towards the north, but in a few hours the wooden animal had to slacken his pace because the farm houses had become few and far between and often there were no paths at all in the direction they wished to follow. At such times they crossed the fields, avoiding groups of trees and fording the streams and rivulets whenever they came to them. But finally they reached a broad hillside closely covered with scrubby brush, through which the wagon could not pass.

"It will be difficult even for you and me to get through without tearing our dresses," said Ozma, "so we must leave the Sawhorse and the Wagon here until our return."

"That's all right," Dorothy replied, "I'm tired riding, anyhow. Do you s'pose, Ozma, we're anywhere near the Skeezer Country?"

"I cannot tell, Dorothy dear, but I know we've been going in the right direction, so we are sure to find it in time."

The scrubby brush was almost like a grove of small trees, for it reached as high as the heads of the two girls, neither of whom was very tall. They were obliged to thread their way in and out, until Dorothy was afraid they would get lost, and finally they were halted by a curious thing that barred their further progress. It was a huge web—as if woven by gigantic spiders—and the delicate, lacy film was fastened stoutly to the branches of the bushes and continued to the right and left in the form of a half circle. The threads of this web were of a brilliant purple color and woven into numerous artistic patterns, but it reached from the ground to branches above the heads of the girls and formed a sort of fence that hedged them in.

"It doesn't look very strong, though," said Dorothy. "I wonder if we couldn't break through." She tried but found the web stronger than it seemed. All her efforts could not break a single thread.

"We must go back, I think, and try to get around this peculiar web," Ozma decided.

So they turned to the right and, following the web found that it seemed to spread in a regular circle. On and on they went until finally Ozma said they had returned to the exact spot from which they had started. "Here is a handkerchief you dropped when we were here before," she said to Dorothy.

"In that case, they must have built the web behind us, after we walked into the trap," exclaimed the little girl.

"True," agreed Ozma, "an enemy has tried to imprison us."

"And they did it, too," said Dorothy. "I wonder who it was."

"It's a spider-web, I'm quite sure," returned Ozma, "but it must be the work of enormous spiders."

"Quite right!" cried a voice behind them. Turning quickly around they beheld a huge purple spider sitting not two yards away and regarding them with its small bright eyes.

Then there crawled from the bushes a dozen more great purple spiders, which saluted the first one and said:

"The web is finished, O King, and the strangers are our prisoners."

Dorothy did not like the looks of these spiders at all. They had big heads, sharp claws, small eyes and fuzzy hair all over their purple bodies.

"They look wicked," she whispered to Ozma. "What shall we do?"

Ozma gazed upon the spiders with a serious face.

"What is your object in making us prisoners?" she inquired.

"We need someone to keep house for us," answered the Spider King.[3] "There is sweeping and dusting to be done, and polishing and washing of dishes, and that is work my people dislike to do. So we decided that if any strangers came our way we would capture them and make them our servants."

"I am Princess Ozma, Ruler of all Oz," said the girl with dignity.

"Well, I am King of all Spiders," was the reply, "and that makes me your master. Come with me to my palace and I will instruct you in your work."

"I won't," said Dorothy indignantly. "We won't have anything to do with you."

"We'll see about that," returned the Spider in a severe tone, and the next instant he made a dive straight at Dorothy, opening the claws in his legs as if to grab and pinch her with the sharp points. But the girl was wearing her Magic Belt and was not harmed. The Spider King could not even touch her.

He turned swiftly and made a dash at Ozma, but she held her Magic Wand over his head and the monster recoiled as if it had been struck.

"You'd better let us go," Dorothy advised him, "for you see you can't hurt us."

"So I see," returned the Spider King angrily. "You magic is greater than mine. But I'll not help you to escape. If you can break the magic web my people have woven you may go; if not you must stay here and starve." With that the Spider King uttered a peculiar whistle and all the spiders disappeared.

"There is more magic in my fairyland than I dreamed of,"[4] remarked the beautiful Ozma, with a sigh of regret. "It seems that my laws have not been obeyed, for even these monstrous spiders defy me by means of magic."

"Never mind that now," said Dorothy; "let's see what we can do to get out of this trap."

They now examined the web with great care and were amazed at its strength. Although finer than the finest silken hairs, it resisted all their efforts to work through, even though both girls threw all their weight against it.

"We must find some instrument which will cut the threads of the web," said Ozma, finally. "Let us look about for such a tool."

So they wandered among the bushes and finally came to a shallow pool of water, formed by a small bubbling spring. Dorothy stooped to get a drink and discovered in the water a green crab, about as big as her hand. The crab had two big, sharp claws, and as soon as Dorothy saw them she had an idea that those claws could save them.

"Come out of the water," she called to the crab; "I want to talk to you."

Rather lazily the crab rose to the surface and caught hold of a bit of rock. With his head above the water he said in a cross voice:

"What do you want?"

"We want you to cut the web of the purple spiders with your claws, so we can get through it," answered Dorothy. "You can do that, can't you?"

"I suppose so," replied the crab. "But if I do what will you give me?"

"What do you wish?" Ozma inquired.

"I wish to be white, instead of green," said the crab. "Green crabs are very common, and white ones are rare; besides the purple spiders, which infest this hillside, are afraid of white crabs. Could you make me white if I should agree to cut the web for you?"

"Yes," said Ozma, "I can do that easily. And, so you may know I am speaking the truth, I will change your color now."

She waved her silver wand over the pool and the crab instantly became snow-white—all except his eyes, which remained black. The creature saw his reflection in the water and was so delighted that he at once climbed out of the pool and began moving slowly toward the web, by backing away from the pool. He moved so very slowly that Dorothy cried out impatiently: "Dear me, this will never do!" Catching the crab in her hands she ran with him to the web.

She had to hold him up even then, so he could reach with his claws strand after strand of the filmy purple web, which he was able to sever with one nip.

When enough of the web had been cut to allow them to pass, Dorothy ran back to the pool and placed the white crab in the water, after which she rejoined Ozma. They were just in time to escape through the web, for several of the purple spiders now appeared, having discovered that their web had been cut, and had the girls not rushed through the opening the spiders would have quickly repaired the cuts and again imprisoned them.

Ozma and Dorothy ran as fast as they could and although the angry spiders threw a number of strands of web after them, hoping to lasso them or entangle them in the coils, they managed to escape and clamber to the top of the hill.

CHAPTER 3

The Mist Maidens

From the top of the hill Ozma and Dorothy looked down into the valley beyond and were surprised to find it filled with a floating mist that was as dense as smoke. Nothing in the valley was visible except these rolling waves of mist, but beyond, on the other side, rose a grassy hill that appeared quite beautiful.

"Well," said Dorothy, "what are we to do, Ozma? Walk down into that thick fog, an' prob'bly get lost in it, or wait till it clears away?"

"I'm not sure it will clear away, however long we wait," replied Ozma, doubtfully. "If we wish to get on, I think we must venture into the mist."

"But we can't see where we're going, or what we're stepping on," protested Dorothy. "There may be dreadful things mixed up in that fog, an' I'm scared just to think of wading into it."

Even Ozma seemed to hesitate. She was silent and thoughtful for a little while, looking at the rolling drifts that were so gray and forbidding. Finally she said:

"I believe this is a Mist Valley, where these moist clouds always remain, for even the sunshine above does not drive them away. Therefore the Mist Maids must live here, and they are fairies and should answer my call."

She placed her two hands before her mouth, forming a hollow with them, and uttered a clear, thrilling, bird-like cry. It floated far out over the mist waves and presently was answered by a similar sound, as of a far-off echo.

Dorothy was much impressed. She had seen many strange things since coming to this fairy country, but here was a new experience. At ordinary times Ozma was just like any little girl one might chance to meet—simple, merry, lovable as could be—yet with a certain reserve that lent her dignity in her most joyous moods. There were times, however, when seated on her throne and commanding her subjects, or when her fairy powers were called into use, when Dorothy and all others about her stood in awe of their lovely girl Ruler and realized her superiority.

Ozma waited. Presently out from the billows rose beautiful forms, clothed in fleecy, trailing garments of gray that could scarcely be distinguished from the mist. Their hair was mist-color, too; only their gleaming arms and sweet, pallid faces proved they were living, intelligent creatures answering the call of a sister fairy.

Like sea nymphs they rested on the bosom of the clouds, their eyes turned questioningly upon the two girls who stood upon the bank. One came quite near and to her Ozma said:

"Will you please take us to the opposite hillside? We are afraid to venture into the mist. I am Princess Ozma of Oz, and this is my friend Dorothy, a Princess of Oz."

The Mist Maids came nearer, holding out their arms. Without hesitation Ozma advanced and allowed them to embrace her and Dorothy plucked up courage to follow. Very gently the Mist Maids held them. Dorothy thought the arms were cold and misty—they didn't seem real at all—yet they supported the two girls above the surface of the billows and floated with them so swiftly to the green hillside opposite that the girls were astonished to find themselves set upon the grass before they realized they had fairly started.

"Thank you!" said Ozma gratefully, and Dorothy also added her thanks for the service.

The Mist Maids made no answer, but they smiled and waved their hands in good-bye as again they floated out into the mist and disappeared from view.

CHAPTER 4

The Magic Tent

"Well," said Dorothy with a laugh, "that was easier than I expected. It's worth while, sometimes, to be a real fairy. But I wouldn't like to be that kind, and live in a dreadful fog all the time."

They now climbed the bank and found before them a delightful plain that spread for miles in all directions. Fragrant wild flowers were scattered throughout the grass; there were bushes bearing lovely blossoms and luscious fruits; now and then a group of stately trees added to the beauty of the landscape. But there were no dwellings or signs of life.

The farther side of the plain was bordered by a row of palms, and just in front of the palms rose a queerly shaped hill that towered above the plain like a mountain. The sides of this hill were straight up and down; it was oblong in shape and the top seemed flat and level.

"Oh, ho!" cried Dorothy; "I'll bet that's the mountain Glinda told us of, where the Flatheads live."

"If it is," replied Ozma, "the Lake of the Skeezers must be just beyond the line of palm trees. Can you walk that far, Dorothy?"

"Of course, in time," was the prompt answer. "I'm sorry we had to leave the Sawhorse and the Red Wagon behind us, for they'd come in handy just now; but with the end of our journey in sight a tramp across these pretty green fields won't tire us a bit."

It was a longer tramp than they suspected, however, and night overtook them before they could reach the flat mountain. So Ozma proposed they camp for the night and Dorothy was quite ready to approve. She didn't like to admit to her friend she was tired, but she told herself that her legs "had prickers in 'em," meaning they had begun to ache.

Usually when Dorothy started on a journey of exploration or adventure, she carried with her a basket of food, and other things that a traveler in a strange country might require, but to go away with Ozma was quite a different thing, as experience had taught her. The fairy Ruler of Oz only needed her silver wand—tipped at one end with a great sparkling emerald—to provide through its magic all that they might need. Therefore Ozma, having halted with her companion and selected a smooth, grassy spot on the plain, waved her wand in graceful curves and chanted some mystic words in her sweet voice, and in an instant a handsome tent appeared before them. The canvas was striped purple and white, and from the center pole fluttered the royal banner of Oz.

"Come, dear," said Ozma, taking Dorothy's hand, "I am hungry and I'm sure you must be also; so let us go in and have our feast."

On entering the tent they found a table set for two, with snowy linen, bright silver and sparkling glassware, a vase of roses in the center and many dishes of delicious food, some smoking hot, waiting to satisfy their hunger. Also, on either side of the tent were beds, with satin sheets, warm blankets and pillows filled with swansdown. There were chairs, too, and tall lamps that lighted the interior of the tent with a soft, rosy glow.

Dorothy, resting herself at her fairy friend's command, and eating her dinner with unusual enjoyment, thought of the wonders of magic. If one were a fairy and knew the secret laws of nature and the mystic words and ceremonies that commanded those laws, then a simple wave of a silver wand would produce instantly all that men work hard and anxiously for through weary years. And Dorothy wished in her kindly, innocent heart, that all men and women could be fairies with silver wands, and satisfy all their needs without so much work and worry, for then, she imagined, they would have all their working hours to be happy in. But Ozma, looking into her friend's face and reading those thoughts, gave a laugh and said:

"No, no, Dorothy, that wouldn't do at all. Instead of happiness your plan would bring weariness to the world. If every one could wave a wand and have his wants fulfilled there would be little to wish for. There would be no eager striving to obtain the difficult, for nothing would then be difficult, and the pleasure of earning something longed for, and only to be secured by hard work and careful thought, would be utterly lost. There would be nothing to do, you see, and no interest in life and in our fellow creatures. That is all that makes life worth our while—to do good deeds and to help those less fortunate than ourselves."

"Well, you're a fairy, Ozma. Aren't you happy?" asked Dorothy.

"Yes, dear, because I can use my fairy powers to make others happy. Had I no kingdom to rule, and no subjects to look after, I would be miserable. Also, you must realize that while I am a more powerful fairy than any other inhabitant of Oz, I am not as powerful as Glinda the Sorceress, who has studied many arts of magic that I know nothing of. Even the little Wizard of Oz can do some things I am unable to accomplish, while I can accomplish things unknown to the Wizard.

This is to explain that I am not all-powerful, by any means. My magic is simply fairy magic, and not sorcery or wizardry."

"All the same," said Dorothy, "I'm mighty glad you could make this tent appear, with our dinners and beds all ready for us."

Ozma smiled.

"Yes, it is indeed wonderful," she agreed. "Not all fairies know that sort of magic, but some fairies can do magic that fills me with astonishment. I think that is what makes us modest and unassuming— the fact that our magic arts are divided, some being given each of us. I'm glad I don't know everything, Dorothy, and that there still are things in both nature and in wit for me to marvel at."

Dorothy couldn't quite understand this, so she said nothing more on the subject and presently had a new reason to marvel. For when they had quite finished their meal table and contents disappeared in a flash.

"No dishes to wash, Ozma!" she said with a laugh. "I guess you'd make a lot of folks happy if you could teach 'em just that one trick."

For an hour Ozma told stories, and talked with Dorothy about various people in whom they were interested. And then it was bedtime, and they undressed and crept into their soft beds and fell asleep almost as soon as their heads touched their pillows.

CHAPTER 5

The Magic Stairway

The flat mountain looked much nearer in the clear light of the morning sun, but Dorothy and Ozma knew there was a long tramp before them, even yet. They finished dressing only to find a warm, delicious breakfast awaiting them, and having eaten they left the tent and started toward the mountain which was their first goal. After going a little way Dorothy looked back and found that the fairy tent had entirely disappeared. She was not surprised, for she knew this would happen.

"Can't your magic give us a horse an' wagon, or an automobile?" inquired Dorothy.

"No, dear; I'm sorry that such magic is beyond my power," confessed her fairy friend.

"Perhaps Glinda could," said Dorothy thoughtfully.

"Glinda has a stork chariot that carries her through the air," said Ozma, "but even our great Sorceress cannot conjure up other modes of travel. Don't forget what I told you last night, that no one is powerful enough to do everything."

"Well, I s'pose I ought to know that, having lived so long in the Land of Oz," replied Dorothy; "but *I* can't do any magic at all, an' so I can't figure out e'zactly how you an' Glinda an' the Wizard do it."

"Don't try," laughed Ozma. "But you have at least one magical art, Dorothy: you know the trick of winning all hearts."

"No, I don't," said Dorothy earnestly. "If I really can do it, Ozma, I am sure I don't know *how* I do it."

It took them a good two hours to reach the foot of the round, flat mountain, and then they found the sides so steep that they were like the wall of a house.

"Even my purple kitten couldn't climb 'em," remarked Dorothy, gazing upward.

"But there is some way for the Flatheads to get down and up again," declared Ozma; "otherwise they couldn't make war with the Skeezers, or even meet them and quarrel with them."

"That's so, Ozma. Let's walk around a ways; perhaps we'll find a ladder or something."

They walked quite a distance, for it was a big mountain, and as they circled around it and came to the side that faced the palm trees, they suddenly discovered an entrance way cut out of the rock wall. This entrance was arched overhead and not very deep because it merely led to a short flight of stone stairs.

"Oh, we've found a way to the top at last," announced Ozma, and the two girls turned and walked straight toward the entrance. Suddenly they bumped against something and stood still, unable to proceed farther.

"Dear me!" exclaimed Dorothy, rubbing her nose, which had struck something hard, although she could not see what it was; "this isn't as easy as it looks. What has stopped us, Ozma? Is it magic of some sort?"

Ozma was feeling around, her hands outstretched before her.

"Yes, dear, it is magic," she replied. "The Flatheads had to have a way from their mountain top from the plain below, but to prevent enemies from rushing up the stairs to conquer them, they have built, at a small distance before the entrance a wall of solid stone, the stones being held in place by cement, and then they made the wall invisible."

"I wonder why they did that?" mused Dorothy. "A wall would keep folks out anyhow, whether it could be seen or not, so there wasn't any use making it invisible. Seems to me it would have been better to have left it solid, for then no one would have seen the entrance behind it. Now anybody can see the entrance, as we did. And prob'bly anybody that tries to go up the stairs gets bumped, as we did."

Ozma made no reply at once. Her face was grave and thoughtful.

"I think I know the reason for making the wall invisible," she said after a while. "The Flatheads use the stairs for coming down and going up. If there was a solid stone wall to keep them from reaching the plain they would themselves be imprisoned by the wall. So they had to leave some place to get around the wall, and, if the wall was visible, all strangers or enemies would find the place to go around it and then the wall would be useless. So the Flatheads cunningly made their wall invisible, believing that everyone who saw the entrance to the mountain would walk straight toward it, as we did, and find it impossible to go any farther. I suppose the wall is really high and thick, and can't be broken through, so those who find it in their way are obliged to go away again."

"Well," said Dorothy, "if there's a way around the wall, where is it?"

"We must find it," returned Ozma, and began feeling her way along the wall. Dorothy followed and began to get discouraged when Ozma had walked nearly a quarter of a mile away from the entrance. But now the invisible wall curved in toward the side of the mountain and suddenly ended, leaving just space enough between the wall and the mountain for an ordinary person to pass through.

The girls went in, single file, and Ozma explained that they were now behind the barrier and could go back to the entrance. They met no further obstructions.

"Most people, Ozma, wouldn't have figured this thing out the way you did," remarked Dorothy. "If I'd been alone the invisible wall surely would have stumped me."

Reaching the entrance they began to mount the stone stairs. They went up ten stairs and then down five stairs, following a passage cut from the rock. The stairs were just wide enough for the two girls to walk abreast, arm in arm. At the bottom of the five stairs the passage turned to the right, and they ascended ten more stairs, only to find at the top of the flight five stairs leading straight down again. Again the passage turned abruptly, this time to the left, and ten more stairs led upward.

The passage was now quite dark, for they were in the heart of the mountain and all daylight had been shut out by the turns of the passage. However, Ozma drew her silver wand from her bosom and the great jewel at its end gave out a lustrous, green-tinted light which lighted the place well enough for them to see their way plainly.

Ten steps up, five steps down, and a turn, this way or that. That was the program, and Dorothy figured that they were only gaining five stairs upward each trip that they made.

"Those Flatheads must be funny people," she said to Ozma. "They don't seem to do anything in a bold straightforward manner. In making this passage they forced everyone to walk three times as far as is necessary. And of course this trip is just as tiresome to the Flatheads as it is to other folks."

"That is true," answered Ozma; "yet it is a clever arrangement to prevent their being surprised by intruders. Every time we reach the tenth step of a flight, the pressure of our feet on the stone makes a bell ring on top of the mountain, to warn the Flatheads of our coming."

"How do you know that?" demanded Dorothy, astonished.

"I've heard the bell ever since we started," Ozma told her. "You could not hear it, I know, but when I am holding my wand in my hand I can hear sounds a great distance off."

"Do you hear anything on top of the mountain 'cept the bell?" inquired Dorothy.

"Yes. The people are calling to one another in alarm and many footsteps are approaching the place where we will reach the flat top of the mountain."

This made Dorothy feel somewhat anxious.

"I'd thought we were going to visit just common, ordinary people," she remarked, "but they're pretty clever, it seems, and they know some kinds of magic, too. They may be dangerous, Ozma. P'raps we'd better stayed at home."

Finally the upstairs-and-downstairs passage seemed coming to an end, for daylight again appeared ahead of the two girls and Ozma replaced her wand in the bosom of her gown. The last ten steps brought them to the surface, where they found themselves surrounded by such a throng of queer people that for a time they halted, speechless, and stared into the faces that confronted them.

Dorothy knew at once why these mountain people were called Flatheads. Their heads were really flat on top, as if they had been cut off just above the eyes and ears. Also the heads were bald, with no hair on top at all, and the ears were big and stuck straight out, and the noses were small and stubby, while the mouths of the Flatheads were well shaped and not unusual. Their eyes were perhaps their best feature, being large and bright and a deep violet in color.

The costumes of the Flatheads were all made of metals dug from their mountain. Small gold, silver, tin and iron discs, about the size of pennies, and very thin, were cleverly wired together and made to form knee trousers and jackets for the men and skirts and waists for the women. The colored metals were skillfully mixed to form stripes and checks of various sorts, so that the costumes were quite gorgeous and reminded Dorothy of pictures she had seen of Knights of old clothed armor.

Aside from their flat heads, these people were not really bad looking. The men were armed with bows and arrows and had small axes of steel stuck in their metal belts. They wore no hats nor ornaments.

CHAPTER 6

Flathead Mountain

When they saw that the intruders on their mountain were only two little girls, the Flatheads grunted with satisfaction and drew back, permitting them to see what the mountain top looked like. It was shaped like a saucer, so that the houses and other buildings—all made of rocks—could not be seen over the edge by anyone standing in the plain below.

But now a big fat Flathead stood before the girls and in a gruff voice demanded.

"What are you doing here? Have the Skeezers sent you to spy upon us?"

"I am Princess Ozma, Ruler of all the Land of Oz."

"Well, I've never heard of the Land of Oz, so you may be what you claim," returned the Flathead.

"This is the Land of Oz—part of it, anyway," exclaimed Dorothy. "So Princess Ozma rules you Flathead people, as well as all the other people in Oz."

The man laughed, and all the others who stood around laughed, too. Some one in the crowd called:

"She'd better not tell the Supreme Dictator about ruling the Flatheads. Eh, friends?"

"No, indeed!" they all answered in positive tones.

"Who is your Supreme Dictator?" answered Ozma.

"I think I'll let him tell you that himself," answered the man who had first spoken. "You have broken our laws by coming here; and whoever you are the Supreme Dictator must fix your punishment. Come along with me."

He started down a path and Ozma and Dorothy followed him without protest, as they wanted to see the most important person in this queer country. The houses they passed seemed pleasant enough and each had a little yard in which were flowers and vegetables. Walls of rock separated the dwellings, and all the paths were paved with smooth slabs of rock. This seemed their only building material and they utilized it cleverly for every purpose.

Directly in the center of the great saucer stood a larger building which the Flathead informed the girls was the palace of the Supreme Dictator. He led them through an entrance hall into a big reception room, where they sat upon stone benches and awaited the coming of the Dictator. Pretty soon he entered from another room—a rather lean and rather old Flathead, dressed much like the others of this strange race, and only distinguished from them by the sly and cunning expression of his face. He kept his eyes half closed and looked through the slits of them at Ozma and Dorothy, who rose to receive him.

"Are you the Supreme Dictator of the Flatheads?" inquired Ozma.

"Yes, that's me," he said, rubbing his hands slowly together. "My word is law. I'm the head of the Flatheads on this flat headland."

"I am Princess Ozma of Oz, and I have come from the Emerald City to—"

"Stop a minute," interrupted the Dictator, and turned to the man who had brought the girls there. "Go away, Dictator Felo Flathead!" he commanded. "Return to your duty and guard the Stairway. I will look after these strangers." The man bowed and departed, and Dorothy asked wonderingly:

"Is *he* a Dictator, too?"

"Of course," was the answer. "Everybody here is a dictator of something or other. They're all office holders. That's what keeps them contented. But I'm the Supreme Dictator of all, and I'm elected once a year. This is a democracy, you know, where the people are allowed to vote for their rulers. A good many others would like to be Supreme Dictator, but as I made a law that I am always to count the votes myself, I am always elected."

"What is your name?" asked Ozma.

"I am called the Su-dic, which is short for Supreme Dictator. I sent that man away because the moment you mentioned Ozma of Oz, and the Emerald City, I knew who you are. I suppose I'm the only Flathead that ever heard of you, but that's because I have more brains than the rest."

Dorothy was staring hard at the Su-dic.

"I don't see how you can have any brains at all," she remarked, "because the part of your head is gone where brains are kept."

"I don't blame you for thinking that," he said. "Once the Flatheads had no brains because, as you say, there is no upper part to their heads, to hold brains. But long, long ago a band of fairies flew over this country and made it all a fairyland, and when they came to the Flatheads the fairies were sorry to find them all very stupid and quite unable to think. So, as there was no good place in their bodies in which to put brains the Fairy Queen gave each one of us a nice can of brains to carry in his pocket and that made us just as intelligent as other people. See," he continued, "here is one of the cans of brains the fairies gave us." He took from a pocket a bright tin can having a pretty red label on it which said: "Flathead Concentrated Brains, Extra Quality."

"And does every Flathead have the same kind of brains?" asked Dorothy.

"Yes, they're all alike. Here's another can." From another pocket he produced a second can of brains.

"Did the fairies give you a double supply?" inquired Dorothy.

"No, but one of the Flatheads thought he wanted to be the Su-dic and tried to get my people to rebel against me, so I punished him by taking away his brains. One day my wife scolded me severely, so I took away her can of brains. She didn't like that and went out and robbed several women of *their* brains. Then I made a law that if anyone stole another's brains, or even tried to borrow them, he would forfeit his own brains to the Su-dic. So each one is content with his own canned brains and my wife and I are the only ones on the mountain with more than one can. I have three cans and that makes me very clever—so clever that I'm a good Sorcerer, if I do say it myself. My poor wife had four cans of brains and became a remarkable witch, but alas! that was before those terrible enemies, the Skeezers, transformed her into a Golden Pig."

"Good gracious!" cried Dorothy; "is your wife really a Golden Pig?"

"She is. The Skeezers did it and so I have declared war on them. In revenge for making my wife a Pig I intend to ruin their Magic Island and make the Skeezers the slaves of the Flatheads!"

The Su-dic was very angry now; his eyes flashed and his face took on a wicked and fierce expression. But Ozma said to him, very sweetly and in a friendly voice:

"I am sorry to hear this. Will you please tell me more about your troubles with the Skeezers? Then perhaps I can help you."

She was only a girl, but there was dignity in her pose and speech which impressed the Su-dic.

"If you are really Princess Ozma of Oz," the Flathead said, "you are one of that band of fairies who, under Queen Lurline, made all Oz a Fairyland. I have heard that Lurline left one of her own fairies to rule Oz, and gave the fairy the name of Ozma."

"If you knew this why did you not come to me at the Emerald City and tender me your loyalty and obedience?" asked the Ruler of Oz.

"Well, I only learned the fact lately, and I've been too busy to leave home," he explained, looking at the floor instead of into Ozma's eyes. She knew he had spoken a falsehood, but only said:

"Why did you quarrel with the Skeezers?"

"It was this way," began the Su-dic, glad to change the subject. "We Flatheads love fish, and as we have no fish on this mountain we would sometimes go to the Lake of the Skeezers to catch fish. This made the Skeezers angry, for they declared the fish in their lake belonged to them and were under their protection and they forbade us to catch them. That was very mean and unfriendly in the Skeezers, you must admit, and when we paid no attention to their orders they set a guard on the shore of the lake to prevent our fishing.

"Now, my wife, Rora Flathead, having four cans of brains, had become a wonderful witch, and fish being brain food, she loved to eat fish better than any one of us. So she vowed she would destroy every fish in the lake, unless the Skeezers let us catch what we wanted. They defied us, so Rora prepared a kettleful of magic poison and went down to the lake one night to dump it all in the water and poison the fish. It was a clever idea, quite worthy of my dear wife, but the Skeezer Queen—a young lady named Coo-ee-oh—hid on the bank of the lake and taking Rora unawares, transformed her into a Golden

Pig. The poison was spilled on the ground and wicked Queen Coo-ee-oh, not content with her cruel transformation, even took away my wife's four cans of brains, so she is now a common grunting pig without even brains enough to know her own name."

"Then," said Ozma thoughtfully, "the Queen of the Skeezers must be a Sorceress."

"Yes," said the Su-dic, "but she doesn't know much magic, after all. She is not as powerful as Rora Flathead was, not half as powerful as I am now, as Queen Coo-ee-oh will discover when we fight our great battle and destroy her."

"The Golden Pig can't be a witch any more, of course," observed Dorothy.

"No; even had Queen Coo-ee-oh left her the four cans of brains, poor Rora, in a pig's shape, couldn't do any witchcraft. A witch has to use her fingers, and a pig has only cloven hoofs."

"It seems a sad story," was Ozma's comment, "and all the trouble arose because the Flatheads wanted fish that did not belong to them."

"As for that," said the Su-dic, again angry, "I made a law that any of my people could catch fish in the Lake of the Skeezers, whenever they wanted to. So the trouble was through the Skeezers defying my law."

"You can only make laws to govern your own people," asserted Ozma sternly. "I, alone, am empowered to make laws that must be obeyed by all the peoples of Oz."

"Pooh!" cried the Su-dic scornfully. "You can't make *me* obey your laws, I assure you. I know the extent of your powers, Princess Ozma of Oz, and I know that I am more powerful than you are.[1] To prove it I shall keep you and your companion prisoners in this mountain until after we have fought and conquered the Skeezers. Then, if you promise to be good, I may let you go home again."

Dorothy was amazed by this effrontery and defiance of the beautiful girl Ruler of Oz, whom all until now had obeyed without question. But Ozma, still unruffled and dignified, looked at the Su-dic and said:

"You did not mean that. You are angry and speak unwisely, without reflection. I came here from my palace in the Emerald City to prevent war and to make peace between you and the Skeezers. I do not approve of Queen Coo-ee-oh's action in transforming your wife Rora into a pig, nor do I approve of Rora's cruel attempt to poison the fishes in the lake. No one has the right to work magic in my dominions without my consent, so the Flatheads and the Skeezers have both broken my laws—which must be obeyed."

"If you want to make peace," said the Su-dic, "make the Skeezers restore my wife to her proper form and give back her four cans of brains. Also make them agree to allow us to catch fish in their lake."

"No," returned Ozma, "I will not do that, for it would be unjust. I will have the Golden Pig again transformed into your wife Rora, and give her one can of brains, but the other three cans must be restored to those she robbed. Neither may you catch fish in the Lake of the Skeezers, for it is their lake and the fish belong to them. This arrangement is just and honorable, and you must agree to it."

"Never!" cried the Su-dic. Just then a pig came running into the room, uttering dismal grunts. It was made of solid gold, with joints at the bends of the legs and in the neck and jaws. The Golden Pig's eyes were rubies, and its teeth were polished ivory.

"There!" said the Su-dic, "gaze on the evil work of Queen Coo-ee-oh, and then say if you can prevent my making war on the Skeezers. That grunting beast was once my wife—the most beautiful Flathead on our mountain and a skillful witch. Now look at her!"

"Fight the Skeezers, fight the Skeezers, fight the Skeezers!" grunted the Golden Pig.

"I *will* fight the Skeezers," exclaimed the Flathead chief, "and if a dozen Ozmas of Oz forbade me I would fight just the same."

"Not if I can prevent it!" asserted Ozma.

"You can't prevent it. But since you threaten me, I'll have you confined in the bronze prison until the war is over," said the Su-dic. He whistled and four stout Flatheads, armed with axes and spears, entered the room and saluted him. Turning to the men he said: "Take these two girls, bind them with wire ropes and cast them into the bronze prison."

The four men bowed low and one of them asked:

"Where are the two girls, most noble Su-dic?"

The Su-dic turned to where Ozma and Dorothy had stood but they had vanished!

CHAPTER 7

The Magic Isle

Ozma, seeing it was useless to argue with the Supreme Dictator of the Flatheads, had been considering how best to escape from his power.

She realized that his sorcery might be difficult to overcome, and when he threatened to cast Dorothy and her into a bronze prison she slipped her hand into her bosom and grasped her silver wand. With the other hand she grasped the hand of Dorothy, but these motions were so natural that the Su-dic did not notice them. Then when he turned to meet his four soldiers, Ozma instantly rendered both herself and Dorothy invisible and swiftly led her companion around the group of Flatheads and out of the room. As they reached the entry and descended the stone steps, Ozma whispered:

"Let us run, dear! We are invisible, so no one will see us."

Dorothy understood and she was a good runner. Ozma had marked the place where the grand stairway that led to the plain was located, so they made directly for it. Some people were in the paths but these they dodged around. One or two Flatheads heard the pattering of footsteps of the girls on the stone pavement and stopped with bewildered looks to gaze around them, but no one interfered with the invisible fugitives.

The Su-dic had lost no time in starting the chase. He and his men ran so fast that they might have overtaken the girls before they reached the stairway had not the Golden Pig suddenly run across their path. The Su-dic tripped over the pig and fell flat, and his four men tripped over him and tumbled in a heap. Before they could scramble up and reach the mouth of the passage it was too late to stop the two girls.

There was a guard on each side of the stairway, but of course they did not see Ozma and Dorothy as they sped past and descended the steps. Then they had to go up five steps and down another ten, and so on, in the same manner in which they had climbed to the top of the mountain. Ozma lighted their way with her wand and they kept on without relaxing their speed until they reached the bottom. Then they ran to the right and turned the corner of the invisible wall just as the Su-dic and his followers rushed out of the arched entrance and looked around in an attempt to discover the fugitives.

Ozma now knew they were safe, so she told Dorothy to stop and both of them sat down on the grass until they could breathe freely and become rested from their mad flight.

As for the Su-dic, he realized he was foiled and soon turned and climbed his stairs again. He was very angry—angry with Ozma and angry with himself—because, now that he took time to think, he remembered that he knew very well the art of making people invisible, and visible again, and if he had only thought of it in time he could have used his magic knowledge to make the girls visible and so have captured them easily. However, it was now too late for regrets and he determined to make preparations at once to march all his forces against the Skeezers.

"What shall we do next?" asked Dorothy, when they were rested.

"Let us find the Lake of the Skeezers," replied Ozma. "From what that dreadful Su-dic said I imagine the Skeezers are good people and worthy of our friendship, and if we go to them we may help them to defeat the Flatheads."

"I s'pose we can't stop the war now," remarked Dorothy reflectively, as they walked toward the row of palm trees.

"No; the Su-dic is determined to fight the Skeezers, so all we can do is to warn them of their danger and help them as much as possible."

"Of course you'll punish the Flatheads," said Dorothy.

"Well, I do not think the Flathead people are as much to blame as their Supreme Dictator," was the answer. "If he is removed from power and his unlawful magic taken from him, the people will probably be good and respect the laws of the Land of Oz, and live at peace with all their neighbors in the future."

"I hope so," said Dorothy with a sigh of doubt.

The palms were not far from the mountain and the girls reached them after a brisk walk. The huge trees were set close together, in three rows, and had been planted so as to keep people from passing them, but the Flatheads had cut a passage through this barrier and Ozma found the path and led Dorothy to the other side.

Beyond the palms they discovered a very beautiful scene. Bordered by a green lawn was a great lake fully a mile from shore to shore, the waters of which were exquisitely blue and sparkling, with little wavelets breaking its smooth surface where the breezes touched it. In the center of this lake appeared a lovely island, not of great extent but almost entirely covered by a huge round building with glass walls and a high glass dome which glittered brilliantly in the sunshine. Between the glass building and the edge of the island was no grass, flowers or shrubbery, but only an expanse of highly polished white marble. There were no boats on either shore and no signs of life could be seen anywhere on the island.

"Well," said Dorothy, gazing wistfully at the island, "we've found the Lake of the Skeezers and their Magic Isle. I guess the Skeezers are in that big glass palace, but we can't get at 'em."

CHAPTER 8

Queen Coo-ee-oh

Princess Ozma considered the situation gravely. Then she tied her handkerchief to her wand and, standing at the water's edge, waved the handkerchief like a flag, as a signal. For a time they could observe no response.

"I don't see what good that will do," said Dorothy. "Even if the Skeezers are on that island and see us, and know we're friends, they haven't any boats to come and get us."

But the Skeezers didn't need boats, as the girls soon discovered. For on a sudden an opening appeared at the base of the palace and from the opening came a slender shaft of steel, reaching out slowly but steadily across the water in the direction of the place where they stood. To the girls this steel arrangement looked like a triangle, with the base nearest the water. It came toward them in the form of an arch, stretching out from the palace wall until its end reached the bank and rested there, while the other end still remained on the island.

Then they saw that it was a bridge, consisting of a steel footway just broad enough to walk on, and two slender guide rails, one on either side, which were connected with the foot-way by steel bars. The bridge looked rather frail and Dorothy feared it would not bear their weight, but Ozma at once called, "Come on!" and started to walk across, holding fast to the rail on either side. So Dorothy summoned her courage and followed after. Before Ozma had taken three steps she halted and so forced Dorothy to halt, for the bridge was again moving and returning to the island.

"We need not walk after all," said Ozma. So they stood still in their places and let the steel bridge draw them onward. Indeed, the bridge drew them well into the glass-domed building which covered the island, and soon they found themselves standing in a marble room where two handsomely dressed young men stood on a platform to receive them.

Ozma at once stepped from the end of the bridge to the marble platform, followed by Dorothy, and then the bridge disappeared with a slight clang of steel and a marble slab covered the opening from which it had emerged.

The two young men bowed profoundly to Ozma, and one of them said:

"Queen Coo-ee-oh bids you welcome, O Strangers. Her Majesty is waiting to receive you in her palace."

"Lead on," replied Ozma with dignity.

But instead of "leading on," the platform of marble began to rise, carrying them upward through a square hole above which just fitted it. A moment later they found themselves within the great glass dome that covered almost all of the island.

Within this dome was a little village, with houses, streets, gardens and parks. The houses were of colored marbles, prettily designed, with many stained-glass windows, and the streets and gardens seemed well cared for. Exactly under the center of the lofty dome was a small park filled with brilliant flowers, with an elaborate fountain, and facing this park stood a building larger and more imposing than the others. Toward this building the young men escorted Ozma and Dorothy.

On the streets and in the doorways or open windows of the houses were men, women and children, all richly dressed. These were much like other people in different parts of the Land of Oz, except that instead of seeming merry and contented they all wore expressions of much solemnity or of nervous irritation. They had beautiful homes, splended clothes, and ample food, but Dorothy at once decided something was wrong with their lives and that they were not happy. She said nothing, however, but looked curiously at the Skeezers.

At the entrance of the palace Ozma and Dorothy were met by two other young men, in uniform and armed with queer weapons that seemed about halfway between pistols and guns, but were like neither. Their conductors bowed and left them, and the two in uniforms led the girls into the palace.

In a beautiful throne room, surrounded by a dozen or more young men and women, sat the Queen of the Skeezers, Coo-ee-oh. She was a girl who looked older than Ozma or Dorothy—fifteen or sixteen, at least—and although she was elaborately dressed as if she were going to a ball she was too thin and plain of feature to be pretty. But evidently Queen Coo-ee-oh did not realize this fact, for her air and manner betrayed her as proud and haughty and with a high regard for her own importance. Dorothy at once decided she was "snippy" and that she would not like Queen Coo-ee-oh as a companion.

The Queen's hair was as black as her skin was white and her eyes were black, too. The eyes, as she calmly examined Ozma and Dorothy, had a suspicious and unfriendly look in them, but she said quietly:

"I know who you are, for I have consulted my Magic Oracle, which told me that one calls herself Princess Ozma, the Ruler of all the Land of Oz, and the other is Princess Dorothy of Oz, who came from a country called Kansas. I know nothing of the Land of Oz, and I know nothing of Kansas."

"Why, *this* is the Land of Oz!" cried Dorothy. "It's a *part* of the Land of Oz, anyhow, whether you know it or not."

"Oh, in-deed!" answered Queen Coo-ee-oh, scornfully. "I suppose you will claim next that this Princess Ozma, ruling the Land of Oz, rules me!"

"Of course," returned Dorothy. "There's no doubt of it."

The Queen turned to Ozma.

"Do you dare make such a claim?" she asked.

By this time Ozma had made up her mind as to the character of this haughty and disdainful creature, whose self-pride evidently led her to believe herself superior to all others.

"I did not come here to quarrel with your Majesty," said the girl Ruler of Oz, quietly. "What and who I am is well established, and my authority comes from the Fairy Queen Lurline,[1] of whose band I was a member when Lurline made all Oz a Fairyland. There are several countries and several different peoples in this broad land, each of which has its separate rulers, Kings, Emperors and Queens. But all these render obedience to my laws and acknowledge me as the supreme Ruler."

"If other Kings and Queens are fools that does not interest me in the least," replied Coo-ee-oh, disdainfully. "In the Land of the Skeezers I alone am supreme. You are impudent to think I would defer to you—or to anyone else."

"Let us not speak of this now, please," answered Ozma. "Your island is in danger, for a powerful foe is preparing to destroy it."

"Pah! The Flatheads. I do not fear them."

"Their Supreme Dictator is a Sorcerer."

"My magic is greater than his. Let the Flatheads come! They will never return to their barren mountain-top. I will see to that."

Ozma did not like this attitude, for it meant that the Skeezers were eager to fight the Flatheads, and Ozma's object in coming here was to prevent fighting and induce the two quarrelsome neighbors to make peace. She was also greatly disappointed in Coo-ee-oh, for the reports of Su-dic had led her to imagine the Queen more just and honorable than were the Flatheads. Indeed Ozma reflected that the girl might be better at heart than her self-pride and overbearing manner indicated, and in any event it would be wise not to antagonize her but to try to win her friendship.

"I do not like wars, your Majesty," said Ozma. "In the Emerald City, where I rule thousands of people, and in the countries near to the Emerald City, where thousands more acknowledge my rule, there is no army at all, because there is no quarreling and no need to fight. If differences arise between my people, they come to me and I judge the cases and award justice to all. So, when I learned there might be war between two faraway people of Oz, I came here to settle the dispute and adjust the quarrel."

"No one asked you to come," declared Queen Coo-ee-oh. "It is *my* business to settle this dispute, not yours. You say my island is a part of the Land of Oz, which you rule, but that is all nonsense, for I've never heard of the Land of Oz, nor of you. You say you are a fairy, and that fairies gave you command over me. I don't believe it! What I *do* believe is that you are an impostor and have come here to stir up trouble among my people, who are already becoming difficult to manage. You two girls may even be spies of the vile Flatheads, for all I know, and may be trying to trick me. But understand this," she added, proudly rising from her jeweled throne to confront them, "I have magic powers greater than any fairy possesses, and greater than any Flathead possesses. I am a Krumbic Witch—the only Krumbic Witch in the world—and I fear the magic of no other creature that exists! You say you rule thousands. I rule one hundred and one Skeezers. But every one of them trembles at my word. Now that Ozma of Oz and Princess Dorothy are here, I shall rule one hundred and three subjects, for you also shall bow before my power. More than that, in ruling you I also rule the thousands you say you rule."

Dorothy was very indignant at this speech.

"I've got a pink kitten that sometimes talks like that," she said, "but after I give her a good whipping she doesn't think she's so high and mighty after all. If you only knew who Ozma is you'd be scared to death to talk to her like that!"

Queen Coo-ee-oh gave the girl a supercilious look. Then she turned again to Ozma.

"I happen to know," said she, "that the Flatheads intend to attack us tomorrow, but we are ready for them. Until the battle is over, I shall keep you two strangers prisoners on my island, from which there is no chance for you to escape."

She turned and looked around the band of courtiers who stood silently around her throne.

"Lady Aurex," she continued, singling out one of the young women, "take these children to your house and care for them, giving them food and lodging. You may allow them to wander anywhere under the Great Dome, for they are harmless. After I have attended to the Flatheads I will consider what next to do with these foolish girls."

She resumed her seat and the Lady Aurex bowed low and said in a humble manner:

"I obey your Majesty's commands." Then to Ozma and Dorothy she added, "Follow me," and turned to leave the throne room.

Dorothy looked to see what Ozma would do. To her surprise and a little to her disappointment Ozma turned and followed Lady Aurex. So Dorothy trailed after them, but not without giving a parting, haughty look toward Queen Coo-ee-oh, who had her face turned the other way and did not see the disapproving look.

CHAPTER 9

Lady Aurex

Lady Aurex led Ozma and Dorothy along a street to a pretty marble house near to one edge of the great glass dome that covered the village. She did not speak to the girls until she had ushered them into a pleasant room, comfortably furnished, nor did any of the solemn people they met on the street venture to speak.

When they were seated Lady Aurex asked if they were hungry, and finding they were summoned a maid and ordered food to be brought.

This Lady Aurex looked to be about twenty years old, although in the Land of Oz where people have never changed in appearance since the fairies made it a fairyland—where no one grows old or dies—it is always difficult to say how many years anyone has lived. She had a pleasant, attractive face, even though it was solemn and sad as the faces of all Skeezers seemed to be, and her costume was rich and elaborate, as became a lady in waiting upon the Queen.

Ozma had observed Lady Aurex closely and now asked her in a gentle tone:

"Do you, also, believe me to be an impostor?"

"I dare not say," replied Lady Aurex in a low tone.

"Why are you afraid to speak freely?" inquired Ozma.

"The Queen punishes us if we make remarks that she does not like."

"Are we not alone then, in this house?"

"The Queen can hear everything that is spoken on this island—even the slightest whisper," declared Lady Aurex. "She is a wonderful witch, as she has told you, and it is folly to criticize her or disobey her commands."

Ozma looked into her eyes and saw that she would like to say more if she dared. So she drew from her bosom her silver wand, and having muttered a magic phrase in a strange tongue, she left the room and walked slowly around the outside of the house, making a complete circle and waving her wand in mystic curves as she walked. Lady Aurex watched her curiously and, when Ozma had again entered the room and seated herself, she asked:

"What have you done?"

"I've enchanted this house in such a manner that Queen Coo-ee-oh, with all her witchcraft, cannot hear one word we speak within the magic circle I have made," replied Ozma. "We may now speak freely and as loudly as we wish, without fear of the Queen's anger."

Lady Aurex brightened at this.

"Can I trust you?" she asked.

"Ev'rybody trusts Ozma," exclaimed Dorothy. "She is true and honest, and your wicked Queen will be sorry she insulted the powerful Ruler of all the Land of Oz."

"The Queen does not know me yet," said Ozma, "but I want you to know me, Lady Aurex, and I want you to tell me why you, and all the Skeezers, are unhappy. Do not fear Coo-ee-oh's anger, for she cannot hear a word we say, I assure you."

Lady Aurex was thoughtful a moment; then she said: "I shall trust you, Princess Ozma, for I believe you are what you say you are—our Supreme Ruler. If you knew the dreadful punishments our Queen inflicts upon us, you would not wonder we are so unhappy. The Skeezers are not bad people; they do not care to quarrel and fight, even with their enemies the Flatheads; but they are so cowed and fearful of Coo-ee-oh that they obey her slightest word, rather than suffer her anger."

"Hasn't she any heart, then?" asked Dorothy.

"She never displays mercy. She loves no one but herself," asserted Lady Aurex, but she trembled as she said it, as if afraid even yet of her terrible Queen.

"That's pretty bad," said Dorothy, shaking her head gravely. "I see you've a lot to do here, Ozma, in this forsaken corner of the Land of Oz. First place, you've got to take the magic away from Queen Coo-ee-oh, and from that awful Su-dic, too. *My* idea is that neither of them is fit to rule anybody, 'cause they're cruel and hateful. So you'll have to give the Skeezers and Flatheads new rulers and teach all their people that they're part of the Land of Oz and must obey, above all, the lawful Ruler, Ozma of Oz. Then, when you've done that, we can go back home again."

Ozma smiled at her little friend's earnest counsel, but Lady Aurex said in an anxious tone:

"I am surprised that you suggest these reforms while you are yet prisoners on this island and in Coo-ee-oh's power. That these things should be done, there is no doubt, but just now a dreadful war is likely to break out, and frightful things may happen to us all. Our Queen has such conceit that she thinks she can overcome the Su-dic and his people, but it is said Su-dic's magic is very powerful, although not as great as that possessed by his wife Rora, before Coo-ee-oh transformed her into a Golden Pig."

"I don't blame her very much for doing that," remarked Dorothy, "for the Flatheads were wicked to try to catch your beautiful fish and the Witch Rora wanted to poison all the fishes in the lake."

"Do you know the reason?" asked the Lady Aurex.

"I don't s'pose there *was* any reason, 'cept just wickedness," replied Dorothy.

"Tell us the reason," said Ozma earnestly.

"Well, your Majesty, once—a long time ago—the Flatheads and the Skeezers were friendly. They visited our island and we visited their mountain, and everything was pleasant between the two peoples. At that time the Flatheads were ruled by three Adepts in Sorcery, beautiful girls who were not Flatheads, but had wandered to the Flat Mountain and made their home there. These three Adepts used their magic only for good, and the mountain people gladly made them their rulers. They taught the Flatheads how to use their canned brains and how to work metals into clothing that would never wear out, and many other things that added to their happiness and content.

"Coo-ee-oh was our Queen then, as now, but she knew no magic and so had nothing to be proud of. But the three Adepts were very kind to Coo-ee-oh. They built for us this wonderful dome of glass and our houses of marble and taught us to make beautiful clothing and many other things. Coo-ee-oh pretended to be very grateful for these favors, but it seems that all the time she was jealous of the three Adepts and secretly tried to discover their arts of magic. In this she was more clever than anyone suspected. She invited the three Adepts to a banquet one day, and while they were feasting Coo-ee-oh stole their charms and magical instruments and transformed them into three fishes—a gold fish, a silver fish and a bronze fish. While the poor fishes were gasping and flopping helplessly on the floor of the banquet room one of them said reproachfully: 'You will be punished for this, Coo-ee-oh, for if one of us dies or is destroyed, you will become shrivelled and helpless, and all your stolen magic will depart from you.' Frightened by this threat, Coo-ee-oh at once caught up the three fish and ran with them to the shore of the lake, where she cast them into the water. This revived the three Adepts and they swam away and disappeared.

"I, myself, witnessed this shocking scene," continued Lady Aurex, "and so did many other Skeezers. The news was carried to the Flatheads, who then turned from friends to enemies. The Su-dic and his wife Rora were the only ones on the mountain who were glad the three Adepts had been lost to them, and they at once became Rulers of the Flatheads and stole their canned brains from others to make themselves the more powerful. Some of the Adepts' magic tools had been left on the mountain, and these Rora seized and by the use of them she became a witch.

"The result of Coo-ee-oh's treachery was to make both the Skeezers and the Flatheads miserable instead of happy. Not only were the Su-dic and his wife cruel to their people, but our Queen at once became proud and arrogant and treated us very unkindly. All the Skeezers knew she had stolen her magic powers and so she hated us and made us humble ourselves before her and obey her slightest word. If we disobeyed, or did not please her, or if we talked about her when we were in our own homes she would have us dragged to the whipping post in her palace and lashed with knotted cords. That is why we fear her so greatly."

This story filled Ozma's heart with sorrow and Dorothy's heart with indignation.

"I now understand," said Ozma, "why the fishes in the lake have brought about war between the Skeezers and the Flatheads."

"Yes," Lady Aurex answered, "now that you know the story it is easy to understand. The Su-dic and his wife came to our lake hoping to catch the silver fish, or gold fish, or bronze fish—any one of them *would* do—and by destroying it deprive Coo-ee-oh of her magic. Then they could easily conquer her. Also they had another reason for want-ing to catch the fish—they feared that in some way the three Adepts might regain their proper forms and then they would be sure to return to the mountain and punish Rora and the Su-dic. That was why Rora finally tried to poison all the fishes in the lake, at the time Coo-ee-oh transformed her into a Golden Pig. Of course this attempt to destroy the fishes frightened the Queen, for her safety lies in keeping the three fishes alive."

"I s'pose Coo-ee-oh will fight the Flatheads with all her might," observed Dorothy.

"And with all her magic," added Ozma, thoughtfully.

"I do not see how the Flatheads can get to this island to hurt us," said Lady Aurex.

"They have bows and arrows, and I guess they mean to shoot the arrows at your big dome, and break all the glass in it," suggested Dorothy.

But Lady Aurex shook her head with a smile.

"They cannot do that," she replied.

"Why not?"

"I dare not tell you why, but if the Flatheads come to-morrow morning you will yourselves see the reason."

"I do not think they will attempt to harm the island," Ozma declared. "I believe they will first attempt to destroy the fishes, by poi-son or some other means. If they succeed in that, the conquest of the island will not be difficult."

"They have no boats," said Lady Aurex, "and Coo-ee-oh, who has long expected this war, has been preparing for it in many astonishing ways. I almost wish the Flatheads would conquer us, for then we would be free from our dreadful Queen; but I do not wish to see the three transformed fishes destroyed, for in them lies our only hope of future happiness."

"Ozma will take care of you, whatever happens," Dorothy assured her. But the Lady Aurex, not knowing the extent of Ozma's power—which was, in fact, not so great as Dorothy imagined—could not take much comfort in this promise.

It was evident there would be exciting times on the morrow, if the Flatheads really attacked the Skeezers of the Magic Isle.

CHAPTER 10

Under Water

When night fell all the interior of the Great Dome, streets and houses, became lighted with brilliant incandescent lamps, which rendered it bright as day. Dorothy thought the island must look beautiful by night from the outer shore of the lake. There was revelry and feasting in the Queen's palace, and the music of the royal band could be plainly heard in Lady Aurex's house, where Ozma and Dorothy remained with their hostess and keeper. They were prisoners, but treated with much consideration.

Lady Aurex gave them a nice supper and when they wished to retire showed them to a pretty room with comfortable beds and wished them a good night and pleasant dreams.

"What do you think of all this, Ozma?" Dorothy anxiously inquired when they were alone.

"I am glad we came," was the reply, "for although there may be mischief done to-morrow, it was necessary I should know about these people, whose leaders are wild and lawless and oppress their subjects with injustice and cruelties. My task, therefore, is to liberate the Skeezers and the Flatheads and secure for them freedom and happiness. I have no doubt I can accomplish this in time."

"Just now, though, we're in a bad fix," asserted Dorothy. "If Queen Coo-ee-oh conquers to-morrow, she won't be nice to us, and if the Su-dic conquers, he'll be worse."

"Do not worry, dear," said Ozma, "I do not think we are in danger, whatever happens, and the result of our adventure is sure to be good."

Dorothy was not worrying, especially. She had confidence in her friend, the fairy Princess of Oz, and she enjoyed the excitement of the events in which she was taking part. So she crept into bed and fell asleep as easily as if she had been in her own cosy room in Ozma's palace.

A sort of grating, grinding sound awakened her. The whole island seemed to tremble and sway, as it might do in an earthquake. Dorothy sat up in bed, rubbing her eyes to get the sleep out of them, and then found it was daybreak.

Ozma was hurriedly dressing herself.

"What is it?" asked Dorothy, jumping out of bed.

"I'm not sure," answered Ozma "but it feels as if the island is sinking."

As soon as possible they finished dressing, while the creaking and swaying continued. Then they rushed into the living room of the house and found Lady Aurex, fully dressed, awaiting them.

"Do not be alarmed," said their hostess. "Coo-ee-oh has decided to submerge the island, that is all. But it proves the Flatheads are coming to attack us."

"What do you mean by sub-sub-merging the island?" asked Dorothy.

"Come here and see," was the reply.

Lady Aurex led them to a window which faced the side of the great dome which covered all the village, and they could see that the island was indeed sinking, for the water of the lake was already half way up the side of the dome. Through the glass could be seen swimming fishes, and tall stalks of swaying seaweeds, for the water was clear as crystal and through it they could distinguish even the farther shore of the lake.

"The Flatheads are not here yet," said Lady Aurex. "They will come soon, but not until all of this dome is under the surface of the water."

"Won't the dome leak?" Dorothy inquired anxiously.

"No, indeed."

"Was the island ever sub-sub-sunk before?"

"Oh, yes; on several occasions. But Coo-ee-oh doesn't care to do that often, for it requires a lot of hard work to operate the machinery. The dome was built so that the island could disappear. I think," she continued, "that our Queen fears the Flatheads will attack the island and try to break the glass of the dome."

"Well, if we're under water, they can't fight us, and we can't fight them," asserted Dorothy.

"They could kill the fishes, however," said Ozma gravely.

"We have ways to fight, also, even though our island is under water," claimed Lady Aurex. "I cannot tell you all our secrets, but this island is full of surprises. Also our Queen's magic is astonishing."

"Did she steal it all from the three Adepts in Sorcery that are now fishes?"

"She stole the knowledge and the magic tools, but she has used them as the three Adepts never would have done."

By this time the top of the dome was quite under water and suddenly the island stopped sinking and became stationary.

"See!" cried Lady Aurex, pointing to the shore. "The Flatheads have come."

On the bank, which was now far above their heads, a crowd of dark figures could be seen.

"Now let us see what Coo-ee-oh will do to oppose them," continued Lady Aurex, in a voice that betrayed her excitement.

The Flatheads, pushing their way through the line of palm trees, had reached the shore of the lake just as the top of the island's dome disappeared beneath the surface. The water now flowed from shore to shore, but through the clear water the dome was still visible and the houses of the Skeezers could be dimly seen through the panes of glass.

"Good!" exclaimed the Su-dic, who had armed all his followers and had brought with him two copper vessels, which he carefully set down upon the ground beside him. "If Coo-ee-oh wants to hide instead of fighting our job will be easy, for in one of these copper vessels I have enough poison to kill every fish in the lake."

"Kill them, then, while we have time, and then we can go home again," advised one of the chief officers.

"Not yet," objected the Su-dic. "The Queen of the Skeezers has defied me, and I want to get her into my power, as well as to destroy her magic. She transformed my poor wife into a Golden Pig, and I must have revenge for that, whatever else we do."

"Look out!" suddenly exclaimed the officers, pointing into the lake; "something's going to happen."

From the submerged dome a door opened and something black shot swiftly out into the water. The door instantly closed behind it and the dark object cleaved its way through the water, without rising to the surface, directly toward the place where the Flatheads were standing.

"What is that?" Dorothy asked the Lady Aurex.

"That is one of the Queen's submarines,"[1] was the reply. "It is all enclosed, and can move under water. Coo-ee-oh has several of these boats which are kept in little rooms in the basement under our village. When the island is submerged, the Queen uses these boats to reach the shore, and I believe she now intends to fight the Flatheads with them."

The Su-dic and his people knew nothing of Coo-ee-oh's submarines, so they watched with surprise as the under-water boat approached them. When it was quite near the shore it rose to the surface and the top parted and fell back, disclosing a boat full of armed

Skeezers. At the head was the Queen, standing up in the bow and holding in one hand a coil of magic rope that gleamed like silver.

The boat halted and Coo-ee-oh drew back her arm to throw the silver rope toward the Su-dic, who was now but a few feet from her. But the wily Flathead leader quickly realized his danger and before the Queen could throw the rope he caught up one of the copper vessels and dashed its contents full in her face!

CHAPTER 11

The Conquest of the Skeezers

Queen Coo-ee-oh dropped the rope, tottered and fell headlong into the water, sinking beneath the surface, while the Skeezers in the submarine were too bewildered to assist her and only stared at the ripples in the water where she had disappeared. A moment later there arose to the surface a beautiful White Swan.[1] This Swan was of large size, very gracefully formed, and scattered all over its white feathers were tiny diamonds, so thickly placed that as the rays of the morning sun fell upon them the entire body of the Swan glistened like one brilliant diamond. The head of the Diamond Swan had a bill of polished gold and its eyes were two sparkling amethysts.

"Hooray!" cried the Su-dic, dancing up and down with wicked glee. "My poor wife, Rora, is avenged at last. You made her a Golden Pig, Coo-ee-oh, and now I have made you a Diamond Swan. Float on your lake forever, if you like, for your web feet can do no more magic and you are as powerless as the Pig you made of my wife!"

"Villain! Scoundrel!" croaked the Diamond Swan. "You will be punished for this. Oh, what a fool I was to let you enchant me!"

"A fool you were, and a fool you are!" laughed the Su-dic, dancing madly in his delight. And then he carelessly tipped over the other copper vessel with his heel and its contents spilled on the sands and were lost to the last drop.

The Su-dic stopped short and looked at the overturned vessel with a rueful countenance.

"That's too bad—too bad!" he exclaimed sorrowfully. "I've lost all the poison I had to kill the fishes with, and I can't make any more because only my wife knew the secret of it, and she is now a foolish Pig and has forgotten all her magic."

"Very well," said the Diamond Swan scornfully, as she floated upon the water and swam gracefully here and there. "I'm glad to see you are foiled. Your punishment is just beginning, for although you have enchanted me and taken away my powers of sorcery you have still the three magic fishes to deal with, and they'll destroy you in time, mark my words."

The Su-dic stared at the Swan a moment. Then he yelled to his men:

"Shoot her! Shoot the saucy bird!"

They let fly some arrows at the Diamond Swan, but she dove under the water and the missiles fell harmless. When Coo-ee-oh rose to the surface she was far from the shore and she swiftly swam across the lake to where no arrows or spears could reach her.

The Su-dic rubbed his chin and thought what to do next. Near by floated the submarine in which the Queen had come, but the Skeezers who were in it were puzzled what to do with themselves. Perhaps they were not sorry their cruel mistress had been transformed into a Diamond Swan, but the transformation had left them quite helpless. The under-water boat was not operated by machinery, but by certain mystic words uttered by Coo-ee-oh. They didn't know how to submerge it, or how to make the water-tight shield cover them again, or how to make the boat go back to the castle, or make it enter the little basement room where it was usually kept. As a matter of fact, they were now shut out of their village under the Great Dome and could not get back again. So one of the men called to the Supreme Dictator of the Flatheads, saying:

"Please make us prisoners and take us to your mountain, and feed and keep us, for we have nowhere to go."

Then the Su-dic laughed and answered:

"Not so. I can't be bothered by caring for a lot of stupid Skeezers. Stay where you are, or go wherever you please, so long as you keep away from our mountain." He turned to his men and added: "We have conquered Queen Coo-ee-oh and made her a helpless swan. The Skeezers are under water and may stay there. So, having won the war, let us go home again and make merry and feast, having after many years proved the Flatheads to be greater and more powerful than the Skeezers."

So the Flatheads marched away and passed through the row of palms and went back to their mountain, where the Su-dic and a few of his officers feasted and all the others were forced to wait on them.

"I'm sorry we couldn't have roast pig," said the Su-dic, "but as the

only pig we have is made of gold, we can't eat her. Also the Golden
Pig happens to be my wife, and even were she not gold I am sure she
would be too tough to eat."

CHAPTER 12

The Diamond Swan

When the Flatheads had gone away the Diamond Swan swam back
to the boat and one of the young Skeezers named Ervic said to her
eagerly:

"How can we get back to the island, your Majesty?"

"Am I not beautiful?" asked Coo-ee-oh, arching her neck gracefully and spreading her diamond-sprinkled wings. "I can see my reflection in the water, and I'm sure there is no bird nor beast, nor human
as magnificent as I am!"

"How shall we get back to the island, your Majesty?" pleaded
Ervic.

"When my fame spreads throughout the land, people will travel
from all parts of this lake to look upon my loveliness," said Coo-ee-
oh, shaking her feathers to make the diamonds glitter more brilliantly.

"But, your Majesty, we must go home and we do not know how to
get there," Ervic persisted.

"My eyes," remarked the Diamond Swan, "are wonderfully blue
and bright and will charm all beholders."

"Tell us how to make the boat go—how to get back into the
island," begged Ervic and the others cried just as earnestly: "Tell us,
Coo-ee-oh; tell us!"

"I don't know," replied the Queen in a careless tone.

"You are a magic-worker, a sorceress, a witch!"

"I was, of course, when I was a girl," she said, bending her head
over the clear water to catch her reflection in it; "but now I've forgotten all such foolish things as magic. Swans are lovelier than girls, especially when they're sprinkled with diamonds. Don't you think so?"
And she gracefully swam away, without seeming to care whether they
answered or not.

Ervic and his companions were in despair. They saw plainly that
Coo-ee-oh could not or would not help them. The former Queen had

no further thought for her island, her people, or her wonderful magic; she was only intent on admiring her own beauty.

"Truly," said Ervic, in a gloomy voice, "the Flatheads have conquered us!"

Some of these events had been witnessed by Ozma and Dorothy and Lady Aurex, who had left the house and gone close to the glass of the dome, in order to see what was going on. Many of the Skeezers had also crowded against the dome, wondering what would happen next. Although their vision was to an extent blurred by the water and the necessity of looking upward at an angle, they had observed the main points of the drama enacted above. They saw Queen Coo-ee-oh's submarine come to the surface and open; they saw the Queen standing erect to throw her magic rope; they saw her sudden transformation into a Diamond Swan, and a cry of amazement went up from the Skeezers inside the dome.

"Good!" exclaimed Dorothy. "I hate that old Su-dic, but I'm glad Coo-ee-oh is punished."

"This is a dreadful misfortune!" cried Lady Aurex, pressing her hands upon her heart.

"Yes," agreed Ozma, nodding her head thoughtfully; "Coo-ee-oh's misfortune will prove a terrible blow to her people."

"What do you mean by that?" asked Dorothy in surprise. "Seems to me the Skeezers are in luck to lose their cruel Queen."

"If that were all you would be right," responded Lady Aurex; "and if the island were above water it would not be so serious. But here we all are, at the bottom of the lake, and fast prisoners in this dome."

"Can't you raise the island?" inquired Dorothy.

"No. Only Coo-ee-oh knew how to do that," was the answer.

"We can try," insisted Dorothy. "If it can be made to go down, it can be made to come up. The machinery is still here, I suppose."

"Yes; but the machinery works by magic, and Coo-ee-oh would never share her secret power with any one of us."

Dorothy's face grew grave; but she was thinking.

"Ozma knows a lot of magic," she said.

"But not that kind of magic," Ozma replied.

"Can't you learn how, by looking at the machinery?"

"I'm afraid not my dear. It isn't fairy magic at all; it is witchcraft."

"Well," said Dorothy, turning to Lady Aurex, "you say there are other sub-sub-sinking boats. We can get in one of those, and shoot out to the top of the water, like Coo-ee-oh did, and so escape. And then we can help to rescue all the Skeezers down here."

"No one knows how to work the under-water boats but the Queen," declared Lady Aurex.

"Isn't there any door or window in this dome that we could open?"

"No; and, if there were, the water would rush in to flood the dome, and we could not get out."

"The Skeezers," said Ozma, "could not drown; they only get wet and soggy and in that condition they would be very uncomfortable and unhappy. But *you* are a mortal girl, Dorothy, and if your Magic Belt protected you from death you would have to lie forever at the bottom of the lake."

"No, I'd rather die quickly," asserted the little girl. "But there are doors in the basement that open—to let out the bridges and the boats—and that would not flood the dome, you know."

"Those doors open by a magic word, and only Coo-ee-oh knows the word that must be uttered," said Lady Aurex.

"Dear me!" exclaimed Dorothy, "that dreadful Queen's witchcraft upsets all my plans to escape. I guess I'll give it up, Ozma, and let *you* save us!"

Ozma smiled, but her smile was not so cheerful as usual. The Princess of Oz found herself confronted with a serious problem, and although she had no thought of despairing she realized that the Skeezers and their island, as well as Dorothy and herself, were in grave trouble and that unless she could find a means to save them they would be lost to the Land of Oz for all future time.

"In such a dilemma," said she, musingly, "nothing is gained by haste. Careful thought may aid us, and so may the course of events. The unexpected is always likely to happen, and cheerful patience is better than reckless action."

"All right," returned Dorothy; "take your time, Ozma; there's no hurry. How about some breakfast, Lady Aurex?"

Their hostess led them back to the house, where she ordered her trembling servants to prepare and serve breakfast. All the Skeezers were frightened and anxious over the transformation of their Queen into a swan. Coo-ee-oh was feared and hated, but they had depended on her magic to conquer the Flatheads and she was the only one who could raise their island to the surface of the lake again.

Before breakfast was over several of the leading Skeezers came to Aurex to ask her advice and to question Princess Ozma, of whom they knew nothing except that she claimed to be a fairy and the Ruler of all the land, including the Lake of the Skeezers.

"If what you told Queen Coo-ee-oh was the truth," they said to her, "you are our lawful mistress, and we may depend on you to get us out of our difficulties."

"I will try to do that," Ozma graciously assured them, "but you must remember that the powers of fairies are granted them to bring comfort and happiness to all who appeal to them. On the contrary, such magic as Coo-ee-oh knew and practiced is unlawful witchcraft and her arts are such as no fairy would condescend to use. However, it is sometimes necessary to consider evil in order to accomplish good, and perhaps by studying Coo-ee-oh's tools and charms of witchcraft I may be able to save us. Do you promise to accept me as your Ruler and to obey my commands?"

They promised willingly.

"Then," continued Ozma, "I will go to Coo-ee-oh's palace and take possession of it. Perhaps what I find there will be of use to me. In the meantime tell all the Skeezers to fear nothing, but have patience. Let them return to their homes and perform their daily tasks as usual. Coo-ee-oh's loss may not prove a misfortune, but rather a blessing."

This speech cheered the Skeezers amazingly. Really, they had no one now to depend upon but Ozma, and in spite of their dangerous position their hearts were lightened by the transformation and absence of their cruel Queen.

They got out their brass band and a grand procession escorted Ozma and Dorothy to the palace, where all of Coo-ee-oh's former servants were eager to wait upon them. Ozma invited Lady Aurex to stay at the palace also, for she knew all about the Skeezers and their island and had also been a favorite of the former Queen, so her advice and information were sure to prove valuable.

Ozma was somewhat disappointed in what she found in the palace. One room of Coo-ee-oh's private suite was entirely devoted to the practice of witchcraft, and here were countless queer instruments and jars of ointments and bottles of potions labeled with queer names, and strange machines that Ozma could not guess the use of, and pickled toads and snails and lizards, and a shelf of books that were written in blood, but in a language which the Ruler of Oz did not know.

"I do not see," said Ozma to Dorothy, who accompanied her in her search, "how Coo-ee-oh knew the use of the magic tools she stole from the three Adept Witches. Moreover, from all reports these

Adepts practiced only good witchcraft, such as would be helpful to their people, while Coo-ee-oh performed only evil."

"Perhaps she turned the good things to evil uses?" suggested Dorothy.

"Yes, and with the knowledge she gained Coo-ee-oh doubtless invented many evil things quite unknown to the good Adepts, who are now fishes," added Ozma. "It is unfortunate for us that the Queen kept her secrets so closely guarded, for no one but herself could use any of these strange things gathered in this room."

"Couldn't we capture the Diamond Swan and make her tell the secrets?" asked Dorothy.

"No; even were we able to capture her, Coo-ee-oh now has forgotten all the magic she ever knew. But until we ourselves escape from this dome we could not capture the Swan, and were we to escape we would have no use for Coo-ee-oh's magic."

"That's a fact," admitted Dorothy. "But—say, Ozma, here's a good idea! Couldn't we capture the three fishes—the gold and silver and bronze ones, and couldn't you transform 'em back to their own shapes, and then couldn't the three Adepts get us out of here?"

"You are not very practical, Dorothy dear. It would be as hard for us to capture the three fishes, from among all the other fishes in the lake, as to capture the Swan."

"But if we could, it would be more help to us," persisted the little girl.

"That is true," answered Ozma, smiling at her friend's eagerness. "You find a way to catch the fish, and I'll promise when they are caught to restore them to their proper forms."

"I know you think I can't do it," replied Dorothy, "but I'm going to try."

She left the palace and went to a place where she could look through a clear pane of the glass dome into the surrounding water. Immediately she became interested in the queer sights that met her view.

The Lake of the Skeezers was inhabited by fishes of many kinds and many sizes. The water was so transparent that the girl could see for a long distance and the fishes came so close to the glass of the dome that sometimes they actually touched it. On the white sands at the bottom of the lake were star-fish, lobsters, crabs and many shell fish of strange shapes and with shells of gorgeous hues. The water foliage was of brilliant colors and to Dorothy it resembled a splendid garden.

But the fishes were the most interesting of all. Some were big and lazy, floating along or lying at rest with just their fins waving. Many with big round eyes looked full at the girl as she watched them and Dorothy wondered if they could hear her through the glass if she spoke to them. In Oz, where all the animals and birds can talk, many fishes are able to talk also, but usually they are more stupid than birds and animals because they think slowly and haven't much to talk about.

In the Lake of the Skeezers the fish of smaller size were more active than the big ones and darted quickly in and out among the swaying weeds, as if they had important business and were in a hurry. It was among the smaller varieties that Dorothy hoped to spy the gold and silver and bronze fishes. She had an idea the three would keep together, being companions now as they were in their natural forms, but such a multitude of fishes constantly passed, the scene shifting every moment, that she was not sure she would notice them even if they appeared in view. Her eyes couldn't look in all directions and the fishes she sought might be on the other side of the dome, or far away in the lake.

"P'raps, because they were afraid of Coo-ee-oh, they've hid themselves somewhere, and don't know their enemy has been transformed," she reflected.

She watched the fishes for a long time, until she became hungry and went back to the palace for lunch. But she was not discouraged.

"Anything new, Ozma?" she asked.

"No, dear. Did you discover the three fishes?"

"Not yet. But there isn't anything better for me to do, Ozma, so I guess I'll go back and watch again."

CHAPTER 13

The Alarm Bell

Glinda, the Good, in her palace in the Quadling Country, had many things to occupy her mind, for not only did she look after the weaving and embroidery of her bevy of maids, and assist all those who came to her to implore her help—beasts and birds as well as people—but she was a close student of the arts of sorcery and spent much time in her

Magical Laboratory, where she strove to find a remedy for every evil and to perfect her skill in magic.

Nevertheless, she did not forget to look in the Great Book of Records each day to see if any mention was made of the visit of Ozma and Dorothy to the Enchanted Mountain of the Flatheads and the Magic Isle of the Skeezers. The Records told her that Ozma had arrived at the mountain, that she had escaped, with her companion, and gone to the island of the Skeezers, and that Queen Coo-ee-oh had submerged the island so that it was entirely under water. Then came the statement that the Flatheads had come to the lake to poison the fishes and that their Supreme Director had transformed Queen Coo-ee-oh into a swan.

No other details were given in the Great Book and so Glinda did not know that since Coo-ee-oh had forgotten her magic none of the Skeezers knew how to raise the island to the surface again. So Glinda was not worried about Ozma and Dorothy until one morning, while she sat with her maids, there came a sudden clang of the great alarm bell. This was so unusual that every maid gave a start and even the Sorceress for a moment could not think what the alarm meant.

Then she remembered the ring she had given Dorothy when she left the palace to start on her venture. In giving the ring Glinda had warned the little girl not to use its magic powers unless she and Ozma were in real danger, but then she was to turn it on her finger once to the right and once to the left and Glinda's alarm bell would ring.

So the Sorceress now knew that danger threatened her beloved Ruler and Princess Dorothy, and she hurried to her magic room to seek information as to what sort of danger it was. The answer to her question was not very satisfactory, for it was only: "Ozma and Dorothy are prisoners in the great Dome of the Isle of the Skeezers, and the Dome is under the water of the lake."

"Hasn't Ozma the power to raise the island to the surface?" inquired Glinda.

"No," was the reply, and the Record refused to say more except that Queen Coo-ee-oh, who alone could command the island to rise, had been transformed by the Flathead Su-dic into a Diamond Swan.

Then Glinda consulted the past records of the Skeezers in the Great Book. After diligent search she discovered that Coo-ee-oh was a powerful sorceress, who had gained most of her power by treacherously transforming the Adepts of Magic, who were visiting her, into three fishes—gold, silver and bronze—after which she had them cast into the lake.

Glinda reflected earnestly on this information and decided that someone must go to Ozma's assistance. While there was no great need of haste, because Ozma and Dorothy could live in a submerged dome a long time, it was evident they could not get out until someone was able to raise the island.

The Sorceress looked through all her recipes and books of sorcery, but could find no magic that would raise a sunken island. Such a thing had never before been required in sorcery. Then Glinda made a little island, covered by a glass dome, and sunk it in a pond near her castle, and experimented in magical ways to bring it to the surface. She made several such experiments, but all were failures. It seemed a simple thing to do, yet she could not do it.

Nevertheless, the wise Sorceress did not despair of finding a way to liberate her friends. Finally she concluded that the best thing to do was to go to the Skeezer country and examine the lake. While there she was more likely to discover a solution to the problem that bothered her, and to work out a plan for the rescue of Ozma and Dorothy.

So Glinda summoned her storks and her aerial chariot, and telling her maids she was going on a journey and might not soon return, she entered the chariot and was carried swiftly to the Emerald City.

In Princess Ozma's palace the Scarecrow was now acting as Ruler of the Land of Oz. There wasn't much for him to do, because all the affairs of state moved so smoothly, but he was there in case anything unforeseen should happen.

Glinda found the Scarecrow playing croquet with Trot and Betsy Bobbin, two little girls who lived at the palace under Ozma's protection and were great friends of Dorothy and much loved by all the Oz people.

"Something's happened!" cried Trot, as the chariot of the Sorceress descended near them. "Glinda never comes here 'cept something's gone wrong."

"I hope no harm has come to Ozma, or Dorothy," said Betsy anxiously, as the lovely Sorceress stepped down from her chariot.

Glinda approached the Scarecrow and told him of the dilemma of Ozma and Dorothy and she added: "We must save them, somehow, Scarecrow."

"Of course," replied the Scarecrow, stumbling over a wicket and falling flat on his painted face.

The girls picked him up and patted his straw stuffing into shape, and he continued, as if nothing had occurred: "But you'll have to tell me what to do, for I never have raised a sunken island in all my life."

"We must have a Council of State as soon as possible," proposed the Sorceress. "Please send messengers to summon all of Ozma's counsellors to this palace. Then we can decide what is best to be done."

The Scarecrow lost no time in doing this. Fortunately most of the royal counsellors were in the Emerald City or near to it, so they all met in the throne room of the palace that same evening.

CHAPTER 14

Ozma's Counsellors

No Ruler ever had such a queer assortment of advisers as the Princess Ozma had gathered about her throne. Indeed, in no other country could such amazing people exist. But Ozma loved them for their peculiarities[1] and could trust every one of them.

First there was the Tin Woodman. Every bit of him was tin, brightly polished. All his joints were kept well oiled and moved smoothly. He carried a gleaming axe to prove he was a woodman, but seldom had cause to use it because he lived in a magnificent tin castle in the Winkie Country of Oz and was the Emperor of all the Winkies. The Tin Woodman's name was Nick Chopper. He had a very good mind, but his heart was not of much account, so he was very careful to do nothing unkind or to hurt anyone's feelings.

Another counsellor was Scraps, the Patchwork Girl of Oz,[2] who was made of a gaudy patchwork quilt, cut into shape and stuffed with cotton. This Patchwork Girl was very intelligent, but so full of fun and mad pranks that a lot of more stupid folks thought she must be crazy. Scraps was jolly under all conditions, however grave they might be, but her laughter and good spirits were of value in cheering others and in her seemingly careless remarks much wisdom could often be found.

Then there was the Shaggy Man—shaggy from head to foot, hair and whiskers, clothes and shoes—but very kind and gentle and one of Ozma's most loyal supporters.

Tik-Tok was there, a copper man with machinery inside him, so cleverly constructed that he moved, spoke and thought by three separate clock-works. Tik-Tok was very reliable because he always did exactly what he was wound up to do, but his machinery was liable to run down at times and then he was quite helpless until wound up again.

A different sort of person was Jack Pumpkinhead, one of Ozma's oldest friends and her companion on many adventures. Jack's body was very crude and awkward, being formed of limbs of trees of different sizes, jointed with wooden pegs. But it was a substantial body and not likely to break or wear out, and when it was dressed the clothes covered much of its roughness. The head of Jack Pumpkinhead was, as you have guessed, a ripe pumpkin, with the eyes, nose and mouth carved upon one side. The pumpkin was stuck on Jack's wooden neck and was liable to get turned sidewise or backward and then he would have to straighten it with his wooden hands.

The worst thing about this sort of a head was that it did not keep well and was sure to spoil sooner or later. So Jack's main business was to grow a field of fine pumpkins each year, and always before his old head spoiled he would select a fresh pumpkin from the field and carve the features on it very neatly, and have it ready to replace the old head whenever it became necessary. He didn't always carve it the same way, so his friends never knew exactly what sort of an expression they would find on his face. But there was no mistaking him, because he was the only pumpkin-headed man alive in the Land of Oz.

A one-legged sailor-man was a member of Ozma's council. His name was Cap'n Bill[3] and he had come to the Land of Oz with Trot, and had been made welcome on account of his cleverness, honesty and good-nature. He wore a wooden leg to replace the one he had lost and was a great friend of all the children in Oz because he could whittle all sorts of toys out of wood with his big jack-knife.

Professor H. M. Wogglebug, T. E., was another member of the council. The "H. M." meant Highly Magnified, for the Professor was once a little bug, who became magnified to the size of a man and always remained so. The "T. E." meant that he was Thoroughly Educated. He was at the head of Princess Ozma's Royal Athletic College, and so that the students would not have to study and so lose much time that could be devoted to athletic sports, such as football, baseball and the like, Professor Wogglebug had invented the famous Educational Pills. If one of the college students took a Geography Pill after breakfast, he knew his geography lesson in an instant; if he took a Spelling Pill he at once knew his spelling lesson, and an Arithmetic Pill enabled the student to do any kind of sum without having to think about it.

These useful pills made the college very popular and taught the boys and girls of Oz their lessons in the easiest possible way. In spite of this, Professor Wogglebug was not a favorite outside his college, for he was very conceited and admired himself so much and displayed his cleverness and learning so constantly, that no one cared to associate with him. Ozma found him of value in her councils, nevertheless.

Perhaps the most splendidly dressed of all those present was a great frog as large as a man, called the Frogman,[4] who was noted for his wise sayings. He had come to the Emerald City from the Yip Country of Oz and was a guest of honor. His long-tailed coat was of velvet, his vest of satin and his trousers of finest silk. There were diamond buckles on his shoes and he carried a gold-headed cane and a high silk hat. All of the bright colors were represented in his rich attire, so it tired one's eyes to look at him for long, until one became used to his splendor.

The best farmer in all Oz was Uncle Henry, who was Dorothy's own uncle, and who now lived near the Emerald City with his wife Aunt Em. Uncle Henry taught the Oz people how to grow the finest vegetables and fruits and grains and was of much use to Ozma in keeping the Royal Storehouses well filled. He, too, was a counsellor.

The reason I mention the little Wizard of Oz last is because he was the most important man in the Land of Oz. He wasn't a big man in size, but he was a big man in power and intelligence and second only to Glinda the Good in all the mystic arts of magic. Glinda had taught him, and the Wizard and the Sorceress were the only ones in Oz permitted by law to practice wizardry and sorcery, which they applied only to good uses and for the benefit of the people.

The Wizard wasn't exactly handsome but he was pleasant to look at. His bald head was as shiny as if it had been varnished; there was always a merry twinkle in his eyes and he was as spry as a schoolboy. Dorothy says the reason the Wizard is not as powerful as Glinda is because Glinda didn't teach him all she knows, but what the Wizard knows he knows very well and so he performs some very remarkable magic.

The ten I have mentioned assembled, with the Scarecrow and Glinda, in Ozma's throne room, right after dinner that evening, and the Sorceress told them all she knew of the plight of Ozma and Dorothy.

"Of course we must rescue them," she continued, "and the sooner they are rescued the better pleased they will be; but what we must now determine is how they can be saved. That is why I have called you together in council."

"The easiest way," remarked the Shaggy Man, "is to raise the sunken island of the Skeezers to the top of the water again."

"Tell me how?" said Glinda.

"I don't know how, your Highness, for I have never raised a sunken island."

"We might all get under it and lift," suggested Professor Woggle-bug.

"How can we get under it when it rests on the bottom of the lake?" asked the Sorceress.

"Couldn't we throw a rope around it and pull it ashore?" inquired Jack Pumpkinhead.

"Why not pump the water out of the lake?" suggested the Patch-work Girl with a laugh.

"Do be sensible!" pleaded Glinda. "This is a serious matter, and we must give it serious thought."

"How big is the lake and how big is the island?" was the Frog-man's question.

"None of us can tell, for we have not been there."

"In that case," said the Scarecrow, "it appears to me we ought to go to the Skeezer country and examine it carefully."

"Quite right," agreed the Tin Woodman.

"We-will-have-to-go-there-any-how," remarked Tik-Tok in his jerky machine voice.

"The question is which of us shall go, and how many of us?" said the Wizard.

"I shall go of course," declared the Scarecrow.

"And I," said Scraps.

"It is my duty to Ozma to go," asserted the Tin Woodman.

"I could not stay away, knowing our loved Princess is in danger," said the Wizard.

"We all feel like that," Uncle Henry said.

Finally one and all present decided to go to the Skeezer country, with Glinda and the little Wizard to lead them. Magic must meet magic in order to conquer it, so these two skillful magic-workers were necessary to insure the success of the expedition.

They were all ready to start at a moment's notice, for none had any affairs of importance to attend to. Jack was wearing a newly made Pumpkin-head and the Scarecrow had recently been stuffed with fresh straw. Tik-Tok's machinery was in good running order and the Tin Woodman always was well oiled.

"It is quite a long journey," said Glinda, "and while I might travel quickly to the Skeezer country by means of my stork chariot the rest of you will be obliged to walk. So, as we must keep together, I will send my chariot back to my castle and we will plan to leave the Emerald City at sunrise to-morrow."

CHAPTER 15

The Great Sorceress

Betsy and Trot, when they heard of the rescue expedition, begged the Wizard to permit them to join it and he consented. The Glass Cat,[1] overhearing the conversation, wanted to go also and to this the Wizard made no objection.

This Glass Cat was one of the real curiosities of Oz. It had been made and brought to life by a clever magician named Dr. Pipt,[2] who was not now permitted to work magic and was an ordinary citizen of the Emerald City. The cat was of transparent glass, through which one could plainly see its ruby heart beating and its pink brains whirling around in the top of the head.

The Glass Cat's eyes were emeralds; its fluffy tail was of spun glass and very beautiful. The ruby heart, while pretty to look at, was hard and cold and the Glass Cat's disposition was not pleasant at all times. It scorned to catch mice, did not eat, and was extremely lazy. If you complimented the remarkable cat on her beauty, she would be very friendly, for she loved admiration above everything. The pink brains were always working and their owner was indeed more intelligent than most common cats.

Three other additions to the rescue party were made the next morning, just as they were setting out upon their journey. The first was a little boy called Button Bright,[3] because he had no other name that anyone could remember. He was a fine, manly little fellow, well mannered and good humored, who had only one bad fault. He was continually getting lost. To be sure, Button Bright got found as often as he got lost, but when he was missing his friends could not help being anxious about him.

"Some day," predicted the Patchwork Girl, "he won't be found, and that will be the last of him." But that didn't worry Button Bright, who was so careless that he did not seem to be able to break the habit of getting lost.

The second addition to the party was a Munchkin boy of about Button Bright's age, named Ojo.[4] He was often called "Ojo the Lucky," because good fortune followed him wherever he went. He and Button Bright were close friends, although of such different natures, and Trot and Betsy were fond of both.

The third and last to join the expedition was an enormous lion, one of Ozma's regular guardians and the most important and intelligent beast in all Oz. He called himself the Cowardly Lion, saying that every little danger scared him so badly that his heart thumped against his ribs, but all who knew him knew that the Cowardly Lion's fears were coupled with bravery and that however much he might be frightened he summoned courage to meet every danger he encountered. Often he had saved Dorothy and Ozma in times of peril, but afterward he moaned and trembled and wept because he had been so scared.

"If Ozma needs help, I'm going to help her," said the great beast. "And, I suspect the rest of you may need me on the journey—especially Trot and Betsy—for you may pass through a dangerous part of the country. I know that wild Gillikin country pretty well. Its forests harbor many ferocious beasts."

They were glad the Cowardly Lion was to join them, and in good spirits the entire party formed a procession and marched out of the Emerald City amid the shouts of the people, who wished them success and a safe return with their beloved Ruler.

They followed a different route from that taken by Ozma and Dorothy, for they went through the Winkie Country and up north toward Oogaboo. But before they got there they swerved to the left and entered the Great Gillikin Forest, the nearest thing to a wilderness in all Oz. Even the Cowardly Lion had to admit that certain parts of this forest were unknown to him, although he had often wandered among the trees, and the Scarecrow and Tin Woodman, who were great travelers, never had been there at all.

The forest was only reached after a tedious tramp, for some of the Rescue Expedition were quite awkward on their feet. The Patchwork Girl was as light as a feather and very spry; the Tin Woodman covered the ground as easily as Uncle Henry and the Wizard; but Tik-Tok moved slowly and the slightest obstruction in the road would halt him until the others cleared it away. Then, too, Tik-Tok's machinery kept running down, so Betsy and Trot took turns in winding it up.

The Scarecrow was more clumsy but less bother, for although he often stumbled and fell he could scramble up again and a little patting of his straw-stuffed body would put him in good shape again.

Another awkward one was Jack Pumpkinhead, for walking would jar his head around on his neck and then he would be likely to go in the wrong direction. But the Frogman took Jack's arm and then he followed the path more easily.

Cap'n Bill's wooden leg didn't prevent him from keeping up with the others and the old sailor could walk as far as any of them.

When they entered the forest the Cowardly Lion took the lead. There was no path here for men, but many beasts had made paths of their own which only the eyes of the Lion, practiced in woodcraft, could discern. So he stalked ahead and wound his way in and out, the others following in single file, Glinda being next to the Lion.

There are dangers in the forest, of course, but as the huge Lion headed the party he kept the wild denizens of the wilderness from bothering the travelers. Once, to be sure, an enormous leopard sprang upon the Glass Cat and caught her in his powerful jaws, but he broke several of his teeth and with howls of pain and dismay dropped his prey and vanished among the trees.

"Are you hurt?" Trot anxiously inquired of the Glass Cat.

"How silly!" exclaimed the creature in an irritated tone of voice; "nothing can hurt glass, and I'm too solid to break easily. But I'm annoyed at that leopard's impudence. He has no respect for beauty or intelligence. If he had noticed my pink brains work, I'm sure he would have realized I'm too important to be grabbed in a wild beast's jaws."

"Never mind," said Trot consolingly; "I'm sure he won't do it again."

They were almost in the center of the forest when Ojo, the Munchkin boy, suddenly said: "Why, where's Button Bright?"

They halted and looked around them. Button Bright was not with the party.

"Dear me," remarked Betsy, "I expect he's lost again!"

"When did you see him last, Ojo?" inquired Glinda.

"It was some time ago," replied Ojo. "He was trailing along at the end and throwing twigs at the squirrels in the trees. Then I went to talk to Betsy and Trot, and just now I noticed he was gone."

"This is too bad," declared the Wizard, "for it is sure to delay our journey. We must find Button Bright before we go any farther, for this forest is full of ferocious beasts that would not hesitate to tear the boy to pieces."

"But what shall we do?" asked the Scarecrow. "If any of us leaves the party to search for Button Bright he or she might fall a victim to the beasts, and if the Lion leaves us we will have no protector."

"The Glass Cat could go," suggested the Frogman. "The beasts can do her no harm, as we have discovered."

The Wizard turned to Glinda.

"Cannot your sorcery discover where Button Bright is?" he asked.

"I think so," replied the Sorceress.

She called to Uncle Henry, who had been carrying her wicker box, to bring it to her, and when he obeyed she opened it and drew out a small round mirror. On the surface of the glass she dusted a white powder and then wiped it away with her handkerchief and looked in the mirror. It reflected a part of the forest, and there, beneath a wide-spreading tree, Button Bright was lying asleep. On one side of him crouched a tiger, ready to spring; on the other side was a big gray wolf, its bared fangs glistening in a wicked way.

"Goodness me!" cried Trot, looking over Glinda's shoulder. "They'll catch and kill him sure."

Everyone crowded around for a glimpse at the magic mirror.

"Pretty bad—pretty bad!" said the Scarecrow sorrowfully.

"Comes of getting lost!" said Cap'n Bill, sighing.

"Guess he's a goner!" said the Frogman, wiping his eyes on his purple silk handkerchief.

"But where is he? Can't we save him?" asked Ojo the Lucky.

"If we knew where he is we could probably save him," replied the little Wizard, "but that tree looks so much like all the other trees, that we can't tell whether it's far away or near by."

"Look at Glinda!" exclaimed Betsy.

Glinda, having handed the mirror to the Wizard, had stepped aside and was making strange passes with her outstretched arms and reciting in low, sweet tones a mystical incantation. Most of them watched the Sorceress with anxious eyes, despair giving way to the hope that she might be able to save their friend. The Wizard, however, watched the scene in the mirror, while over his shoulders peered Trot, the Scarecrow and the Shaggy Man.

What they saw was more strange than Glinda's actions. The tiger started to spring on the sleeping boy, but suddenly lost its power to move and lay flat upon the ground. The gray wolf seemed unable to lift its feet from the ground. It pulled first at one leg and then at another, and finding itself strangely confined to the spot began to bark and snarl angrily. They couldn't hear the barkings and snarls, but they could see the creature's mouth open and its thick lips move. Button Bright, however, being but a few feet away from the wolf, heard its cries of rage, which wakened him from his untroubled sleep.

The boy sat up and looked first at the tiger and then at the wolf. His face showed that for a moment he was quite frightened, but he soon saw that the beasts were unable to approach him and so he got upon his feet and examined them curiously, with a mischievous smile upon his face. Then he deliberately kicked the tiger's head with his foot and catching up a fallen branch of a tree he went to the wolf and gave it a good whacking. Both the beasts were furious at such treatment but could not resent it.

Button Bright now threw down the stick and with his hands in his pockets wandered carelessly away.

"Now," said Glinda, "let the Glass Cat run and find him. He is in that direction," pointing the way, "but how far off I do not know. Make haste and lead him back to us as quickly as you can."

The Glass Cat did not obey everyone's orders, but she really feared the great Sorceress, so as soon as the words were spoken the crystal animal darted away and was quickly lost to sight.

The Wizard handed the mirror back to Glinda, for the woodland scene had now faded from the glass. Then those who cared to rest sat down to await Button Bright's coming. It was not long before he appeared through the trees and as he rejoined his friends he said in a peevish tone:

"Don't ever send that Glass Cat to find me again. She was very impolite and, if we didn't all know that she had no manners, I'd say she insulted me."

Glinda turned upon the boy sternly.

"You have caused all of us much anxiety and annoyance," said she. "Only my magic saved you from destruction. I forbid you to get lost again."

"Of course," he answered. "It won't be *my* fault if I get lost again; but it wasn't my fault *this* time."

CHAPTER 16

The Enchanted Fishes

I must now tell you what happened to Ervic and the three other Skeezers who were left floating in the iron boat after Queen Coo-ee-oh had been transformed into a Diamond Swan by the magic of the Flathead Su-dic.

The four Skeezers were all young men and their leader was Ervic. Coo-ee-oh had taken them with her in the boat to assist her if she captured the Flathead chief, as she hoped to do by means of her silver rope. They knew nothing about the witchcraft that moved the submarine and so, when left floating upon the lake, were at a loss what to do. The submarine could not be submerged by them or made to return to the sunken island. There were neither oars nor sails in the boat, which was not anchored but drifted quietly upon the surface of the lake.

The Diamond Swan had no further thought or care for her people. She had sailed over to the other side of the lake and all the calls and pleadings of Ervic and his companions were unheeded by the vain bird. As there was nothing else for them to do, they sat quietly in their boat and waited as patiently as they could for someone to come to their aid.

The Flatheads had refused to help them and had gone back to their mountain. All the Skeezers were imprisoned in the Great Dome and could not help even themselves. When evening came, they saw the Diamond Swan, still keeping to the opposite shore of the lake, walk out of the water to the sands, shake her diamond-sprinkled feathers, and then disappear among the bushes to seek a resting place for the night.

"I'm hungry," said Ervic.

"I'm cold," said another Skeezer.

"I'm tired," said a third.

"I'm afraid," said the last one of them.

But it did them no good to complain. Night fell and the moon rose and cast a silvery sheen over the surface of the water.

"Go to sleep," said Ervic to his companions. "I'll stay awake and watch, for we may be rescued in some unexpected way."

So the other three laid themselves down in the bottom of the boat and were soon fast asleep.

Ervic watched. He rested himself by leaning over the bow of the boat, his face near to the moonlit water, and thought dreamily of the day's surprising events and wondered what would happen to the prisoners in the Great Dome.

Suddenly a tiny goldfish popped its head above the surface of the lake, not more than a foot from his eyes. A silverfish then raised its head beside that of the goldfish, and a moment later a bronzefish lifted its head beside the others. The three fish, all in a row, looked earnestly with their round, bright eyes into the astonished eyes of Ervic the Skeezer.

"We are the three Adepts whom Queen Coo-ee-oh betrayed and wickedly transformed," said the goldfish, its voice low and soft but distinctly heard in the stillness of the night.

"I know of our Queen's treacherous deed," replied Ervic, "and I am sorry for your misfortune. Have you been in the lake ever since?"

"Yes," was the reply.

"I—I hope you are well—and comfortable," stammered Ervic, not knowing what else to say.

"We knew that some day Coo-ee-oh would meet with the fate she so richly deserves," declared the bronzefish. "We have waited and watched for this time. Now if you will promise to help us and will be faithful and true, you can aid us in regaining our natural forms, and save yourself and all your people from the dangers that now threaten you."

"Well," said Ervic, "you can depend on my doing the best I can. But I'm no witch, nor magician, you must know."

"All we ask is that you obey our instructions," returned the silverfish. "We know that you are honest and that you served Coo-ee-oh only because you were obliged to in order to escape her anger. Do as we command and all will be well."

"I promise!" exclaimed the young man. "Tell me what I am to do first."

"You will find in the bottom of your boat the silver cord which dropped from Coo-ee-oh's hand when she was transformed," said the goldfish. "Tie one end of that cord to the bow of your boat and drop the other end to us in the water. Together we will pull your boat to the shore."

Ervic much doubted that the three small fishes could move so heavy a boat, but he did as he was told and the fishes all seized their end of the silver cord in their mouths and headed toward the nearest shore, which was the very place where the Flatheads had stood when they conquered Queen Coo-ee-oh.

At first the boat did not move at all, although the fishes pulled with all their strength. But presently the strain began to tell. Very slowly the boat crept toward the shore, gaining more speed at every moment. A couple of yards away from the sandy beach the fishes dropped the cord from their mouths and swam to one side, while the iron boat, being now under way, continued to move until its prow grated upon the sands.

Ervic leaned over the side and said to the fishes: "What next?"

"You will find upon the sand," said the silverfish, "a copper kettle, which the Su-dic forgot when he went away. Cleanse it thoroughly in the water of the lake, for it has had poison in it. When it is cleaned, fill it with fresh water and hold it over the side of the boat, so that we three may swim into the kettle. We will then instruct you further."

"Do you wish me to catch you, then?" asked Ervic in surprise.

"Yes," was the reply.

So Ervic jumped out of the boat and found the copper kettle. Carrying it a little way down the beach, he washed it well, scrubbing away every drop of the poison it had contained with sand from the shore.

Then he went back to the boat.

Ervic's comrades were still sound asleep and knew nothing of the three fishes or what strange happenings were taking place about them. Ervic dropped the kettle in the lake, holding fast to the handle until it was under water. The gold and silver and bronze fishes promptly swam into the kettle. The young Skeezer then lifted it, poured out a little of the water so it would not spill over the edge, and said to the fishes: "What next?"

"Carry the kettle to the shore. Take one hundred steps to the east, along the edge of the lake, and then you will see a path leading through the meadows, up hill and down dale. Follow the path until you come to a cottage which is painted a purple color with white trimmings. When you stop at the gate of this cottage we will tell you what to do next. Be careful, above all, not to stumble and spill the water from the kettle, or you would destroy us and all you have done would be in vain."

The goldfish issued these commands and Ervic promised to be careful and started to obey. He left his sleeping comrades in the boat, stepping cautiously over their bodies, and on reaching the shore took exactly one hundred steps to the east. Then he looked for the path and the moonlight was so bright that he easily discovered it, although it was hidden from view by tall weeds until one came full upon it. This path was very narrow and did not seem to be much used, but it was quite distinct and Ervic had no difficulty in following it. He walked through a broad meadow, covered with tall grass and weeds, up a hill and down into a valley and then up another hill and down again.

It seemed to Ervic that he had walked miles and miles. Indeed the moon sank low and day was beginning to dawn when finally he discovered by the roadside a pretty little cottage, painted purple with white trimmings. It was a lonely place—no other buildings were anywhere about and the ground was not tilled at all. No farmer lived here, that was certain. Who would care to dwell in such an isolated place?

But Ervic did not bother his head long with such questions. He went up to the gate that led to the cottage, set the copper kettle carefully down and bending over it asked:

"What next?"

CHAPTER 17

Under the Great Dome

When Glinda the Good and her followers of the Rescue Expedition came in sight of the Enchanted Mountain of the Flatheads, it was away to the left of them, for the route they had taken through the Great Forest was some distance from that followed by Ozma and Dorothy.

They halted awhile to decide whether they should call upon the Supreme Dictator first, or go on to the Lake of the Skeezers.

"If we go to the mountain," said the Wizard, "we may get into trouble with that wicked Su-dic, and then we would be delayed in rescuing Ozma and Dorothy. So I think our best plan will be to go to the Skeezer Country, raise the sunken island and save our friends and the imprisoned Skeezers. Afterward we can visit the mountain and punish the cruel magician of the Flatheads."

"That is sensible," approved the Shaggy Man. "I quite agree with you."

The others, too, seemed to think the Wizard's plan the best, and Glinda herself commended it, so on they marched toward the line of palm trees that hid the Skeezers' lake from view.

Pretty soon they came to the palms. These were set closely together, the branches, which came quite to the ground, being so tightly interlaced that even the Glass Cat could scarcely find a place to squeeze through. The path which the Flatheads used was some distance away.

"Here's a job for the Tin Woodman," said the Scarecrow.

So the Tin Woodman, who was always glad to be of use, set to work with his sharp, gleaming axe, which he always carried, and in a surprisingly short time had chopped away enough branches to permit them all to pass easily through the trees.

Now the clear waters of the beautiful lake were before them and by looking closely they could see the outlines of the Great Dome of the sunken island, far from shore and directly in the center of the lake.

Of course every eye was at first fixed upon this dome, where Ozma and Dorothy and the Skeezers were still fast prisoners. But soon their attention was caught by a more brilliant sight, for here was the Diamond Swan swimming just before them, its long neck arched proudly, the amethyst eyes gleaming and all the diamond-sprinkled feathers glistening splendidly under the rays of the sun.

"That," said Glinda, "is the transformation of Queen Coo-ee-oh, the haughty and wicked witch who betrayed the three Adepts at Magic and treated her people like slaves."

"She's wonderfully beautiful now," remarked the Frogman.

"It doesn't seem like much of a punishment," said Trot. "The Flathead Su-dic ought to have made her a toad."

"I am sure Coo-ee-oh is punished," said Glinda, "for she has lost all her magic power and her grand palace and can no longer misrule the poor Skeezers."

"Let us call to her, and hear what she has to say," proposed the Wizard.

So Glinda beckoned the Diamond Swan, which swam gracefully to a position near them. Before anyone could speak Coo-ee-oh called to them in a rasping voice—for the voice of a swan is always harsh and unpleasant—and said with much pride:

"Admire me, Strangers! Admire the lovely Coo-ee-oh, the handsomest creature in all Oz. Admire me!"

"Handsome is as handsome does," replied the Scarecrow. "Are your deeds lovely, Coo-ee-oh?"

"Deeds? What deeds can a swan do but swim around and give pleasure to all beholders?" said the sparkling bird.

"Have you forgotten your former life? Have you forgotten your magic and witchcraft?" inquired the Wizard.

"Magic—witchcraft? Pshaw, who cares for such silly things?" retorted Coo-ee-oh. "As for my past life, it seems like an unpleasant dream. I wouldn't go back to it if I could. Don't you admire my beauty, Strangers?"

"Tell us, Coo-ee-oh," said Glinda earnestly, "if you can recall enough of your witchcraft to enable us to raise the sunken island to the surface of the lake. Tell us that and I'll give you a string of pearls to wear around your neck and add to your beauty."

"Nothing can add to my beauty, for I'm the most beautiful creature anywhere in the whole world."

"But how can we raise the island?"

"I don't know and I don't care. If ever I knew I've forgotten, and I'm glad of it," was the response. "Just watch me circle around and see me glitter!"

"It's no use," said Button Bright; "the old Swan is too much in love with herself to think of anything else."

"That's a fact," agreed Betsy with a sigh; "but we've got to get Ozma and Dorothy out of that lake, somehow or other."

"And we must do it in our own way," added the Scarecrow.

"But how?" asked Uncle Henry in a grave voice, for he could not bear to think of his dear niece Dorothy being out there under water; "how shall we do it?"

"Leave that to Glinda," advised the Wizard, realizing he was helpless to do it himself.

"If it were just an ordinary sunken island," said the powerful Sorceress, "there would be several ways by which I might bring it to the surface again. But this is a Magic Isle, and by some curious art of witchcraft, unknown to any but Queen Coo-ee-oh, it obeys certain commands of magic and will not respond to any other. I do not despair in the least, but it will require some deep study to solve this difficult problem. If the Swan could only remember the witchcraft that she invented and knew as a woman, I could force her to tell me the secret, but all her former knowledge is now forgotten."

"It seems to me," said the Wizard after a brief silence had followed Glinda's speech, "that there are three fishes in this lake that used to be Adepts at Magic and from whom Coo-ee-oh stole much of her knowledge. If we could find those fishes and return them to their former shapes, they could doubtless tell us what to do to bring the sunken island to the surface."

"I have thought of those fishes," replied Glinda, "but among so many fishes as this lake contains how are we to single them out?"

You will understand, of course, that had Glinda been at home in her castle, where the Great Book of Records was, she would have known that Ervic the Skeezer already had taken the gold and silver and bronze fishes from the lake. But that act had been recorded in the Book after Glinda had set out on this journey, so it was all unknown to her.

"I think I see a boat yonder on the shore," said Ojo the Munchkin boy, pointing to a place around the edge of the lake. "If we could get that boat and row all over the lake, calling to the magic fishes, we might be able to find them."

"Let us go to the boat," said the Wizard.

They walked around the lake to where the boat was stranded upon the beach, but found it empty. It was a mere shell of blackened steel, with a collapsible roof that, when in position, made the submarine watertight, but at present the roof rested in slots on either side of the magic craft. There were no oars or sails, no machinery to make the boat go, and although Glinda promptly realized it was meant to be operated by witchcraft, she was not acquainted with that sort of magic.

"However," said she, "the boat is merely a boat, and I believe I can make it obey a command of sorcery, as well as it did the command of witchcraft. After I have given a little thought to the matter, the boat will take us wherever we desire to go."

"Not all of us," returned the Wizard, "for it won't hold so many. But, most noble Sorceress, provided you can make the boat go, of what use will it be to us?"

"Can't we use it to catch the three fishes?" asked Button Bright.

"It will not be necessary to use the boat for that purpose," replied Glinda. "Wherever in the lake the enchanted fishes may be, they will answer to my call. What I am trying to discover is how the boat came to be on this shore, while the island on which it belongs is under water yonder. Did Coo-ee-oh come here in the boat to meet the Flatheads before the island was sunk, or afterward?"

No one could answer that question, of course; but while they pondered the matter three young men advanced from the line of trees, and rather timidly bowed to the strangers.

"Who are you, and where did you come from?" inquired the Wizard.

"We are Skeezers," answered one of them, "and our home is on the Magic Isle of the Lake. We ran away when we saw you coming, and hid behind the trees, but as you are Strangers and seem to be friendly we decided to meet you, for we are in great trouble and need assistance."

"If you belong on the island, why are you here?" demanded Glinda.

So they told her all the story: How the Queen had defied the Flatheads and submerged the whole island so that her enemies could not get to it or destroy it; how, when the Flatheads came to the shore, Coo-ee-oh had commanded them, together with their friend Ervic, to go with her in the submarine to conquer the Su-dic, and how the boat had shot out from the basement of the sunken isle, obeying a magic word, and risen to the surface, where it opened and floated upon the water.

Then followed the account of how the Su-dic had transformed Coo-ee-oh into a swan, after which she had forgotten all the witch-craft she ever knew. The young men told how, in the night when they were asleep, their comrade Ervic had mysteriously disappeared, while the boat in some strange manner had floated to the shore and stranded upon the beach.

That was all they knew. They had searched in vain for three days for Ervic. As their island was under water and they could not get back to it, the three Skeezers had no place to go, and so had waited patiently beside their boat for something to happen.

Being questioned by Glinda and the Wizard, they told all they knew about Ozma and Dorothy and declared the two girls were still in the village under the Great Dome. They were quite safe and would be well cared for by Lady Aurex, now that the Queen who opposed them was out of the way.

When they had gleaned all the information they could from these Skeezers, the Wizard said to Glinda:

"If you find you can make this boat obey your sorcery, you could have it return to the island, submerge itself, and enter the door in the basement from which it came. But I cannot see that our going to the sunken island would enable our friends to escape. We would only join them as prisoners."

"Not so, friend Wizard," replied Glinda. "If the boat would obey my commands to enter the basement door, it would also obey my commands to come out again, and I could bring Ozma and Dorothy back with me."

"And leave all of our people still imprisoned?" asked one of the Skeezers reproachfully.

"By making several trips in the boat, Glinda could fetch all your people to the shore," replied the Wizard.

"But what could they do then?" inquired another Skeezer. "They would have no homes and no place to go, and would be at the mercy of their enemies, the Flatheads."

"That is true," said Glinda the Good. "And as these people are Ozma's subjects, I think she would refuse to escape with Dorothy and leave the others behind, or to abandon the island which is the lawful home of the Skeezers. I believe the best plan will be to summon the three fishes and learn from them how to raise the island."

The little Wizard seemed to think that this was rather a forlorn hope.

"How will you summon them," he asked the lovely Sorceress, "and how can they hear you?"

"That is something we must consider carefully," responded stately Glinda, with a serene smile. "I think I can find a way."

All of Ozma's counsellors applauded this sentiment, for they knew well the powers of the Sorceress.

"Very well," agreed the Wizard. "Summon them, most noble Glinda."

CHAPTER 18

The Cleverness of Ervic

We must now return to Ervic the Skeezer, who, when he had set down the copper kettle containing the three fishes at the gate of the lonely cottage, had asked, "What next?"

The goldfish stuck its head above the water in the kettle and said in its small but distinct voice:

"You are to lift the latch, open the door, and walk boldly into the cottage. Do not be afraid of anything you see, for however you seem to be threatened with dangers, nothing can harm you. The cottage is the home of a powerful Yookoohoo, named Reera the Red,[1] who assumes all sorts of forms, sometimes changing her form several times in a day, according to her fancy. What her real form may be we do not know. This strange creature cannot be bribed with treasure, or coaxed through friendship, or won by pity. She has never assisted anyone, or done wrong to anyone, that we know of. All her wonderful powers are used for her own selfish amusement. She will order you out of the house but you must refuse to go. Remain and watch Reera closely and try to see what she uses to accomplish her transformations. If you can discover the secret whisper it to us and we will then tell you what to do next."

"That sounds easy," returned Ervic, who had listened carefully. "But are you sure she will not hurt me, or try to transform me?"

"She may change your form," replied the goldfish, "but do not worry if that happens, for we can break that enchantment easily. You may be sure that nothing will harm you, so you must not be frightened at anything you see or hear."

Now Ervic was as brave as any ordinary young man, and he knew the fishes who spoke to him were truthful and to be relied upon, nevertheless he experienced a strange sinking of the heart as he picked up the kettle and approached the door of the cottage. His hand trembled as he raised the latch, but he was resolved to obey his instructions. He pushed the door open, took three strides into the middle of the one room the cottage contained, and then stood still and looked around him.

The sights that met his gaze were enough to frighten anyone who had not been properly warned. On the floor just before Ervic lay a great crocodile, its red eyes gleaming wickedly and its wide open mouth displaying rows of sharp teeth. Horned toads hopped about; each of the four upper corners of the room was festooned with a thick cobweb, in the center of which sat a spider as big around as a washbasin, and armed with pincher-like claws; a red-and-green lizard was stretched at full length on the window-sill and black rats darted in and out of the holes they had gnawed in the floor of the cottage.

But the most startling thing was a huge gray ape which sat upon a bench and knitted. It wore a lace cap, such as old ladies wear, and a little apron of lace, but no other clothing. Its eyes were bright and looked as if coals were burning in them. The ape moved as naturally as an ordinary person might, and on Ervic's entrance stopped knitting and raised its head to look at him.

"Get out!" cried a sharp voice, seeming to come from the ape's mouth.

Ervic saw another bench, empty, just beyond him, so he stepped over the crocodile, sat down upon the bench and carefully placed the kettle beside him.

"Get out!" again cried the voice.

Ervic shook his head.

"No," said he, "I'm going to stay."

The spiders left their four corners, dropped to the floor and made a rush toward the young Skeezer, circling around his legs with their pinchers extended. Ervic paid no attention to them. An enormous black rat ran up Ervic's body, passed around his shoulders and uttered piercing squeals in his ears, but he did not wince. The green-and-red lizard, coming from the window-sill, approached Ervic and began spitting a flaming fluid at him, but Ervic merely stared at the creature and its flame did not touch him.

The crocodile raised its tail and, swinging around, swept Ervic off the bench with a powerful blow. But the Skeezer managed to save the kettle from upsetting and he got up, shook off the horned toads that were crawling over him and resumed his seat on the bench.

All the creatures, after this first attack, remained motionless, as if awaiting orders. The old gray ape knitted on, not looking toward Ervic now, and the young Skeezer stolidly kept his seat. He expected something else to happen, but nothing did. A full hour passed and Ervic was growing nervous.

"What do you want?" the ape asked at last.

"Nothing," said Ervic.

"You may have that!" retorted the ape, and at this all the strange creatures in the room broke into a chorus of cackling laughter.

Another long wait.

"Do you know who I am?" questioned the ape.

"You must be Reera the Red—the Yookoohoo," Ervic answered.

"Knowing so much, you must also know that I do not like strangers. Your presence here in my home annoys me. Do you not fear my anger?"

"No," said the young man.

"Do you intend to obey me, and leave this house?"

"No," replied Ervic, just as quietly as the Yookoohoo had spoken.

The ape knitted for a long time before resuming the conversation.

"Curiosity," it said, "has led to many a man's undoing. I suppose in some way you have learned that I do tricks of magic, and so through curiosity you have come here. You may have been told that I do not injure anyone, so you are bold enough to disobey my commands to go away. You imagine that you may witness some of the rites of witchcraft, and that they may amuse you. Have I spoken truly?"

"Well," remarked Ervic, who had been pondering on the strange circumstances of his coming here, "you are right in some ways, but not in others. I am told that you work magic only for your own amusement. That seems to me very selfish. Few people understand magic. I'm told that you are the only real Yookoohoo in all Oz. Why don't you amuse others as well as yourself?"

"What right have you to question my actions?"

"None at all."

"And you say you are not here to demand any favors of me?"

"For myself I want nothing from you."

"You are wise in that. I never grant favors."

"That doesn't worry me," declared Ervic.

"But you are curious? You hope to witness some of my magic transformations?"

"If you wish to perform any magic, go ahead," said Ervic. "It may interest me and it may not. If you'd rather go on with your knitting, it's all the same to me. I am in no hurry at all."

This may have puzzled Red Reera, but the face beneath the lace cap could show no expression, being covered with hair. Perhaps in all her career the Yookoohoo had never been visited by anyone who, like this young man, asked for nothing, expected nothing, and had no reason for coming except curiosity. This attitude practically disarmed the witch and she began to regard the Skeezer in a more friendly way. She knitted for some time, seemingly in deep thought, and then she arose and walked to a big cupboard that stood against the wall of the room. When the cupboard door was opened Ervic could see a lot of drawers inside, and into one of these drawers—the second from the bottom— Reera thrust a hairy hand.

Until now Ervic could see over the bent form of the ape, but suddenly the form, with its back to him, seemed to straighten up and blot out the cupboard of drawers. The ape had changed to the form of a woman, dressed in the pretty Gillikin costume, and when she turned around he saw that it was a young woman, whose face was quite attractive.

"Do you like me better this way?" Reera inquired with a smile.

"You *look* better," he said calmly, "but I'm not sure I *like* you any better."

She laughed, saying: "During the heat of the day I like to be an ape, for an ape doesn't wear any clothes to speak of. But if one has gentlemen callers it is proper to dress up."

Ervic noticed her right hand was closed, as if she held something in it. She shut the cupboard door, bent over the crocodile and in a moment the creature had changed to a red wolf. It was not pretty even now, and the wolf crouched beside its mistress as a dog might have done. Its teeth looked as dangerous as had those of the crocodile.

Next the Yookoohoo went about touching all the lizards and toads, and at her touch they became kittens. The rats she changed into chipmunks. Now the only horrid creatures remaining were the four great spiders, which hid themselves behind their thick webs.

"There!" Reera cried, "now my cottage presents a more comfortable appearance. I love the toads and lizards and rats, because most people hate them, but I would tire of them if they always remained the same. Sometimes I change their forms a dozen times a day."

"You are clever," said Ervic. "I did not hear you utter any incantations or magic words. All you did was to touch the creatures."

"Oh, do you think so?" she replied. "Well, touch them yourself, if you like, and see if you can change their forms."

"No," said the Skeezer, "I don't understand magic and if I did I would not try to imitate your skill. You are a wonderful Yookoohoo, while I am only a common Skeezer."

This confession seemed to please Reera, who liked to have her witchcraft appreciated.

"Will you go away now?" she asked. "I prefer to be alone."

"I prefer to stay here," said Ervic.

"In another person's home, where you are not wanted?"

"Yes."

"Is not your curiosity yet satisfied?" demanded Reera, with a smile.

"I don't know. Is there anything else you can do?"

"Many things. But why should I exhibit my powers to a stranger?"

"I can think of no reason at all," he replied.

She looked at him curiously.

"You want no power for yourself, you say, and you're too stupid to be able to steal my secrets. This isn't a pretty cottage, while outside are sunshine, broad prairies and beautiful wildflowers. Yet you insist on sitting on that bench and annoying me with your unwelcome presence. What have you in that kettle?"

"Three fishes," he answered readily.

"Where did you get them?"

"I caught them in the Lake of the Skeezers."

"What do you intend to do with the fishes?"

"I shall carry them to the home of a friend of mine who has three children. The children will love to have the fishes for pets."

She came over to the bench and looked into the kettle, where the three fishes were swimming quietly in the water.

"They're pretty," said Reera. "Let me transform them into something else."

"No," objected the Skeezer.

"I love to transform things; it's so interesting. And I've never transformed any fishes in all my life."

"Let them alone," said Ervic.

"What shapes would you prefer them to have? I can make them turtles, or cute little sea-horses; or I could make them piglets, or rabbits, or guinea-pigs; or, if you like I can make chickens of them, or eagles, or bluejays."

"Let them alone!" repeated Ervic.

"You're not a very pleasant visitor," laughed Red Reera. "People accuse *me* of being cross and crabbed and unsociable, and they are quite right. If you had come here pleading and begging for favors, and half afraid of my Yookoohoo magic, I'd have abused you until you ran away; but you're quite different from that. *You're* the unsociable and crabbed and disagreeable one, and so I like you, and bear with your grumpiness. It's time for my midday meal; are you hungry?"

"No," said Ervic, although he really desired food.

"Well, I am," Reera declared and clapped her hands together. Instantly a table appeared, spread with linen and bearing dishes of various foods, some smoking hot. There were two plates laid, one at each end of the table, and as soon as Reera seated herself all her creatures gathered around her, as if they were accustomed to be fed when she ate. The wolf squatted at her right hand and the kittens and chipmunks gathered at her left.

"Come, Stranger, sit down and eat," she called cheerfully, "and while we're eating let us decide into what forms we shall change your fishes."

"They're all right as they are," asserted Ervic, drawing up his bench to the table. "The fishes are beauties—one gold, one silver and one bronze. Nothing that has life is more lovely than a beautiful fish."

"What! Am *I* not more lovely?" Reera asked, smiling at his serious face.

"I don't object to you—for a Yookoohoo, you know," he said, helping himself to the food and eating with good appetite.

"And don't you consider a beautiful girl more lovely than a fish, however pretty the fish may be?"

"Well," replied Ervic, after a period of thought, "that might be. If you transformed my three fish into three girls—girls who would be Adepts at Magic, you know they might please me as the fish do. You won't do that of course, because you can't, with all your skill. And, should you be able to do so, I fear my troubles would be more than I

could bear. They would not consent to be my slaves—especially if
they were Adepts at Magic—and so they would command *me* to obey
them. No, Mistress Reera, let us not transform the fishes at all."

The Skeezer had put his case with remarkable cleverness. He realized that if he appeared anxious for such a transformation the
Yookoohoo would not perform it, yet he had skillfully suggested that
they be made Adepts at Magic.

CHAPTER 19

Red Reera, the Yookoohoo

After the meal was over and Reera had fed her pets, including the four
monster spiders which had come down from their webs to secure their
share, she made the table disappear from the floor of the cottage.

"I wish you'd consent to my transforming your fishes," she said, as
she took up her knitting again.

The Skeezer made no reply. He thought it unwise to hurry matters.
All during the afternoon they sat silent. Once Reera went to her cupboard and after thrusting her hand into the same drawer as before,
touched the wolf and transformed it into a bird with gorgeous colored
feathers. This bird was larger than a parrot and of a somewhat different form, but Ervic had never seen one like it before.

"Sing!" said Reera to the bird, which had perched itself on a big
wooden peg—as if it had been in the cottage before and knew just
what to do.

And the bird sang jolly, rollicking songs with words to them—just
as a person who had been carefully trained might do. The songs were
entertaining and Ervic enjoyed listening to them. In an hour or so the
bird stopped singing, tucked its head under its wing and went to sleep.
Reera continued knitting but seemed thoughtful.

Now Ervic had marked this cupboard drawer well and had concluded that Reera took something from it which enabled her to perform her transformations. He thought that if he managed to remain in
the cottage, and Reera fell asleep, he could slyly open the cupboard,
take a portion of whatever was in the drawer, and by dropping it into
the copper kettle transform the three fishes into their natural shapes.
Indeed, he had firmly resolved to carry out this plan when the
Yookoohoo put down her knitting and walked toward the door.

"I'm going out for a few minutes," said she; "do you wish to go with me, or will you remain here?"

Ervic did not answer but sat quietly on his bench. So Reera went out and closed the cottage door.

As soon as she was gone, Ervic rose and tiptoed to the cupboard.

"Take care! Take care!" cried several voices, coming from the kittens and chipmunks. "If you touch anything we'll tell the Yookoohoo!"

Ervic hesitated a moment but, remembering that he need not consider Reera's anger if he succeeded in transforming the fishes, he was about to open the cupboard when he was arrested by the voices of the fishes, which stuck their heads above the water in the kettle and called out:

"Come here, Ervic!"

So he went back to the kettle and bent over it.

"Let the cupboard alone," said the goldfish to him earnestly. "You could not succeed by getting that magic power, for only the Yookoohoo knows how to use it. The best way is to allow her to transform us into three girls, for then we will have our natural shapes and be able to perform all the Arts of Magic we have learned and well understand. You are acting wisely and in the most effective manner. We did not know you were so intelligent, or that Reera could be so easily deceived by you. Continue as you have begun and try to persuade her to transform us. But insist that we be given the forms of girls."

The goldfish ducked its head down just as Reera re-entered the cottage. She saw Ervic bent over the kettle, so she came and joined him.

"Can your fishes talk?" she asked.

"Sometimes," he replied, "for all fishes in the Land of Oz know how to speak. Just now they were asking me for some bread. They are hungry."

"Well, they can have some bread," said Reera. "But it is nearly supper-time, and if you would allow me to transform your fishes into girls they could join us at the table and have plenty of food much nicer than crumbs. Why not let me transform them?"

"Well," said Ervic, as if hesitating, "ask the fishes. If they consent, why—why, then, I'll think it over."

Reera bent over the kettle and asked:

"Can you hear me, little fishes?"

All three popped their heads above water.

"We can hear you," said the bronzefish.

"I want to give you other forms, such as rabbits, or turtles or girls or something; but your master, the surly Skeezer, does not wish me to. However, he has agreed to the plan if you will consent."

"We'd like to be girls," said the silverfish.

"No, no!" exclaimed Ervic.

"If you promise to make us three beautiful girls, we will consent," said the goldfish.

"No, no!" exclaimed Ervic again.

"Also make us Adepts at Magic," added the bronzefish.

"I don't know exactly what that means," replied Reera musingly, "but as no Adept at Magic is as powerful as Yookoohoo, I'll add that to the transformation."

"We won't try to harm you, or to interfere with your magic in any way," promised the goldfish. "On the contrary, we will be your friends."

"Will you agree to go away and leave me alone in my cottage, whenever I command you to do so?" asked Reera.

"We promise that," cried the three fishes.

"Don't do it! Don't consent to the transformation," urged Ervic.

"They have already consented," said the Yookoohoo, laughing in his face, "and you have promised me to abide by their decision. So, friend Skeezer, I shall perform the transformation whether you like it or not."

Ervic seated himself on the bench again, a deep scowl on his face but joy in his heart. Reera moved over to the cupboard, took something from the drawer and returned to the copper kettle. She was clutching something tightly in her right hand, but with her left she reached within the kettle, took out the three fishes and laid them carefully on the floor, where they gasped in distress at being out of water.

Reera did not keep them in misery more than a few seconds, for she touched each one with her right hand and instantly the fishes were transformed into three tall and slender young women, with fine, intelligent faces and clothed in handsome, clinging gowns. The one who had been a goldfish had beautiful golden hair and blue eyes and was exceedingly fair of skin; the one who had been a bronzefish had dark brown hair and clear gray eyes and her complexion matched these lovely features. The one who had been a silverfish had snow-white hair of the finest texture and deep brown eyes. The hair contrasted exquisitely with her pink cheeks and ruby-red lips, nor did it make her look a day older than her two companions.

As soon as they secured these girlish shapes, all three bowed low to the Yookoohoo and said:

"We thank you, Reera."

Then they bowed to the Skeezer and said:

"We thank you, Ervic."

"Very good!" cried the Yookoohoo, examining her work with critical approval. "You are much better and more interesting than fishes, and this ungracious Skeezer would scarcely allow me to do the transformations. You surely have nothing to thank *him* for. But now let us dine in honor of the occasion."

She clapped her hands together and again a table loaded with food appeared in the cottage. It was a longer table, this time, and places were set for the three Adepts as well as for Reera and Ervic.

"Sit down, friends, and eat your fill," said the Yookoohoo, but instead of seating herself at the head of the table she went to the cupboard, saying to the Adepts: "Your beauty and grace, my fair friends, quite outshine my own. So that I may appear properly at the banquet table I intend, in honor of this occasion, to take upon myself my natural shape."

Scarcely had she finished this speech when Reera transformed herself into a young woman fully as lovely as the three Adepts. She was not quite so tall as they, but her form was more rounded and more handsomely clothed, with a wonderful jeweled girdle and a necklace of shining pearls. Her hair was a bright auburn red, and her eyes large and dark.

"Do you claim this is your natural form?" asked Ervic of the Yookoohoo.

"Yes," she replied. "This is the only form I am really entitled to wear. But I seldom assume it because there is no one here to admire or appreciate it and I get tired admiring it myself."

"I see now why you are named Reera the Red," remarked Ervic.

"It is on account of my red hair," she explained smiling. "I do not care for red hair myself, which is one reason I usually wear other forms."

"It is beautiful," asserted the young man; and then remembering the other women present he added: "But, of course, all women should not have red hair, because that would make it too common. Gold and silver and brown hair are equally handsome."

The smiles that he saw interchanged between the four filled the poor Skeezer with embarrassment, so he fell silent and attended to

eating his supper, leaving the others to do the talking. The three Adepts frankly told Reera who they were, how they became fishes and how they had planned secretly to induce the Yookoohoo to transform them. They admitted that they had feared, had they asked her to help, that she would have refused them.

"You were quite right," returned the Yookoohoo. "I make it my rule never to perform magic to assist others, for if I did there would always be crowds at my cottage demanding help and I hate crowds and want to be left alone.

"However, now that you are restored to your proper shapes, I do not regret my action and I hope you will be of use in saving the Skeezer people by raising their island to the surface of the lake, where it really belongs. But you must promise me that after you go away you will never come here again, nor tell anyone what I have done for you."

The three Adepts and Ervic thanked the Yookoohoo warmly. They promised to remember her wish that they should not come to her cottage again and so, with a good-bye, took their departure.

CHAPTER 20

A Puzzling Problem

Glinda the Good, having decided to try her sorcery upon the abandoned submarine so that it would obey her commands, asked all of her party, including the Skeezers, to withdraw from the shore of the lake to the line of palm trees. She kept with her only the little Wizard of Oz, who was her pupil and knew how to assist her in her magic rites. When they two were alone beside the stranded boat, Glinda said to the Wizard:

"I shall first try my magic recipe No. 1163, which is intended to make inanimate objects move at my command. Have you a skeropythrope with you?"

"Yes, I always carry one in my bag," replied the Wizard. He opened his black bag of magic tools and took out a brightly polished skeropythrope, which he handed to the Sorceress. Glinda had also brought a small wicker bag, containing various requirements of sorcery, and from this she took a parcel of powder and a vial of liquid. She poured the liquid into the skeropythrope and added the powder.

At once the skeropythrope began to sputter and emit sparks of a violet color, which spread in all directions. The Sorceress instantly stepped into the middle of the boat and held the instrument so that the sparks fell all around her and covered every bit of the blackened steel boat. At the same time Glinda crooned a weird incantation in the language of sorcery, her voice sounding low and musical.

After a little the violet sparks ceased, and those that had fallen upon the boat had disappeared and left no mark upon its surface. The ceremony was ended and Glinda returned the skeropythrope to the Wizard, who put it away in his black bag.

"That ought to do the business all right," he said confidently.

"Let us make a trial and see," she replied.

So they both entered the boat and seated themselves.

Speaking in a tone of command the Sorceress said to the boat: "Carry us across the lake, to the farther shore."

At once the boat backed off the sandy beach, turned its prow and moved swiftly over the water.

"Very good—very good indeed!" cried the Wizard, when the boat slowed up at the shore opposite from that whence they had departed. "Even Coo-ee-oh, with all her witchcraft, could do no better."

The Sorceress now said to the boat:

"Close up, submerge and carry us to the basement door of the sunken island—the door from which you emerged at the command of Queen Coo-ee-oh."

The boat obeyed. As it sank into the water the top sections rose from the sides and joined together over the heads of Glinda and the Wizard, who were thus enclosed in a water-proof chamber. There were four glass windows in this covering, one on each side and one on either end, so that the passengers could see exactly where they were going. Moving under water more slowly than on the surface, the submarine gradually approached the island and halted with its bow pressed against the huge marble door in the basement under the Dome. This door was tightly closed and it was evident to both Glinda and the Wizard that it would not open to admit the underwater boat unless a magic word was spoken by them or someone from within the basement of the island. But what was this magic word? Neither of them knew.

"I'm afraid," said the Wizard regretfully, "that we can't get in, after all. Unless your sorcery can discover the word to open the marble door."

"That is probably some word only known to Coo-ee-oh," replied the Sorceress. "I may be able to discover what it is, but that will require time. Let us go back again to our companions."

"It seems a shame, after we have made the boat obey us, to be balked by just a marble door," grumbled the Wizard.

At Glinda's command the boat rose until it was on a level with the glass dome that covered the Skeezer village, when the Sorceress made it slowly circle all around the Great Dome.

Many faces were pressed against the glass from the inside, eagerly watching the submarine, and in one place were Dorothy and Ozma, who quickly recognized Glinda and the Wizard through the glass windows of the boat. Glinda saw them, too, and held the boat close to the Dome while the friends exchanged greetings in pantomime. Their voices, unfortunately, could not be heard through the Dome and the water and the side of the boat. The Wizard tried to make the girls understand, through signs, that he and Glinda had come to their rescue, and Ozma and Dorothy understood this from the very fact that the Sorceress and the Wizard had appeared. The two girl prisoners were smiling and in safety, and knowing this Glinda felt she could take all the time necessary in order to effect their final rescue.

As nothing more could be done just then, Glinda ordered the boat to return to shore, and it obeyed readily. First it ascended to the surface of the water, then the roof parted and fell into the slots at the side of the boat, and then the magic craft quickly made the shore and beached itself on the sands at the very spot from which it had departed at Glinda's command.

All the Oz people and the Skeezers at once ran to the boat to ask if they had reached the island, and whether they had seen Ozma and Dorothy. The Wizard told them of the obstacle they had met in the way of a marble door, and how Glinda would now undertake to find a magic way to conquer the door.

Realizing that it would require several days to succeed in reaching the island raising it and liberating their friends and the Skeezer people, Glinda now prepared a camp half way between the lake shore and the palm trees.

The Wizard's wizardry made a number of tents appear and the sorcery of the Sorceress furnished these tents all complete, with beds, chairs, tables, rugs, lamps and even books with which to pass idle hours. All the tents had the Royal Banner of Oz flying from the centerpoles and one big tent, not now occupied, had Ozma's own banner moving in the breeze.

Betsy and Trot had a tent to themselves, and Button Bright and Ojo had another. The Scarecrow and the Tin Woodman paired together in one tent and so did Jack Pumpkinhead and the Shaggy Man, Cap'n Bill and Uncle Henry, Tik-Tok and Professor Wogglebug. Glinda had the most splendid tent of all, except that reserved for Ozma, while the Wizard had a little one of his own. Whenever it was meal time, tables loaded with food magically appeared in the tents of those who were in the habit of eating, and these complete arrangements made the rescue party just as comfortable as they would have been in their own homes.

Far into the night Glinda sat in her tent studying a roll of mystic scrolls in search of a word that would open the basement door of the island and admit her to the Great Dome. She also made many magical experiments, hoping to discover something that would aid her. Yet the morning found the powerful Sorceress still unsuccessful.

Glinda's art could have opened any ordinary door, you may be sure, but you must realize that this marble door of the island had been commanded not to open save in obedience to one magic word, and therefore all other magic words could have no effect upon it. The magic word that guarded the door had probably been invented by Coo-ee-oh, who had now forgotten it. The only way, then, to gain entrance to the sunken island was to break the charm that held the door fast shut. If this could be done no magic would be required to open it.

The next day the Sorceress and the Wizard again entered the boat and made it submerge and go to the marble door, which they tried in various ways to open, but without success.

"We shall have to abandon this attempt, I think," said Glinda. "The easiest way to raise the island would be for us to gain admittance to the Dome and then descend to the basement and see in what manner Coo-ee-oh made the entire island sink or rise at her command. It naturally occurred to me that the easiest way to gain admittance would be by having the boat take us into the basement through the marble door from which Coo-ee-oh launched it. But there must be other ways to get inside the Dome and join Ozma and Dorothy, and such ways we must find by study and the proper use of our powers of magic."

"It won't be easy," declared the Wizard, "for we must not forget that Ozma herself understands considerable magic, and has doubtless tried to raise the island or find other means of escape from it and failed."

"That is true," returned Glinda, "but Ozma's magic is fairy magic, while you are a Wizard and I am a Sorceress. In this way the three of us have a great variety of magic to work with, and if we should all fail it will be because the island is raised and lowered by a magic power none of us is acquainted with. My idea therefore is to seek—by such magic as we possess—to accomplish our object in another way."

They made the circle of the Dome again in their boat, and once more saw Ozma and Dorothy through their windows and exchanged signals with the two imprisoned girls.

Ozma realized that her friends were doing all in their power to rescue her and smiled an encouragement to their efforts. Dorothy seemed a little anxious but was trying to be as brave as her companion.

After the boat had returned to the camp and Glinda was seated in her tent, working out various ways by which Ozma and Dorothy could be rescued, the Wizard stood on the shore dreamily eyeing the outlines of the Great Dome which showed beneath the clear water, when he raised his eyes and saw a group of strange people approaching from around the lake. Three were young women of stately presence, very beautifully dressed, who moved with remarkable grace. They were followed at a little distance by a good-looking young Skeezer.

The Wizard saw at a glance that these people might be very important, so he advanced to meet them. The three maidens received him graciously and the one with the golden hair said:

"I believe you are the famous Wizard of Oz, of whom I have often heard. We are seeking Glinda the Sorceress, and perhaps you can lead us to her."

"I can, and will, right gladly," answered the Wizard. "Follow me, please."

The little Wizard was puzzled as to the identity of the three lovely visitors but he gave no sign that might embarrass them.

He understood they did not wish to be questioned, and so he made no remarks as he led the way to Glinda's tent.

With a courtly bow the Wizard ushered the three visitors into the gracious presence of Glinda, the Good.

CHAPTER 21

The Three Adepts

The Sorceress looked up from her work as the three maidens entered, and something in their appearance and manner led her to rise and bow to them in her most dignified manner. The three knelt an instant before the great Sorceress and then stood upright and waited for her to speak.

"Whoever you may be," said Glinda, "I bid you welcome."

"My name is Audah," said one.

"My name is Aurah," said another.

"My name is Aujah," said the third.

Glinda had never heard these names before, but looking closely at the three she asked:

"Are you witches or workers in magic?"

"Some of the secret arts we have gleaned from Nature," replied the brownhaired maiden modestly, "but we do not place our skill beside that of the Great Sorceress, Glinda the Good."

"I suppose you are aware it is unlawful to practice magic in the Land of Oz, without the permission of our Ruler, Princess Ozma?"

"No, we were not aware of that," was the reply. "We have heard of Ozma, who is the appointed Ruler of all this great fairyland, but her laws have not reached us, as yet."

Glinda studied the strange maidens thoughtfully; then she said to them:

"Princess Ozma is even now imprisoned in the Skeezer village, for the whole island with its Great Dome, was sunk to the bottom of the lake by the witchcraft of Coo-ee-oh, whom the Flathead Su-dic transformed into a silly swan. I am seeking some way to overcome Coo-ee-oh's magic and raise the isle to the surface again. Can you help me do this?"

The maidens exchanged glances, and the white-haired one replied:

"We do not know; but we will try to assist you."

"It seems," continued Glinda musingly, "that Coo-ee-oh derived most of her witchcraft from three Adepts at Magic, who at one time ruled the Flatheads. While the Adepts were being entertained by Coo-ee-oh at a banquet in her palace, she cruelly betrayed them and after transforming them into fishes cast them into the lake.

"If I could find these three fishes and return them to their natural shapes—they might know what magic Coo-ee-oh used to sink the island. I was about to go to the shore and call these fishes to me when you arrived. So, if you will join me, we will try to find them."

The maidens exchanged smiles now, and the golden-haired one, Audah, said to Glinda:

"It will not be necessary to go to the lake. We are the three fishes."

"Indeed!" cried Glinda. "Then you are the three Adepts at Magic, restored to your proper forms?"

"We are the three Adepts," admitted Aujah.

"Then," said Glinda, "my task is half accomplished. But who destroyed the transformation that made you fishes?"

"We have promised not to tell," answered Aurah; "but this young Skeezer was largely responsible for our release; he is brave and clever, and we owe him our gratitude."

Glinda looked at Ervic, who stood modestly behind the Adepts, hat in hand. "He shall be properly rewarded," she declared, "for in helping you he has helped us all, and perhaps saved his people from being imprisoned forever in the sunken isle."

The Sorceress now asked her guests to seat themselves and a long talk followed, in which the Wizard of Oz shared.

"We are quite certain," said Aurah, "that if we could get inside the Dome we could discover Coo-ee-oh's secrets, for in all her work, after we became fishes, she used the formulas and incantations and arts that she stole from us. She may have added to these things, but they were the foundation of all her work."

"What means do you suggest for our getting into the Dome?" inquired Glinda.

The three Adepts hesitated to reply, for they had not yet considered what could be done to reach the inside of the Great Dome. While they were in deep thought, and Glinda and the Wizard were quietly awaiting their suggestions, into the tent rushed Trot and Betsy, dragging between them the Patchwork Girl.

"Oh, Glinda," cried Trot, "Scraps has thought of a way to rescue Ozma and Dorothy and all of the Skeezers."

The three Adepts could not avoid laughing merrily, for not only were they amused by the queer form of the Patchwork Girl, but Trot's enthusiastic speech struck them as really funny. If the Great Sorceress and the famous Wizard and the three talented Adepts at Magic were unable as yet to solve the important problem of the sunken isle, there was little chance for a patched girl stuffed with cotton to succeed.

But Glinda, smiling indulgently at the earnest faces turned toward her, patted the children's heads and said:

"Scraps is very clever. Tell us what she has thought of, my dear."

"Well," said Trot, "Scraps says that if you could dry up all the water in the lake the island would be on dry land, an' everyone could come and go whenever they liked."

Glinda smiled again, but the Wizard said to the girls:

"If we should dry up the lake, what would become of all the beautiful fishes that now live in the water?"

"Dear me! That's so," admitted Betsy, crestfallen; "we never thought of that, did we Trot?"

"Couldn't you transform 'em into polliwogs?" asked Scraps, turning a somersault and then standing on one leg. "You could give them a little, teeny pond to swim in, and they'd be just as happy as they are as fishes."

"No indeed!" replied the Wizard, severely. "It is wicked to transform any living creatures without their consent, and the lake is the home of the fishes and belongs to them."

"All right," said Scraps, making a face at him; "I don't care."

"It's too bad," sighed Trot, "for I thought we'd struck a splendid idea."

"So you did," declared Glinda, her face now grave and thoughtful. "There is something in the Patchwork Girl's idea that may be of real value to us."

"I think so, too," agreed the golden-haired Adept. "The top of the Great Dome is only a few feet below the surface of the water. If we could reduce the level of the lake until the Dome sticks a little above the water, we could remove some of the glass and let ourselves down into the village by means of ropes."

"And there would be plenty of water left for the fishes to swim in," added the white-haired maiden.

"If we succeed in raising the island we could fill up the lake again," suggested the brown-haired Adept.

"I believe," said the Wizard, rubbing his hands together in delight, "that the Patchwork Girl has shown us the way to success."

CHAPTER 22

The Sunken Island

As soon as they had breakfasted the next morning, Glinda and the Wizard and the three Adepts went down to the shore of the lake and formed a line with their faces toward the submerged island. All the others came to watch them, but stood at a respectful distance in the background.

At the right of the Sorceress stood Audah and Aurah, while at the left stood the Wizard and Aujah. Together they stretched their arms over the water's edge and in unison the five chanted a rhythmic incantation.

This chant they repeated again and again, swaying their arms gently from side to side, and in a few minutes the watchers behind them noticed that the lake had begun to recede from the shore. Before long the highest point of the dome appeared above the water. Gradually the water fell, making the dome appear to rise. When it was three or four feet above the surface Glinda gave the signal to stop, for their work had been accomplished.

The blackened submarine was now entirely out of water, but Uncle Henry and Cap'n Bill managed to push it into the lake. Glinda, the Wizard, Ervic and the Adepts got into the boat, taking with them a coil of strong rope, and at the command of the Sorceress the craft cleaved its way through the water toward the part of the Dome which was now visible.

"There's still plenty of water for the fish to swim in," observed the Wizard as they rode along. "They might like more but I'm sure they can get along until we have raised the island and can fill up the lake again."

The boat touched gently on the sloping glass of the Dome, and the Wizard took some tools from his black bag and quickly removed one large pane of glass, thus making a hole large enough for their bodies to pass through. Stout frames of steel supported the glass of the Dome, and around one of these frames the Wizard tied the end of a rope.

"I'll go down first," said he, "for while I'm not as spry as Cap'n Bill I'm sure I can manage it easily. Are you sure the rope is long enough to reach the bottom?"

"Quite sure," replied the Sorceress.

So the Wizard let down the rope and climbing through the opening lowered himself down, hand over hand, clinging to the rope with his legs and feet. Below in the streets of the village were gathered all the Skeezers, men, women and children, and you may be sure that Ozma and Dorothy, with Lady Aurex, were filled with joy that their friends were at last coming to their rescue.

The Queen's palace, now occupied by Ozma, was directly in the center of the Dome, so that when the rope was let down the end of it came just in front of the palace entrance. Several Skeezers held fast to the rope's end to steady it and the Wizard reached the ground in safety. He hugged first Ozma and then Dorothy, while all the Skeezers cheered as loud as they could.

The Wizard now discovered that the rope was long enough to reach from the top of the Dome to the ground when doubled, so he tied a chair to one end of the rope and called to Glinda to sit in the chair while he and some of the Skeezers lowered her to the pavement. In this way the Sorceress reached the ground quite comfortably and the three Adepts and Ervic soon followed

The Skeezers quickly recognized the three Adepts at Magic, whom they had learned to respect before their wicked Queen betrayed them, and welcomed them as friends. All the inhabitants of the village had been greatly frightened by their imprisonment under water, but now realized that an attempt was to be made to rescue them.

Glinda, the Wizard and the Adepts followed Ozma and Dorothy into the palace, and they asked Lady Aurex and Ervic to join them. After Ozma had told of her adventures in trying to prevent war between the Flatheads and the Skeezers, and Glinda had told all about the Rescue Expedition and the restoration of the three Adepts by the help of Ervic, a serious consultation was held as to how the island could be made to rise.

"I've tried every way in my power," said Ozma, "but Coo-ee-oh used a very unusual sort of magic which I do not understand. She seemed to have prepared her witchcraft in such a way that a spoken word is necessary to accomplish her designs, and these spoken words are known only to herself."

"That is a method we taught her," declared Aurah the Adept.

"I can do no more, Glinda," continued Ozma, "so I wish you would try what your sorcery can accomplish."

"First, then," said Glinda, "let us visit the basement of the island, which I am told is underneath the village."

A flight of marble stairs led from one of Coo-ee-oh's private rooms down to the basement, but when the party arrived all were puzzled by what they saw. In the center of a broad, low room, stood a mass of great cog-wheels, chains and pulleys, all interlocked and seeming to form a huge machine; but there was no engine or other motive power to make the wheels turn.

"This, I suppose, is the means by which the island is lowered or raised," said Ozma, "but the magic word which is needed to move the machinery is unknown to us."

The three Adepts were carefully examining the mass of wheels, and soon the golden-haired one said:

"These wheels do not control the island at all. On the contrary, one set of them is used to open the doors of the little rooms where the submarines are kept, as may be seen from the chains and pulleys used. Each boat is kept in a little room with two doors, one to the basement room where we are now and the other letting into the lake.

"When Coo-ee-oh used the boat in which she attacked the Flat-heads, she first commanded the basement door to open and with her followers she got into the boat and made the top close over them. Then the basement door being closed, the outer door was slowly opened, letting the water fill the room to float the boat, which then left the island, keeping under water."

"But how could she expect to get back again?" asked the Wizard.

"Why the boat would enter the room filled with water and after the outer door was closed a word of command started a pump which pumped all the water from the room. Then the boat would open and Coo-ee-oh could enter the basement."

"I see," said the Wizard. "It is a clever contrivance, but won't work unless one knows the magic words."

"Another part of this machinery," explained the white-haired Adept, "is used to extend the bridge from the island to the mainland. The steel bridge is in a room much like that in which the boats are kept, and at Coo-ee-oh's command it would reach out, joint by joint, until its far end touched the shore of the lake. The same magic command would make the bridge return to its former position. Of course the bridge could not be used unless the island was on the surface of the water."

"But how do you suppose Coo-ee-oh managed to sink the island, and make it rise again?" inquired Glinda.

This the Adepts could not yet explain. As nothing more could be learned from the basement they mounted the steps to the Queen's private suite again, and Ozma showed them to a special room where Coo-ee-oh kept her magical instruments and performed all her arts of witchcraft.

CHAPTER 23

The Magic Words

Many interesting things were to be seen in the Room of Magic, including much that had been stolen from the Adepts when they were transformed to fishes, but they had to admit that Coo-ee-oh had a rare genius for mechanics, and had used her knowledge in inventing a lot of mechanical apparatus that ordinary witches, wizards and sorcerers could not understand.

They all carefully inspected this room, taking care to examine every article they came across.

"The island," said Glinda thoughtfully, "rests on a base of solid marble. When it is submerged, as it is now, the base of the island is upon the bottom of the lake. What puzzles me is how such a great weight can be lifted and suspended in the water, even by magic."

"I now remember," returned Aujah, "that one of the arts we taught Coo-ee-oh was the way to expand steel, and I think that explains how the island is raised and lowered. I noticed in the basement a big steel pillar that passed through the floor and extended upward to this palace. Perhaps the end of it is concealed in this very room. If the lower end of the steel pillar is firmly embedded in the bottom of the lake, Coo-ee-oh could utter a magic word that would make the pillar expand, and so lift the entire island to the level of the water."

"I've found the end of the steel pillar. It's just here," announced the Wizard, pointing to one side of the room where a great basin of polished steel seemed to have been set upon the floor.

They all gathered around, and Ozma said:

"Yes, I am quite sure that is the upper end of the pillar that supports the island. I noticed it when I first came here. It has been hollowed out, you see, and something has been burned in the basin, for the fire has left its marks. I wondered what was under the great basin and got several of the Skeezers to come up here and try to lift it for me. They were strong men, but could not move it at all."

"It seems to me," said Audah the Adept, "that we have discovered the manner in which Coo-ee-oh raised the island. She would burn some sort of magic powder in the basin, utter the magic word, and the pillar would lengthen out and lift the island with it."

"What's this?" asked Dorothy, who had been searching around with the others, and now noticed a slight hollow in the wall, near to where the steel basin stood. As she spoke Dorothy pushed her thumb into the hollow and instantly a small drawer popped out from the wall.

The three Adepts, Glinda and the Wizard sprang forward and peered into the drawer. It was half filled with a grayish powder, the tiny grains of which constantly moved as if impelled by some living force.

"It may be some kind of radium," said the Wizard.

"No," replied Glinda, "it is more wonderful than even radium, for I recognize it as a rare mineral powder called Gaulau by the sorcerers. I wonder how Coo-ee-oh discovered it and where she obtained it."

"There is no doubt," said Aujah the Adept, "that this is the magic powder Coo-ee-oh burned in the basin. If only we knew the magic word. I am quite sure we could raise the island."

"How can we discover the magic word?" asked Ozma, turning to Glinda as she spoke.

"That we must now seriously consider," answered the Sorceress.

So all of them sat down in the Room of Magic and began to think. It was so still that after a while Dorothy grew nervous. The little girl never could keep silent for long, and at the risk of displeasing her magic-working friends she suddenly said:

"Well, Coo-ee-oh used just three magic words, one to make the bridge work, and one to make the submarines go out of the holes, and one to raise and lower the island. Three words. And Coo-ee-oh's name is made up of just three words. One is 'Coo,' and one is 'ee,' and one is 'oh.' "

The Wizard frowned but Glinda looked wonderingly at the young girl and Ozma cried out:

"A good thought, Dorothy dear! You may have solved our problem."

"I believe it is worth a trial," agreed Glinda. "It would be quite natural for Coo-ee-oh to divide her name into three magic syllables, and Dorothy's suggestion seems like an inspiration."

The three Adepts also approved the trial but the brown-haired one said:

"We must be careful not to use the wrong word, and send the bridge out under water. The main thing, if Dorothy's idea is correct, is to hit upon the one word that moves the island."

"Let us experiment," suggested the Wizard.

In the drawer with the moving gray powder was a tiny golden cup, which they thought was used for measuring. Glinda filled this cup with the powder and carefully poured it into the shallow basin, which was the top of the great steel pillar supporting the island. Then Aurah the Adept lighted a taper and touched it to the powder, which instantly glowed fiery red and tumbled about the basin with astonishing energy. While the grains of powder still glowed red the Sorceress bent over it and said in a voice of command: "Coo!"

They waited motionless to see what would happen. There was a grating noise and a whirl of machinery, but the island did not move a particle.

Dorothy rushed to the window, which overlooked the glass side of the dome.

"The boats!" she exclaimed. "The boats are all loose an' sailing under water."

"We've made a mistake," said the Wizard gloomily.

"But it's one which shows we are on the right track," declared Aujah the Adept. "We know now that Coo-ee-oh used the syllables of her name for the magic words."

"If 'Coo' sends out the boats, it is probable that 'ee' works the bridge," suggested Ozma. "So the last part of the name may raise the island."

"Let us try that next then," proposed the Wizard.

He scraped the embers of the burned powder out of the basin and Glinda again filled the golden cup from the drawer and placed it on top the steel pillar. Aurah lighted it with her taper and Ozma bent over the basin and murmured the long drawn syllable: "Oh-h-h!"

Instantly the island trembled and with a weird groaning noise it moved upward—slowly, very slowly, but with a steady motion, while all the company stood by in awed silence. It was a wonderful thing, even to those skilled in the arts of magic, wizardry and sorcery, to realize that a single word could rise that great, heavy island, with its immense glass Dome.

"Why, we're way *above* the lake now!" exclaimed Dorothy from the window, when at last the island ceased to move.

"That is because we lowered the level of the water," explained Glinda.

They could hear the Skeezers cheering lustily in the streets of the village as they realized that they were saved.

"Come," said Ozma eagerly, "let us go down and join the people."

"Not just yet," returned Glinda, a happy smile upon her lovely face, for she was overjoyed at their success. "First let us extend the bridge to the mainland, where our friends from the Emerald City are waiting."

It didn't take long to put more powder in the basin, light it and utter the syllable "EE!" The result was that a door in the basement opened and the steel bridge moved out, extended itself joint by joint, and finally rested its far end on the shore of the lake just in front of the encampment.

"Now," said Glinda, "we can go up and receive the congratulations of the Skeezers and of our friends of the Rescue Expedition."

Across the water, on the shore of the lake, the Patchwork Girl was waving them a welcome.

CHAPTER 24

Glinda's Triumph

Of course all those who had joined Glinda's expedition at once crossed the bridge to the island, where they were warmly welcomed by the Skeezers. Before all the concourse of people Princess Ozma made a speech from a porch of the palace and demanded that they recognize her as their lawful Ruler and promise to obey the laws of the Land of Oz. In return she agreed to protect them from all future harm and declared they would no longer be subjected to cruelty and abuse.

This pleased the Skeezers greatly, and when Ozma told them they might elect a Queen to rule over them, who in turn would be subject to Ozma of Oz, they voted for Lady Aurex, and that same day the ceremony of crowning the new Queen was held and Aurex was installed as mistress of the palace.

For her Prime Minister the Queen selected Ervic, for the three Adepts had told of his good judgment, faithfulness and cleverness, and all the Skeezers approved the appointment.

Glinda, the Wizard and the Adepts stood on the bridge and recited an incantation that quite filled the lake with water again, and the Scarecrow and the Patchwork Girl climbed to the top of the Great Dome and replaced the pane of glass that had been removed to allow Glinda and her followers to enter.

When evening came Ozma ordered a great feast prepared, to which every Skeezer was invited. The village was beautifully decorated and brilliantly lighted and there was music and dancing until a late hour to celebrate the liberation of the people. For the Skeezers had been freed, not only from the water of the lake but from the cruelty of their former Queen.

As the people from the Emerald City prepared the next morning to depart Queen Aurex said to Ozma:

"There is only one thing I now fear for my people, and that is the enmity of the terrible Su-dic of the Flatheads. He is liable to come here at any time and try to annoy us, and my Skeezers are peaceful folks and unable to fight the wild and wilful Flatheads."

"Do not worry," returned Ozma, reassuringly. "We intend to stop on our way at the Flatheads' Enchanted Mountain and punish the Su-dic for his misdeeds."

That satisfied Aurex and when Ozma and her followers trooped over the bridge to the shore, having taken leave of their friends, all the Skeezers cheered them and waved their hats and handkerchiefs, and the band played and the departure was indeed a ceremony long to be remembered.

The three Adepts at Magic, who had formerly ruled the Flatheads wisely and considerately, went with Princess Ozma and her people, for they had promised Ozma to stay on the mountain and again see that the laws were enforced.

Glinda had been told all about the curious Flatheads and she had consulted with the Wizard and formed a plan to render them more intelligent and agreeable.

When the party reached the mountain Ozma and Dorothy showed them how to pass around the invisible wall—which had been built by the Flatheads after the Adepts were transformed—and how to gain the up-and-down stairway that led to the mountain top.

The Su-dic had watched the approach of the party from the edge of the mountain and was frightened when he saw that the three Adepts had recovered their natural forms and were coming back to their former home. He realized that his power would soon be gone and yet he determined to fight to the last. He called all the Flatheads together and armed them, and told them to arrest all who came up the stairway and hurl them over the edge of the mountain to the plain below. But although they feared the Supreme Dictator, who had threatened to punish them if they did not obey his commands, as soon as they saw the three Adepts they threw down their arms and begged their former rulers to protect them.

The three Adepts assured the excited Flatheads that they had nothing to fear.

Seeing that his people had rebelled the Su-dic ran away and tried to hide, but the Adepts found him and had him cast into a prison, all his cans of brains being taken away from him.

After this easy conquest of the Su-dic, Glinda told the Adepts of her plan, which had already been approved by Ozma of Oz, and they joyfully agreed to it. So, during the next few days, the great Sorceress transformed, in a way, every Flathead on the mountain.

Taking them one at a time, she had the can of brains that belonged to each one opened and the contents spread on the flat head, after which, by means of her arts of sorcery, she caused the head to grow over the brains—in the manner most people wear them—and they were thus rendered as intelligent and good looking as any of the other inhabitants of the Land of Oz.

When all had been treated in this manner there were no more Flatheads at all, and the Adepts decided to name their people Mountaineers. One good result of Glinda's sorcery was that no one could now be deprived of the brains that belonged to him and each person had exactly the share he was entitled to.

Even the Su-dic was given his portion of brains and his flat head made round, like the others, but he was deprived of all power to work further mischief, and with the Adepts constantly watching him he would be forced to become obedient and humble.

The Golden Pig, which ran grunting about the streets, with no brains at all, was disenchanted by Glinda, and in her woman's form was given brains and a round head. This wife of the Su-dic had once been even more wicked than her evil husband, but she had now forgotten all her wickedness and was likely to be a good woman thereafter.

These things being accomplished in a satisfactory manner, Princess Ozma and her people bade farewell to the three Adepts and departed for the Emerald City, well pleased with their interesting adventures.

They returned by the road over which Ozma and Dorothy had come, stopping to get the Sawhorse and the Red Wagon where they had left them.

"I'm very glad I went to see these peoples," said Princess Ozma, "for I not only prevented any further warfare between them, but they have been freed from the rule of the Su-dic and Coo-ee-oh and are now happy and loyal subjects of the Land of Oz. Which proves that it is always wise to do one's duty, however unpleasant that duty may seem to be."

THE END

EXPLANATORY NOTES

THE WIZARD OF OZ

INTRODUCTION

1. *the old-time fairy tale:* Baum is referring to the classical fairy-tale tradition: Charles Perrault (1628–1703), *Tales of Times Past* (1697); Jacob (1785–1863) and Wilhelm (1786–1859) Grimm, *Children's and Household Tales* (1812–15), and the fairy tales of Hans Christian Andersen (1805–75), published in a series of collections from 1835 until the year he died. By the time Baum began writing his tales, the works of Perrault, the Grimms, and Andersen had already assumed classical status, and though he admired their works, he rejected some of the more gruesome aspects of their tales and sought to update and "Americanize" their tales with less violence. Clearly, the structure of *The Wonderful Wizard of Oz* is indebted to the classical fairy tale. Like the typical protagonist of a Grimms' tale, Dorothy goes on a quest and needs three helpers to assist her on the way. After she apparently reaches her destination, she is deceived—the peripety, or sudden fall in fortunes of the heroine—and she must continue her journey with her three helpers to triumph—in this case, to conquer the Wicked Witch of the West and return home. By introducing American characters, inventions, and settings, Baum transformed the classical fairy tale into a utopian fantasy.

2. *Modern education:* Though it is difficult to determine whether Baum knew the works of John Dewey (1859–1952), he was certainly aware of the new trends in American education. In 1899, Dewey published *The School and Society*, and he placed great emphasis on democracy as an ethical value and learning through experimentation and practice. Dewey's works initiated the progressive movement in American modern education. In many respects, Dorothy and her friends are representative of "American" democracy in contrast to the European monarchical values upheld by the heroes of the Perrault's and the Grimms' tales, and they solve their problems through experiments and common sense.

358

3. *modernized fairy tale:* Baum's views on this subject can be found in his short essays, "Fairy Tales on the Stage" (*Chicago Record-Herald,* June 18, 1905) and "Modern Fairy Tales" (*The Advance,* August 19, 1909). Indeed, Baum was the first American writer of fairy tales to use American colloquialisms and settings along with a strong democratic if not socialist message that was at odds with the patriarchal and authoritarian ideology of many classical fairy tales. Both Frank Stockton (1834–1902) and Howard Pyle (1853–1911), two of Baum's contemporaries, had made great strides toward changing the classical fairy tale in America, but Baum was the first to truly "modernize" it.

CHAPTER 1: THE CYCLONE

1. *Dorothy:* Clearly influenced by Lewis Carroll's *Alice in Wonderland,* Baum stated in his article on "Modern Fairy Tales" that "the secret of Alice's success lay in the fact that she was a real child, and any normal child could sympathize with her all through her adventures" (*The Best of The Baum Bugle, 1965–1966,* p. 52). Dorothy, too, is an average sweet and compassionate girl, whom one might encounter in any town in America. It is interesting to note that Dorothy's age is never mentioned—she could be anywhere from seven to twelve—and her physical features are never described. Baum sought to make Dorothy an "everyman," and the reason he chose a young girl as his "everyman" may be due to the fact that he had four sons and had always hoped that he might have a daughter, whom he intended to name Dorothy. Moreover, Baum was very much influenced by the suffragette views of his wife, Maud, and the universe of Oz that he gradually conceives is very much a matriarchal one in contrast to the "tainted" patriarchal American society.

2. *cyclone cellar:* Given the frequency of cyclones and tornadoes in the Midwest, many farmers dug little cellars to escape the turbulent storms.

3. *gray mass:* Baum begins to set up his color scheme in the novel by associating Kansas with gray. He will use different colors to distinguish the regions of Oz and their peculiar qualities. For Baum, gray was the color of dreariness, bland routines, and life without dreams. In keeping with naturalist writers of the time like Hamlin Garland (1860–1940) and Frank Norris (1870–1902) he was interested in depicting the hard life of American farmers and

workers. Of course, Baum was not at all a naturalist, but he did share their concerns, and he was critical of the Darwinian philosophy "survival of the fittest."

4. *Toto:* Ironically, this was the name for a dog in the Victorian Age, as Michael Hearn points out in *The Annotated Wizard of Oz.* Such a name would be strange for a dog from the American Midwest. "Toto" was also a common nickname for little boys in France.

5. *the house whirled:* The entire house with Dorothy and Toto are transported to Oz. Baum forgets about the house at the end of the novel, and apparently Aunt Em and Uncle Henry were not so much upset by the loss of the house as they were by the disappearance of Dorothy. Indeed, they rebuilt their home before Dorothy returned. The 1939 MGM film tried to deal with this inconsistency by having Dorothy's journey to Oz turn out to be a dream. However, this defeats Baum's conception of Oz as a real place.

CHAPTER 2: THE COUNCIL WITH THE MUNCHKINS

1. *in the midst of a country of marvelous beauty:* Since Baum never stated where Oz was located, readers and critics have speculated that it is either another planet or that it is a hidden continent on earth. In *The Tin Woodman of Oz* (1918) we learn that it was once an ordinary country and became a fairyland when it was enchanted by Queen Lurline, a powerful fairy. Only "chosen" people are allowed to visit and stay in this country. Though realistically described by Baum, Oz is a utopian projection of a paradise that is intended to serve as a contrast to the America that Baum knew so well. With each novel that he wrote, the contours of Oz became more defined.

2. *Dorothy, who was a well-grown child for her age:* W. W. Denslow's illustrations make it appear that she is five or six years old, whereas John R. Neill's drawings make her look somewhat older. Baum never states her age. Judy Garland portrays a Dorothy in her teens. Throughout the Oz novels, Dorothy remains the same age, and she will stay the same age as long as she lives in Oz. Her actions and demeanor throughout the series lead one to believe that she is about ten.

3. *blue:* This is the color associated with the land of the Munchkins. Though Baum was probably not familiar with the "blue flower,"

the symbol of hope and yearning conceived by the German romantic poet Novalis, he may have known other works that continued this tradition. As the first pleasing color that Dorothy sees, blue stands in contrast to the gray of Kansas. It is connected to the heavens, infinity, and openness, and the blue Munchkin country is a welcoming place that introduces Dorothy to the possibility of exploring herself and her talents.

Baum developed an elaborate color code for Oz. Munchkin Country was blue; Quadling Country, red; Winkie Country, yellow. Gillikin Country in the north is not described, but the Emerald City in the center is green, and the area right below it is brown. Baum wrote about color theory in *The Art of Decorating Dry Goods Windows and Interiors*. It is interesting to see how the change of colors parallels the time and action of the story. It begins in a gray winter and gray landscape in Kansas. Then Dorothy encounters the colors blue, red, and green of spring in Munchkin Country and the Emerald City. Next she travels to the yellow country of the Winkies in summer, and ends in the browns and reds of the Quadling Country before she returns to the gray winter of Kansas. Her journey appears to cover a one-year cycle.

4. *the land of the Munchkins:* Baum never explained the origins of the names he invented, and one can only speculate about their meaning. Obviously the suffix "kin" refers to the diminutive size of the little people, and since they are small, they might take little bites or "munchkins" when they eat. The word "munchkin" has made its way into the tenth edition of Merriam-Webster's Collegiate Dictionary to define "a person who is notably small and often endearing."

5. *the wicked Witch of the East:* Baum associated the banking and business world with the East, but it is unclear why he made the two wicked witches stem from the East and the West.

6. *I have not killed anything:* Baum endeavored to keep violence and killing out of his tales as much as possible. Therefore, his heroine, Dorothy, does not kill directly. Rather, it is always by accident that she manages to cause the wicked witches to perish.

7. *shod in silver shoes:* These shoes have magical powers, but Dorothy does not realize this at the time. The silver may have referred to the debate at the time as to whether American money should be based on a gold or silver standard or a bimetallic standard. In "*The Wizard of Oz*: Parable of Populism," *American Quarterly* 16 (Spring 1964): 47–58, Henry Littlefield draws paral-

lels in Baum's work with the sociopolitical conditions of the 1890s. In "The 'Wizard of Oz' as a Monetary Allegory," *Journal of Political Economy* 41 (1990): 739–759, Hugh Rockoff goes much further and interprets all the symbols as direct references to the monetary crises and political campaigns of the times. In *Land of Desire: Merchants, Power, and the Rise of a New American Culture* (New York: Pantheon, 1993, pp. 249–50), William Leach argues that the silver shoes have more to do with Baum's theosophical beliefs and that they are a direct reference to John Bunyan's *The Pilgrim's Progress*, which Baum knew quite well. In Bunyan's work, Christian meets "By-ends," who has no interest in religion except when it benefits him. He tells Christian that we are always most zealous when religion goes in silver slippers. Christian answers that religion must be accepted in rags as well as in silver slippers.

8. *But I thought all witches were wicked:* Baum liked to play with the characters and motifs of the classical fairy tales. Therefore, he endowed two of the witches with wicked powers; they were the exploiters of other people. But the witches from the North and the South helped people and thus were considered good. The wicked witches were not linked to the devil, nor did they have any religious significance. The good witches were models of kindness and generosity who sought to maintain harmony in Oz. They were completely secular, and in some respects, Baum was ahead of his times in arguing that there were good and bad witches and that the entire concept of witchcraft should be reconsidered. Here he may have been influenced by his suffragette mother-in-law, Matilda Gage, who argued in *Woman, Church, and State* (1893) that witchcraft was part of a modern technological revolution and could help humankind. She insisted that the witch as hag was representative of the assertive, independent woman who can triumph over nature and her own body and can provide secular nurturing that opposes the "nurturing" of the church. It is only in recent times with the rise of feminist history that witchcraft has been linked with healing.

9. *four witches:* In the first novel of the series, it is true that there are only four witches, but Baum introduced several more as the series progressed: Mombi, the Wicked Witch of the North, who was overthrown by the good Witch of the North; Blinkie, the Wicked Witch of the South, who was toppled by Glinda the Good; Mrs. Yoop, who is turned into a Green Monkey by Ozma (*The*

Tin Woodman of Oz, 1918); and Reera the Red and Coo-ee-oh (*Glinda of Oz*, 1920).

10. *the Land of Oz:* In an interview published in the *St. Louis Republic* (May 10, 1903), Baum stated: "I have a little cabinet letter file on my desk in front of me. I was thinking and wondering about a title for my story, and I had settled on 'Wizard' as part of it. My gaze was caught by the gilt letters on the three drawers of the cabinet. The first was A–G; the next drawer was labeled H–N; and on the last were the letters O–Z. And Oz it at once became." Whether there is any truth to this story is somewhat dubious. On the other hand, it is likely that Baum conceived the name through association. In *The Annotated Wizard of Oz*, Michael Hearn points out there are several theories about the origination of the name Oz. Baum may have associated it with the biblical Land of Uz in the Book of Job. He admired Dickens, whose nickname was "Boz." Jack Snow, author of some Oz sequels and *Who's Who in Oz*, believes the name was due to Baum's preference for stories that caused readers to exclaim with "ohs!" Finally, the meaning of Oz as "great and good" is given in *Dorothy and the Wizard of Oz*.

11. *the Land of Oz has never been civilized:* This remark recalls the famous words of Huck Finn at the end of Mark Twain's novel, when Huck indicates that he is about to light out for the free territory in the West because he doesn't wanted to be adopted or "sivilized." Like many American writers at the end of the nineteenth century, when the frenzied migration west had come to a close, Baum believed that the "the virgin land" of America would become a wasteland, and of course, Kansas itself with its gray tones and mortgaged farms is a result of "civilization." On the other hand, the rainbow colors of Oz and the simple, naive, and tolerant ways of its inhabitants suggest a primitive and magical paradise. Throughout the series, Baum compels Dorothy and other visitors from America, especially Aunt Em and Uncle Henry, to compare their Oz experiences with their way of life. Civilized America always loses in the end!

12. *Oz himself is the Great Wizard:* The ruler of Oz is always called "Oz" or "Ozma." The Wizard of Oz is not the ruler of Oz. Rather, he rules over the Emerald City. The Witch of the North is under the same misapprehension as the rest of the people who have been "conned" into believing that he has great powers.

13. *the City of Emeralds:* It was probably named by Baum to honor his mother's ancestral country, the Emerald Isle.
14. *The South is the Quadlings country:* There is no definite explanation for the name of the Quadlings. Like the name of the Munchkins, it is a diminutive and suggests little quarter people. In *Who's Who in Oz*, Jack Snow suggests that this country, ruled by Glinda the Good, has wild unexplored regions and may have been given its name because it is the fourth of the four countries of Oz.
15. *Winkies:* This name may stem from the expression "in the wink of an eye" or from the nursery rhyme, "Wee Willie Winkie."
16. *no one will dare injure a person who has been kissed by the Witch of the North:* Baum constantly made up his own magic spells, arbitrary rules, and special qualities. In the classical fairy tales, the kiss was generally given to a young woman to save her and to a man to transform him from beast to handsome prince. Glinda's kiss is for protection, but it does not completely shield Dorothy from danger.
17. *yellow brick:* There are many yellow brick roads in Oz. Like the veins of a gold mine, they form networks and connect many different places of the land. At the time that Baum wrote the Oz books, yellow brick was often used to construct buildings throughout America. Henry Littlefield and Hugh Rockoff link the yellow brick road to the debate about the gold standard in the 1890s. See note 7 in this chapter.

CHAPTER 3: HOW DOROTHY SAVED THE SCARECROW

1. *put the key carefully in the pocket of her dress:* Dorothy has been brought up to be very responsible, and her locking the house is a sign of her good upbringing. Yet, there is no need to lock the house because she never returns to it. For all we know, the house is still standing in Munchkin Country.
2. *only witches and sorceresses wear white:* Once again, Baum is playing with the traditional motifs of the classical fairy tale. Instead of black, the usual color of witches, he has the good witches wear white.
3. *Scarecrow:* These figures were very common at the end of the nineteenth and beginning of the twentieth centuries. Baum's creation is similar to the dunce, stupid Hans, or bungling Jack in folk and fairy tales. These characters do not appear to be clever, and

yet, with good fortune, they stumble through life and manage to overcome obstacles and succeed in the end. The good-natured Scarecrow is the brightest figure that Dorothy will meet, but ironically he is not aware of how smart he is. It is Dorothy who both brings out his talents and needs his brains to help her in difficult situations.

4. *If you will come with me I'll ask Oz to do all he can for you:* This line is reminiscent of the request made by the discharged soldier in the Grimms' tale "How Six Made their Way through the World." In need of help, the soldier enlists the aid of a strong man, sharpshooter, runner, blower, and swallower, who use their talents to help the soldier fulfill his quest. Dorothy collects specific qualities—brains, heart, and courage—that she will need to mature and return home on her own footing. In this instance, however, Dorothy promises them help if they come with her. Symbolically, the Scarecrow, Tin Woodman, and Lion represent the inner characteristics that Dorothy must develop, and at the same time, these figures need to cultivate what they have but do not recognize.

5. *it's a lighted match:* From the beginning the Scarecrow demonstrates that he is wise and has no need of brains.

CHAPTER 4: THE ROAD THROUGH THE FOREST

1. *That is because you have no brains:* Throughout the novel, Baum pokes fun at Dorothy and other characters in ironic fashion. It is Dorothy who has no brains, not the Scarecrow: one would have to be "brainless" to choose Kansas over Oz.

2. *There is no place like home:* Dorothy's attachment to Kansas is dependent on her love for Aunt Em and Uncle Henry. This becomes clear when she prompts them to move to Oz in *The Emerald City of Oz,* and Oz becomes her home. Not only does she have her aunt and uncle with her, but she has a sense of community and has formed a bond with Ozma and Glinda the Good, not to mention all the other zany characters of Oz. Home is a key theme in Baum's works, and Oz as utopia becomes his ideal vision of existence, and thus of "home."

3. *story:* Baum published a separate but slightly different version of this story titled "The Scarecrow Tells a Fairy Tale to Children and Hears an Equally Marvelous True Story" on November 27, 1905. It was reprinted in *The Baum Bugle* (Spring 1969) as follows:

You must know, my dears, that in the Land of Oz everything has life that can become of any use by living. Now, I do not know of what use a live Scarecrow can be unless he serves to amuse children; but it is a fact that, as soon as the farmer had stuffed me into the shape of a man and made me a head by using this excellent cotton sack, I began to realize that I was part of the big world and had come to life.

Of course, I could not see, nor hear, nor talk at first, but the farmer brought a paint pot and a brush, and upon the surface of my head, where a face properly belongs, he began to paint. First he made this left eye, which you observe is a beautiful circle, with a dot in the centre of it. The first object I saw with this eye was the farmer himself, and, you may be sure, I watched him carefully as he painted my other eye. I have always considered that man an artist; otherwise he could not have made me so handsome. My right eye is even finer than the left; and, after making it, the farmer gave me this exquisite nose, with which I gathered the scent of the wild flowers and the new-mown hay and the furrows of sweet and fertile earth. Next my mouth was manufactured so excellently shaped that I have never ceased to be proud of it; but I could not then speak, for I knew no words by which to express my feelings. Then followed these lovely ears, which completed my features. And now I heard the loud breathing of the farmer, who was fat and inclined to asthma, and the twittering songs of the birds and the whisper of the winds as they glided through the meadows, and the chatter of the field mice—and many other pleasant and delightful sounds.

Indeed, I now believed myself fully the equal of the man who had made me; but the idea was soon dispelled when the farmer sat me upon a stout pole in the cornfield and then walked away with his paint pot and left me. I tried at once to follow, but my feet would not touch the earth, and so I could not escape from the pole.

Near me was a stile, and people crossing the fields would often stop at the stile and converse; so that by listening to them I soon learned how to speak properly. I had a fine view of the country from my elevation, and plenty of time to examine it curiously. Moreover, the crows often came and perched upon my head and shoulders and talked of the big world they had seen; so my education was unusually broad and diverse. But I longed to see the big world of Oz for myself, and my real mission in life—to scare the crows seemed to be a failure. The crows even grew fond of me and spoke to me pleasantly while they dug up the grains of the corn the farmer had planted.

4. *Brains are the only things worth having in this world, no matter whether one is a crow or a man:* Throughout the Oz series, the

Scarecrow will utter truisms, platitudes, and proverbs, indicating that he is more insightful than he thinks he is and much brighter than the others around him.

CHAPTER 5: THE RESCUE OF THE TIN WOODMAN

1. *a man made entirely of tin:* Throughout his life, Baum tinkered with all sorts of objects and invented mechanical toys and creatures. This was very much in keeping with the times, and when he worked as a window-dresser for stores in Chicago, he actually invented a mechanical figure with washboilers and stovepipe legs that may have been the model for the Tin Woodman. In the fairy-tale tradition, the introduction of mechanical creatures begins with E. T. A. Hoffmann's (1776–1822) automata and mechanical dolls, his most famous appearing in "The Sandman" (1819). For the best account of the Tin Woodman's history, see Martin Gardner, "The Tin Woodman of Oz: An Appreciation."

2. *Do you suppose Oz could give me a heart?:* Like the Scarecrow, the Tin Woodman already has what he thinks he needs. He simply hasn't yet realized how great a heart he has. For Baum, the importance of having a good heart was connected to the heart defect with which he was born.

3. *the following story:* Baum liked to insert fairy tales into his fairy-tale novels. They are often ironic fantastic stories that enrich the plot and explain the past of certain characters. The Tin Woodman's background will be elaborated in greater detail in *The Tin Woodman of Oz* (1918).

4. *I too became a woodchopper:* In *The Marvelous Land of Oz* (1904), Baum notes that the name of the Tin Woodman is Nick Chopper.

5. *father died:* Both the Tin Woodman's father and mother die. According to Baum's history of Oz, no one dies a natural death, and everyone remains the same age. (See note 3, chapter 18.) This inconsistency can be attributed to the temporary reign of the Wizard, who could not prevent death. Or it may be due to the fact that Baum was not certain at this stage in his conception of Oz whether all creatures would have eternal life.

6. *the girl:* Her name is Nimmie Aimee, and in *The Tin Woodman of Oz* (1918), Nick Chopper tells a slightly different version of his life.

7. *tinsmith:* His name is Ku-Klip, and he reappears in *The Tin Woodman of Oz* (1918) and is responsible for the construction of other mechanical figures. In fact, he also does some genetic engineering and invents a human being made out of flesh and bones who is named Chofyte. Nimmie Aimee marries Chofyte because he is made out of the abandoned parts of the Tin Woodman and the Tin Soldier, the two men she at one time loved.

CHAPTER 6: THE COWARDLY LION

1. *a big coward:* Although there are cowardly lions in *Aesop's Fables* and other fables, he is generally considered the king of the beasts, something that the Cowardly Lion tells us a few paragraphs later. Baum is playing on the traditional belief that children held in those times—and still hold today. For a lion to be cowardly would be regarded ridiculous, and Baum pokes fun at this huge creature who roars because he is frightened.

2. *Perhaps you have heart disease:* This remark is, of course, a reference to Baum's own heart defect, and he is mocking himself. Interestingly, both the Tin Woodman and the Lion think that they need "new" hearts, one for love, the other for courage. Knowing one's heart is a central theme in all the Oz books.

CHAPTER 7: THE JOURNEY TO THE GREAT OZ

1. *I should certainly weep:* The Tin Woodman constantly shows that he has much more of a compassionate heart than most people.

2. *Then we are all right:* Typically, the Scarecrow finds the solution to the desperate situation.

3. *there is nothing to do but try it:* This is the lion's first display of bravery, and he will continue to show courage throughout the journey. He is even prepared to fight the Kalidahs to death.

4. *Kalidahs:* The origin of this name is unclear. These dreadful beasts are killed because they are so evil, but they are killed in the usual accidental Baum fashion: they fall to their death in pursuit of Dorothy and her friends. They reappear in *The Magic of Oz* (1919) and are a kind of conglomerate beast that appear in many other fairy tales. Frank Stockton depicted a fearsome and mysterious beast in "The Griffin."

CHAPTER EIGHT: THE DEADLY POPPY FIELD

1. *Stork:* Like most storks in literature, this one is helpful, and as the stork states, she always likes to help anyone in trouble.
2. *scarlet poppies:* In this episode, the poppies have a deadly effect. In Greek myth poppies are linked to sleep and death. When Ceres became exhausted during her quest for Persephone, she was granted sleep by smelling a poppy sent by the gods. In traditional folklore throughout the world, poppies are associated with death; they are said to grow from blood and are especially prolific on battlefields. As is known, opium (the base for heroin and morphine) can be extracted from the seeds of scarlet poppies, and during the nineteenth century, the use of opium was not illegal. It was used for pleasure by many people, particularly in affluent and intellectual circles, and as a medicinal painkiller. At the time that Baum wrote his novel, the poppy was also used in Art Nouveau designs.

CHAPTER 9: THE QUEEN OF THE FIELD MICE

1. *two pieces:* This is one of the few incidents of violence in Baum's Oz books. Whenever he could, he avoided horror and cruelty. But his tales would have been boring without dangerous and evil creatures seeking to undermine the utopian principles of democracy in Oz. Therefore, at times, wicked and sadistic characters are graphically destroyed.
2. *Only a mouse!:* Baum follows the traditional fairy tale and fable ("The Lion and the Mouse") by endowing "small" oppressed heroes with special powers. In addition, good deeds are always repaid. Not only do the mice rescue Dorothy and their friends from the poppy field, but also, in *The Land of Oz*, the mice frighten the girl soldiers of General Jinjur's Army of Revolt and help the Scarecrow regain his throne.

CHAPTER 10: THE GUARDIAN OF THE GATES

1. *take on any form he wishes:* In the fairy-tale tradition, witches and wizards are dangerous because they can assume many different forms. But other evil characters can do this, too. In Charles Perrault's "Puss in Boots," the ogre can take on different forms,

and the cat tricks him by asking the boastful ogre to turn himself into a mouse. This he does, and he is quickly devoured by the cat. The wizard cannot actually turn himself into other creatures, but he is a master of deception.

2. *he could not speak:* Later, in *Tik-Tok of Oz*, we learn that Toto has the gift of speaking once he enters the Land of Oz and that the reason he does not talk in the early episodes is because he just did not feel like it.

3. *spectacles:* As we learn later, the Wizard has everyone wear spectacles to deceive them. Even though the city is built out of emeralds, they are not as dazzling as they might seem. Therefore, by wearing glasses, people think that everything is greener than it actually is. Nevertheless, the city must have been radiant. The meaning of the spectacles is connected to the theme of recognition and cognition. Dorothy and her friends must learn to know who they are and what they can do before they can recognize their innate qualities. Their experiences enable them to uncover the frauds in their lives, and they also learn from their differences to gain insight into human nature. Of course, it is difficult to talk about "human" nature in Oz, but for Dorothy, this journey to another land and her adventures with bizarre and eccentric creatures enable her to gain distance from herself and Kansas. In the future, she will see herself and Kansas more clearly, and in the sequels to *The Wizard of Oz*, her insights compel her to recognize that life in Kansas is mere survival, whereas life in Oz offers her and her family more hope and more justice.

CHAPTER 11: THE WONDERFUL EMERALD CITY OF OZ

1. *many people:* In *The Emerald City of Oz* (1910), we are told that there are 57,318 citizens and 9,654 buildings. The name of a citizen of the city is Ozmite, and the name of an inhabitant of the country is Ozite.

2. *the shape of a most terrible Beast:* The Wizard wants to inspire fear in everyone, and the disguises he assumes are intended to confuse Dorothy and her friends. He does not model the beast on any particular mythological animal.

3. *a Ball of Fire:* The terrifying sight of fire might be associated with the flames of hell.

CHAPTER 12: THE SEARCH FOR THE WICKED WITCH

1. *forty wolves:* Probably a biblical reference to the forty days and nights of the great flood and Noah's Ark and Christ's forty days and nights of fasting. Baum will repeat this reference with forty crows and forty bees. They may also be related to the forty thieves in *Ali Baba and the Forty Thieves.*

2. *Golden Cap:* There are many magical caps in folklore and fairy tales. Whoever wears such a cap (or sometimes a cape) can become invisible or can be transported to any place the wearer desires. Andrew Lang (1844–1912) published a fascinating version of "Little Red Riding Hood" called "The True History of Little Goldenhood" in *The Red Fairy Book* (London: Longmans, Green, 1890). The golden hood is made of a ray of sunshine and protects the girl, Blanchette, from the wolf, whose tongue is burned when he touches it.

3. *Winged Monkeys:* These monkeys appear to be related to the genii of *The Arabian Nights* and can be used for good or evil by the possessor of the Golden Cap. This is also true of genii, who are at the beck and call of their master three times.

4. *the Witch bade her clean the pots and kettles and sweep the floor and keep the fire fed with wood:* Dorothy is treated somewhat like Cinderella or Gretel. Forced to do menial chores in the household, she cannot be killed by the evil Witch of the West because she is protected by the kiss of the Good Witch of the North.

5. *old umbrella:* Instead of a broomstick, this witch carries an umbrella which is used more as a weapon than as a magical vehicle of transportation. It is also intended to protect her from water.

6. *bucket of water:* Dorothy is unaware of the power of water. During the European witch-hunts in the sixteenth and seventeenth centuries, women and men were tested in various ways to discover whether they were witches. They had to walk over hot coals, or they were tied up and thrown into water. If they did not survive these ordeals unscathed, they were declared witches. The Wicked Witch of the West dies because water can also be a cleansing or purifying agent. It is, of course, strange that the water melts the witch. The fact that Dorothy throws another bucket of water on the floor after the Witch's death indicates that she is going through some kind of purifying ritual.

CHAPTER 13: THE RESCUE

1. *a beautiful bracelet, studded with diamonds:* Evidently Dorothy never brought this gift back to Kansas with her. Otherwise, it might have helped Aunt Em and Uncle Henry to solve their money problems.

CHAPTER 14: THE WINGED MONKEYS

1. *a long story:* Baum's fairy tale about the origins of the Winged Monkeys serves to provide history for the reader. The Winged Monkeys do not appear in subsequent Oz books.

CHAPTER 15: THE DISCOVERY OF OZ, THE TERRIBLE

1. *a little, old man, with a bald head and a wrinkled face:* In contrast to the Wizard's terrifying features that he had shown before, Baum cleverly depicts him as a harmless, if not banal person. He has neither great brains, beauty, ferocity, nor courage, qualities that Dorothy and her friends have needed to complete their quest. The little old man is not even a sinister con man, but some helpless soul stuck in Oz, to which he, too, will return in a later story.
2. *I am a humbug:* When confronted, the Wizard is honest, and he shows Dorothy and her friends the theatrical tricks he used to con people. Baum himself had a great deal of experience in the theater, and there is a vaudeville aspect to the Wizard, also a ventriloquist, and to the entire cast of characters in this novel.
3. *I was born in Omaha:* Baum was, of course, much more familiar with Omaha than he was with Kansas. In *Dorothy and the Wizard of Oz*, he provides much more background information about the Wizard, whose father named him "Oscar Zoroaster Phadrig Isaac Norman Henkle Emmanuel Ambroise Diggs. Fearful that he might be insulted and called "Pinhead," the name spelled by the other initials after O and Z, he shortened his name to O.Z. which he painted on all his possessions including the balloon that took him to the Land of Oz. Indeed, when he arrived in Oz, the people thought he was the true ruler when they saw the balloon.
4. *No more than in any other city:* This is not exactly true. When the Wizard arrived in Oz, he used emeralds and other precious stones to construct the city. It is in fact a unique city.

5. *I am a very old man now:* In *The Annotated Wizard of Oz*, Michael Hearn rightly contends that the Wizard could not be much older than fifty, about as old as Baum was when he wrote his novel. Moreover, there is something of Baum in the Wizard— his love for stage magic, invention, and the theater in general.

CHAPTER 17: HOW THE BALLOON WAS LAUNCHED

1. *I can't come back, my dear:* The Wizard cannot control the flight of the balloon. Apparently he does not have a rope or valve to let out the air so he can land. For this reason, it is not clear whether he will actually return to America.
2. *And that was the last any of them ever saw of Oz, the Wonderful Wizard:* Although this is true for this episode, Oz returns in the fourth book, *Dorothy and the Wizard of Oz* (1908), and he continues to play a role in other Oz books as the "official Wizard of Oz."

CHAPTER 18: AWAY TO THE SOUTH

1. *we cannot cross the desert:* Oz is surrounded by deserts and wastelands on all sides, and the magic that works within the confines of Oz cannot function outside it. Even within Oz, there are limits placed on the characters, and Baum made up the laws of magic as he developed his stories. Many of the magical qualities of the characters seem arbitrary, but once he endowed a character with a certain trait, Baum tried consistently to have the character act accordingly.
2. *Glinda:* She rules the Quadling Country in the South and is the most powerful good witch in Oz. She is a close friend of the Princess of Ozma (introduced in the second book) and studies magic to find new ways to improve the happiness of the people of Oz. She also keeps the Great Book of Records that provides an account of all the events that take place in Oz.
3. *a beautiful woman, who knows how to keep young in spite of the many years she has lived:* Like most of the characters and animals in Oz, Glinda does not age. It seems that the aging process occurs only in America, while in Oz everyone achieves a certain age and then remains that age. Even though Dorothy goes back and forth between Kansas and Oz, she does not get older. If anything, her

language becomes more childlike if not childish. The entire question of age and aging is addressed in *The Tin Woodman of Oz* (1918, pp. 156–57):

> Oz was not always a fairyland, I am told. Once it was much like other lands, except it was shut in by a dreadful desert of sandy wastes that lay all around it, thus preventing its people from all contact with the rest of the world. Seeing this isolation, the fairy band of Queen Lurline left one of her fairies to rule this enchanted Land of Oz, and then passed on and forgot all about it.
>
> From that moment on no one in Oz ever died. Those who were old remained old; those who were young and strong did not change as years passed them by; the children remained children always, and played and romped to their hearts' content, while all the babies lived in their cradles and were tenderly cared for and never grew up. So people in Oz stopped counting how old they were in years, for years made no difference in their appearance and could not alter their station. They did not get sick, so there were no doctors among them. Accidents might happen to some, on rare occasions, it is true, and while no one could die naturally, as other people do, it was possible that one might be totally destroyed. Such incidents, however, were very unusual, and so seldom was there anything to worry over that the Oz people were as happy and contented as can be.

There is a slight contradiction in Baum's account because people do die during the Wizard's reign. Once the Princess Ozma rules the entire country, there are no more natural deaths, although creatures can be destroyed.

CHAPTER 19: ATTACKED BY THE FIGHTING TREES

1. *The trees seem to have made up their minds to fight us, and stop our journey:* One never knows what will happen in fairy-tale forests. It is not unusual for trees and woods to be endowed with magical qualities. In "Sleeping Beauty" the hedge of briars grows to protect the princess's castle. In Shakespeare's *Macbeth*, the king proclaims that he will not be defeated until Great Birnam wood to high Dunsinae Hill shall come against him. And, of course, it does. There is a wonderful stanza in Gilbert Keith Chesterton's (1874–1936) poem "The Donkey," which also relates to this theme:

When fishes flew and forests walked
And figs grew upon thorn,
Some moment when the moon was blood
Then surely I was born.

2. *a high wall, which seemed to be made of white china:* A reference to the Great Wall of China. Baum's pun does not appear to have much significance. It anticipates the care that Dorothy and her friends will have to take as they enter the Dainty China Country.

CHAPTER 20: THE DAINTY CHINA COUNTRY

1. *Mr. Joker:* The fact that this clown is a piece of cracked china makes him somewhat more zany than the other characters in China Country.
2. *You'd eaten up a poker!:* The influence of Lewis Carroll (1832–98) and Edward Lear (1812–88) is evident here. Baum introduces nonsense rhymes and puns throughout his works to liven the dialogue. Baum knew a great deal about flowers and plants, and poker may refer to a species of liliaceous plants bearing spikes of scarlet or yellow flowers—known as the flame flower—or to the metal rod used for poking a fire.
3. *he upset a china church:* This is the only reference to a church in the entire Oz series. Baum was against organized religion. Raised a Methodist, he rebelled against his religious upbringing and developed his own peculiar kind of theosophical beliefs that included reincarnation.

CHAPTER 21: THE LION BECOMES THE KING OF THE BEASTS

1. *the biggest of the tigers:* This creature anticipates the Hungry Tiger, who appears later in *Ozma of Oz* (1907). The hungry tiger's conscience is so strong that it prevents him from devouring other animals and satisfying his appetite. Ruth Plumly Thompson developed this character in *The Hungry Tiger of Oz* (1926).
2. *The great spider:* Spiders do not fare well in the Oz series, probably because Baum had an aversion to them. Later, in *Glinda of Oz* (1920), the purple Spider King captures Ozma and Dorothy, who are fortunately freed by a crab.

CHAPTER 22: THE COUNTRY OF THE QUADLINGS

1. *Hammer-Heads:* Though not vicious, the Hammer-Heads are tough, and they are invincible. Nobody knows what they are protecting on their hill because the Hammer-Heads have never allowed anyone to enter their terrain. Their name reminds one of "blockhead," and they act like wild jack-in-the-boxes.

2. *country of the Quadlings:* Set in the south, this country is associated with the red of autumn. It is the final phase of Dorothy's journey before she returns to the gray of Kansas.

CHAPTER 23: GLINDA GRANTS DOROTHY'S WISH

1. *Your Silver Shoes will carry you over the desert:* The seven-league boots were a stock motif in folk and fairy tales. They are generally stolen from giants but shrink to fit the feet of the wearer. Dorothy "won" her shoes from the evil witch.

2. *If you had known their power:* But the point of the entire story is that Dorothy does not realize her own powers. It is through the journey of exploration that she comes to recognize how powerful she is and what her qualities are. By gathering and summoning brains, compassion, and courage in the form of the Scarecrow, the Tin Woodman, and the Cowardly Lion, she becomes a mature young woman. In other words, she finds home in herself.

3. *the new farmhouse:* The old one remained locked up in Munchkin Country and was never mentioned again.

4. *the Silver Shoes had fallen off:* Nothing magical can exist in Kansas. The Silver Shoes served their purpose, and Dorothy must use her own newly developed powers in America.

CHAPTER 24: HOME AGAIN

1. *I'm so glad to be at home again!:* This is true at this point in her development, but both Baum and Dorothy will continually miss Oz. The notion of what home is shifts during the course of the series to a conception of Oz as eternal home.

THE EMERALD CITY OF OZ

INTRODUCTION

1. *editor or private secretary:* Though he is being slightly ironic here, Baum did profit a great deal from the responses of his readers, and he often included some of their ideas in his stories and books.
2. *dissolve partnership:* In fact, Baum was about to dissolve the partnership, for he had moved to Hollywood, California, in 1909, and had become involved in some film projects. When he was forced to declare bankruptcy in 1911, he turned to Oz for help. In 1913, three years after the publication of *The Emerald City of Oz*, he produced *The Patchwork Girl of Oz*.

CHAPTER 1: HOW THE NOME KING BECAME ANGRY

1. *Nome King:* The Nome King makes his first appearance in *Ozma of Oz* (1907), in which Dorothy helps liberate the Queen of Ev from the nasty Nome King and takes away his magic belt that gives him the power to transform people and creatures as he wishes. The Nome King is a greedy monarch who also goes by the name of Roquat the Red and Roquat of the Rocks. Here Baum might be playing with the name Riquet from Charles Perrault's "Riquet with the Tuft," in which a misshapen character associated with gnomes forces himself on a princess. In *Ozma of Oz*, it is a queen who is held captive. After the Nome King fails in his attempt to take over Oz, he forgets his name because he has drunk from the Water of Oblivion. In *Tik-Tok of Oz* (1914) he assumes the name of Ruggedo the Metal Monarch and again is up to no good, holding the Shaggy Man's brother captive. However, Tik-Tok and friends manage to rescue the brother, and Ruggedo promises to reform as an ordinary Nome.
2. *Chief Steward Kaliko:* When the Nome King is banished from the underground kingdom in *Tik-Tok of Oz* (1914), Kaliko takes over and promises not to misbehave. However, he does not always keep his promise, and Ozma and Glinda have to keep him in line.
3. *Magic Belt:* This belt was taken from him in *Ozma of Oz* (1907) because he used it to transform people into ornaments and for other evil purposes. After the belt is captured, Dorothy gives it to Ozma, who uses it to wish the girl back to Kansas.
4. *Ozma:* Introduced in *Ozma of Oz* (1907), Princess Ozma quickly

becomes Dorothy's best friend. At one time she had been held captive by the evil witch Mombi, but Glinda the Good managed to set her free, and then she became the ruler of Oz. In *Ozma of Oz*, she uses kindness and love to triumph over the Nome King, and though she has magical powers, it is her generous heart and her belief in justice that endears her to the people of Oz. Like most of the major characters in the Oz series, she represents the best qualities of a socialist matriarchal society. Under Ozma's reign, nobody needs to work, and everything is shared. Differences are recognized and tolerated. There is no such thing as poverty or money. Ozma is most adept in the art of gentle persuasion.

5. *secret tunnel:* The Nome Kingdom is outside Oz, and since the desert is formidable—nobody has ever crossed it—the Nome King's decision to go under the desert is a logical choice.

6. *Land of Ev:* This country is also outside Oz and plays a major role in *Ozma of Oz*.

CHAPTER 2: HOW UNCLE HENRY GOT INTO TROUBLE

1. *mortgage his farm:* Baum alludes to the 1890s in the Midwest when the depression caused many farmers to abandon their farms. Baum had first-hand experience of the farmer's plight when he lived in Aberdeen. See Matilda Gage, "The Dakota Days of L. Frank Baum," *The Best of the Baum Bugle* (1965–66), pp. 71–74, 92–94, 111–13.

2. *banker:* In Baum's America, bankers play a role similar to that of the witches and Nome Kings. Greedy and heartless, they will drive Aunt Em and Uncle Henry from the country to seek refuge in Oz. There is no hope in America, and the government does not provide adequate protection from the bankers.

3. *many other girls of her age:* Of course we do not know her age, and we shall never know it. See note 1, Chapter 1 of *The Wizard of Oz*. Baum continues to suggest that Dorothy is "every girl."

4. *No one wants to employ old people who are broken down in health, as we are:* Baum reflects on the plight of old people in America, especially farmers. At that time there was no Social Security and Medicare.

5. *Magic Picture:* At the end of *Ozma of Oz*, Dorothy gives the Magic Belt to Ozma, who uses it to bring Dorothy back to Oz whenever she chooses, and whenever Dorothy gives her a signal.

Ozma looks into the Magic Picture at the agreed-upon time, four o'clock, when school is finished and the work day is almost over.

CHAPTER 3: HOW OZMA GRANTED DOROTHY'S REQUEST

1. *Dorothy Gale:* This is the first time that Baum refers to Dorothy's last name, obviously associating it with the cyclone. As usual, though, Baum is ironic in his choice of name, as Dorothy is anything but tempestuous and stormy.
2. *I'd like to live here in the Land of Oz:* It now becomes clear that home is not Kansas per se, but where Aunt Em and Uncle Henry are. More important, Dorothy explains to Ozma that she prefers Oz to Kansas.
3. *Jellia Jamb:* As Ozma's personal maid, she is actually a friend and personal secretary and had been a member of the royal staff even before Ozma was princess. Nevertheless, she remains the same age as Ozma. She has many responsibilities, and in *The Land of Oz* she even acts as interpreter for Jack Pumpkinhead, who cannot understand the Scarecrow language.

CHAPTER 4: HOW THE NOME KING PLANNED REVENGE

1. *torture chamber:* Though Baum rarely introduced violence in his works, he does so in this novel to indicate how evil the Nome King is. Yet, even here there is a certain irony that undercuts the violence. The Nome King uses "please" and asks his servants to "kindly" slice General Crinkle, who "may" be fed to the seven-headed dogs.
2. *Guph:* There is no history to this name. If it is pronounced "guff," it indicates a nasty character, and Guph is certainly conniving and deceitful.
3. *Whimsies:* Since Whimsey Land is next to the Kingdom of the Nomes, it makes sense that Guph would seek the help of the Whimsies first. As their name suggests, they are somewhat flaky and foolish.

CHAPTER 5: HOW DOROTHY BECAME A PRINCESS

1. *Shaggy Man:* Dorothy encounters him in *The Road to Oz* (1909) in America. He is on his way to a town called Butterfield to collect money from someone, but he does not really want to collect the

money. As he says to Dorothy, "Money makes people proud and haughty; I don't want to be proud and haughty. All I want is to have people love me; and as long as I own the Love Magnet every-one I meet is sure to love me dearly." He eventually brings the Love Magnet to the Emerald City where he hangs it by the portal so that all who pass through its gates will be loving and loved.

2. *Billina:* This famous hen is introduced in *Ozma of Oz* while Dorothy is taking a trip to Australia with Uncle Henry. A storm interrupts the voyage, and Dorothy is washed overboard with the yellow hen. In the Land of Ev and the Nome Kingdom she pro-ceeds to have very unusual adventures with Billina who proves to be a trustworthy and smart companion. When she discovers that the Nomes are afraid of eggs—they are like poison for them—she is able to use her eggs to save the royal family of Ev and to help Dorothy capture the Magic Belt. Baum had a special fondness for hens and wrote a book about raising chickens. In 1878 he raised and bred chickens in New York and helped found the Empire State Poultry Association. The next year he started the journal *The Poultry Record*. In 1882, he wrote a long article for *The Poultry Record* about breeding chickens that eventually became his first published book, *The Book of Hamburgs* (Hartford, Conn.: H. H. Stoddard, 1886).

3. *Tiktok:* He makes his first appearance in *Ozma of Oz*. Built by Smith and Tinker's in the town of Evna in the Land of Ev, Tiktok, who has all the features of a robot, was bought by Ev-ol-do, the evil King of Ev, as a servant. After Ev-ol-do sold his family to the Nome King in exchange for a long life, he regretted this action but could not get his family back. So, he locked Tiktok in a cave and eventually drowned himself by accident. Dorothy came across Tiktok in the cave and rescued him. From that time on, he becomes her "obedient servant" out of gratitude.

4. *Jack Pumpkinhead:* Tip, the famous young boy, who becomes Ozma in *The Land of Oz*, makes Jack out of sticks of wood with a pumpkin for a head. Tip created Jack Pumpkinhead to scare Mombi the Witch, who had originally transformed Ozma into Tip. But Mombi is not frightened and tests her Powder of Life on Jack Pumpkinhead, inadvertently bringing him to life. From that point on, he is Tip/Ozma's faithful friend and regards her as his parent. At first he lives in constant fear that his head could easily be smashed until he realizes that he can always carve a new head from a fresh pumpkin whenever he needs it. Unlike the Scarecrow,

however, his head is not filled with brains, and he is not particularly clever.

5. *Hungry Tiger:* His conscience prevents him from devouring other animals. See Chapter 21, note 1, in *The Wizard of Oz.*

6. *Professor H. M. Wogglebug, T. E.:* The letters H. M. mean "Highly Magnified" and T. E., "Thoroughly Educated." Professor Wogglebug first shows up in *The Land of Oz.* Originally a mere bug, he took refuge from the cold in a red schoolhouse where he listened to the lessons of Professor Notwitall as he taught the children. One day he is caught and magnified onto a screen through a screen and becomes a professor himself. A pompous character, Professor Wogglebug becomes Dean of the Royal College of Oz, and he regards himself as the most important educator in the Land of Oz. He is clearly Baum's spoof of egotistical scholars.

CHAPTER 7: HOW AUNT EM CONQUERED THE LION

1. *Topeka Hotel:* The reference is to a small hotel in Topeka, Kansas.

2. *died of the pip:* This disease is peculiar to birds and is marked by a scale or crust on the tongue. Generally, nobody or nothing dies in Oz, so this is one of the many little contradictions in the series.

CHAPTER 8: HOW THE GRAND GAILLIPOOT JOINED THE NOMES

1. *Growleywogs:* Baum's wordplay is difficult to decipher. Given the mean characters of the Growleywogs, it would seem that he wants to emphasize their "growling" nature.

2. *Ripple Land:* Like most countries in which repulsive creatures reside, this one is outside Oz.

3. *Grand Gallipoot:* Again, given the nastiness of the Growleywogs, Baum appears to be playing with the words "gall" and "pout."

CHAPTER 9: HOW THE WOGGLEBUG TAUGHT ATHLETICS

1. *The old people were chiefly troubled by the fact that there was no work for them to do:* Aunt Em and Uncle Henry represent the dedicated American farmers who are accustomed to working long hours and believe that you develop good values through hard work.

2. *Omby Amby:* Originally the guardian of the gates in *The Wizard of Oz,* this soldier with the green whiskers is placed in charge of the Royal Army and Royal Police Force by Ozma.

3. *Sawhorse:* In *The Land of Oz* Tip wants to get to the Emerald City as quickly as he can, but Jack Pumpkinhead slows him down. So, along the way, he transforms a carpenter's sawhorse with Mombi's magic Powder of Life, and from that point on the sawhorse, which carries Tip and Jack, becomes the royal steed of Tip/Princess Ozma.

4. *Cuttenclips:* Baum's pun will become clearer once Dorothy and company arrive at Miss Cuttenclip's place.

5. *scientific College Athletics:* Although sports at American schools and universities were not yet as professionalized as they are now, there were already indications in Baum's time that sports would take precedence over studies. In this regard, Baum was somewhat prophetic, and his mock university in which "it is easier to swallow knowledge than to acquire it laboriously from books," has unfortunately become somewhat real in our own day and age.

CHAPTER 11: HOW THE GENERAL MET THE FIRST AND FOREMOST

1. *Phanfasms:* If the Phanfasms are Erbs, Baum may be referring to erbia or erbium, a metallic element of the rare-earth group that occurs with yttrium. Associated with the dread Mountain of Phantastico, the Phanfasms are connected to horrifying nightmares.

CHAPTER 12: HOW THEY MATCHED THE FUDDLES

1. *Fuddles:* This name evokes puzzle and befuddle. The Fuddles must be put together like puzzles and therefore befuddle the people who are given the task to put them together.

2. *Grandmother Gnit:* The play upon "knit" is evident here. Typically, Grandmother Gnit cannot even knit herself together, and even when she is in one piece, she knits mittens for the silly kangaroo, who really does not need them.

CHAPTER 13: HOW THE GENERAL TALKED TO THE KING

1. *china ornaments:* In *Ozma of Oz* the Nome King used the Magic Belt to transform the Queen of Ev and her children into ornaments and bric-a-brac.

CHAPTER 14: HOW THE WIZARD PRACTICED SORCERY

1. *Rigmaroles:* The origin of their name is clear: when they talk, they always beat around the bush and can never answer any question simply and directly.

CHAPTER 15: HOW DOROTHY HAPPENED TO GET LOST

1. *Utensia:* Though Dorothy has never heard of this kingdom, ruled by King Kleaver, it exists in the Quadling Country. Since Baum kept inventing kingdoms and regions, he also had to explain that Dorothy (and even Ozma) were not and could not be familiar with everything in a fairy realm. Utensia is marked by the fact that, despite the abundance of utensils, there is not a single cook or anything to eat in the kingdom.

CHAPTER 19: HOW BUNNYBURY WELCOMED THE STRANGERS

1. *Your size:* This episode is reminiscent of Alice's adventures in Wonderland. Here, however, Dorothy must voluntarily reduce her size.

CHAPTER 22: HOW THE WIZARD FOUND DOROTHY

1. *Flutterbudgets:* They are alarmists who live in a remote corner of the Quadling Country. Since they are always expecting terrible things to happen, they are constantly warning strangers that they are in danger.
2. *Gump:* The Wizard is referring to a contraption that was built by the Scarecrow and his companions in *The Land of Oz.* When the Scarecrow and his friends sought to flee from the Royal Palace in Oz surrounded by General Jinjur's Army of Revolt, they built a flying machine. As they were constructing it, they noticed a creature's head resembling that of an elk hanging on a wall of the Royal Palace. They took the head from the wall and placed it on the front of their flying machine. With the use of the magic Powder of Life, the machine was brought to life, and they were carried to safety. Later the head was restored to the wall of the Royal Palace, and occasionally the Gump speaks to visitors.

CHAPTER 26: HOW OZMA REFUSED TO FIGHT FOR HER
KINGDOM

1. *I will not fight—even to save my kingdom:* Ozma is the ultimate
   pacifist, and in contrast to the male leaders of the real world, she
   refuses to employ weapons or to be aggressive. Baum's views were
   similar to those of Ozma, but he was not a radical pacifist.
2. *I've been a slave all my life:* Aunt Em's remark is an interesting
   self-revelation. Clearly, she understands how much the farm and
   the bankers have held her in bondage.
3. *Forbidden Fountain:* Again, Baum is very innovative. Instead of a
   Fountain of Youth, he creates this unusual fountain with the
   Water of Oblivion that will enable him to bring about a peaceful
   resolution to the conflict.

CHAPTER 29: HOW GLINDA WORKED A MAGIC SPELL

1. *visitors who would ruin our lovely, secluded fairyland:* Later,
   Baum would change his mind about visitors when he thought
   about transforming an island off the coast of California into Oz,
   which would have been a kind of Disneyland in need of visitors.
2. *Johnny Dooit:* This fairy friend of the Shaggy Man appears in *The
   Road to Oz.* The Shaggy Man always carries a tool kit with him,
   and whenever he needs to build some extraordinary thing, he
   calls upon Johnny Dooit, who once built a sandboat that carried
   Shaggy and his friends across the Deadly Desert to Oz.
3. *I believe we must not hesitate to separate ourselves forever from
   all the rest of the world:* Philip José Farmer plays upon the threat
   to Oz in his superb novel *A Barnstormer in Oz* (New York: Berke-
   ley, 1982). Farmer sets his story in 1923 and has Hank Stover,
   Dorothy's son, discover Oz, while he is on a flying mission. Once
   he is there, he falls in love and is captivated by the utopian society. But Stover discovers that the American military wants to
   occupy and use Oz as an outpost in space. So he helps Glinda
   thwart the U.S. government and keep Oz invisible. Baum has
   other reasons for isolating Oz, but there is no doubt that he saw
   an "American" invasion as one that would destroy the altruism
   and socialism of Oz.

CHAPTER 30: HOW THE STORY OF OZ CAME TO AN END

1. *You will never hear anything more about Oz:* It is evident from this statement and other remarks in this short chapter that Baum had planned to end the Oz series with *The Emerald City of Oz.*

GLINDA OF OZ

INTRODUCTION: TO OUR READERS

1. *letters:* Baum was very conscientious about answering the letters of his readers.
2. *he went away:* This is a reference to his death on May 6, 1919.

CHAPTER 1: THE CALL TO DUTY

1. *it's against the law for anyone but Glinda and the Wizard to work magic in the Land of Oz:* There is no constitution in Oz, nor are the laws published. They seem to be spread by word of mouth. But Baum constantly had his characters proclaim that magic was sacred and only to be used by Ozma, Glinda, and the Wizard, who has limited powers.

CHAPTER 2: OZMA AND DOROTHY

1. *Trot:* She is a little girl who lives with her mother and Cap'n Bill on the coast of California. She and the Captain get caught in a whirlpool and eventually have many adventures in Jinxland and Oz, where Dorothy befriends them. In the end, Little Trot and the Captain stay in the Emerald City. All this takes place in *The Scarecrow of Oz.*
2. *Betsy Bobbin:* She comes from Oklahoma and is the same age as Dorothy. In *Tik-Tok of Oz* she finds her way to Oz after a shipwreck, and after numerous adventures with her friend Hank the Mule, she is invited by Ozma to stay in the Royal Palace so that Dorothy will have a friend her own age.
3. *Spider King:* The threatening spiders are anticipated in *The Wizard of Oz.* See Chapter 21, note 2.
4. *There is more magic in my fairyland than I dreamed of:* This is

what makes the Oz series so fascinating. Baum kept changing the rules and inventing new unusual characters. It appears that there are laws that Baum and his characters tried to follow, but whenever the plot demanded changes, Baum did not hesitate to break his own laws.

CHAPTER 6: FLATHEAD MOUNTAIN

1. *I know that I am more powerful than you are:* In fact, the Su-dic is correct. Ozma rules more through the gentle art of persuasion than by force. Even though she knows some magic, as we have just seen, she relies more on Glinda and the Wizard to employ magic.

CHAPTER 8: QUEEN COO-EE-OH

1. *Fairy Queen Lurline:* She was the powerful fairy who transformed Oz from an ordinary country into an enchanted fairyland and is mentioned in *The Tin Woodman of Oz.*

CHAPTER 10: UNDER WATER

1. *submarines:* Though submarines had already been invented by this time, Baum's imagination endows these vessels with even more extraordinary powers than they had at that time. He was always interested in new gadgets and inventions that he conceived for the series.

CHAPTER 11: THE CONQUEST OF THE SKEEZERS

1. *White Swan:* In contrast to the traditional beautiful swan in Hans Christian Andersen's "The Ugly Duckling," Baum uses the image of a Diamond Swan to suggest how vain, greedy, and haughty Coo-ee-oh is.

CHAPTER 14: OZMA'S COUNSELLORS

1. *But Ozma loved them for their peculiarities:* One of the striking features about all the Oz books is the theme of "multiculturalism" and tolerance. Baum created all kinds of characters and things

that represented the most different sorts of races, religions, and sexes. They were all greeted in Oz and were expected to accept and respect each other's differences.

2. *Scraps, the Patchwork Girl of Oz:* She was made from an old crazy quilt by Margolotte, the wife of Dr. Pipt, the Crooked Magician, in *The Patchwork Girl of Oz*. Due to Dr. Pipt's magic Powder of Life, the Patchwork Girl develops a will of her own and refuses to be Margolotte's servant. Indeed, she runs off with Ojo, a poor boy from Munchkin Country, who accidentally had given her a great deal of brains when she was made. Together they have numerous adventures, and Scraps is eventually invited to live in the Royal Palace.

3. *Cap'n Bill:* Little Trot's companion from California; the Captain loves to tell stories, and he ends up in Oz after being caught in a whirlpool. See Chapter 2, note 1.

4. *Frogman:* This creature is featured in *The Lost Princess of Oz*. Once an ordinary frog, he was picked up by a bird and carried to a pool in Yip Land (located in Winkie Country). This pool happened to have magic skosh, and when the frog ate it, he grew to be as large as a man and very wise to boot.

CHAPTER 15: THE GREAT SORCERESS

1. *Glass Cat:* Thanks to Dr. Pipt's Powder of Life, the Glass Cat comes to life. She accompanies Scraps and Ojo on their journey in *The Patchwork Girl of Oz*. Somewhat rambunctious, she becomes modest and well behaved by the end of the novel.

2. *Dr. Pipt:* In *The Patchwork Girl of Oz* he used magic illegally and caused disastrous things to happen. By the end of the novel, Dr. Pipt is "straightened out" and is no longer allowed to practice magic.

3. *Button Bright:* He is from Philadelphia and is always getting lost. In *The Road to Oz* he wanders into Oz and attends one of Ozma's famous birthday parties. Though he is sent home in a magic bubble by the Wizard, he gets lost again and returns to Oz, where he remains and still gets lost from time to time.

4. *Ojo:* He used to be unlucky and visits Dr. Pipt in *The Patchwork Girl of Oz* to see if the Crooked Magician can help him change his luck. Yet, Ojo causes a few accidents and takes a trip to seek some remedies for all the trouble he has caused. With the help of

Scraps and the Glass Cat, he manages to restore order to the lives he had changed.

CHAPTER 18: THE CLEVERNESS OF ERVIC

1. *a powerful Yookoohoo, named Reera the Red:* She is another one of the various witches in Oz. Located in Gillikin Country, she uses magic primarily for her own entertainment and never seeks to harm anyone. The other Yookoohoo Witch is Mrs. Yoop, the wife of the tremendous giant Mr. Yoop, who is 21 feet tall, weighs 1,640 pounds, and is 400 years old. Since Mrs. Yoop causes a lot of trouble in *The Patchwork Girl of Oz*, Ozma turns her into a Green Monkey.